I0665644

EXSAR

HAILEY KRALLES

Exsar

Copyright © 2025 by Hailey Kralles.

All rights reserved. No part of this publication may be reproduced, distributed, or transmitted in any form or by any means, including photocopying, recording, or other electronic or mechanical methods, without the written consent of the publisher. The only exceptions are for brief quotations included in critical reviews and other noncommercial uses permitted by copyright law.

MILTON & HUGO L.L.C.
4407 Park Ave., Suite 5
Union City, NJ 07087, USA

Website: *www. miltonandhugo.com*
Hotline: *1- 888-778-0033*
Email: *info@miltonandhugo.com*

Ordering Information:
Quantity sales. Special discounts are granted to corporations, associations, and other organizations. For more information on these discounts, please reach out to the publisher using the contact information provided above.

ISBN-13:   979-8-89285-567-9   [Paperback Edition]
               979-8-89285-568-6   [Hardback Edition]
               979-8-89285-566-2   [Digital Edition]

Rev. date: 10/28/2025

DEDICATION

To the dreamers trapped in their own Iverness:
May you find a home in Exsar.

To my Windsor:
For helping me reclaim my power and embrace the fire within.

PROLOGUE

In the depths of the Atraxian ocean, on the seafloor lied *the Gold Pearl*. It thrummed with the planet's life force rushing through it. The gold light shining within grew slowly for hundreds of years before purring with the need to be harvested. It vibrated against the sand, glowing brighter and brighter by the passing second. The sea shook, the world around it melted and alas, the light exploded and swept the ocean away with its force. The Pearl sat in a sandy bed for centuries, untouched by any animal as they scurried past when the power roared at them.

After sitting, filtering and harvesting the planet's energy, for *seven hundred and sixty eight years*, the Gold Pearl glittered in the wake of the child approaching it. The dusky skinned girl giggled as her Cerulean eyes danced with wonder. She reached for it. Her golden-brown hair was cast behind her as The Pearl beamed even more intensely, calling her name in a whisper of wind. The girl, Princess Kanika of the Tunate Empire, toppled forward and knelt before it. She lifted it into her lap with a grunt. The orb purred at her, much like her domesticated cat at home and she smiled.

"Kanika?" Her mother, Empress Kiwi of Tunate, called.

Kanika turned to see her mother walking down the beach. She turned back to the Orb and placed it back in the sand. *Hide me*, it cooed. The Princess giggled and started digging as fast as her small, five year old hands could manage. She had just placed the Orb into the hole and covered it when she felt a hand on her shoulder. She looked up and smiled at her mother. The sand beside her hummed satisfactorily.

"Hi, Mommy," she stood up from the ground.

The woman scoffed as she brushed the dirt from Kanika's pale pink dress. "You had me worried sick. Let's go back to the palace, hm?" She hums, straightening her spine and extended a hand to the child.

Kanika nodded and took her mother's hand. She glanced over her shoulder as the Orb called her name again and again. She hummed happily as they ascended the steps to the castle.

Kanika had visited the precious Pearl every chance she got in the following 10 years. The Orb had glowed with anything she asked to see, from her wildest dreams to other countries throughout the world.

On Kanika's fifteenth birthday, just after her parents had informed her she was to be wed, she ran to her secret with tears pricking the backs of her eyes. The Orb sung to her *louder* than usual as she approached. *Kanika*, it called. *Come closer.* She lifted the Orb to her face and stared at her reflection. *I have a gift for you*, it stretched out a stream of gold light toward her face. Light blinded Kanika as she felt her body erupt into flames. She screamed, dropping the Orb into the sand. She continued crying out at the feeling of pure agony coursing through her veins. The light surged through her, twisting and turning with her veins. It embedded into her bones and seeped into her soul. Her eyes burned as she stared at the now dormant object at her feet. She dropped to her knees, bracing herself with her palms in the sand. Kanika gasped for air and looked over her shoulder to the Golden Pearl. *Sweet child*, it purred, *unlock your potential and release your rage.*

A troop of royal guards ran toward the Princess. "Milady, are you alright?"

She rose onto her knees and exhaled with closed eyes. When she opened her eyes, the men were reduced to piles of ash. *That's it*, the Pearl hissed. Kanika stormed back toward the palace, her irises flaring bright red.

That night, Kanika reduced the entire capitol to rubble. Kanika rose from the ash in the morning, using the new energy coursing through her to take to the skies. She would go on to capture the entire continent, divided into three countries and their surrounding isles, over the next twenty five years. She ruled over the continent of Deteron for seven hundred and sixty eight years, forming hundreds of orbs below the surface to harvest the planet's power. She ruled the continent with all of her subjects bowing to her very breath. She raised an army of dragons, creating life from ash, before training her people and conquering every country in the hemisphere. Her people worshipped her. She cared for her dragons like her own children. She rose thousands of dragons from the ashes of those who opposed her. She filtered her rage through them, letting them feast on her every pain and grow strong with every rampage.

Kanika stood atop the hill, watching the lower class workers move blocks of granite. She felt a presence behind her and turned. "My Queen," Pekhi bowed at the waist.

Kanika looked her most trusted advisor up and down before looking back to the building. "What is it, Pekhi?" Her low voice sent shivers down his spine.

"The outer build will be completed by the end of the week," he informed her.

She nodded, intertwining her fingers in front of her. "And the build in the land we call Crunia?"

"It is completed, we will be able to get you settled upon our arrival at sunset." Kanika nodded and followed Pekhi to the horses. Their journey had only lasted a few hours. The people of Crunia rejoiced with their Ruler's return. Thousands danced in the streets, offering her gifts as she passed. By the time she'd arrived at the palace, dinner had been served.

Kanika spent the week seeing her loyal followers of Crunia and granting them whatever she could. She took care of her followers, she rewarded their loyalty with peaceful lives. There was no wars under one ruler. There was no struggle if she provided. She was the Mother of the Land.

Kanika laid awake one night, watching the cracks in the ceiling grow. She closed her eyes, feeling a pull toward her desk. She pushed herself out of her bed and walked to her desk. The ceiling began crumbling around her as she began writing on a scroll with a feather and ink.

Kanika knew she was going to die that night. She knew that her dragons would die out with her, her *rage* being their life source. She scribbled out her soul's destiny as it fractured into two, the small piece of parchment being the only thing recovered from the rubble by her four sons; Uhzana, Nox, Sihon, and Ri-Zahn.

Kanika's Prophecy

Two kingdoms will become one.
Two souls will twine as one.
One will be fire,
The other ice
One will soar as a bird,
The other will harvest from Tretanov,
Resurrecting my children.
Neither will know solace until they are one.
The world will not know peace until two becomes one.
Fire will burn the kingdoms down,
Ice will resurrect an empire.
Two will become one when the suppression is blinded.
Two will become one when suppression is hanged.
Two will love as one.

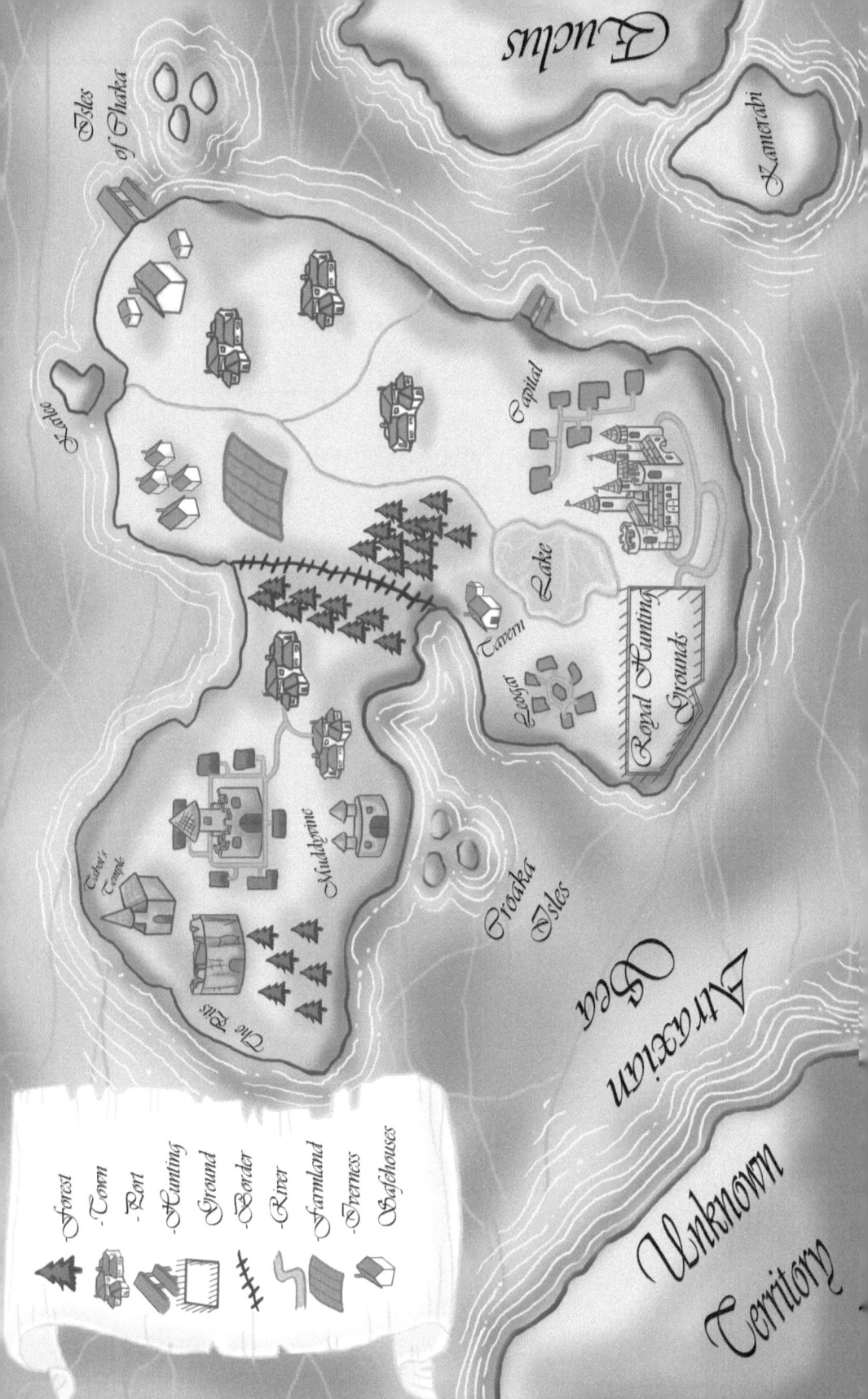

1

EOWYN

Maude, the Princess's appointed Lady-In-Waiting, adjusts her hair. She pulls it over her right shoulder, letting half fall down her torso and past her waist. She steps back and nods, her hands on her hips. Eowyn stands before her with an impassive expression. Maude looks over the Princess.

The Emerald encrusted Golden crown atop her silver hair sits perfectly straight. The earrings she dons match both her crown and the necklace gifted to her by her Father. The matching metallic green ball gown harbored a sweeping golden embroidered neckline. The matching Gold Spaulder-like sleeve caps covered the red swirls of the twin marks on each of her arms. The heavy gown contoured to her waist before flaring into a tremendous ball gown skirt with a train trailing elegantly behind her.

"Today is your Eighteenth birthday," Maude finally says, her voice old and scratchy. "You will pick a suitor." Eowyn dips her chin in a single nod. Her mother had prepared her for this day. "You will choose well." Eowyn's eyes dart between Maude's. "You will... *do* well," she knocks on the ballroom door to signal the Princess is ready. Eowyn's marks burn under the shoulder pads, her eyes flaring red beneath the color distortion enchantment. Maude smiles gently. "You are not alone," she whispers as she walks past The Princess.

"Princess Eowyn Alnwick of Iverness!" The secretary of the state, Blaine Cromwell, announces from the other side of the door. He motions to the Royal Guard to open the ball room doors.

She clenches her jaw and lifts her chin, taking slow steps into the dark ball room. The room falls into an eerie silence when she crosses the threshold. Her flowing silver hair glows in the dim palace. The black granite walls absorb all light, yet she glows as she steps in. The crowd parts, some recoiling with the heat flaring off of her markings beneath the gold Spaulders.

The ashes of the candles mounted throughout the room whisper to her with each step she takes toward her parent's thrones. *There is another,* they hiss as she passes. She keeps her expression neutral, holding her Father's stare defiantly. *One who mirrors thee.* Her eyes glow red beneath the gray hue from the enchantment of the *collar* he called a necklace around her neck. His nostrils flare in a silent confirmation of punishment. She notices her Mother's slight smirk out of the corner of her eye. She turns her attention toward her Mother, stopping at the bottom of the steps. Queen Alice holds a blank stare, meeting her daughter's eyes. King Tabot motions to the small wooden chair between their colossal black granite thrones, adorned with Gold and Emeralds. Eowyn's eyes flare brighter this time and her Father's fingers angrily curl around the arms of his throne. She turns back toward the crowd and curtsies, bowing her head deeply.

This was her first public appearance *in 10 years* and she defied every royal protocol under Tabot's reign, from bowing before commoners to demonstrating her magic.

She lifts her head to see the *entire* room on one knee. The soldiers positioned around the room even bow their heads. Her eyes sweep along the crowd, meeting a glowing pair of ice blue eyes. *That's him,* the ashes in the torch beside her whisper. She rises to her feet. He holds her gaze as he follows suit. She watches his shoulders rise and fall with a single breath. A brutal cold brushes against her skin as if it were his exhale across her skin. The crowd rises and he disappears in the sea of her subjects.

The Princess turns back toward the King and Queen. Her Father points to the chair between them demandingly. She holds his stare with each step up. The rage inside of her ignited a fire in the pit of her stomach. The familiar feeling of the suppressed power boils over under the heat of her anger. She lowers into the chair, positioning herself on the edge with her hands delicately folded in her lap.

"You will choose a suitor tonight or you will die in those dungeons," Tabot's grating voice is like throwing wood into the fire within her.

"She will choose a suitor," Alice hums, tapping her fingers on the stone throne.

Eowyn keeps her chin straight despite how her eyes drop to her Mother's frail hand. *An approval.* She drags her eyes back to the rest of the ballroom when the orchestra begins playing the opening symphony. "And of Zanna?" The Princess keeps her voice low.

The Queen's pinky stretches toward Eowyn, grabbing her attention. She keeps her head straight and glances at her Mother through her peripheral vision once more. Alice moves her pinky side to side, telling her to quiet.

"Zanna will stay where she belongs," Tabot growls, his foot tapping angrily.

The swirls of Eowyn's markings sizzle against her skin, fire coursing through her veins. "She will die without me," she keeps her voice even. The song ends and the orchestra flawlessly starts into a faster paced ballad.

"Then her scales will be harvested for armor and her meat will be consumed during a royal feast," his gaze burns into the back of her head. "You've spent a year in the dungeons for using magic, a form of *high treason*, dare to *flare* it as if my chains do not bind you this very moment, and now *demand* your dragon follows you? I ought to throw you back in the dungeons and make you eat her eggs."

Eowyn's toes curl inside of her heels as her spine stiffens slightly. "Eggs," she repeats.

"Zanna laid five eggs two moons ago," Alice says dully. The Princess's eyes dart around the room, the only thing to show her Mother her shock. "You've been in the Dungeons a long time, little bird."

Tabot rises from his throne. "I shall return," he says gruffly, already starting down the steps.

Both Eowyn and Alice's eyes follow him. Two soldiers flank to his sides once he reaches the bottom of the platform stairs. They watch the three of them walk to the doors and exit the ballroom. Eowyn holds her posture but turns her head to look at her Mother. "There is another element wielder," she declares quietly. "The ashes confirmed it."

Alice hums, tapping her index finger on the arm of her seat. She scans the room. "You're dressed in his suppressive collar, yet the ashes still speak to you, interesting," she hums, not meeting her daughter's gaze. "Did you see them?"

Eowyn turns back to the mass of chatter. "I did," she confirms. "His eyes were nearly white."

Alice cocks an eyebrow, looking at her side profile. "Charlotte," she turns her head to call her Lady-In-Waiting.

The young woman rushes up the steps. "Your Majesty," she curtsies.

"Please fetch me a man with eyes so blue they appear white," she commands.

Charlotte straightens and nods. "Yes, Milady," she smiles nervously before rushing down the stairs again.

"His chains are not holding you," Alice says to her daughter. "Your eyes still glow beneath the gray."

The Princess brings a hand up, dragging her fingers along the warded necklace. "I've felt like I am engulfed in flames since he placed it on me," she confesses. "Though, I cannot light a flame or summon my wings."

Alice taps her finger again. "I will find a way to get it off of you to release the tension."

Eowyn's hair swings with her as she cocks her head to look at her Mother again. "You have yet to find a way to remove yours and have fallen ill from the effects," she affirms.

"My health is of no concern to you, my love," she meets her daughter's eyes. "I will consult with Flare Meadowglade. You may be able to release small bursts of power since the effects are yielding," she turns back to the scene before them.

The Princess blinks, another bout of anger brewing at her Mother's avoidance of the topic. "I was unaware Zanna would not follow me," she stares at the side of her mother's gaunt face. "I was unaware she had laid eggs."

Alice's eyes snap to the doors, her shoulders relaxing slightly when another group of noble women enter the room. "Zanna will not die in your absence," Alice meets Eowyn's eyes once more. "You have my word."

"Your Majesty," a resonant voice calls from below the throne platform. Both of the women turn toward the sound, Eowyn's ears ringing loudly. The man with iced over eyes stands before them, his spine snapping straight as his eyes meet Eowyn's. The scars on her back from the past year's punishments burn against her skin, her markings flanking her shoulders hissing louder as they gleam beneath the glamor. His nostrils flare. Eowyn holds his stare blankly, inwardly screaming in pain. "Your Highness," he kneels, bowing his head. "I was honored to witness how you greeted your people, Princess," he says as he rises once again. He takes another step forward.

Eowyn lays her hands, one over the other, in her lap. "Thank you."

"To what do I owe the pleasure of the Queen's request for my presence?" He turns toward her Mother.

She studies him silently for a moment, watches him as if she knew him. His long, jet black hair signified a status of wealth or possibly a high ranking military officer. His sharp jawline and broad shoulders screamed intense training with the sword sheathed at his side. The white suit and cobalt blue cape encrusted with precious red stones shimmer in the dim torch light.

"You are Prince Windsor of Exsar," Alice claims, cocking an eyebrow.

His full lips spread into a smile and he bows at the waist. "It's a pleasure, *Your Majesty*." His voice drips like venom, something taunting in his tone.

Eowyn's eyes flick between the Queen and the Prince of another Kingdom. The Kingdom that Iverness revolted against and quashed their alliance with after The Mother's death. *The Kingdom of the Free.*

Eowyn keeps her revelation to herself, using her skill of masking her features to convey boredom when her Mother looks to her once more. "I'd like you to dance with Prince Windsor," she opines.

Realization sets into Eowyn's gut as her eyes dart between her Mother's and she nods. She slowly rises from the chair, her gaze meeting his again. He extends a hand to her when she begins descending toward him. She delicately lays her fingers against his palm, standing one step above him. He wraps his hand around her fingers and kneels, holding her gaze while he presses his lips to the back of her hand. His lips leave a glacial burn on her searing skin. She feels the fire shoot through her veins to her hand, her eyes widening slightly. His expression mirrors her, his lips parting as if he felt the same rush of power lurching toward him. Windsor slowly rises to his feet and clears his throat. He keeps a feeble grasp on her hand to lead her toward the middle of the room. The crowd seems to recoil from her again, though she assumes the other half moved away from the coldness seeping from his pores.

He leads her to the front of the ballroom, stopping and facing her just as the orchestra finishes another song. He brings his other hand to her waist and she settles hers on his shoulder. The orchestra starts up again, a slower tempo ballad. "This is a great honor, Your Highness," The Prince remarks softly, taking the lead of a slow waltz.

"Likewise," Eowyn says shortly, craning her neck slightly to meet his gaze.

His eyes drop to the chain disguised as a necklace around her neck. "Iverness has some of the most beautiful Emeralds," he looks back to her face.

Eowyn dips her chin in agreement. "Thank you, Your Highness."

He takes a step back, dropping his hand from her waist and twirling her once. She spins lightly on her toes, gracefully stepping back into him. "You don the marks of a chosen house yet your eyes are gray," he observes. Eowyn glances down to see her markings on her arms fully covered. "I can smell them burning against a magical boundary," he explains.

Smell her markings in distress. He's her opposite chosen house. "You're an ice wielder." She raises her eyebrows. He presses his lips in a thin line and nods. She gives him a nod back and concedes. "I live in a land where magic is forbidden," The Princess states bluntly, circling back to his remark, "I am to show no signs of my abilities."

A smile quirks the corner of his lips as they continue to dance. "Iverness is the only land in this half of the world where magic is forbidden," he denotes.

Eowyn raises a challenging brow. "You come into my territory and insult my lands," she retorts.

"On the contrary, Princess," he steps back and watches her with an amused glint, ghosting his features as she twirls again. His smile widens once she steps back into him. "I am insulting the ruler of your territory."

Eowyn slides her tongue across her teeth. "The rulers that invited you into this territory."

He lets out a short laugh, something Eowyn had rarely heard in her eighteen years. Her head tilts slightly, something that could be portrayed as an expression of offense but was pure curiosity. "It was merely an observation, Your Highness," he gently pulls her forward and speeds up their steps with the bridge of the song. "My, my, your Mother was correct. You are enchanting to speak with."

Eowyn feels a soft hum skate through her, *her power was calming.* She blinks, effortlessly gliding with him across the floor. "You enjoy being accused of treason?" She nearly drawls.

"I have diplomatic immunity from the Queen herself, Your Highness," he fires back. She notes the way the corners of his eyes crinkle with his broadened smile. He slows them to a halt with the music. "This has been absolutely delightful," he takes both of her hands in his. He presses a kiss to the backs of each of her hands. "I do hope you'll reserve another dance for me later in the evening."

Eowyn steps back, a faint smile gracing over her face. "I look forward to it, Prince Windsor." She doesn't miss the slight blaze of his eyes when his name falls from her lips. She holds his gaze, also noting how his fingertips ice over.

He takes a step back, bowing at the waist. She gathers the skirt of her dress and curtsies in response. The ballroom erupts into a fit of applause and cheering as Eowyn stands upright. Windsor holds her stare as a high class noble of Iverness steps between them. His eyes flare again when the man extends a hand to the Princess. "May I have the next dance?" The man smiles broadly.

Eowyn places her hand in his palm, dragging her eyes from Windsor to the man before her. "Most certainly," she plasters a smile onto her lips and steps into rhythm with the man. She keeps her attention on Windsor through her peripheral vision, watching him stalk toward the thrones where her Mother sat. She turned her attention back to the man before him and continued the dully silent dance.

2

WINDSOR

The Prince holds the Princess's gaze over the unnamed noble's shoulder, still feeling his magic coo and purr for her. The ice gracing his fingertips drips off of him, melting in her presence. He turns his head to see the Queen still alone on the platform. He takes one last glance at Eowyn before bounding toward Alice. His feet carry him through the crowd of people, still staring at the Princess in awe. "Your Majesty," Windsor bows when he approaches the thrones.

Alice dips her chin, a silent invitation to approach. Windsor climbs the steps and stands beside her throne, his fingers intertwined in front of him. "Do we have a deal?" Alice keeps her eyes glued to her daughter.

"We do," Windsor's voice rumbles lowly.

The ballroom doors open and Tabot walks in, clearly disheveled. The Prince cocks an eyebrow at the sight, his eyes drifting toward Alice who sits with a stone cold expression. The King makes his way through the crowd, Windsor's eyes never leaving him or the men by his sides.

"You will tell him you wish to take her to Exsar immediately," Alice says in a hushed tone. "You will leave and not return until I've summoned you."

"Prince Windsor," Tabot stumbles over the first step. He clears his throat, obviously drunk, and composes himself before continuing up.

"Your Majesty," Windsor keeps his tone level while bowing. He doesn't miss the satisfied smirk on the King's face as he positions himself lower than him.

"To what do I owe the pleasure of hosting the Prince of *Exsar*?" He lowers himself into his throne.

Windsor straightens, letting his hands fall to his sides. "I wish to take the Princess's hand in marriage in exchange for a treaty," the Prince answers bluntly. "Exsar as an ally for the Princess."

Alice taps her finger in approval as the orchestra ends a song and Eowyn takes another's hand for the next. A blood-curdling smile curves the King's lips. "I've already told my daughter she may choose her suitor," he leans back, drunkenly crossing one leg over the other.

The Prince swallows, his jaw clenching slightly with the words he'd be forced to spew to do this dance with the Ruler of this forsaken territory. "You will turn away a peace treaty, an offer not extended within nearly one thousand years, to allow *her* to make her own decision," Windsor plays into the King's hand, his words guided by the information fed to him by the Queen.

Tabot's eyebrows raise, the feral display of his teeth making Windsor's body tense. But he wasn't tensing, she'd prepared him for this over the last year. Alice leans forward on the throne slightly and Windsor glances over his shoulder to see Eowyn staring at him. Her body is rigid, her eyes glowing brightly despite the glamor. Her flames called out to his ice. The sound, only to be heard by the pair, felt like *home* to him.

Alice rises from her seat, her hands falling to her sides. Eowyn keeps her eyes locked on Windsor's, his own zeroing on the muscles of her jaw while she clenches and unclenches her teeth. He turns back toward her dazed Father. "My offer walks away with me," Windsor says sharply.

"Cromwell," Tabot snaps, his stare never leaving Windsor. The secretary of the state takes a few steps up, awaiting the King's command. "Fetch my daughter."

Alice stays on her feet, watching Windsor expectantly. He challengingly holds Tabot's gaze as he speaks. "I wish to bring her with me upon my return to Exsar," the Prince asserts.

Tabot raises an eyebrow, looking at his wife. "He wishes to take your bird home with him," his scratchy voice drones, "what say you?"

The Queen turns her gaze back toward her daughter where she walks with her chin held high beside Blaine Cromwell. "I've no qualms," she responds after a silent moment.

Tabot drags his head toward Windsor, his eyes just a beat behind the movement. "You may take her with you in a week's time," he avows as Eowyn starts up the steps.

"You wished to see me," her voice rakes over the Prince's soul, making his fingers twitch. A wave of heat washes over him, his adrenaline spikes and makes his body feel like it's vibrating. He glances at her out of the corner of his eye. *She is wearing an enchanted necklace to suppress her magic, yet her power is gathering around them.* He watches a condemned soul slither from a nearby flame and curl around her neck. Whether or not it spoke to her, she'd not led on.

"You will marry the Prince of Exsar," Tabot all but demands. "You will depart for his kingdom in one week's time."

Windsor's muscles twitch as she stiffens beside him. The scent of her magic completely engulfs him when the unmistakable anger settles into her stomach. He keeps his expression blank, his nostrils flaring with the inability to inhale the sweet smell of her building rage quick enough. The hints of blood, burnt hair, and cinnamon fill his lungs. He holds in the urge to turn the whole room to ice just to cease her fire, blowing a heavy breath out of his nose. Eowyn's shoulders relax slightly and the smells plaguing him withdraws from his senses.

The Queen's eyes dart between the pair, the small amount of power she still possesses recoiling from the silent exchange. Windsor meets her eyes and watches her gaze follow the shadow.

"You do not oppose?" Tabot shifts in his seat, planting both feet on the floor and leaning forward. He was taunting her and Windsor's nostrils flared again, this time with his own stirring rage. Eowyn's power snakes around Alice in an invisible barrier.

Windsor notices the Queen's light tap on the arm of the chair again. He watches Eowyn's eyes dart to the signal before she relaxes again. *A silent communication tactic.* "I do not oppose," Eowyn says slowly to her Father.

He bares his teeth with a feral grin. "Cromwell," he calls darkly, "the Princess is ready to retire for the night. She has found herself a suitor."

The man walks up the steps and grabs Eowyn by the arm, just above her elbow. Alice's features harden. "She may stay and enjoy her celebrations," she decrees. Windsor's eyes slide from the King to the Queen, not passing over how Eowyn's own eyes widen. "She does not retire until the festivities conclude," Alice maintains eye contact with her daughter as she speaks.

Tabot hesitates but nods and Blaine Cromwell releases Eowyn's arm. "Enjoy it while it lasts, bird," Tabot hisses. "You return to confinement at the end of the night." Eowyn holds her chin high, boldly challenging him in silence. "Go before I change my mind," he leans forward, baring his teeth with a soundless snarl. Without another word, the defiant Princess turns on her heels and makes her way back to the crowd. His eyes glow opaquely as he summons a shadow to trail her. "My wife will tend to the matter of the treaty with you now," Tabot gabbles gruffly, waving a dismissal at Windsor.

The Prince nods with his eyes still locked on the retreating Princess. Alice steps to his side. "You did well," she whispers, "come." She motions to the stairs.

The Prince wordlessly follows the Queen from the ballroom. He keeps a few paces behind her as she leads him to the Queen's wing of the Palace. The first thing he despised about the Castle upon his arrival was the layout. In Exsar, there was a wing for the Royal Family's residence, a wing for guests, a diplomatic wing, and the public wing. In Iverness, it was the King's ward, the Queen suite, guests and public wings. He blinks, pulling himself back to Tretanov as she pushes open a door just before the staircase leading to the bedrooms. He steps into the office, noticing how it matches the rest of the palace, dark and dreary. She closes the door and locks it behind them. He watches every movement as she crosses the distance to the desk and shuffles through a drawer. She pulls out a piece of parchment and lays it on top of the desk.

"This is an ironclad treaty that will be filed as soon as you sign it. It expires upon my death," she slides a quill standing in an inkwell toward him. "He is too drunk to care about the details and I will inform him tomorrow that the matter has been cared for."

Windsor steps toward the desk and grabs the quill. He silently signs his name. He places the metal tipped feather back into the inkwell. "She will remain safe, Your Majesty, you have my word," he places a hand over his heart, snowflakes gathering at his fingertips.

The Queen nods, "I am counting on it." She glances to the door, then back to the Prince of Exsar. "You need to find out how to get that collar off of her."

"I agree." He lowers his hand to his side. "I suppose contacting Flare Meadowglade for assistance is not possible as he is being held in the warded prison."

Alice glances at the door again. "I want you to leave with her tonight," she whispers. "Her Lady has been preparing her things for departure.

They've been loaded along with everything in your room into a carriage that is on its way to your Capital." Windsor cocks an eyebrow questioningly. "He will have her returned to the dungeons after the festivities end. I will tend to my husband while Blaine Cromwell sees you out. I fear if she stays the week, he will kill her."

She watches a shadow curve around Windsor's neck, seeming to whisper something into his ear before recoiling. He holds the Queen's gaze as she opens her mouth, but snaps it shut. She knows better than to ask about magic out loud and it made his jaw clench. Windsor extends a hand, showing her how he calls to and commands the shadows, just as her daughter does.

"Shadow wielder," she whispers, bracing her hands on the edge of the desk and sitting in the chair behind it. "Just as Eowyn."

"Soul seeker," he corrects, flicking the shadows away from his fingers.

Her eyes widen slightly. "That is a hunted gift," she swallows, "all over the world."

His eyes watch the shadows slither back into the walls. "To speak to the dead is a powerful thing," he nods. His eyes revert back to the Queen's. He lets the silence surround them for a moment as he tries to gauge whether or not there was any indication of Eowyn being a soul seeker as well. Alice stares at him, as if awaiting him to disclose what the soul had. "The Princess has been placed in the dungeons," he repeats what it whispered to him.

She slides open a drawer and extracts an envelope. She glides it across the wood. "Give her this once she is across the border." Windsor takes the envelope and nods. "I'd like to make one more request of you, Your Grace." His eyes flicker in silent acknowledgement. The hair on his arms rose under his sleeves. A wave of anger washes over him, briefly but enough to assume Eowyn was speaking with the King. He held Alice's gaze in silence. "Please do not tell her of our agreement until after my death," she says in a hushed voice. "Show her my letters after my death."

Windsor swallows, nodding with his lips pressed into a thin line. "Of course, Your Majesty," he accepts. "I will focus on her edification until then." He knew agreeing to it added to the bond between them. But he'd not come to Iverness to leave the Queen with doubts.

A single knock on the door rings through the room. Alice sucks in a sharp breath and uses the desk to help her lift herself from the chair. Windsor steps to her side, grabbing her arm and helping her up. "It's time," she murmurs. His hand drops to his side and he starts toward the door, pulling it open for Her Majesty. She gives him a weak smile, "thank you."

He steps out behind her and his eyes fall on Blaine Cromwell rounding the corner and disappearing. He follows the Queen through the corridor, back to the main palace. The stone spiral staircase was behind a locked and warded door. Windsor has to keep himself from scoffing as he feels the strain of his magic against the barrier when he starts down the steps behind the Queen. The subdued lighting makes it seem like the tunnel stretched on for miles.

"Your Majesty," Blaine stands in front of a cell. "Sir Meadowglade has information for you."

Windsor's eyes dart toward the enclosure where the one and only former Headmaster of Muddyvine Institute of Magic sat chained to a wall. He clenches his jaw, lifting a single finger and freezing the cuffs on his wrists. A soul comes from the shadows and shatters the ice, freeing the omniscient man.

All three look at Windsor, disconcerted. "You are wielding in the dungeon," Meadowglade rises to his feet. "There are spells and wards... How are you wielding your power?" He rushes forward and wraps his sickly slender fingers around the bars.

Windsor opens his mouth to respond, only to be cut off by a feral scream coming from deeper in the dungeons. "Eowyn," Alice gasps, looking at Blaine.

The Prince steps around the Queen and starts down the tunnel. Blaine grabs his arm, pulling him back. Windsor's eyes flash and he looks at the man warningly. Blaine lifts a key. Windsor takes it and rushes off into the darkness.

3

EOWYN

Blaine Cromwell holds her arm loosely as they descend the cobblestones steps. She keeps her eyes forward, feeling the bubbling anger in her gut start to boil when she passes the full cells on either side of the hallway. He releases her arm when she stops in front of the last cell at the end of the tunnel. She watches him pull the key from his pocket and shove it into the lock. He twists, making the metal click and the door swings open. She steps in, her back to him, waiting for him to take the collar off. The door closes behind her and she whirls around.

"This isn't part of the deal," The Princess snarls through the bars.

"My apologies, Your Highness," he whispers solemnly. "His Majesty has instructed me to leave it on."

Her jaw clenches, power reeling with anticipation of blowing the whole kingdom to dust. *Help is coming. Make him leave,* something whispers on a breath of brisk air, pushing past her ear. Her spine straightens and she steps away from the bars. Blaine stands on the other side, watching her walk to the cot and sit on the edge. He lets out a frustrated sigh, turning on his heels to start down the hall.

"Cromwell," Flare Meadowglade hisses, his hands yanking at the chains holding him to the wall. Blaine halts in his tracks, not turning to the former headmaster. "The King knows not, how to remove the collars." Blaine dips his chin in a single nod. "Tell the Queen there is a way."

Blaine finally turns to meet his gaze in acknowledgement, starting toward the stairs again.

Eowyn waits for his footsteps to fade into silence. "Flare," she whispers down the hall.

"Princess," he turns his head to smile at her.

"How do I get this off?" I tug at the enchanted necklace.

The familiar clack of shoes against the cobblestones makes them both snap their mouths shut. Eowyn steps back to the cot and lays down, her back to the gate that holds her. The steps grow louder and louder, the other prisoners whispering curiously at the sudden presence. Metal clanks and the door groans as it opens. "Get up," the guttural voice demands curtly. Eowyn clenches her jaw but does not defy the King's order. She stands before him, her eyes blazing red. "My fiery daughter dares to challenge me?" He growls resoundingly. She keeps her features tight, only blinking in response. "I should kill you," he slurs angrily. "You have been down here for a year for using magic and you continue to break my laws by blatantly flaring it at me." He sucks in a dramatic breath. "High treason, *daughter*," he spits the name so venomously that his saliva clings to her face. "Yet, I took mercy and let you live."

"Many men born with no powers choose to live as mages, you did not. That is not a burden your Kingdom should bear," she fumes, flames now dancing at her fingertips.

Tabot reaches out and lays an open hand slap to her cheek. The fire burns brighter, rising to her forearms. He steps back with his teeth bared. "Away with it, Eowyn," he barks, "or you'll be executed in the morning for your treachery." The words hit the anger within her just right and the flames swallow her whole. She charges toward him, an irate scream tearing through her. Tabot steps to the side and watches her hit the wall. He steps out of the cell and slams the door shut. Eowyn whirls on her feet, the flames dying out completely as the door seals her into the warded cage. "I'll have your head at dawn."

The Princess watches him retreat. As soon as he's disappeared up the stairs, she lets out a guttural scream. She paces back and forth, clenching and unclenching her fists for a few moments. "I can't wait to rip his head off with my bare hands," she mutters. She turns to the wall, grinding her teeth angrily. She lets out another scream and sends her fist into the stone wall beside her.

"That's not very ladylike."

Eowyn cradles her hand to her chest and turns to face the voice. "What are you doing here?" She breathes out.

His eyes shine brighter in the darkness, the icy blue of his irises lighting nearly the whole dungeon. "Saving you," he waves a hand in front of the door and the lock freezes over. He brings his leg up and kicks his boot against it, the door shattering on impact. "Come on, we don't have much time," he motions for her to step out.

Eowyn's feet stay cemented to the ground, her features blank. "This is a test," she states. She takes a step back. "I will not go with you."

"Your Highness, please, we do not have much time. Your Mother is –"

"My Mother?" Her fingers flash with the smallest hint of a blaze.

Windsor's eyes drop to her hands. "You are wielding as well," he observes, shaking his head and looking back at her face. "Your mother is with Flare Meadowglade. We have to go, *now*," his tone is low and serious.

The Princess chews on the inside of her cheek for a few seconds before nodding. If Alice truly was in the dungeons, she had to make sure she got out before her Father knew. She follows his brisk pace, her eyes widening when her Mother comes into view. Alice steps back from Flare Meadowglade's cell and Eowyn's eyes go even wider when she sees him free of his shackles. "Mother, he will kill you for undoing his binds," she pushes past the Prince to get to her.

Alice shakes her head and grabs Eowyn's hand. "Windsor did it, he has diplomatic immunity." She speaks with rushed finality. "We need to get you out of here," she says hurriedly.

"What about you? And Flare and Amethyst?" Eowyn asks, keeping a tight grip on her hand as they start toward the stairs.

Alice glances back to Blaine who walks behind her, Windsor on his heels. "Flare and Amethyst will be alright," she starts to walk faster. "I will send a message as soon as I can. Windsor has a letter from me to you for when you cross the border." She leads them to turn down a corridor, back toward the Queen's Palace. Windsor falls into step beside Eowyn. "You need to trust Windsor and the King and Queen of Exsar. I have been in contact with Elenor for four years and Prince Windsor since you were sentenced to spend the year in the dungeons. I am trusting them with my little bird," she stops in front of the door leading out to the path toward the hunting grounds. She turns to face her daughter and the Prince, tears streaking down her cheeks. She grabs both of Eowyn's in hers, feeling the fire dance below the skin of her palms. "You need to promise me you will not return."

"Mother," Eowyn's voice cracks on a whisper.

Alice shakes her head. "Promise me, Eowyn. I promise I will be at your wedding, but you need to promise me not to come back here. Not for me, not for Flare or Amethyst, not for Zanna." The Princess's eyes blaze at the mention of her dragon. "Now, Eowyn," Alice snaps, squeezing her daughter's fingers tightly.

"I promise," Eowyn grits out, dropping her Mother's hands and wrapping her arms around her tightly.

Alice hugs her back firmly, inhaling the scent of her anger one last time. Her eyes connect with Windsor and she nods once against Eowyn's shoulder. "Don't move, sweet girl. We're going to get this damned thing off of you."

Eowyn feels ice cold fingers dance along the back of her neck. The fire within the pit of her stomach slowly fades. He lays his palms on the back of the chain, making her gasp as the whole thing turns to ice around her neck. Something seeps from a shadow behind her Mother and it winds around the necklace. The necklace shatters around her neck, falling to the floor in millions of pieces. Windsor steps back, his hands moving from her neck.

Alice pulls back from the embrace, watching her only child's eyes glow bright red and illuminate the hallway. "Once you are over the border, soar high for me, little bird," she tucks a strand of hair behind Eowyn's ear. "You are my greatest accomplishment."

"Your Majesty!" Charlotte yells from down the hall.

Alice looks from the Princess to Charlotte, nodding before kissing her forehead. "It's time to go. I love you more than anything," she takes a step back and looks over her daughter one more time. "You will do great things."

Eowyn watches with tears in her eyes as her Mother steps around her and dashes down the hall. Blaine hooks his arm through the Princess's and pulls her toward the door. "We must go," he murmurs.

Eowyn turns, her eyes connecting with Windsor's. Now flowing freely, her power reaches toward him. She takes a step away from him, the clean and crisp scent of the ice pumping through his veins nearly overwhelming her. Blaine pushes the door open and she snaps out of her momentary daze. She follows him out onto the trail, glancing back as Windsor matches their accelerating speed.

"Blaine," she glances over at him, breathing heavily. "He ordered my execution." Another wave of iciness wash over her, his own anger seeping into her veins and feeding the fire in her.

Cromwell nods, "I made Her Majesty aware. She is going to keep him drinking and convince him it was a dream and that he let you leave after your ball."

Eowyn nods once, seeing Windsor speed up to pass them. He extends a hand and shadows pool in his palm. "Make sure the way is clear," he commands. The shadows fly from his palm and weave through the trees ahead.

Eowyn silently commands her own shadows to follow his. "I need to free Zanna," she says to Blaine.

They are safe, her shadows whisper through the wind.

He keeps running, shaking his head. "You cannot move a dragon and her eggs." Eowyn rolls her eyes. "She will return to you, Your Highness. Her Majesty and I will make sure of it."

"*Her Majesty* is in no shape to make sure of anything but staying alive," she snaps.

He starts to slow as they approach two horses. One was so white she glowed in the moonlight, the other so black he could've been a shadow. "We will await our Queen's return," he holds her gaze, grabbing her by the waist and sitting her on the black stallion.

Windsor mounts the white mare beside her, grabbing her reins. Eowyn's eyes blaze brighter as she grabs her own reins. "Until then, Cromwell," she dips her chin with a teary nod. He takes a knee beside the horse and bows his head, his right hand over his heart.

"We must go," the Prince insists in a hushed tone.

She sucks in a sharp breath, finally meeting his eyes again. She nods, jerking the reins to make the horse start into a trot. Windsor faces ahead of them, squeezing his legs on either side of the mare. She bursts into a sprint. The stallion races after them and keeps pace with the female.

"It's a six hour journey," Windsor says loud enough for her to hear over the wind. "That's including an hour and a half to rest once we are over the border." Eowyn swallows, her eyes narrowing on the dark trail ahead of them. She points a finger, small torches appearing as far as the trail extends and dying out when she passes them. Windsor looks over his shoulder to see the torches disappearing once she no longer needed them. He lets out an amused laugh. "That was marvelous," he beams.

The flames in her coo at his appraisal and she clears her throat, lifting her chin. "The three of you seem to have done plenty of work on my behalf, the least I can do is make the journey... tolerable."

Windsor cocks an eyebrow, an enliven smile spreading over his lips. "Your Mother told me that she knows not the extent of your powers," he looks over to see her expression still blank. "She wishes for you to work with the Headmaster of Drexrerth, Draven Idris."

"Flare Meadowglade's prodigy," she mumbles.

"Precisely," he studies the side of her face. Eowyn let's out a deep exhale, tightening her grip on the reins. She leans forward, her eyes fluttering shut. She allows the warm night air to wash over her. "Do you enjoy riding horses?"

Her eyes snap open and she turns to look at Windsor. "I've been in a dungeon for eleven months, seven days, six hours, and eight minutes," she says bluntly. "I enjoy fresh air." He turns his attention forward, making her cock an eyebrow. "I do not mean to offend, Your Highness, but I do not dip my words in honey before serving them on a gold platter."

Another laugh erupts from his chest, the sound ringing through her ears. It was a sound that was unusually calming to her. "That is why I am here, Princess. Your Mother feared you would suffer the same fate once he locked you away for not being able to contain your magic," he meets her eyes again.

Eowyn's features harden and she looks back to the path. "You signed a treaty with him," she says lowly.

"I signed a treaty with the Queen," he corrects. "You may see it once the King and Queen of Exsar have seen it."

She scans the darkness around them, the whispers of shadows letting her know they are not being watched. "She said she has been in contact with you since my sentencing," she keeps her tone level, "why?"

Prince Windsor blows out a breath. "Her Majesty needed allies who could claim you," he admits, "somewhere you would be safe."

"And she convinced the King and Queen to sign a peace treaty with my kingdom, which does not benefit them in anyway, while also harboring her fugitive daughter."

She notices the corners of his mouth start to quirk upwards again from her periphery. "There is more to it, but simply put, yes. Though Exsar is benefitting from this greatly," he turns to look at her.

She feels his icy gaze burning into her skin as the horses start to run faster. "In what manner?" She keeps her eyes forward, seeing more shadows seep from the trees. They rush forward, making her eyes narrow.

"We will have a powerful Queen to rule our lands," he says as soon as her question leaves her lips. "We will have leverage over Iverness as the treaty expires with Her Majesty."

Royal guards, a shadow hisses in her ear. She watches it dart to Windsor, coiling around his neck. Her eyes widen at both facts: there are Ivernese soldiers ahead and that *his* shadow reported to her *first*. She blinks, focusing back ahead of them. Three shadowy figures emerge from the darkness, making the horses skid to a halt. "Princess Eowyn," the General of the Iverness army, Perceval Hagan, drawls sarcastically. "You are out of the dungeons three weeks early." His eyes slide to Windsor.

"And with a foreign Prince," he tsks, turning back to her. "His Majesty will be delighted to put two of *your kind* to death."

The other two soldiers step forward, making the horses take a few steps backward. Eowyn holds Hagan's stare challengingly. "He approved my departure as I am to be wed to the Prince of Exsar," she lies coolly.

He lets out a bitter laugh, grabbing at his abdomen as if he knew it was a lie. Though tomorrow, he would suffer some sort of punishment from the Queen. "Seize them," he growls. The soldiers lurch forward. The mare kicks back, causing Windsor to fall backward. He lands on his back with a groan. The soldier yanks him up by his arm, the other ripping Eowyn off of the horse.

4

WINDSOR

The Princess bares her teeth as the soldiers shove the pair toward the General. Windsor watches her closely, waiting to see her overpower them like her Mother had written she'd done in one of her first letters. The reason she was sentenced to spend a year in the dungeons, manipulating the soldiers into letting her into Tabot's safe space even though she held the intention of ending him. Then she burned the temple dedicated to him, to the ground around them. "He should've killed you when you burned down the temple," Hagan's voice rips through the Prince's thoughts and his attention zeros back on the General when he grabs her by the hair and spits in her face.

A low, warning growl rumbles from the Prince. He looks to Eowyn and watches her chest heave with angry, ragged breaths. The smell of blood and cinnamon overwhelms him as her power gathers with her anger. *Good girl*, his magic purrs. A shiver travels up his spine when he feels her flames coo back to his ice. She lets out a guttural noise and her arms burst into flames. The soldier releases her, stumbling back with a scream while he goes up in flames. Windsor freezes the sweat coating his skin, making the soldier holding him hiss in pain. He drops Windsor's arms and tucks his hands under his armpits. Eowyn narrows her eyes at him and bright flames swallow him whole. He turns, seeing Perceval Hagan gone.

"Are you hurt?" Her voice washes over him.

"No," he turns to look at her before glancing at the piles of ash before them. "Are you?" He rakes his eyes over her frame and meets her eyes.

"No," she shakes her head. She looks around skeptically, her markings flaring once more under the spaulders. "we should go." He nods, motioning toward the horses.

He watches her mount the stallion gracefully, his tongue darting out to wet his lips. He clears his throat and looks down to the ground as he makes his way back to the mare. He mounts her silently, grabbing her reins and wordlessly commanding her to start into a sprint once more.

For the next hour, neither uttered a word. Windsor sat, consumed by... *her*. The way she knew exactly what to do, so quickly. The fact that one of *his* commanded souls warned *her* before *him*. He tries to quell the thoughts but they continue to rage on.

How much does she know about her powers? Does she know the difference between a Soul Seeker from the House of the infinite and a Manipulator born to that of the Planets? Does she even know how the Houses were formed?

"Princess," he decides to break the silence, about an hour away from the border. "I am curious about something."

She raises an eyebrow but keeps her stare forward. "You may ask," she glances at him from the corner of her eyes.

"Why does your Mother call you *little bird*?" He questions, his eyes falling to the gold plates covering her chosen Shifter markings.

She finally turns to look at him, her expression *still* void of emotion. "I am a shifter," she denotes.

His eyebrows shoot to his hairline and he smiles, though he could already smell that fact. "As am I," he avers. "I am a lion shifter."

He watches as her eyes travel to his hair, probably imaging him as a midnight black lion. She'd be right to do so. She directs her attention forward again. "I do not speak of my shifted form," she states plainly.

That piques his interest. There are no shifters that are hunted any longer. All of the serpents died out when Iverness cut ties with Exsar, seven hundred and sixty-seven years ago. "Your Highness?" He quirks a brow.

"I belong to the aves," she says concisely. A bird? Birds are not hunted, why would she have been told not to speak of her shifted form?

He lets out another laugh and nods. "I concede," he hums. *I'll see that pretty little bird soon enough*, he snickers inwardly.

Another silence inundates the pair. He watches her scan their surroundings every few moments, the incandescent light of her eyes never dulling. He calls on the souls stuck in this realm silently. The luminescent of her blaring red eyes flicking in his direction. She quickly focuses forward once more, making him cock an eyebrow. The souls swirl around him, buzzing with anticipation. He keeps his eyes trained on the side of her face, waiting to see if it was a coincidence.

"They are growing impatient," she unenthusiastically observes.

The Prince's jaw slackens slightly. "The Queen told me you were a shadow wielder," his power cooing at her in amazement.

"I am," she finally meets his gaze.

He holds her stare, despite the harsh glare of her coiling power shining through her eyes. "These are not shadows, Princess," he responds quietly.

Eowyn's expression remains blank, making his magic now weep for hers. "They come from the ashes, they are shadows." He's taken aback by her stubbornness, even more so by her lack of knowledge despite what she bears. Then it clicks. *Alice wouldn't have told her she harbors a hunted gift*

"My parents will ask to see your markings," he decides it best to avoid the conversation until they are at the palace. "Of your chosen house."

Her eyes slide over his face as if she were searching his features for something. She turns her head forward again and nods. "I understand," she hums plainly.

Windsor can't help but let his eyes roam over her side profile. Her high cheekbones glow under her eyes, casting shadows down her cheeks. His eyes land on her soft, resting pout. *You're staring*, a soul hisses in his ear. He ignores it, instead listening to the power reaching for her, calling for her. His eyes slide up to her button nose and behind her, watching her frosty silver hair flow in the wind. His fingertips involuntarily ice over and his eyes start to gleam.

He catches her gaze when she glances at him from the corner of her eye again. She doesn't say anything but he doesn't miss her grip on the reins loosening slightly. He feels a sense of static skate across his skin. His breath hitches and his magic quiets, settling back into his veins. She holds his stare from her peripheral vision, watching his shoulders slacken before looking ahead again. A smile spreads across Windsor's face. He lifts a hand, extending it toward her. He summons a ball of ice into his palm with a small snow storm swirling in the center. Eowyn looks to his face, then his hand. She hesitatingly brings her hand to hover over the ball. A small flame blooms in the center of the microscopic storm and lightning flashes in the cloud. His smile widens into a grin.

The corners of Eowyn's mouth quirk upward and she turns to look straight ahead again. "Temperature manipulator," she says in a soft tone, "ice and shadow wielder, shifter." He swallows, not bothering to correct her as he thinks it safe to assume she doesn't know what a soul seeker is. "Three chosen ones."

He tosses the ball of ice beside him, watching it disappear before it hits the ground. "Fire, electricity and shadow wielding as well as shifter." He can't hide the astonishment from his tone or his features, mainly because she was a soul seeker and didn't even know it. He was curious to know what she knew about the chosen ones. "You belong to three also."

"Does that mean we hold two of the same markings?" Her question caught him off guard. She'd seemed so confident, so- "My Mother and I hold the same marking of electricity but my mark is altered because it is my secondary in the *House of Light*." He blinks, *she's so-* "Though my other imprints are the same size of the fire."

"Mine as well," he nods, turning toward the path. They're about thirty minutes away from the border now, his soldiers should be crossing their path at any moment. "Your fire markings sizzled at the palace. Do you know why that happened?" He clears his throat, "I only ask because I know not if that is normal for a fire wielder."

She raises her chin slightly. "Those are not a house marking," she clarifies, "those are the markings of being born with a dragon attached to my life."

The Queen had told him about her dragon in her letters, she'd mentioned the dragon's egg hatched at the same time Eowyn was born and that much like Kanika's dragons, Eowyn's feasted on her anger. Now the dragon has laid five eggs of her own.

"I will return for her one day," the red light flicks in his direction again with another glance from her.

A ghost of a smile graces his face, it was admirable really, the way she'd vowed to return. But she needn't worry about anything from this point on. "I've given your Mother my word that I will free Zanna and the babes as well," he admits.

Her eyes turn back toward the trail. "You gave my Mother your word for a lot of things." It comes out as a sneer, catching him off guard.

Another soft laugh pushes past Windsor's lips and his ears perk up with the sound of a strained, barely-there laugh coming from her as well. His shoulders slacken at the melodic sound. "Your Mother is an ally of Exsar," he shrugs, "we take care of our own."

She clicks her tongue. "I was taught that Exsar and Iverness are continuously at war." Her gaze sweeps over their surroundings again. "Not since Iverness cut ties with Exsar almost eight hundred years ago."

His smile falters into a smirk. "That is correct, Your Highness," he couldn't help but sound almost jocular. "Your Mother as a seer, subjected to a life as a prisoner in her own home is our ally. The King is not." So, she *does* know about the relationship between the two nations to some extent.

Eowyn cocks an eyebrow, her eyes darting to her left. He watches her nostrils flare as she scans the area before turning her attention forward again. "You sympathize with my Mother," her features, despite the heat blazing from her skin, return to a cold expression.

"Your Mother was of a noble Exsarian bloodline, we protect our own." He drops one of his hands from the reins and strokes the mare's main. "I used to think she had the brightest hair I'd ever seen."

Appreciative of the subject change, Eowyn indulges. "Used to think?"

Windsor smirks, his eyes flaring as they meet hers. "Yours, Princess Eowyn," he licks his lips when she shivers at his name falling from his mouth. "Your hair glowed in a palace of black granite and no electricity stores."

She holds his gaze, her power flashing at his words. His smirk only widens at the almost unbearable glow of red challenging him. "My Mother siphoned from Tretanov when she gave birth to me," she divulges. "Flare Meadowglade told me, when I was in the dungeon, that she resurrected me from dead. He told me the reason Zanna's egg hatched the moment I took that first breath was because my soul was enraged to not be freed."

Siphoned from Tretanov? No, she must've used a Stone of Malice.

The words sing to his power like a beautiful melody and his eyes flash cobalt blue. Her body stiffens. His eyes pierce hers, his powering diving into her and hunting for her soul. He slightly recoiled at the way she roars against him before willing himself deeper into the rawest form of her being. The closer his power gets to the deepest part of her soul, the louder it sings.

The Princess is stunned, she doesn't know what was happening. His eyes changed, he's staring at her, and now he bares his teeth at her. She watches his K9 teeth start to elongate, stretching to the size of a lion's.

Windsor stares into her, addlepated. Her rawest form mirrors his. The aura around her was much larger, nearly double his, but her soul was identical. *Home*, his power stretches for her. He reels back, blinking once, back to reality.

His eyes returned to their nearly white color. He examines her face. She stares at his fangs, one hand lifted from the reins with a flame in her palm. He retracts his fangs. "Princess," he starts. "I did not intend to- you have my deepest apologies," he was unsure of whether or not she'd sensed him reading her soul. His eyes drift to the small red and gold glimmers of light gathering around her shoulders. "I will not hurt you," he catches her gaze again. Eowyn closes her hand, putting out the flame and turns forward. The sparkles still dance close to her back and he quirks an eyebrow. "You were preparing to shift." He watches her throat bob as she swallows.

"I was," she responds drably.

"You would have fought a lion... as a bird?" His question drips with hesitation, as if anticipating her to take offense.

Her eyes flare and she whips her head toward him, flames dancing behind her irises. "You underestimate me?" Her voice came out just as scorching.

He tilts his head slightly. "I am *amazed* by you." Her lips part slightly, her eyes widening. "I'd say I am intrigued to know what kind of bird shifter is confident enough to take on a lion, but you've already said you do not wish to speak of your shifted form." He watches her power dim, the scent of her anger retreating for the first time since they'd left the Palace of Iverness.

A tension filled silence settled over the pair. Eowyn's expression was taut, her markings, under the shoulder coverings, starts to sizzle. Windsor leans over, pressing his fingertips to the metal. He freezes it and lifts it off of her shoulder. He freezes the other one and gestures for her to take it off. She holds his gaze, not moving. The ice bursts into a flame and the ashes get swept away with the wind.

His smile returns. "Absolutely astonishing," he whispers, his eyes dropping to the mark on her arm. A pale pink line starts in the middle of her bicep, it swirls into a deep purple before spreading into a thicker metallic green line. The green went into a pale blue, the line thinning and connecting to a purple arrow looking shape. Four white lines flanking each side of the arrowhead. "That is your dragon's marking?" He lifts his eyes to hers again.

She dips her chin in a nod, turning forward. "There are soldiers," she whispers.

Windsor follows her gaze and his shoulders drop. "They are Exsarian," he rolls his neck. "We are at the border."

5

EOWYN

"Your Highnesses," the men bow deeply as the horses approach.

The Princess bows her head at them in acknowledgement. The soldiers straighten and turn their focus to Prince Windsor. "There is a tavern with water and hay for the horses just up the road. They've been informed of your arrival and have been paid handsomely by the King and Queen to close for the evening." The man with brown eyes and short brown hair informs him. His warm skin and sprawling black feathered wings made her want to fly once she crossed into Exsar.

Her eyes slide past the men toward the other realm. Hundreds of pink bleeding heart flowers line both sides of the one road into the Kingdom. Massive multi-colored trees line either side in a sprawling forest. Her eyes dart from a light blue leafed tree to a deep green, then to a yellow and orange tree.

The stallion starts into a slow trot again, pulling her back to reality. "Welcome, Your Highness," the other soldier, with rich brown skin and yellow eyes, whispers as she passes.

She sends him a small smile, glancing back over her shoulder. She cranes her neck, stretching to look at the trees over the stone path. A purple limbed tree stretches from the right, clashing with a dusty rose colored sapling and concealing it from any sunshine during the day. Without thinking, Eowyn raises a hand, manipulating the purple limbs to move upward and allow a decent size clearance for sunlight to filter to the smaller tree.

"Wow," Windsor breathes out beside her. Her head swivels to look at him, the small smile still gracing her features. "You can manipulate life."

"I can manipulate plants," she turns back to take in her surroundings. "Living things," he muses on a chuckle.

Eowyn cocks her head even more, hiding her broadening smile at the sound. She scans the endless expanse of beautifully colored trees, spotting a clearing a short distance ahead. She squints, noticing a small sign hanging outside and assumes it is the mentioned tavern. The bleeding hearts move into deep red dahlias, her eyes flaring with the hum of her power's contentment.

"The House of Light was said to be Exsar during Kanika's reign," Windsor broaches the silence. "Your Mother is Exsarian as well, your power will thrive here." She meets his gaze, still caught off guard by how well he could understand her power. His eyes drift to her shoulders where the gold and red sparkles flash behind her again. He returns his eyes to hers. "You wish to fly," he says quietly.

The Princess turns her head to look at the sparkles aligning themselves in the shape of wings. "I do," she nods once.

He looks forward, seeing the horses approaching the tavern. "Do you wish to eat first?"

"I do not."

A smirk crosses his face and he licks his lips. "You may do as you please in my territory, Your Highness."

Eowyn wastes no time, tugging on the reins until the stallion comes to a halt. Windsor watches as she dismounts the horse. She hums three notes, the small melody calling to something deep within him. He watches, the sound of bones cracking and snapping filling his ears as she summons two monumental red feathered wings. His eyes dip to her lips when she *finally* smiles. The sight makes his spine snap straight.

Eowyn flaps her wings once, twice, and then launches toward the sky. Her heartbeat thrums in her ears as she beats her wings faster. She pushes past the clouds, a loud laugh erupting from her chest. The wind flows through her hair, the strands absorbing the light of the moon. She extends her arms, spreading her fingers to feel the wind through the webbing of her hands. The markings of the House of Shifters reverberates against her skin. She tears the sleeves of her dress clean off, watching the grey swirls encasing her porcelain wrists glow. Her wings cease their beating for just a moment and she dips below the clouds. She peers down to the vibrant blue blaze rushing through the trees. Her eyes narrow, glowing brightly. The black lion's eyes meet hers and Windsor lets out a thunderous roar.

Her guffaw echoes through the forest, ringing through his ears. He growls, craning his neck to bare his teeth at her. She lowers even more, hovering just above his back. Windsor turns his head forward again, running even faster. She pushes harder, her chest heaving with tired breaths. She bites her lip and falls back. Windsor skids to a halt, digging all four of his paws into the dirt.

Eowyn stands in the moonlight, her wings sprawled. She holds his gaze and slowly lifts her chin until its pointed toward the sky. Her whole body erupts into flames and he steps forward, lifting a paw encased in ice. He shoots a line of ice toward her, freezing the flame. A deafening squawk pierces the silence as a bird shoots through the ice, leaving a pile of ash. Windsor's eyes widen, his tongue falling from his mouth as he watches the Phoenix extends her wings. From the angle he observes, she sprawls in the center of the moon, the light creating a halo around her. Her long, yellow tail glides along the breeze. The feathers encasing her abdomen shift into a blood orange tone. Her neck and wings gleaming like blood, a crown of yellow feathers sat just above her eyes and long pointed beak.

She caws again, dropping to Windsor. He starts into a sprint again, ducking his head when she glides past him. She glances back and chirps. Another growl rumbles through him and he scampers on. She feels his power approaching quickly, noting a shadow skating past her. Her pupils contract into slits and she watches the shadows trap a jackrabbit. A whistle pushes past her beak, sending a flame to char the small animal. Windsor grunts in approval, running past her to snatch the cooked creature. She feels the fire within her bones bombinate with satisfaction at the sound of his jaws snapping what's left of the bones.

Eowyn bounds for the sky again, emitting another happy shriek. She closes her eyes and lifts her head to part the clouds. She blows a breath through them, watching as lightning crackles around her. Her eyes flare crimson and she flaps her wings faster. Then she arches back, pulling her wings taut. She falls backward, plummeting toward the ground.

Windsor pauses under her, his paws tapping nervously.

She kicks her feet, one nail grazing along the Prince's spine before she pushes off the back of his neck and flies back toward the tavern. He snarls and turns around, following closely behind her. Another scream explodes from the fire bird when the velvety black lion catches up to her. His eyes flick upward, snagging on the gold blossoms fulgurating in her eyes. The gold flares brighter when she leans down, pecking at his ear playfully. His eyes gleam brighter when her wings thrust harder.

Eowyn was showing off. She felt the electricity start to spark behind her ears and she purposely pushed her aching muscles harder. His cobalt light shone brighter than hers as her red feathers turn gold. He keeps running after her, the scent of a crisp dewy morning flooding her senses as he grows nearer. Her eyelids flutter, the fire in her whispering inaudibly. Her wings slow just as they approach the trail. Windsor slows to a stop a few feet behind her. She lands on her feet, letting out one last ecstatic sound before she shifts back. She lets out a laugh and watches the Prince alter himself.

His lips spread into a wide grin. "Your Highness," he bows at the waist. "Thank you for the snack." He straightens with a smirk settling on his face.

Eowyn produces a breathier laugh this time. "You would have eaten it anyway," she retorts, glancing toward the tavern a few paces down the road.

"Allow me to accommodate your appetite now, Princess." He takes a step toward the Princess and gestures forward.

She turns to meet his gaze, their eyes locking as his hand settles on the small of her back. He steps to her side and his eyes flare. Eowyn holds his gaze, her power mirroring his. He slides his hand to her hip, his nose a hair's breadth away from hers. Her magic purrs when his fingers trail to her elbow and slide down her forearm. He grasps her searing fingers in his frosty hand, his eyes never leaving hers as he kneels before her.

The Princess watches with parted lips as he presses his lips to her shifter mark, then another to the back of her hand. His lips leave a frosted outline on her hand. She snaps her mouth shut before he rises to his feet. "This has been my honor," he brings his other hand to his chest and places it over his heart. "I am eager to see the power you hold, *My Queen.*"

She slides her tongue along her teeth, maintaining a neutral expression while her abilities gather and sing in unison for him. She dips her chin in a single nod. She quirks a brow when his shoulders slump, noting the distaste for her lack of reaction gracing his features. He turns, yet not to let go of her hand. She steps to his side, closing her thumb around his ice-covered fingers. She wills small embers to her thumb as they start toward the alehouse. Her attention is drawn to the small, satisfied twinkle ghosting over his face when she slowly drags her thumb along his fingers. The ice begins to melt away, small drops of water leaving a path in their wake.

Eowyn raises her chin, turning forward. They walk to the establishment in a peaceful silence, *The Puzzled Monkey*. The Princess can't help but stroke the stallion's mane as they pass by. He huffs in appreciation. Windsor opens the door for her, his cheeks tinged pink. He stares at her as she walks past, her eyes catching his awestricken expression. He clears his throat and she feels him will ice back to his face.

"Your Highness," a bold orange haired woman curtsies to Eowyn. "Welcome to Exsar," she slowly rises, her brown irises meeting the scarlet eyes. "And welcome to The Puzzled Monkey."

Eowyn takes a moment to take in the woman's features. Her bright orange hair is chopped to her chin, framing her heart shaped face flawlessly. Her pinched nose is littered with deep brown freckles, matching her powerless eyes. "Thank you," The Princess finally drops her chin in greeting. "Both your Kingdom and Tavern are lovely," she glances around.

"Gramercy, Princess," she bows her head. "Sit anywhere you please," she gestures around to the many empty tables. "I will fetch the finest *aqua vitae* and two glasses."

Eowyn watches her quickly disappear behind a wall. Her head tilts to the side curiously before her eyes drift to the candle just inside the doorway. The ashes call to her, *wine cellar*. She blinks, turning to look at Windsor as his hand settles on the small of her back again. "You needn't be so apprehensive," he says lowly. "My people anxiously await your arrival."

Her stone cold expression drops for a brief moment as her brows pinch together in confusion. He gently ushers her to a wooden booth situated in the farthest corner. Her eyes rake over the detailed carvings and the hand embroidered cushions. She drags her fingers along the edge of the oiled wooden table as she walks around it, catching the Prince's stare over her shoulder. His jaw slackens slightly and her eyes drop to where his breath hitches in his chest.

Averting her gaze, the Princess slides into the booth. She rests her back against the soft cushion, her muscles slowly releasing the tension. She hadn't realized how much she would ache after flying for the first time in nearly a year. She keeps her focus on Windsor while he slides into the adjacent seat, though her eyes move to the fiery haired woman making her way to them.

Eowyn straightens her spine, carefully following her hands as she places a bottle of amber liquid in the center of the dark oak table. She places her hand on the woman's, a calming heat radiating from her finger tips. "I did not apprehend your name, Madam," she smiles warmly.

The walnut colored eyes met the soothing glow of the golden blossoms blooming in Eowyn's eyes. "Bryanna Grizel," the woman's orbs move between Eowyn's.

"Thank you, Lady Bryanna," Eowyn retracts her hand. It falls delicately on into her lap and she points her fingertips at Windsor below the surface, easing the thumps of his power beckoning her. She watches a muscle in his jaw tick, his eye flare dimly, from her periphery.

"You Highness," Bryanna curtsies, hiding the reddening of her cheeks.

Eowyn matches the woman's breathing, sucking in a sharp breath. Her fire pulls the perturbation from Bryanna's lungs and swallows it whole. The twin markings on her biceps shimmer contently. Eowyn rolls her neck, willing the woman to rise again.

"May I fetch you anything else to drink before I bring supper? A pitcher of water, perhaps?" She offers gleefully, all evidence of nervousness wiped from her being.

"That would be marvelous," The Prince says briefly, his eyes watching Bryanna walk toward the kitchen not a moment later. The Princess turns to observe him, an eyebrow raising when his eyes change from ice blue to a deep, vibrant blue. He narrows his eyes at the woman before his eyes return to normal and he whips his head toward her. Her other

41

eyebrow lifts to match the other, *a challenge*. The radiancy of his eyes dims in acceptance. She raises her chin with a slight smirk.

Windsor reaches for the bottle in the middle of the table. He pulls the cork free from the glass and fills both cups halfway. Eowyn takes in his actions, her eyes tracing over the outline of the veins protruding from his muscular hands. He slides a glass toward her. She grabs it with delicate fingers, swirling the contents. "What is *aqua vitae*?" Her eyes move up his arm, over the epaulette, to his curious expression.

A smile tugs at the corners of his lips and he reclines back against the bolsters. "Pixie Whiskey," he drawls, bringing the glass to his mouth. He ices over the glass before taking a long swig. "It means *water of life*."

Bryanna walks back toward the table with a tray resting on her palm. A pitcher of water, two fresh glasses and a basket of bread rest atop the platter. She moves smoothly, placing each item on the table. "Just a few more moments on the venison. May I get you anything else?"

Eowyn looks to the Prince, still awaiting to see any interaction between him and his citizen. "You have been a superb hostess, Bryanna," he flashes her a bright smile. "We will never forget your hospitality."

She watches as the woman bows her head gratefully. "You are too kind, Your Grace," her eyes move to Eowyn. "It has been a true honor to be the one who welcomes your bloodline home, Princess."

6

WINDSOR

The Prince knew she was reading him, he could feel her soul reaching for him. He holds her gaze as he chews the bite of meat slowly. Her eyes dim and he smirks. "Find anything interesting, Princess?" He purrs.

Eowyn's eyes rake over his frame, her eyes dull and expression unconcerned. "You are drawn to me," she says blandly. "Why?"

He uses the fork to pierce another piece of venison. *He could get used to this dance.* "I'm assuming you're aware of what you just did," the Prince brings the fork to his lips. Her eyes drop and he watches her focus on him pull the meat off of the utensil with his teeth. His smirk widens. Her gaze returns to his. "I'll take that as a *yes,*" he chuckles, looking toward the table. He swaps the fork for his napkin and nods. "She taught you well," he dabs his mouth with the cloth.

A silence falls over them for a brief moment. He could feel her staring at him, observing. He turns, his stare falls to her lips when she speaks. "Your soul mirrors mine," she circles back to her food. "That is why your power howls?"

Windsor smiles amusedly. "You are insinuating that yours does not?"

She pauses, her irises flicker. "Part of it," she bobs her head in acknowledgment. "Though I recognize all of you, you do not recognize all of me."

He reaches for the aqua vitae, "verily." He finishes the second glass of the sweet burning whiskey. "That would be the blood of the light," he leers over her features. "But the House of Light was chosen from the House of the Infinite."

Windsor feels the tension around them weaken. He watches her numb expression crack slightly, the corner of her mouth tugging upward. "All four Houses were born from the House of the Infinite," she murmurs.

Her indulgence makes his fingers twitch on the tabletop. "Indeed," he hums, his head swimming with the need to push further, to know what she knows. "And the Houses were chosen as protectors of the magicless, The Mother's own blood."

She licks her lips, he watches the movement carefully. Her smirk lifts into a smile. *She likes this*, a soul warbles in his ear. "*Said* to be The Mother's own children," her voice susurrates past his ears. "What a time to live in," she meets his stare.

"Certainly," Windsor affirms. "I am curious to know if Flare Meadowglade taught you anything about the House of Infinite." She averts a brow. He clenches his jaw, his eyes gleaming. He clears his throat and lifts his finger. A shadow swirls around it before darting past Eowyn's ear.

Good girl, it murmurs before disappearing again. Still, her expression remains glacial. Those born of the House of the Infinite do not speak of it and it satisfies him to no end that she held that boundary with another finite being.

The Prince reaches into his jacket and pulls out an envelope. He slides it across the table, his fingers tapping lightly. "Your Mother wishes for you to open this now that you are over the border." The gold flowers bloom within her ruby pools again when they meet his white orbs. He rolls his neck, holding her enchanting stare. Those eyes pull the darkest parts of him out and her eyes flare. "You're staring," he clicks his tongue. The Princess raises her eyebrows, plucking the letter from the table with delicate fingers. "We should start heading toward the palace," he grabs the glass of water and gulps down the rest of the contents.

His power pulls and yelps. He'd gotten too close, let her read his soul. Now it *yearns* for her.

He clenches his jaw when he sees her unaffected as he pushes himself out of the booth. He stands in front of the table, watching her lift her cloth napkin from her lap and dab the corners of her mouth. She rises from the seat and walks past him. A smirk appears on his lips, his feet seeming to float along the compacted dirt below them.

Eowyn goes straight for the door but stops before Bryanna Grizel. She turns slowly toward her. "I truly will never forget your kindness," her eyes glow a flash of yellow. The Prince cocks his head to the side.

"Your Highness," Bryanna bows her head, confusing the Prince even more. She was speaking to the Princess as if they were friends. "Welcome to Exsar." Eowyn smiles, turning and walking out of the doors.

Windsor blinks, gaze meeting the establishment owner's. "Thank you for your hospitality, Lady Bryanna." She curtsies to him, holding until the door closes behind him. Eowyn mounting the stallion catches his attention and he strides toward the mare. He unties the reins from the hitch post. "Your Mother said you'd not interacted with the public since you were a child. Yet, you seem at ease in public settings."

A shadow ghosts over her eyes, almost as dark as the horse's hair. "I was raised to be a Queen," she says directly.

He smirks, swinging the reins over the mare's head. He walks to her side and lifts one foot to the stirrup bar. "A Queen does not get sentenced to a year in a warded dungeon," he taunts as he settles on the saddle.

The horses start into a trot and Eowyn stares forward. "I committed treason," her tone is even, unbothered.

"Yes," Windsor hums. Something inside of the lion growled. "How so?"

A red sparkle appears just at the tip of his nose. The Phoenix cawing back. "The King ordered the execution of Zanna," her voice did not waiver nor crack. "He was in his temple when I found him. I burned it to the ground around us."

His heart rate increases, seemingly with the horse's speed. "The dragon lives?" He calls over the wind.

A wicked grin breaks out across her lips and she leans forward, soaking in the feeling of the rushing wind. "*My* dragon lives," she confirms. His eyes drop from the side of her face to her bicep. He commits every line of the intricate marking to memory. "My Mother called upon you after my sentencing, why?" She glances over her shoulder at him.

The air hitches in the Prince's throat and his hands tighten around the leather. The way her hair falls down her back, the platinum curls splaying as the breeze flows through it, the way her eyes flicker with curiosity... Something inside of him wanted to take the innocent picture and rip it to shreds, embrace the coldness that lies beneath the fire.

"Queen Alice and Queen Elenor had planned this based on a vision your mother had three years ago. I am merely a tool," his tongue darts out to wet his lips. "Your Mother and I have been in contact for eleven months. We planned this evening down to the minute."

Skepticism graces over her features as she turns forward. "Why was the Prince of a Kingdom that has been at war for seven hundred and sixty-seven years so eager to help the opposing Queen with my escape?"

A shock ran up his spine and he growled lowly. "I was given an order by the Queen," he feels ice dance along the curves of his ears. It's his turn in their game but he can't form a thought. Something inside of him, reeling, like it feels proud. He rolls his shoulders. His head whips toward her when she snickers. His time is up.

"Why does my Mother want me in Exsar?" She behests.

He abides, "to thrive, Your Highness." He shivers, *there was no hesitation.* He responded to her command without a single thought. "What binds the dragon?"

It's her turn to swing her gaze to him. "She lies in the slave pits between the castle and the Atraxian. A warded chain around her neck and one on each leg." Her knowledge sears into his brain, his head spinning. She'd seemed to know everything for a Princess locked inside of a granite prison. "She's fed well, by the grace of my Mother."

He smirks, "though she will never truly starve as long as your rage burns."

She raises her chin in acknowledgment. "What exactly was your order from your Queen?" Her eyes drift around them, the light causing the souls hidden in the shadows to scurry away.

"To follow Queen Alice's instructions," he goads. "Did you pull the anxiety from the woman who served us?"

A sarcastic laugh rings through the air and the dragon markings flare in response. "Her name was Bryanna," she huffs out. "What were Alice's instructions?"

He simpers at her, his eyes flashing, "to come to Iverness when called and whisk the Princess away." Her eyes narrow, but her gaze stays forward. The Prince cocks his head at her, his own vision dancing along the outline of her body. He clenches and unclenches his jaw as the horses start moving faster. "If the Queen siphoned the force of Tretanov to resurrect you as a babe, why does she not use it to overpower the King?"

After a few moments, he realizes she was not going to answer. He looks toward the east, the corner of his lips quirking up when he sees the sun begin to rise. The trees span for seventy six miles, another eight miles to the ocean. They would start through Leogar in just a few moments.

"Are you tired, Your Highness?" Windsor turns his attention back to the Princess.

"No," her head swivels in his direction. "What is the name of the city we approach?"

His eyebrows jump to his hairline, *she was waiting for his next question.* "Leogar," his tongue darts out to wet his lips. Her stare makes his blood freeze over. She wastes no time sending a rush of hot air toward him, thawing it instantly. "Have you ever siphoned?" He sucks in a sharp breath, her heat flaring at his prodding.

"My Mother has been collared since then," she glances to her hands.

He follows her gaze and a wave of nausea washes over him when he watches the lightning dance around her wrists. "You siphon her power," he breathes out, nodding.

"*Siphoned*," she corrects. "She no longer bares the markings of the House of Light."

He leans forward, amazement dancing over his features. "You hold both as a Primary," he chuckles, running a hand through his hair. She watches the motion through the corner of her eye and he smirks when he catches her. "My Mother will love you, fire bird," his eyes sparkle.

Windsor's smirks quickly morphs into a grin when Eowyn's lips lift slightly. The dirt path gradually becomes stone and the horses slow to a trot. Leogar, being one of two cities in Exsar, was already bustling with people rushing to work.

"Is there anything you wish to do while in the city, Princess?" He watches her eyes roam over the buildings. Many were shops or restaurants with small tenements above. Her crimson orbs glisten as she takes in the black Fuchsia flowers lining the road. His attention falls to her chest and he watches her chest heave. Her power gathers beneath the surface, her sweet scent overwhelming him nearly to tears. "Eowyn," he reaches out and places his hand on her arm.

A shock runs up his appendage and she lets out a breathy laugh as he recoils. His magic weeps at the sound. "I wish to sit." He leans closer as she speaks, her voice and her scent reeling him in and- "It doesn't have to be for long."

He blinks, something in him flipping. He inhaled sharply as her rage became his.

He draws in another breath and her soul cries out. His chest sputters out another breath, the sound and smell of her so overwhelming, so intoxicating. "We can sit for as long as you'd like," he clears his throat. "Your time is yours now, Princess," he assures.

"Thank you," her voice is smooth, her expression unwavering.

Windsor clenches his jaw. He bites his tongue, swallowing the question of how she remains so unaffected by her magic. Something deep inside of him, hidden in the depths of the darkness, snivels. A shudder wracks through him. He zeros his focus on her physical being rather than the inebriating magic thrumming through her.

He watches with parted lips as she bows her head at each and every person stopping to bow to them. She takes her time to pull on the reins and slow the stallion just to greet those who stop. He can't help but gawk at the way she seems to draw everyone toward her. But then again, he understood. Everything about her was enchanting and he wanted to dig into the deepest parts of her, to consume her in her rawest form. She was calling to him with every breath she took, every gasp a beautiful new melody to his ears. He couldn't wrap his head around the primal need to tear her open and explore every secret she dares to hide.

The Prince's chin jerks as Eowyn dismounts the stallion in front of him. His grip on the lead tightens but he keeps his position. His eyes follow her a short distance to his right. She kneels before a set of identical twin girls, no older than five years old. His eyes flare in approval as he watches the scene unfold in front of him.

She wills a bouquet of white dahlias to both palms and extends them toward the children. The girl's eyes widen and they snatch the flowers from the Princess. She smiles, a genuine toothy grin, a sight making his heart lurch into his throat. He chokes on his own breath when her eyes slide to his, holding the beam. Just as quickly, she turns her gaze toward the children's mother. She wills a cloth sack to her hands and extends it to the woman. Windsor quirks a brow as she makes her way back to him, holding the skirt of her gown in both hands.

"You make a good first impression, *My Queen*," he pushes out an airy laugh.

She stops on the side of the stallion, dragging her eyes up to him. A shiver wracks up his spine at the sight. The golden morning rays project a healthy glow on her pale skin. She raises her chin, her eyes flaring. Everything about her screams power in this moment and for once, his power cowers.

7

EOWYN

The Princess silently watches the various flowers sway in the breeze. The Prince sits a few feet away from her, utterly failing at hiding whatever was making him uneasy. She looks him over once and clicks her tongue. "I require four hours a day in my schedule to fly," she attempts to broker; a start to some sort of conversation to fill the tumultuous silence.

"Your schedule is yours to do with what you please," he says with a nonchalant shrug. She slides her tongue over her top row of teeth, feeling his eyes burn into her face as she stares at the field of various colorful plants. What she remembered of Iverness, outside of the Palace walls all of those years ago, was nothing like this. Things here just feel alive. Exsar feels warm, the air isn't bitten with the scent of dying magic. "That seems to unease you." His statement, though incorrect in his context, is correct to her.

"It is a new concept," she huffs brusquely. He's able to sense the shift within her, *interesting*.

Windsor hesitates, but chuckles. He brings a hand up to rub his palm against his stubble. "A man does not dictate his woman. He gently leads and leaves her room to thrive." He nods to himself, dropping his hand to rest on the ground beside him. He tears his gaze away from her. "I will help you come up with a schedule that suits your needs."

"*His* woman," she muses, "I belong to no one."

He opens his mouth to say something but snaps it shut quickly before forcing out a strained laugh. "I did not mean to offend, Princess. I merely meant you are my partner to aid in this life and I am eager to do it."

"Why?" She looks at him wearily. *A king to be, talking about aiding his queen. If it benefits him, perhaps.*

"I am curious about you, Princess Eowyn." She ignores the quiver that skids along her spine when her name drips from his lips. "You are fascinating," he leans closer to her, "and I have every intention of making you comfortable in my Kingdom. Even more so now that my people are *drawn* to you."

She looks down to the grass below her. The words seep into her pores and her power absorbs the sweet sounds. Something in her *sings* at his promise. She notices a glowing stream of white reaching toward her and lifts her head. Windsor holds a lopsided grin, the light inching even closer to her. She extends her right hand and it begins to swirl in her palm.

He moves closer. She holds his gaze as his power coils like a spring in her hand. "Play with me," he nudges her shoulder with his.

Eowyn looks back to the current of power, a small smile gracing her lips. A vibrant spurt of electrified static twists around the glowing spring as it expands into a ball, small sparks popping every few seconds. Windsor laughs, hovering his hand over the magic twisted in her palm. A cool blue brook flows into the center and ripples much like the stream to her left side. She watches intently, the beam never leaving her expression. A small flame erupts in the center of the swirling manifestation, fluttering in the shape of a butterfly.

"Breathtaking," the Prince breathes out.

Her eyes move from the flame, to him, seeing his eyes locked on her face. He holds her stare and moves his hand from hovering over hers, to brace the underside of her hand. His palm cradles the dorsal side of her hand, a thin layer of verglas coating his skin. His nostrils flare as she melts the ice overlay. He wraps his fingers around hers, the power swirling in their hands now, enthusiastically dancing and... *singing?*

She observes him for a moment. She takes in the sight of his ears perking up, the way his eyes crinkle and how his smile broadens. Her attention drops to his neck where her eyes snag on his pulse point, his heartbeat accelerating rapidly. His head turns and his eyes meet hers, both pairs flaring in response to the other's.

"You can't tell me you don't feel that," he whispers. Her gaze drops to where his other hand moves. He waves a palm over the space between them, showing her how their souls reach for one another. His wails, desperately grasping toward her while hers maintains the distance. The rawest, truest parts of them were reaching toward each other - but she did not allow him to get any closer.

"I feel nothing, Prince Windsor," she looks up at him. "I apologize for saying so, but... my powers, my soul, they do not call to anything. They did not even call to my mother." She'd never been capable of feeling anything, that's why it was so easy for her to harness her magic when others in Iverness could not.

He swallows and drops his eyes to where her soul, exposed only to the both of them, sits stagnant deep inside of her. His lunges toward her, trying to leap from his physical being and hers jolts backward. Her spine snaps straight as she stutters on a shaky breath. "They do," he urges, leaning back on his palms with a smirk, "you do not allow them to yearn."

Eowyn folds her hands in her lap and seals her soul back inside of her where it is protected. "They have no need to pine after anything," she turns her head to look at the horses. She could feel the frustration radiating off of him, but he stayed silent. "Is it painful?" She inquires, "to... allow your soul to... *want* things?"

"No," the Prince says quickly. "No, Princess, it's actually... quite pleasant. It's like dreaming but..." He trails off, a breathy laugh pushing past his lips with a gentle swivel of his head. He drops his chin to his chest and his tongue darts out to wet his lips.

Something flutters in her chest. "But?" She pushes, almost involuntarily leaning closer to him.

He lifts his head, nearly jostling at her proximity. "It's like dreaming but stronger," he whispers, his eyes dancing between both of hers. "It's like my soul has something to hope for." She knew he was speaking of her, knew he was speaking of the cry that his soul was projecting onto hers. Yet, her expression remains stoic. "Another desire I wish to consume without reprimand," he continues, watching contently as her eyes shimmer. "Another selfish hunger in my gut that I would egotistically satisfy," he brings a hand up to push a lock of her ashen hair over her shoulder. His eyes drift to her exposed collarbone. "Within the blink of an eye." His gaze locks on hers again.

The fire in her solar plexus blazes uncontrollably as if the flames are reaching for his hand now resting on her shoulder. She focuses on his extremity out of the corner of her eye while her gaze takes in every line of his face. The fire simmers, a sort of calmness rushes through her as thunder rumbles above them. He rips his attention from her and looks toward the sky. "It was me," she confesses, her tone gentler now. "It happens when I am... *pleased*."

Windsor's nearly white orbs connect with hers once more. "You were pleased with my description?" His power purrs in satisfaction, reaching for her again.

Eowyn's hard shell cracks slightly and she allows the slightest bit of her magic to twine with his between them. "I was," she nods once. His teeth flash in another lopsided grin and she can't help but laugh. His magic enfolds hers, greedily pulling for more. Her features harden again and the magic withdraws, leaving his a howling mess.

His smile only broadens. "My limits have been dually noted, Your Highness," he murmurs. She watches him rise to his feet beside her. He offers his hand. She places her palm against his and shivers when his cold fingers wrap around it. He helps her to her feet, inclining his chin toward where the horses drink from a nearby stream. "The King and Queen anxiously await your arrival, *My Queen*."

She feels chirp from the bird rise through her in approval. Whether it was for the nickname he's chosen for her, or the gesture, she was unsure. But something in her *aches* for him in the way he'd described to her just moments before.

He leads her toward steeds, his hand never unclasping. She'd expected him to drop it as they approached the black stallion, but he catches her off guard by gripping either side of her waist and effortlessly lifting her onto the horse's back. A small gasp escapes her as he settles her onto the saddle, one hand lingering on her hip briefly before he steps back. Her observation narrows on him as he mounts the mare.

"How long until we have reached the capital?" She clears her throat, the horses starting into an unhurried trot.

An amused glint skates through his now dimming eyes. "Just over one hour," he looks over to her. "You maintain a strong hold on the abilities you possess."

The Princess presses her lips into a thin line. "I do." She steals a glance at him out of the corner of her eye.

"Is *that* painful?"

"No."

"Look at me."

Her eyebrow arches at his demand. "I do not take orders," she keeps her chin straight and reinforces her mask of stiffness.

"I do not believe you," he chuckles beside her.

She hums uninterestedly, "that is of no concern of mine, Your Grace." She catches the way his eyes flash blue again from her peripheral vision. "What color are your eyes, *truly?*" The words tumble from her lips just like the bones Zanna regurgitates after feasting on sheep.

"Blue," he answers simply. "They are resting blue, when I am not straining my magic." Her only response is a nod of understanding. He was pulling himself back, staying true to his word of noting his limits.

Yet over the next hour, Eowyn could feel the uncertainty radiating from his core. She had utterly confused the poor man but could not care any less. He'd not pressed for more information, not restarted their game of questions, she'd rocked him to the rawest layer of himself. She pulled his intense emotions from the air, absorbed them and used them to fuel the insatiable arcane swirling within.

At least twenty five royal guards line the steps to the Palace as the Princess ascends with her arm looped through Windsor's. "That's her," she hears one whisper. "She's said to be **uncontrollable.**"

The Prince halts, bringing his hand to rest atop hers. Eowyn raises her chin in acknowledgment. He gracefully turns, offering her his other hand and ushering her to face the men. The Castle doors open behind them as Windsor raises Eowyn's hand into the air, clasped in his. "You will respect my bride," he growls to the lines of men flanking them. Their posture straightens, their eyes on the Prince.

Eowyn cocks a menacing brow. *"Bow,"* she commands.

The *entire* guard drops to a knee, her power seeping into the oxygen around them and manipulating their bones to bend to her will. A satisfied noise rumbles in the Prince's chest. "My Queen," he lowers her hand to his lips and presses a kiss to the back of her hand.

"A force to be reckoned with, indeed," an angelic voice calls over the sound of clicking heels. Eowyn turns her head to see an older couple approaching them, *the King and Queen of Exsar.* "Princess Eowyn," they both bow at the waist as the Queen utters her name. "Welcome *home.*"

Eowyn tugs herself free of Windsor's grip and curtsies deeply to the pair. "It is my honor to be welcomed so openly," her velvety voice sends the Prince's jaw clamping shut.

The man, slightly taller than her father, has dark brown hair with piercing green eyes. He wears a white jacket with a bright blue cape, the shoulders embellished with gorgeous red jewels. The woman stands about her mother's height with chestnut brown hair and beautiful ocean colored eyes, wearing a white gown with red accents and red jewels around her neck.

"I am Elenor Exeter and this is King Gideon Exeter III," she gestures to the male by her side. "We have prepared the west wing of the palace for your arrival. The carriage of your belongings arrived just before dawn and awaits your assortment."

The Princess takes a step back, startled. Windsor's hand falls to the small of her back, a conciliating gesture. "My belongings?" She keeps her tone level, though she knew Windsor could smell the confusion emitting from her pores. She'd assumed Tabot had rid his home of all traces of her, he *had* promised she would die in the dungeons. But she was also confused as to why she was speaking on behalf of the pair.

"Your Mother had your things packed and sent here before we left Iverness," The Prince's hand presses into her back while his Mother continues. She leans into the oddly familiar touch. He takes a step closer to her and slides his arm around her waist.

Eowyn watches the King's eyes drop to where Windsor's hand grips her hip. Her fingers wrap around his *possessively.* "The Prince had mentioned Her Majesty had been in contact with my Mother," she rakes her gaze over Elenor's frame.

The Queen's eyes flash nearly cerulean when they meet the crimson glimmer. A crisp, rain like scent washes over the Princess and her muscles relax slightly. A pleased smile graces over the Queen's face. "Why don't you come inside and sit down, my love?" She steps forward, offering her a hand.

Eowyn's fingers tighten around the Prince's. Her eyes flash and she sees the King recoil slightly. Windsor's hand ices over when flames engulf her hands. "I'm not going anywhere, Eowyn," his lips brush against her ear. "I'm right here."

Elenor's eyes glisten at the scene unfolding, resulting in the Princess stepping forward and taking her hand. Eowyn allows the Queen to lead her toward the Palace doors. "Your Mother left a message with your belongings," she closes her other hand atop Eowyn's. "I am eager to speak with you but I will understand if you wish to rest and recuperate." She offers, seemingly half-heartedly.

Eowyn shakes her head, a soft smile tugging at the corners of her lips. "Thank you, Your Majesty. But I fear I know my Mother well enough to assume what message she left. I will be unable to rest until I have some sort of understanding of what is going on," she divulges. She glances back to see Windsor and his Father whispering among themselves. "I must confess, your son is quite alluring," she looks back to the Queen as they cross the threshold, into her new home.

The white marble of both the floor beneath them and the walls now engluging them gleams in the rising sunlight, a stark contrast from the black granite of Iverness' Castle. A shadow dances along the crevices lined with gold flakes. Her gaze follows it along the walls, noting the family portraits along the corridor. A red wool rug stretches into the endless oblivion of windows and doors.

"We shall sit and chat in the drawing room. I will fetch Marie for refreshments," Elenor stops at a set of glass paned double doors. "Is there anything specific we can retrieve for you?" She turns to face her family and Eowyn.

Eowyn feels a *tap* at the tip of her shoe as she approaches the room. The Prince stiffens behind her when her nostrils flare. Something inside of this room was waiting for her. "A cup of hot tea would be extraordinary," the Princess nods once.

The Prince steps forward and pushes open the doors. Eowyn's hands tremble, the scent of dirt and death making her nose crinkle. The Queen turns and loops her arm through the King's. Eowyn steps back, bringing her hand up to cover her nose. Windsor turns to face her, watching his parents retreat down the corridor. She inhales deeply, the scent turning... *sweet.*

"Princess?" Her attention snaps back to the Prince. "Are you alright?"

Something here needed to escape. She nods, "I need to sit."

"Of course," he offers her his arm. She hooks her arm around his, happily being led further into the room that was buzzing around her. The red velvet wallpaper matched the ruby embroidered white couches, There lies a white oak accent table between the sofas. He leads her to the couch closest to the windows. He sits beside her, his leg pressed against hers. She makes no move to pull her arm from his while she takes in her surroundings. Her eyes glow nearly yellow as she narrows her eyes, looking for what was scratching at her senses. Another wave of ease washes over her and she turns to look at the Prince.

"Thank you," it comes out in a breathy whisper but it's all she manages to push out.

His arm moves from hers and snakes around her waist. He lays his hand on her waist, his thumb dragging along the outline of her hip. Her power calls to him, stretches and fights against her. "Let it go," his voice coaxes more of it out of her.

8

WINDSOR

The Prince's teeth grind together at the sound of the doors opening. Eowyn closes the path to her magic off as his parents step into the room. Marie, the head of the wait staff, follows behind the King and Queen with a cart. He shifts to pull away, but she stops him. Her hand settles on top of his. He flexes his fingers around her hip in acknowledgment and leans back into the sofa.

"Welcome, Princess," Marie bows at the waist before the pair. "I've brought you Xomélo tea and the ripest Brobosu," she hums pleasantly as she straightens. She sets a red and yellow marble tea pot on the table, then four cups with saucers. She sets down a platter of the chopped fruit before excusing herself.

Elenor and Gideon sit on the couch opposite their son and the Princess. Windsor watches his Father's eyes flick to where his hand lays against her side. Gideon's eyes gleam knowingly when they meet the Prince's.

Elenor leans forward and pours a cup full of tea. "This was your Mother's favorite when we were teenagers," she smiles.

The Princess's hand brushes against the Queen's as she takes the teacup. "You knew my Mother growing up?" He watches intently, she brings the cup to her lips and takes a gulp.

"I did," Elenor pours herself a drink. "Alice Azazé," she hums.

Gideon clears his throat, grabbing the Prince's attention. He slowly pulls his arm away from Eowyn and rises from the seat. He watches his father start toward the door.

"Her Mother and mine were the closest of friends. Alice and I spent much of our time together growing up," Elenor says gently.

He feels Eowyn's power coo at the mention of her Mother. He takes a few slow steps across the room before glancing back at her. He wasn't sure if he was worried about her or if he just craved the way she'd seemed to latch onto him. His tongue darts out to wet his lips and he reluctantly makes his way toward the doors. Gideon waits patiently, motioning down the corridor. Windsor falls into step with his father and crosses his arms behind his back.

"The Princess holds a great deal of power," Gideon glances over at his son. "Just as you do."

An asymmetrical smile forms on the Prince's lips. "She does," he laughs nervously. "And every once of mine wishes to devour her whole."

Gideon chuckles, clapping a hand on his son's shoulder. Windsor looks up and watches the corners of his father's eyes crinkle. "Yes, that can happen when you are around the blood of an opposing House," he muses. "She seems to have taken a liking to you."

Windsor rolls his eyes. "Something seemed to have switched in her when we arrived at the Palace," he discloses. "We played a game on our way here. A question for a question and if I prodded too far, we sat in silence. Then we arrived here and she... seemed to give into her shifter instincts," he replays the memory of how possessively she stood by him. Like she *owned* him and no one was allowed to draw near unless *she* commanded it. "She has the blood of all four chosen ones."

"Alice divulged as much," he concurs. "Did she display her powers before what occurred outside?" Windsor drags a tired hand over his face and laughs lazily. Gideon nods, tugging his son into his side. "You did well, son." He kisses the side of Windsor's head. "Why don't you go get some rest? I'll have lunch and supper brought up to your room."

Windsor stops, turning to look back toward the drawing room. "Is there a relic in that room?" He asks, "she reacted oddly when I opened the doors."

Gideon's brows furrow. "No, but I shall double check." He follows Windsor's eyes. "Your Mother will make sure she is well cared for. Olivette will aid her for the time being."

The Prince's shoulders relax slightly at the mention of his childhood friend helping Eowyn adjust. "I'll return to my duties in the morning," he clears his throat.

"Rest now," his Father gestures toward the exorbitant staircase. "Your duties will only grow with complexity from here."

The Prince mulls over the Kings words as he makes his way through the South wing. He'd done everything Alice requested, their bargain remains a secret between them. He'd given the Princess her letter, though she had yet to read it. He rakes a hand through his hair as he trudges up the steps. The white marble reflects the light throughout the Palace, something he'd missed in the few days he spent in Iverness. The walls are lined with wallchieres that glow at night with the power of the electric reserves. He passes by the priceless art pieces his Mother gathered in her travels to Chaka and Karlee, his mind drifting back to Eowyn. There were so many questions swirling through him as his feet carried him toward his chambers. What did she know about the Chosen Houses? Was Alice the one who taught her how to manipulate life? When the hell was he going to clear four hours a day to run with her as she soared above him?

He blinks, stopping in front of his hand painted wooden door. His Mother had painted the markings of the House of Planets in various shades of blue when he was born. Both of his parents were born manipulators, his Father of the ground and Mother of water. They'd not expected their son to be born with the blood of the Shifters and of the Infinite.

Windsor turns the doorknob and steps into the room. The blue and silver damask wallpaper calls to the ice within and soothes the lion. He blows out a breath as the door clicks shut behind him. He slides the jacket off of his shoulders and starts toward the bed. He lays the jacket over one of the chairs, his eyes dancing over the windows that overlook his Mother's rose garden. The sweet scent of cinnamon and blood wafts through the cracked open balcony doors, drawing him out. He steps onto the balcony, his body buzzing with excitement when he finds his Mother and Eowyn walking through the garden, arm in arm. His teeth elongate and his ears perk up, listening to the conversation.

"I'd promised your Mother that you'd start on your studies with Draven Idris upon your arrival. Though, I wish to give you a few days to convalesce." Elenor says softly, rubbing a hand over Eowyn's.

The Princess keeps her chin high. "If my Mother wishes it to be done, Your Majesty, I will start tomorrow."

His half shifted jaw clenches, his eyes flaring. *My Queen will not suffer for her own stubbornness,* the thought only pulls a rough growl from his chest.

The red and gold sparkles appear over Eowyn's shoulders, she knew he was there. He narrows his eyes on her. She jerks the hand not wrapped up with his Mother and waves him derisively. His power recoils from her dismissal and he bares his teeth in a silent snarl. A flame ignites in that godforsaken hand in warning. He retreats, closing the doors behind him but not before sending a rush of ice toward the flame. He watches her snicker silently as his Mother continues speaking when the flame ices over.

Windsor starts to the washroom, not bothering to close the door behind him. He gravitates toward the tub, his hand turning the cold water nozzle as far as it would go. His hands effortlessly undo the buttons of the silk tunic and he lets it drop to the floor. Once he's fully undressed, he sinks himself into the frigid water. He leans his head back against the side of the tub.

"Keep her safe and ride with her when the time comes," Alice's words echo in his mind. "She will not bend, she will not break. Most importantly, she will not vacillate. Do not stand in her way."

How could he stand in her way? After one dance with her in Iverness, he was prepared to give her whatever she asked. He was prepared to bend and break for her, just for a taste of the peace he felt with her. Every breath she exhaled was like a new melody to his hears and he couldn't shake the feeling of-

A soul slithers from the shadows and curls around his neck. *The Queen offers her a chance to fly*, it purrs. His pupils contract, a growl rumbling through him. *She summons the bird.*

Something inside of him fractures and he shifts into the lion before he'd risen from the tub. His paws slip below him as he stumbles out of the tub. He scampers into the bedroom, running straight for the open balcony doors. He pushes off his back legs, clearing the banister and landing beside the Queen on all four legs. His nose raises to the air, his legs bounding toward the scent of the bird.

"Windsor!" His Mother calls after the beast.

He lets out a loud, dominating roar in response. She stumbles back at the deafening sound. He ignores her, ignores the soldiers rushing from inside the palace, just focusing on getting to *her*. The scent of burning hair invades his senses and he runs even faster. He glances up when she caws. It's like music to his ears and he moves even faster. She hovers just above him for a moment before swooping down in front of him. He nips at her wing. She huffs, circling around him to dart back toward the palace. A growl tears through him and he skids to a stop. His heels dig into the ground and he charges after her.

Her wings glimmer in the sunlight, her scent wafting over the breeze. That, *thing*, deep inside of him is crying again and the only thing he can think to do is jump. He leaps into the air, wrapping his front paws around the Phoenix and tackling her to the ground. The bird goes up in a blaze, leaving Eowyn laughing hysterically under the lion.

He doesn't shift, makes no move to gather his magic as he stares down at her. She reaches up and runs a delicate hand through the black mane. He purrs, leaning into her hand. Her eyes flare, not red but gold. Another laugh rings through the air as her fingers thread through the wind stricken hair. His power reaches timidly, but it extends. He feels her hook onto it and his breathing ceases.

A white flash of light engulfs the pair. Her magic encompasses his and a mild calm washes over him. He shifts back, unaware of how he'd become humanoid again. His arms tighten around her as she pulls on his power, demanding more. He holds her stare and gladly relinquishes control over the magic. She keeps her hand in his hair, her fingers gently resting against his scalp. His chest heaves with ragged breaths as thunder rumbles throughout the clear sky above them.

Windsor smirks down at the Princess. "You are pleased with being caught?" He goads, his hands pressing into her back as if he were trying to get closer to her.

"Windsor!" King Gideon's voice booms.

The Prince jumps up and his smirk morphs into a teasing grin when Eowyn's eyes widen as she takes in his naked frame. He shifts back into the lion as his Father approaches, flanked by two of the Royal Guard. He stands dominantly in front of the Princess, his legs bent in an attack stance and teeth bared possessively. Gideon stops and raises his arms to signal to the soldiers to wait. The Princess sits up behind him. Her power releases his and his eyes blaze white with anger, not his, but *hers*.

"Are you hurt, Princess?" His Father asks cautiously.

Her rage burns brighter and he lets out a booming roar. He can't control the way his front left paw lurches forward. She was his and someone dared to insinuate he would ever hurt her. But he did want to hurt her, he wanted to tear her apart until he saw her in her rawest and most pure form. He knows he'd succumbed to the primal being and he could only relish in the sound of her inner bird cawing in approval.

"I am not hurt," Eowyn rises to her feet and steps beside Windsor. Her phlegmatic expression falling over her features again. She places a hand on his head, between his twitching ears, before sliding it down his back. "The Prince was accompanying me on my flight," her touch sends an electric shock down his spine. Gideon's shoulders relax but Eowyn's hand stays firmly planted on Windsor. Her fire grows and the Prince cocks his head, his stare still on his Father. "I do not enjoy those who do not understand the House of the Shifters making... *inferences*," she whispers quietly enough for only him to hear. He bows his head in acknowledgement.

"Very well," Gideon's voice was like daggers driving into the Prince's eardrums. "His Grace will have no opposition showing you to your quarters then," a knowing sparkle flashes in the King's eyes. Windsor huffs in approval. "Well then," he turns his back to the pair. "Gentlemen," he starts back toward the Palace.

The Princess turns towards Windsor, her hand falling to her side. He shifts on his front paws and nudges her hand again, scooping it back onto his head. Her mask cracks and she lets out a breathy chuckle. "You did well, cub," her tone was as soft as he'd heard in the past eight hours. He purrs, closing his eyes when her nails dig into the untamed hair behind his ear. "You keep up well too."

He huffs, craning his head to meet her gaze and narrowing his eyes at her. She only smirks and gestures for him to lead the way. The Princess walks beside him in silence with her hand lightly resting on the back of his neck. The skin below his fur burns at her touch. No amount of summoned ice eased the blissful pain. He leads her through the castle, her new home. Her fingers tap softly against him as they start up the grand staircase in the West Wing. He stalks down the hallway, his eyes drifting up to look at her.

Eowyn's cheeks are flushed a soft pink hue, her crimson irises dimmed contently. She keeps her chin straight despite his obvious stare. He takes in the way her cheekbones seem to be capable of sharpening the most Legendary of Blades within the Kingdom, *HeartSeeker*. Her lips rest in a soft pout.

You're staring, a soul whispers in his ear.

Windsor lets out a huff, scaring the soul back into the shadows. He stops in front of the only open door in the corridor. There are multiple decorated chests and crates in the center of the room. "I assume it is important that I read the letter from the border before the message left with my belongings," Eowyn's voice nearly makes the lion drop to the ground and roll onto his back like a kitten. He nods once. "Thank you," his eyes drop to her throat and he watches the slight movement of a swallow. "For everything, Your Grace." He nods his head again and takes a step back. He holds her emotionless stare for another moment before walking past her. He doesn't take another glance back until he's made it back to the South Wing where the Royal Family resides.

9

EOWYN

"Her Mother and mine were the best of friends. Alice and I spent much of our time together," The Queen spoke fondly of the Princess's mother. "Her and I travelled to Iverness together and attended Muddyvine Academy together," she glances over her shoulder once The King and Windsor had stepped into the hallway. Eowyn's ears perk up curiously as Elenor turns back to her. "Ah, you did not know," she smiles as she brings the teacup to her lips.

Eowyn reaches for her own drink. "My Mother has been forbidden from speaking of the days before the King's reign," she sets the saucer on her thighs. "Any form of magic is considered High Treason in my Kingdom." Her eyes drop to the liquid in her lap. It seemed almost comforting to know there was someone here who knew her Mother.

"Yes," Elenor's voice gathers her attention. "Your Mother had stopped sending letters to the Palace the day after their coronation," she sighs, taking another sip of the Xomélo tea. Eowyn watches her movements intently, searching for any darkness in her soul. Her shoulders slacken slightly and she brings the tea to her lips. She nearly hums with satisfaction at the taste. It's both zesty and floral, a spark of lemon and a dash of lavender, maybe even a hint of cinnamon. "I hadn't heard from her in nearly sixteen years, until your fifteenth birthday."

Eowyn's gold flowers bloom in her crimson irises. The Queen's lips lift into a smile. "What changed?" Her voice is just above a whisper.

Elenor's features soften. "You did, my dear," she leans forward and sets the cup on the table. The Princess's eyes studiously follow her as she rises from the sofa and walks to her side. She takes the seat beside her and grabs both of her hands. "She found a way to get letters to me as soon as she realized you were gifted with more than that of the Light." Eowyn swallows, holding the Queen's gaze and silently commanding her to continue. "I am curious to know if you hold that of the Infinite as Alice and Windsor do."

A satisfied smirk settles on the Princess's lips. She'd been able to manipulate *The Queen*. "I do," Eowyn nods once. "I am the blood of all chosen Houses," she imparts.

"You are truly as your Mother described," Elenor chortles, "would you care to join me for a walk in the Rose Garden, Princess?"

The offer catches Eowyn off guard but her expression remains neutral. "Of course, Your Majesty," she moves her tea from her lap to the table.

Elenor walks toward the door beside her. "May I..." She sighs, "may I ask you something, Princess?" Crossing the threshold into the corridor, Eowyn nods. "What age were you when you started showing signs of being a shifter?"

Her eyes scan the hallway, everything seeming to shine in the morning sun. The light filters through the arched windows and bounces off the white marble floors. Elenor extends her arm to her when they approach a set of double doors. She can't help but smile faintly at the gesture and loop her arm through the Queen's. "I am an Aves shifter, Your Majesty," she drops her guarded tone slightly. "I was flying before I was walking."

Elenor smiles, nodding her head slightly. Her warm, brown waves dance around her. "Windsor started summoning his claws at two. It scared me half to death at first," she laughs softly. The pair fall into a moment of silence, brief but bordering comfortable. "I'd promised your Mother that you'd start on your studies with Draven Idris upon your arrival.

Though, I wish to give you a few days to convalesce." She says softly, rubbing a hand over Eowyn's.

The Princess keeps her chin high. "If my Mother wishes it to be done, Your Majesty, I will start tomorrow." She senses Windsor behind them. Gold and red Phoenix sparks flash over her shoulders at him. She jerks her free hand by her side, waving him off. She feels his power recoil and she smirks, feeling the primal pull of the lion at her back. A small flame ignites in the hand, *that pissed him off.* Half a moment later, the flame is encased in ice. She drops the ice, rolling her lips into a thin line.

Eowyn can't help but notice the peace she felt radiating from the woman when she spoke about her son. "Windsor was much like you in that regard." She reminisces, "always eager to learn more." The Princess silently nods, wondering if she truly was eager to learn or just to abide by her Mother's wishes. The sun is still concealed behind the Palace as they venture through the garden. As her eyes scan over the large area, she takes in the many different colors. She squints, narrowing her vision on the closest ones. They're Eden roses. Her eyes slide along the winding path again and her magic purrs when she sees they're all two colors.

"This was my husband's wedding gift," Elenor says proudly. "He is a terrain manipulator. On our wedding night he summoned all of these from Karlee Island and arranged them before my very eyes."

Eowyn looks over at her, taking in the soft but radiant glow of the Queen. The blue jewels of her crown fit her complexion almost too well, nearly matching her irises. The Princess had sensed the marks of a manipulator, also from the Queen. Her seafoam eyes gave it away all too quickly. Yet, Eowyn was drawn to something else about her. Almost like a new kind of magic. The happiness emanating from her was something so... *new* to the younger female. "It is magnificent," Eowyn utters and looks back toward the beautiful landscaping. "There are so many colors," she observes. Her eyes dart from an Eden Rose with a pink outer layer and a violet inner layer to one with a majestic blue core and a red ring on the edge of the petals.

They continue down the herringbone stone path, arm in arm. After seeing nearly the entire garden, Eowyn feels a slight tug behind her left ear. The Phoenix was clawing to get out, a bright red feather sticking out of the tip of the cartilage. The Queen notices and lets out a small laugh. "Do you wish to fly?" She gently squeezes her arm.

Eowyn stops, turning to look at her. Her pupils dilate as she queries, "may I?"

"Of course," she nods encouragingly. "Just be careful, over the cliff there is an army base."

The Princess wastes no time summoning her wings. Elenor only smiles and Eowyn shifts fully. She pushes off the ground, launching toward the sky. A strained caw echoes through her chest as she flaps her wings as hard as she can. She belts out louder squawk once she breaks through the clouds.

The sun instantly warms feathers, the breeze bristling them gently. She closes her eyes for a brief moment just to enjoy the serenity of the inconsequential flight. There were no punishments waiting for her on the ground, there was no hostile guards ready to drag her to her father. It felt... *good*.

What felt even better was the rush of a darkened crisp scent invading her senses.

She lets out a squawk, dipping back below the clouds. He races after her and she can hear a low growl rumble through him. She coos softly, dropping to hover just above his mane. She flaps her wings a beat faster and sweeps down in front of him. He lurches forward and plucks a feather from her wing. She breaths a huff of approval, swinging around to dart toward the Palace. The ground below the Prince rumbles with his growl. He comes to an abrupt halt, the sound of his nails digging into the ground followed by the rapid footsteps of him charging after her. She lifts her head into the air and sniffs, her dragon markings flaring as she absorbs his desperation from the air. He lets out a sonorous roar and launches toward her. His front paws clap her wings to her sides and he pulls the bird into his chest, tackling her to the ground.

Eowyn hums her melody, going up in flames as the bird and revealed to be herself again. A foreign feeling bubbles in her gut, working its way to her throat and manifests as a fit of laughter under the lion. She reaches up to thread her fingers through his wild, untamed mane. He hums a near purr, her infinite calling to his. She continues to rake her fingers through the fluff gathered on his head. She feels his braided magic reach for her. The Princess releases her own to the call, just that of the Planets, feeling it encase every ounce of his twined power. His chest stills, blood starting to freeze over.

She swallows, a bright flash of silver light surrounding them. She closes her eyes and focuses on unbraiding his streams of chosen blood. His muscles relax above her as she unbinds the magic and tugs on the shifting blood, manipulating him to shift into the Prince again. She leaves her fingers pressed against his scalp. He looks down at her causing thunder to rumble through the clear sky above them.

The Prince smirks, "you are pleased with being caught?" His tone is light, almost teasing as his hands push against her back beneath them.

Her nostrils flare, the scent of intruders making her features harden. Then, a moment later, "WINDSOR!" The King's voice booms through the clearing in the forest.

Windsor moves quickly, rising to his feet. Eowyn's eyes widen as they drag down his indecent form. He shifts back into the lion, his Father approaching a heartbeat later with two soldiers on either side of him. She props herself up on her elbows and watches as the lion lowers himself into an aggressive stance. He bares his teeth possessively when Gideon steps forward, a hand raised to the soldiers to stop their approach. Eowyn's feels Windsor's magic fighting against hers so she releases the raw, primal power. She feeds a bit of her rage into him and his eyes start to glow *white*.

"Are you hurt, Princess?" Gideon's voice cuts through the air hesitantly.

She clenches her jaw and funnels more of her anger into the Prince. He lets out a booming roar, his left paw lurching forward. His own anger rises and the predator in him begins to spiral. He's *livid* someone would ask if he hurt her, then she feels a shift. She narrows her eyes at him and searches for his soul. *He wants to hurt her in all the right ways.* The bird in her caws in approval.

The Princess rises to her feet. "I am not hurt," she says firmly, her hand falling onto the cat's head. Her palm slides down his pain. "The Princess rises was accompanying me on my flight." She begins releasing her power, letting it latch on and manipulate Gideon into easing. Her hand never leaves Windsor. Her anger flares again and the lion cranes his neck to look up at her. "I do not enjoy those who do not understand the House of Shifters making... *inferences*," she spits out the last word, despite her quiet tone.

Windsor dips his head in a single nod. "Very well," The King takes a step back. "His Grace will have no opposition showing you to your Quarters then." Eowyn notes the gleam in his eyes and narrows her own slightly. Windsor huffs beside her. "Well then," Gideon starts toward the Palace.

Eowyn feels the soldiers hesitations and she absorbs it. Her dragon markings flare. She clenches her jaw as she manipulates the men into dashing after the King before turning toward Windsor. She drops her hand to her side and he bends his front legs to nudge his head against her extremity. She can't help but let out a breathy laugh as he scoops her hand back onto his head. "You did well, cub," she speaks softly, her tone nearly tender. He purrs in response, tilting his head toward her when she begins scratching behind his ear. "You keep up well too."

He cranes his neck to meet her gaze, narrowing his eyes at her and blowing out a dramatically exasperated breath. She just smirks and gestures toward the part. She watches him take a step forward, her hand lingering on his back for the duration of their walk. She could feel him trying to ice his skin over butt she wraps her power around his and renders it useless.

Her fingers dance on his back as they ascend the staircase in the west wing. He slows to a predatory stalk. The lion's eyes are wide with amusement while he leads her down the corridor. She keeps her stare forward, though her focus is on the way a shadow slithers from the ashes of a near by scented candle.

The lion's eyes scoffs and the shadow scampers away. The third door on the left is the only ajar. The Prince comes to a halt in front of the doorway.

She takes in the sight of both her's and *her Mother's* chests stacked neatly beside pine crates. She swallows and turns to face Windsor. "I assume it is important that I read the letter from the border before the message left with my belongings," she keeps her tone soft. She feels a rush of cool air, as if he were pleased. He simply nods. "Thank you," she whispers. She narrows her gaze at his dropping to watch the movement of her next swallow. "For everything, Your Grace." He nods again and steps back.

Eowyn keeps her features impassive while he brushes past her. He keeps his head bowed until he disappears from her sight. She cocks a curious brow before turning toward her room. The white, gold and blue marble walls shine brightly in the morning sun, polished to a smooth and flawless finish. The room can't be described as anything less than opulent and graceful. The black tile flooring is adorned with contrasting, luxurious white fur rugs. Her eyes move to the large bed dressed with the finest silk and linens, a white oak headboard with a lustrous finish. She turns her attention back to the center of the room where the chests and crates sit stacked neatly. She raises her chin and sniffs the air. Blaine Cromwell. She follows the scent to a crate.

Eowyn lifts the lid and pulls out six familiar blankets. All are of the same pattern, different colors. The first is white, the blanket she's had since birth. Alice had told Eowyn that it was a gift from the Secretary of State when he had learned of the Queen's pregnancy; she was later wrapped in it after Alice had resurrected her. The second one was from her third birthday, Blaine had chosen a pale yellow color. For her sixth was blue, nine was green, twelve was purple, fifteen was orange. Her eyebrows pull together as she sees a small piece of parchment folded on top of the same fabric, this one red. She lifts the paper and unfolds it gently.

> *I've saved this color for the moment you could spread your wings freely. —Crow*

Blaine Cromwell had sent her on her way with the seventh to add to her collection. She reaches for it, pulling it out and shaking it in the air once. In the middle of the beautiful swirling patterns, a hand stitched firebird. She hugs it close to herself and inhales deeply. Her eyes drift toward the chests, taking a step forward as the blanket drops to the floor.

Her Mother's scent is all over the stacks. She steps closer, hesitantly. She moves her four chests off of the two that held the Azazè family crest. Her fingers dance along the wood before drifting down to the iron latch. It flips up, releasing under her touch. She smirks, *she's still got it*. She lifts the lid to reveal stacks of books beneath a single journal. Her eyebrow arches at the stale smell wafting from the old books. She grabs the leather bound diary from the top and slams the lid shut, the lock clicking into place on its own. Her fingers slide along the envelope and she pulls out her Mother's letter.

> *My sweetest gift,*
>
> *You are safe. Your Father will harbor no ill will and we will be at your wedding, I can assure you of this much. Everything in Iverness will remain as it was, you are in no danger.*
>
> *You are to remain in Exsar until the time is right. You will feel a pull to come home after my inevitable ending. I do not know when, but you will feel an urge to return to Iverness. By now, I have spread word of this vision to those blessed*

with the blood of the chosen. There is an army behind you, they will die for you upon your return.

You are expected to learn all you can from Draven Idris. If you are unaware of who this male is, Flare Meadowglade will need a healer to mend his memories. Queen Elenor will walk you through the tasks expected of you in their kingdom. You will not be alone.

I will leave a book in the chest with your shoes. Elenor will tell you there was a message left with your things. When you have rested and released some of your power, please sit down and read through the book.

I love you more than anything, my little bird.

Eowyn lifts a hand, a shadow dancing from a near by candle to where she left the journal. She sits on the bed and smiles warmly when it places the book on her lap. "Thank you," she whispers. She watches the silhouette scamper back to the ashes. She listens to it call out happily in response to her gratitude. Her soul replies softly as her fingers flip open the cover of the book.

By now, you will have spoken with Elenor.

There are a few things I know she would have divulged:

I did grow up in Exsar. Yes, Elenor and I went to Muddyvine Academy as roommates. We both studied under Flare Meadowglade as you have done for the last eleven months in the dungeons. You have been given my belongings from Muddyvine. Eleneor and Gideon will aid with whatever you need in my absence. However, aside from Draven, you will need to rely on the Prince for assistance. He is born of three Houses, his parents only bleed that of the Planets. Windsor will be able to show you how to nurture the blood of the Shifters and that of the unspoken. Only trust him with the information that you are of the unbleeding. Elenor will not speak of it if you did divulge. Windsor is a lion shifter, a predator. Though there has never been a known predatory shifter amongst the Aves, he will be able to keep you safe while hunting in Estrella's absence. He has bargained with me, his power bound in a single braid. Should one of the houses within him crumble, so will the rest. Use this information wisely, Eowyn.

The Princess snaps the journal shut. *She'd unbraided his power, she'd undone a binding meant to end his life.*

10

WINDSOR

The Prince had slept through the majority of the day, only waking at the sound of a soft knock on the door. When he opened it, as promised, his dinner was waiting on a platter in front of the door. He graciously took it and devoured it on the bed.

His eyes drift to the nightstand drawer when he puts the platter on the surface. He glances toward the windows to see the sun setting on the horizon. A smile spreads across his lips and he reaches for the drawer. He grabs the rolled grit of SuperNova and the pack of matches tucked beside it. He holds it in his palm as he pushes himself up from the bed. He walks toward the dresser holding his training gear and slides on a pair of loose fitting, white linen pants. He doesn't bother with a shirt as he starts toward the door.

Windsor doesn't pass a single person on his way to his Mother's rose garden. He pushes open both of the glass doors and steps out, inhaling the evening air. His muscles relax as the feeling of being back home finally sinks in. He was no longer in the place where magic was forbidden, he was free to do as he pleased and the feeling quelled his soul. He starts toward the bench tucked in the farthest corner from the doors, the closest to the path leading out of the courtyard. He lights the match against the oak under him and lifts the grated drug wrapped in an iris petal to his lips. He brings the flame to the other end and inhales deeply, pulling the oxygen through the roll and lighting it.

The sweet smell of cinnamon wafts over the light breeze and his hands tremble when he meets Eowyn's blazing eyes. He watches her breath hitch as he smirks at her, blowing out his drag of SuperNova.

Excitement dances through his bones as she makes her way toward him. He takes in the way the strapless, white velvet dress hugs her torso tightly and flows from her waist to halfway down her shins. Her luminescent hair was slightly damp as it curled around her features. She dons no jewelry, just the dress and a simple pair of white heels. His mind hazes over and he takes another drag. She stops a few feet away. "Join me," he says lowly, "please." He blows out another puff.

Eowyn does not hesitate, she crosses the distance and takes the spot on the bench beside him. He looks over at her, raising a brow when he sees her gaze locked dead ahead of her. "You are intoxicated," she utters bluntly.

"I am," Windsor laughs, looking down at the roll pinched between his pointer finger and thumb. "Do you wish to... partake?" He lifts it between them.

Her head turns and her eyes drop to the drug, grabbing it between her index and middle finger. His power singes as her hand brushes against his. She holds his stare as she brings it to her lips and inhales deeply. The smoke billows around her upon her exhale. His breath catches in his chest at the sight of the smoke swirling around her like, it too, recognized her as *home.*

The Prince observes with pure amazement while the smoke twirls around a few of her loose curls. She takes another drag, holding the smoke in her lungs and handing it back to him.

Unsure of whether it the high from the drug or *her,* he leans over and takes it from her with his mouth. He breathes in. She tenses beside him, her gaze never wavering as the whites of her eyes darken with the effects. He grins, straightening his spine and clamping his teeth around it. The smoke exits between the gap in his jaws, his K9's elongating at the same time. He barks out a laugh when small sounds of thunder rumble from the smoke around them. "You are pleased," he teases while he plucks the roll from his lips. He flicks the butt of the roll, ashes falling from the tip to the stone beneath them.

Eowyn leans back on the bench. "Why did you bargain with my Mother?"

He narrows his eyes at the ashes below him. "I was following Queen Elenor's orders," he repeats. His bones cry out, begging him to tell her.

She hums, obviously not amused by the same response he'd given her about why he was so eager to help Alice. "Your Mother ordered you to make a deal with a woman you'd never met?"

Windsor shakes his head, pursing his lips and spitting out a chunk of ice. It shatters when it hits the ground. All of the pieces disappear a moment later, vaporizing into blue sparkles and sweeping the ashes away with it. "Alice used to spend one week every moon in the Palace until Tabot claimed the throne. I was seven years of age," he lifts his eyes to hers when her power shrieks.

She holds his stare for a long moment. He couldn't help but notice the glimmer of her Limbal rings turning gold. "You are older than me," she notes, "and unwed. Why?"

"I was betrothed for a year, four years ago," his power was now begging for him to continue. But he had given Alice his word not to speak with Eowyn about it until she died.

"Yet, you remain an unwed Prince." He lifts his gaze to hers. "Why?"

"I'm sorry," he whispers, a slight shake in his head. "I cannot say. It is part of the bargain." He braces for her a magic to flare, for her anger to consume them both. It does not. "Princess?" He studies her blank features for a crack, a nostril flare, a muscle twitch, anything.

"I heard you," Eowyn turns back toward the garden. His eyes glow dimly, a silent attempt to gauge her emotions. "I am not angry," she murmurs.

Windsor's eyebrows jump to his hairline. "You are not," he leans back and stretches his arm across the back of bench. His fingertips brush against her spine, a stream of electricity shooting straight to his heart and stopping it momentarily.

"No," she looks into his eyes once more."I do not care to learn of things that are not mine to glean."

He could feel his tongue trace along the points of his lion fangs, could hear her words and feel his thoughts forming, but he is gobsmacked. She still held herself so poised, talked so elegantly, after smoking. He slumps back, the words flying from that disconnected, still working part of his brain. "You are not curious?" He can't help but *gawk* at her. The way her hair fell over her bare shoulders, the white strapless gown making her silver locks glow against it. His eyes drift over her collar bones, the fangs buzzing with anticipation. "I would be curious," he rips his attention back to her face

She quirks a brow. "And what purpose would curiosity serve me?"

"Mother of Tretanov," he laughs. His chin drops to his chest. "You are one intriguing creature, Eowyn." He lifts the joint to her lips.

The gold rings around her irises gleam against the fogginess settling into her as she leans forward. The skin on his fingers burns when her lips graze him. She draws in a deep breath, his eyes never leaving the side of her face. She sits up, blowing the smoke out of her nose. A primal growl rumbles in his throat. He brings the roll back to own mouth and his blood freezes over when he tastes her on it.

A wave of warmth washes over him and thaws his veins, Eowyn's laughter echoing through the garden. "You are tightly wound, Your Grace," she remarks.

"Windsor," he meets her eyes. "I despise formalities," he inhales the SuperNova once more.

Her smile softens and she nods. "Windsor," his name drips from her lips so naturally. His fingers twitch, blowing out the smoke. "Do you always indulge in drugs on the palace grounds, Windsor?" *Oh, she's teasing now.*

He feels another rush from an increasing high. He nods, passing it back to her. "I do," he shrugs as she takes it between her fingers. "Do you always keep yourself so composed when intoxicated?" The words spill out before he can stop them.

"Yes," she replies shortly. "Do you want to walk with me?"

Windsor smirks, his muscles tightening with her offer. "The glorious Princess wishes to walk beside the Prince who steps out of his room half bare?" He brings a hand to cover his heart teasingly.

She snorts out another chuckle, rising from the bench. "Suit yourself," she quips, taking off down the path leading out of the garden.

His smirk only widens as he tosses his roll to the ground and stands up. He takes a few quick strides to catch up with Eowyn, looping his arm through hers. "Can't let you get lost," he whispers, falling into step with her.

"Right," she angles her head to look up at him.

He feels *something*, unsure of what, settle over him. His muscles relax and hers seem to ease with him. "Did you rest at all?" His other hand twitches by his side when a hoary colored curl falls in front of her face. He clenches his fingers in a fist, holding back from taking it and twirling it around his fingers.

"Yes," she holds his gaze, "did you?"

His eyes are glazed over as he blinks down at her. "I did."

She moves her chin to look ahead of them again. He unclenches his fist when she speaks again. "You are holding back for the first time since we met," she seems to gripe, "why?"

Windsor's eyes twinkle as she shifts closer to him. He stares down at her, his body seemingly igniting on fire with her proximity. "I do not wish to... frighten you... as my father assumes I would," he admits. She only hums, a soft sound rocking him to his core. He clenches his jaw briefly. "You do not believe me?"

"I believe you know I do not feel fear," she doesn't react when his arm tightens around hers, his fingers twitching against the bare skin of her forearm. "I believe you are harming yourself by not feeding into your instincts."

His power roars inside of him. She knew exactly what he wanted to do and it pleased the lion, or the magic, or maybe it was just his soul. Perhaps it was everything, or it was just... *Her.* Maybe she just called to everything he was and he wasn't strong enough to fight it. No, he was. He didn't wish to fight it, he didn't wish to fight *her.*

The Prince stops in his tracks, Eowyn stopping silently beside him. She turns her attention toward him with an expectant stare gracing her features. He looks down to their interlocked arms. "I..." he locks his gaze on hers again. "Eowyn," he breathes out, stepping closer to her. She lifts her chin to keep the shared stare.

Words fail him, he's completely and utterly entranced by her. The way her eyes bore into him, the way her power is creeping around his and encircling it. Her eyes flicker and she tugs on his magic. He releases it, unaware of his other hand sliding to her waist. A small smile tugs at her lips, her fingers dancing over his hand on her hip before sliding it up his arm. Her attention drops to the stones under their feet, a sheet of ice growing around them.

"It happens when I'm pleased," he avows, his voice low and strained.

Eowyn's smile grows and a ring of fire springs around them. The ice melts and the fire burns out as quick as it appeared. His eyes move from hers to her hand on his bicep. "Say it," she coaxes.

Windsor watches her fingers lightly dance on his skin. Her touch burns into him, his whole body reigniting every time she taps against him. "Say what?" He breathes out.

Her gentle touch moves up to rest on his shoulder. He lets out a low growl when her thumb brushes against the side of his neck. "Whatever it is that you wish to say," she swipes her thumb along the length of his neck.

His hand tightens on her hip, pulling her so she is flush against him. "I fear my thoughts are not to be spoken aloud until we are wed," he clears his throat, his eyes moving to her lips. "Even then, I'd be ashamed to admit what runs through my mind in this very moment." His predatory gaze drops even lower when her throat bobs with a simple swallow.

She pulls her other arm away from his and he quickly grabs her wrist, holding her hand up between them. His fangs tingle at the heat radiating off of her body. Her eyes scan his face but she doesn't resist his grip and he would put his life on the fact that he saw curiosity cross over her first the first time since they met. The fingers encircling her wrist spring his claws free. He watches her look at the nails, her breath hitching in her chest again. His eyes nearly roll at the scent of her anticipation. He moves his index finger quickly, slicing the skin on her wrist. She doesn't flinch, doesn't gasp, doesn't move as a single bubble of blood forms on the surface and slowly moves down her arm.

Windsor lowers his head, observing her goggle as his tongue darts between his tusks. He flattens his tongue against her skin, groaning while he slides it over the open wound. She tastes even sweeter than she smells. Her magic wraps around his and she pulls his control from him. His teeth clamp down around her arm and the fangs sink into the skin. She arches a brow, the only display of any emotion. He releases her limb but the scent of her blood makes him dip back down and lick the wound again. He can't get enough of it, it was more addicting than any drug or alcohol he's ever had. She was sweet in the hottest way, like fresh baked Omra pie. His eyelids flutter as he swipes his tongue over it once more.

"Windsor," she whispers as he lifts his head. "Look," she raises her arm between them and a small blue light shines inside of the wound. She releases his power and he stumbles back.

He recoils, watching the deep blue light seal her skin. "You're a healer?" He tilts his head. "There are no schools of magic in Iverness."

"I am *not* a healer." Her stare locks on his. "*You* did that."

"*I* am not a healer," the Prince takes another step back.

11

WINDSOR

The Prince didn't expect much of anything, surely not to be sat next to Eowyn during his shifter lesson with Draven the next morning. They'd not spoken to anyone of the incident on their walk. He was baffled and she couldn't seem to careless. She'd left him in the gardens, alone, and returned to her room. Now, he keeps his head low as he pretends to read from the book in his lap, his eyes darting to her every few seconds. She cocks her head to the side and turns the page. His gaze drops back to the text. "I have a question," her voice cuts through the silence.

He whips his head toward her and stares at the side of her face. He follows her line of sight to the front of the room where Draven sits on the floor surrounded by stacks of parchment. He nearly bares his teeth at the mage when he looks at the Princess. "Ask whatever you like," Draven rises from his position on the floor. His shoulder length white hair swaying with each movement. *"Knowledge can only make you stronger,"* he smiles.

The Prince notices the Princess's spine snap straight, almost as if in recognition, and it only fuels the coldness growing within him. Windsor now lets his teeth show in silent snarl as the headmaster of Drexrerth Academy steps closer to Eowyn. Neither one makes it known if they take notice.

"The Aves in this text are portrayed as prey, why?" She places her left hand, palm down on the cover. The tension in his shoulders eases with her movement and a wave of warmth washes over him. *She did.*

Draven's eyebrows knit together. "The Aves are considered prey in the House of the Shifters."

Eowyn's expression remains neutral but her eyes gleam bright red and her rage burns so sweetly inside of her. Windsor's power cries out as she speaks again. "A firebird is no *prey*," she keeps her tone level.

"A firebird?" The headmaster halts. "There has never been a firebird shifter." The Prince's eyes snap back to the Princess when she hums, almost amusedly. He watches her flip the book back open and resume reading. Draven looks to Windsor then back to her and he asks lowly, "are you a firebird, Your Highness?"

"I am," she keeps her eyes on the text.

"May I see?" Draven's attention turns to the Prince when he audibly snarls at him. His eyes flick between the pair sitting side by side on the sofa. Windsor's hand moves to Eowyn's knee and his fangs start to take form. "It can't be," he murmurs, taking a step back. "Windsor?" His eyes drop to the Prince's teeth.

Eowyn's hand drops to his and he feels the teeth retract. "Of course, Sir Idris," she wraps her fingers around his hand and places it back on the book in his lap. She squeezes his hand firmly, her fingertips singeing his skin in warning. He scoffs, but *Mother of Tretanov, she was easy to obey.* His eyes follow her as she stands from her seat, pushing the book to the side. She takes a few steps toward Draven and Windsor's eyes widen as he *cowers*. He leans forward. His gaze narrows on the slight tense in her right forearm.

The Princess goes up into a flame and is born again as the bird. Windsor feels his power come rushing back to him- *she'd been pulling his power from him?* He rises from the couch when she spreads her wings. Draven's eyes are wide as they dart between Eowyn and Windsor. The Prince's nostrils flare in remonstrance.

"Your Grace," Draven says cautiously. "This is a shifter lesson," he reminds the Prince. He nods once in response. His eyes slide back to Eowyn, his bones singing happily when he sees her head cocked to the side. She blinks and turns to their instructor. His shoulders sag slightly, realizing he'd give up every ounce of his magic to see that look in her eyes again. Draven takes a step closer, keeping half of his attention on the Prince. "You are beautiful, Princess," he brings a hand up to stroke her feathers.

Windsor takes a step forward. "Don't," he growls and his eyes flare briefly. "Please, Sir Idris," he clears his throat.

The instructor's hand drops to his side. "Your Grace?" he steps to the side and moves toward Windsor. He clenches his jaw when he has to shift his focus off of Eowyn but releases it when he realizes it meant no one had their attention on her. "May I... May I ask what you're feeling right now?" He takes another step toward the Prince and Windsor blinks to attention. His eyes flash cobalt, Eowyn's power piercing through him and coiling around him.

"Don't touch her," he grits out. His eyes slide back to the bird as she lowers her wings. Her eyes glow gold back at him and she coaxes the words out of him, "she's mine." A switch flips inside of him and he feels Eowyn retract her invisible grasp. He shifts into the lion, immediately letting out a stentorian roar. He pushes off his front paws and stands on his hind legs, swiping at Draven. Eowyn wraps a wing around him and pulls him back.

Windsor's breaths are ragged as he lowers himself back onto all four legs. Eowyn steps in front of their instructor and coos softly. His blue orbs roam over her frame, not missing a single movement. The door to the den opens and his Mother steps in, surrounded by her Ladies. She stands in the doorway, the same look of shock over her face as Draven dons from behind the Princess.

Eowyn glances toward Elenor and quickly shifts back, the scent of burning feathers making the Prince clamp his mouth shut. Her eyes meet his again. "Windsor," his Mother steps forward. He keeps his main focus on Eowyn but watches every movement from his peripheral vision. He only huffs in acknowledgement. "What is going on?" She asks slowly.

Eowyn narrows her eyes at the Prince and he feels her tug at his shifting blood. He shifts back, looking to Elenor with a stiff expression. "I need to speak with you," his eyes dart to the Princess then back. "Now," he briskly makes his way to the door and follows Elenor into the hall.

"Privately, darling?" She loops her arm through his when they step into the hallway.

"Yes, Mother," he keeps his eyes on the ground as they walk through the corridor.

Elenor glances up at her son briefly."You seem quite attached to the Princess," she tests the topic.

Windsor mulls over her observation. He sucks in a sharp breath but nods. "I feel a pull to her. Father says it is because she is of my opposing House," he sighs. They sit in silence for a moment. He contemplates disclosing what he'd felt her do last night.

"While the House of Light is the Opposing of the Unspoken, the Light was born of the Unspoken," she notes. "It could be familiarity, sweetheart."

"She undid the binding of my bargain with Queen Alice of Iverness," he says as her ladies take off in another direction.

Elenor gives Windsor's arm a gentle squeeze. "That is impossible, my love. Not even a seer can undo their own bargains," she tsks, rubbing her hand along his ice cold forearms. It was something she'd done his whole life, try to warm him up, regardless of the fact that ice coursed through his veins.

The Prince hesitates. He takes a moment to consider the phrasing, careful not to insult his Mother. "Her Majesty had woven my power together, a tactic to exert my power until the bargain is fulfilled. The Princess... she untwined it She took ahold of it, all of it," he breathes out an amazed laugh. "She released it." He's unsure as to why he wants to withhold the bit about her manipulating his power into doing what she willed and respectively how he enjoyed every breath.. He feels something possessive in him snap at the thought of sharing that, that was *his* memory. That was *his* bit of her that no one else had seen. Yet, at least.

"Your Majesty!" The Prince whips around, nearly pushing her over when he hears Draven's voice. He doesn't wait for him to say anything, his legs acting on their own volition and carrying him back to the den.

Eowyn stands in the middle of the room with her wings sprawled out behind her. The rooms melts away as he stares at her. The light blue gown complimented the warm tones of her feathers, the long puffy sleeves adorned in intricate lace detailing and jeweled bodice making her whole form glow. The expansive skirt of tulle falls in graceful waves, the shimmering blue hue fading into white. His jaw clenches while his eyes rake over every inch of her frame. He is completely entranced by her at this moment. Every contour of her muscles and curves captivating him to no end.

She looks at him peculiarly *again* and he rolls his neck. He steps over the threshold and slams the door closed. "You came back," she notes, tucking her wings behind her tightly.

His gaze moves from her wings to her eyes. "I prefer the wings out, Princess." The words hang in the air for several moments but he never drops her stare. He knows she is only going to do what she wants, but his mind is swarming with questions and not a single one will do the favor of cutting through the silence. She doesn't move, her magic seemingly closed off from him. Slowly, the tension in her muscles loosen and her wings hang slackly behind her. "You *are* a manipulator," he finally says while taking a step closer to her. "Blood of all."

"I am not manipulating you, Windsor," she says, almost irrevocably. "You know when I have manipulated you."

"I know you are not," he snaps and runs a hand through his hair. He doesn't miss the golden flowers blooming in her blood red pools. "I know you are not because of how much my... *uncontrollable* behavior *pleases* you," he takes another step closer to her.

She arches her brow. His eyes widen when she crosses the distance. He places his hands on her waist and pulls her into him. She places her hands on his shoulders, the massive feathered wings looming over both of them. "Everything about you pleases me," she imparts. Her words are like music to his ears, even though her tone and face are like stone.

His heartbeat thrums in his ears. "Do tell, *My Queen*," he rasps. His untangled magic reaches for her and cries out.

He watches her lips part while she speaks. "*That,*" she whispers as it strokes against her own magic. "*This,*" her hands slide down his arms, leaving near electric tingles in her wake as she moves to lay her hands on top of his.

"Does it feel good, Princess?" He slides a hand around to the small of her back. He twirls the end of a strand of her silver locks slowly. "Do you like it when I can't control the urge to let everyone know you are *mine*? My bride, my Queen, mine to protect and care for, mine to bend and break for." Her muscles tense below his touch. "Does that please you, Eowyn?" He speaks almost tauntingly. She'd tried to keep her power in check but he can feel it whirring inside of her.

She swallows, a slight nod following a breath later. She releases her abilities and allows them to twine with his. He presses his palm flat on her back and pulls her against his chest. Her eyes drop to his lips and he groans deep in his chest. Her fingers dance along his skin as she moves her hands up to his shoulders. "Nothing has ever pleased me as much as that does." He shudders when she traces a single finger along his jawline, his gaze locked on her lips. "You may-"

Windsor doesn't let the rest of the sentence fall from her lips before he slides his hand up her spine and grips either side of the back of her neck. He leans down, pressing his lips to hers. The kiss is soft, a stark contrast to the tight grip his left hand on her waist and his right hand on the back of her neck. Her lips are warm, she tastes sweet, her hands moving to cup his cheeks. He feels her wings settle around them and pull him in closer. He chuckles against her lips and retreats slightly. Eowyn's hands fall to rest on his chest and she leans her forehead against his chin. He loosens his grip slightly, but keeps his hands in their place.

"I do feel the pull to you, Your Grace," she whispers. "I apologize for prevaricating. My Mother left a message assuring me that I can trust you."

His hand slips down her back, coming around to hook a finger under her chin and tilt her gaze up. He feels her soul hum with the motion but her expression remains stolid. "Something inside of me won't be satisfied until I've given you the world," he professes. "I want to know everything about you and tear everyone to shreds who ever has wronged you. I want to bring your soul peace," he isn't in control of the words or how fast they spill from his lips. "I want to tear you apart layer by layer until I've seen every cracked, vulnerable piece of you. Mother of Tretanov, you fascinate me beyond belief, Eowyn. I just want to sew everyone who dares to look at you eyes shut." His index finger holds her chin up, his thumb gripping her chin just below her bottom lip.

"That seems a tad unfair to your subjects, Windsor," the corner of her lips twitch into a slight smirk.

Windsor lets out a quiet laugh, lifting his thumb to graze her bottom lip. "I wish to watch you burn the world down," he husks, "I wish to watch you unleash your rage." He steadily inches his mouth closer to hers. "And then I wish to devour any leftover rage you wish to unleash in *unspeakable* ways."

12

ELENOR

"Your Majesty!" Draven Idris comes rushing down the hallway behind the Queen and her son. Windsor turns quickly, not releasing her arm quick enough and almost sending her tumbling to the floor. He immediately takes off down the corridor. Draven moves to follow him but she stops him.

"He is fine, Sir Idris. He will find me when he needs me. What has you so frantic?" She folds her hands in front of her mesmerizing gown, the regal purple fabric commanding attention. The detailed bodice and flowing ruffled sleeves complimenting the voluminous skirt cascading elegantly to the floor.

The Headmaster of Drexrerth's shoulders slump. "The Princess is a firebird shifter," he says less frantically. "There has never been a phoenix shifter."

Elenor squares her shoulders. "I am aware of this, Sir Idris. I have Evangeline of Euclus looking into the History of the Aves." She nods down the hall, a silent request for him to walk with her. He falls into step beside the Queen. "I am curious if you know of any way to undo a seer's bargain," she demands.

"No," Idris says with no hesitation. "The only way out of a seers binds are to fulfill the terms or death. Is Prince Windsor unable to fulfill the bargain with Alice Azazè?" His voice is just above a whisper.

Elenor gestures for Draven to take the turn into the primary corridor of the main Palace before her. "My son believes the Princess undid the binds," she divulges, glancing up when she hears footsteps coming from the opposite way. A soft smile appears on her face as her eyes connect with her husband's.

"Queen Alice informed us when Eowyn siphoned her power to lessen the effects of the collar," Draven follows her gaze to the King. "It may be possible that she absorbed more than just that of the Light, Your Majesty," he stops, turning to face her. "I would like to meet with her and explore her powers."

Gideon's hand rests on the small of Elenor's back and he stands with his hip against hers. "Very well," Elenor smiles, "she and I are having lunch together. I will arrange it with her this afternoon." She nods a dismissal to the instructor. He bows to the King and Queen before heading for the front doors. She lifts her head to look at Gideon. "Was your journey into the Capital successful?" She wraps her arm around his waist as he starts to usher her back toward the den.

He lets out a hearty chuckle and leans over to kiss the side of her head. She leans into the simple, yet affectionate gesture. "It was, my love. It would not be an exaggeration to say the people were more excited to meet the Princess than receive their dividends." He turns his attention down the hall. "How was their lesson with Sir Idris?" He inquires softly.

Elenor smiles, "about as well as to be expected."

Her husband's eyes gleam knowingly. "He seems to have become quite... *attached* to her," he gives her waist a gentle squeeze. "Much like the cub he is." She leans her head on her husband's shoulder. He leads her to the door to the den. "They are not here," he laughs and shifts to stand in front of her. He places his hands on either side of her waist, his fingers stroking over the boning in her corset. "Should we fret?" He gazes into her eyes.

"No, Your Majesty," her hands slide up his abdomen to his chest and settle on his shoulders. "I believe our son planned to show his betrothed around the capital after she joins me for lunch," she adjusts the lapels of his jacket. "And you have a meeting with Layne Renhart," she leans up and presses a kiss to the corner of his lips.

He smirks, a slight shake of his head following a moment later. "That boy will be the death of me," he presses his lips to her in a brief kiss. "I will join you after lunch." He reluctantly pulls away from her, grabbing her hand and pressing a kiss to her knuckles.

"I look forward to it," she strokes her thumb along his fingers. The King grins and retracts his hand. "Please speak to Windsor about his behavior before he ventures into the public," she doesn't request, but demands.

He bows his head in acknowledgment as he turns back toward the North Wing. "Yes, Your Majesty," he calls over his shoulder.

The Queen folds her hands in front of her while she watches him go. She takes a step to follow him but turns on her heels and starts toward the patio. She catches a glimpse of Windsor leading the Princess, by the small of her back, through the glass doors. He stares down at her with a grin painted across his lips. Elenor stops, a good distance away but still able to watch them through the windows. Her eyes widen and she starts down the hall again when his hand slides up to her face and he pulls her into him. His ears perk up at the sound of her approach and he pulls away. He takes a step away from Eowyn. A rush of cool air attacks Elenor when she crosses the threshold and his eyes glow near white.

That's new.

Her eyes narrow on the Princess's hand, watching as it moves to Windsor's arm. His eyes dim and his Infinite retreats. *And that is quite interesting.* She clears her throat and glances between the two. "Will you be joining us, Windsor?" She gestures to the table to the left of the door.

Eowyn's features are unnaturally nonreactive, though her hand remains on his arm. Elenor doesn't miss the slight stroke of her thumb under his bicep. "No," he says after a moment of silence. "Layne is waiting for me," he takes another step away from the Princess. Her hand falls to her side. With a slight tilt to her head, the Queen watches their interaction closely. He looks over at Eowyn, contemplation ghosting over his features. She remains stoic despite how her fingers twitch at her side. His eyes flash and within the next breath he's walking past both of them toward the Palace. She watches Eowyn's gaze follow him before drifting to her.

Elenor blinks, a warm smile spreading across her lips. "Please, have a seat, Your Grace," she crosses the distance to the closest chair. Eowyn settles into the chair before her. "I am curious to know how your lesson with Sir Idris went this morning. He was very eager to learn of your shifted form," she says softly as she reaches for the teapot in the middle of the table. She fills both teacups and settles the kettle back on the table before returning her attention to the Princess.

"I learned that I enjoy reading the text by the chosen shifters." *She'd waited to have the Queen's attention to speak. How...* Queenly.

Elenor feels a rush of warmth as the thought flitters through her mind and the words fall from her lips before they even register in her brain. "Exsar's archives hold nearly all the texts written by the chosen children." She reaches for her tea, an attempt to silence herself. Confusion wells within her as she continues. "Along with many of their relics."

Something inside of the Queen quavers when Eowyn hums interestedly. "Relics?" She raises her eyebrows.

Elenor nods and spews the words, once again, before thinking about them. "Exsar holds *Heartseeker* of the *Infinite*... Well, I suppose we protect all of the weapons left by the Unbleeding, the Weapon Catalog of the *Planets*, and the Torch of *light*." Pride swells in her chest as the Princess's eye gleam with approval. "We also hold the blood of the *Infinite*."

Eowyn lifts one eyebrow curiously. Elenor smiles and takes another gulp of tea. *"The blood spilled to become the unbleeding."* The words sound so natural coming from the Princess, like she was one that bled. She places her cup on the saucer. "It resides in Exsar?" She probes, leaning forward interestedly.

Marie pushes a cart through the doors, catching Elenor's stare over her shoulder. She silently places two platters on the table, one in front of each of the Royals. Elenor's held an assortment of vegetables and fruit, Eowyn's the same but with meat off to the side. Marie leaves as quickly as she came. "Yes," Elenor says finally. She lifts her fork and stabs into a piece of Brobosu. "As Queen you will be in charge of their location change every five years." She bites into the piece of fruit. Her eyes widen slightly when Windsor's words pop into her mind.

"She likes to play a game," he mused, *"a question for a question."*

Elenor watches the Eowyn cut into the piece of meat and take a bite. "You and Windsor seem to have... *Prominent Instincts,* when you are around each other," she lifts her fork again. "Is this normal when the blood of the Light meets that of Infinity?" She has so many questions for the Princess, but nothing was more important to her than her son's predatory behavior.

"I've never met one of the Unspoken, I do not know," her tone is even and honest. "Why do you move the relics every five years?" She stabs into another piece of meat and wastes no time popping it into her mouth.

She was truthful and direct about what she wanted, Elenor respected it. She is just as Alice described, enchanting in her own way. "Tabot is not the only one who wishes for the expulsion of magic," she sighs heavily. "We do not know what power the relics hold, if any. But they are treasures nonetheless."

"Your Majesty, Your Grace," a voice drawls behind the Queen. She feels the warm air seem to dissipate and turns toward the doors. "What a beautiful scene to stumble upon." Layne Renhart beams as he starts toward them.

Elenor smiles at the noble, the same blonde hair, orange eyed boy her son spent his childhood with. He takes a few long strides toward her, leaning down and pressing a kiss to the top of her head. "Hello, sweetheart," she coos as he straightens.

"Hello, Mother," he places a hand on her shoulder. He looks toward Eowyn. "And you must be the betrothed," he muses.

"I must," Eowyn rises from her chair.

"Princess Eowyn of Iverness." He grabs her hand and raises it to his lips. "My future Queen."

A loud roar startles the Queen, making her jump and turn her head toward the noise. Windsor, fully shifted, charges toward his friend at lightning speed with his teeth bared. Elenor watches, horrified. Eowyn shoves Renhart aside and crosses her arms over her chest. The cat skids to a stop and sits at her feet. He growls at Layne who stares at him with wide eyes from behind the Princess. Windsor shifts, looking a touch dazed. He blinks a few times and raises to his feet. He wraps his arms around Eowyn's waist and she steps into him.

"Lovely of you to join us, brother," Layne scoffs, stepping forward. The Prince snarls in response. Eowyn's hands move to rest on his shoulders and he visibly relaxes.

Very Interesting.

Elenor clears her throat and moves to stand at Renhart's side. "Why don't you two join us?" She places a hand on his back and narrows her eyes at her son.

Windsor's eyes flare with defiance, his grip on the Princess tightening. "We are expected in the Capital," his voice was low and defensive.

The Queen raises her chin. "We've not finished our conversation," she squares her shoulders and raises a challenging brow.

His jaw clenches and he opens his mouth to retort but Eowyn raises a hand to the side of his face, silencing him immediately. He glances down at her. "Join us," she speaks much more gently than he.

Elenor's eyes widen when Windsor nods instantly. He places his hand on top of hers and kisses her palm. Layne chuckles softly beside her, "oh." He grins while they watch him guide her to the table and pull his chair closer to her. Elenor sits back down and motions for Layne to take the spot beside her.

"Your Majesty," Eowyn smiles, genuinely *smiles*, raising her teacup to the Queen. Windsor settles his arm around her waist.

Elenor offers a piece of fruit to the Hand-to-be. He plucks it off of her fork with his fingers and flicks it into the air, catching it in his mouth. "Why doesn't Alice rise an army against Tabot?" She asks bluntly.

The Princess leans back, lazily stabbing at another piece of meat. She crosses her arms, lifting the fork to Windsor's mouth. She holds Elenor's stare for a long moment. She waits patiently and takes a sip of her tea. "She's not going to answer," Windsor reaches for his betrothed's napkin. He wipes his mouth and swallows his food. "Why don't we start sneaking people over the border and do it on her behalf?" He meets her glare.

"They are collared," Elenor says simply. Marie comes rushing out of the doors with two more plates. She disappears once more, leaving the four of them in silence.

"I was collared," Eowyn cocks her head to the side. "Windsor removed it."

Her eyes widen. *The collars are made of Paronia, a precious metal resistant to everything– including magic.*

"Not that it mattered," Windsor chuckles, "she was speaking to... *shadows*," he almost spits the word. *Curious*. Elenor makes a mental note of it as he continues. "She was still flaring her magic at Tabot all night."

Layne smirks and leans forward. "Feisty?" He glances between Windsor and Eowyn- so does Elenor.

A shiver runs down the Queen's spine as Windsor grins almost wickedly. "Fiery," he whispers, lifting a piece of meat to his mouth and making a show of releasing his fangs.

"How did you remove it, Windsor?" She flicks her gaze to her son and reaches for her tea.

He leans back in his chair, chewing slowly. "Unspoken," he mumbles.

She nods in understanding, turning her attention to the Princess. "Your power was not subdued under the Paronia?" She tilts her head to the side.

Eowyn shakes her head lightly. "Suppressed, slightly."

She didn't give much, but Elenor couldn't blame her. The topic alone was considered High Treason in Iverness. She reaches across the table and offers a hand to the Princess. She places her hand, hesitantly, in the Queen's. "You will thrive here, Darling," she smiles brightly.

13

ALICE

Dearest Mother,

How I miss you immensely.

Exsar is absolutely beautiful, everything from the border to the capital. You can FEEL the magic here and it makes me wonder what it would be like to live here. Well, I suppose I do now.

I've been learning so much from Sir Idris, but even more so from your textbooks. Sir Idris has sat with me until the late evenings many times within the past two months, just explaining things to me. He showed me a text which detailed the first hand account those who bled to become the unbleeding. Reading it felt like I found a missing shoe.

I read through your textbooks every night before I fall asleep. You have such detailed notes and I have made sure to thank Her Majesty, Queen Elenor, excessively for keeping them in such stunning condition for me. My favorite, though, is your four leather bound journals. One for each chosen House, the protectors of Tretanov. You have so much more knowledge than you have ever shared. I hope to have at least one day with you to sit and just listen to things you know.

I cannot wait to see you for the wedding celebrations, thank you for letting me know when it is safe to contact you.

Eowyn.

The carriage halts in front of the Palace and Tabot grumbles beside the Queen. He snatches the parchment from her and crumbles it in his palm before standing from the seat. He steps out of the carriage, wordlessly. She follows suit, bending to grab the crumpled paper and tucking it into the small bag hung on her wrist.

"Alice," Elenor greets her as soon as she steps out. "Mother of Tretanov, it has been *ages*," she pulls Alice into a tight embrace.

"Elenor," Alice relaxes against her old friend and returns the hug. "It has been far too long," she sighs heavily.

Elenor pulls back, gripping Alice's biceps tightly while her eyes move from Alice's to her feet and back up. "Come, let's get you inside," she says after a moment. "I've prepared your room with lots of desserts and Xomélo tea," she whispers excitedly, looping her arm through the other Queen's and leading her up the steps to the Palace.

"Ellie," she laughs softly, "I'd much prefer to see Eowyn first."

Elenor's eyes widen slightly and she shakes her head with her own chuckle. "Of course, Your Majesty," she leads her through the doors. "She has been doing tremendous work with Windsor. They have been practicing in the gardens," she informs. "Oh, it is so lovely to see you back home."

"It is lovely to be home," Alice keeps a smile plastered on her face.

Elenor leads her through the Palace toward the courtyard. "Here, let's watch for a moment," she whispers and slows to stop just in front of the glass doors leading out.

Alice's smile widens into a grin as she sees her daughter, clad in a short metal dress. The metal is painted the color of the Prince's eyes, the perfect practice gear. Eowyn raises the sword above her head and Windsor jumps back, though not quick enough as she strikes his armored abdomen. He gives her a lopsided smile before lunging toward her. Eowyn summons her wings and darts upward. Alice belts out a soft laugh, bringing her right hand to cover her mouth. Eowyn wills her wings away, dropping back down to the ground in front of the Prince. He drops his weapon and grabs her hips. Alice's eyes widen as her daughter drops the sword and places her hands on his shoulders, allowing him to pull her closer. She watches intently while his lips move as he speaks to her. Surprise, shock, and pride wells within her chest as Eowyn's head tilts back and she *laughs.*

"Oh, my sweet little love," Alice drops her hand to cover her heart. "I don't think I've ever seen her so happy, El," she turns to look at Elenor.

She wraps an arm around Alice's waist and lays her head down against her shoulder. "I don't think Windsor has ever been so happy either," she admits, "or so defensive."

"Defensive?" Alice glances down at her friend. "How so?"

The woman at her side sighs and straightens. She motions to their children with her chin. "He *hates* anyone being near her. Very... *territorial,* if you will," she divulges, studying Alice's face. "Eowyn does not seem to react much," she promulgates as Gideon steps to her other side.

Finally removing her gaze from the pair, Alice meets The King's eyes. "Gideon, hello," she beams, "we were just talking about the children," her attention zeros back in on Eowyn, still wrapped up in Windsor's arms. Her arms now locked around his neck, their faces now mere inches apart. "They seem to be enjoying each other's company."

"Yes," Gideon's voice is laced with amusement. "It is hard to not enjoy Eowyn's presence."

Alice's ears perk at the compliment. "Is that so?"

Gideon moves to place his hand on Elenor's lower back. "Indeed, Your Majesty. She has made a habit of joining me in the Capital to disperse the weekly dividends to our people," she could hear the smile in his voice. "Our people were thrilled to meet her when she first arrived and they *still* fight for her attention every week, two moons later." He belts out a hearty laugh. "*Gragion*, we sometimes fight over who gets to teach her about the Planets," he motions between him and his wife.

Alice's heart swelled with pride and nearly exploded with adoration. Her daughter was *home*. She was healing, she was stepping into her own and she was not only the embodiment of *power*, but *beauty*. She'd managed to become even more alluring than when she left Iverness.

Windsor lifts his head slightly, his eyes connecting with Alice's eyes immediately. He lifts one of his hands from her daughter's waist and points at her. Eowyn's turns to glance at the window over her shoulder before disappearing in a massive flame. Alice's eyebrows pinch together momentarily, jumping with a yelp when Eowyn appears beside her. "Mother," Eowyn's voice was softer, kinder than she remembers.

"My word, Eowyn," she breathes out, grabbing her hands. "Look at you. You've been in the sun," her eyes move over her daughter's tanned skin. "You're building muscle," she notes and looks back to the crimson eyes she adores. "And you were wielding a sword," she laughs breathily. She shakes her head and pulls Eowyn into a hug. "You are thriving, little bird," she whispers into her ear before kissing the side of her head.

Eowyn wraps her arms around her Mother's thinning waist. "All because of you," she sighs, her muscles relaxing against Alice's embrace. The Queen's eyes fall closed and she sucks in a deep breath. Eowyn smells... *peaceful*.

A low whistle cuts through the silence and Alice pulls away from Eowyn. She glances at Windsor over Eowyn's shoulder and he jerks his chin toward her. Alice turns, catching a glimpse of Tabot and Blaine walking toward them. Windsor takes a few steps forward and places a hand on Eowyn's back. "Come," he whispers to her, his fingers sliding around to wrap around her hip. He gently pulls her to take a step back and she does, much to Alice's surprise.

"I'll find you soon, darling," Alice reassures her as Windsor continues to usher her back outside. Eowyn holds her stare over her shoulder. Alice feels a warm breeze brush past her when she moves to address her husband. She waves a hand by her side in acknowledgment. "Your Majesty," she curtsies to Tabot.

Elenor and Gideon stand off to the side, silent but hyper focused on the King of Iverness. "Pity, I missed the Princess," he jeers. Alice nods once in acknowledgement. "I wish to retire for the night. I shall see you at the start of the ceremony," he glances between the three royals.

"Very well, my King," Alice says abidingly.

Wordlessly, he turns on his heels and retreats. Blaine holds his Queen's stare for a long moment before following the King. Alice's eyes slide to Elenor and Gideon. "I suppose the three of us have some catching up to do," her once bright eyes flash a mere percent of what they used to.

Alice walks behind the King and Queen of Exsar, following them silently to the North Wing of the Palace. Her eyes dance along the marble floors, up to the massive windows adjacent to lamps. Her shoulders sag slightly, she missed the simplicities of magic. She missed powering electricity stores, the rush of the power leaving her body and the thrill of it regenerating over the coming hours. She missed raw, unfiltered power.

She sinks into the sheepskin chair sideways, draping her legs over the arm. Elenor places her hands over her chest. "Eighteen years it's been and you still look so natural here," she lowers herself onto the sofa across from Alice. Gideon sits beside her, perching on the edge of the seat with his forearms braced on his knees. "How are you? With the..." Elenor gestures her hand aimlessly in front of her as if trying to pull the words from the air. "Sickness," the word comes out on a defeated sigh.

Alice's pulse thrums against the collar subduing her power completely. Well, all but that of which she siphoned into Eowyn. "There is much to be done," she leans her head back and stares at the ceiling, her hair falling toward the floor as she hangs upside down.

Gideon moves to gently pat his wife's knee. "We understand, Your Majesty. Where would you like to start?" He leaves his hand on Elenor as he looks at Alice. She sighs, shifting to sit properly. "Let's start with Eowyn," she looks between them.

Elenor nods and clears her throat. "Draven Idris believes there to be a link between her and Windsor. They have begun working on siphoning each other's power," she discloses. "Eowyn siphons from Windsor easily and he struggles," she looks over Alice's face as she speaks.

"What does Idris say of this?" Alice leans forward slightly.

Gideon leans back on the couch and crosses his arms over his chest. "He does fine with it. It is the Princess who does not allow him to siphon from her. She let him do it once to prove that he could and refuses to let him. But he cannot stop her from siphoning if he tries," he says bluntly. Alice's ears perk up slightly. "Idris believes it to be for the Prince's benefit."

"For-" Alice cuts herself off, her head whipping toward the window at the sound of thunder crackling. She pushes herself from the chair and crosses the distance. Her gaze immediately catches on the firebird flying in circles around a black lion. Her eyes widen.

Windsor. He jumps onto his hind legs and launches himself into the air. The bird squawks just as she's tackled to the ground, thunder rumbling loudly above them. The cat releases her and she darts back to the sky, resuming flying in circles.

"They're playing," she laughs, placing both of her hands on the glass. "She's having... *fun*," she glances over her shoulder at Elenor with tears in her eyes.

"Four hours a day." She looks at Gideon confusedly. "They do this for four hours, everyday, without fail." She swings her attention back toward the window. "He adores her, Alice." She knew, she could see it.

Eowyn takes off toward the sky, spreading her wings fully. She shifts halfway, leaving her wings flapping behind her. She glances down and Alice follows her gaze to see Windsor, back to his natural form, looking up at her with a grin. She looks back to Eowyn and gasps when she watches her start to free fall.

"Eowyn!" She yells, pressing her hands harder against the glass while she watches her daughter plummet toward the ground. Elenor and Gideon rush to her side, peering over her shoulders.

They watch as the Princess flattens her body in the air. She flaps her wings once, slowing her moderately. She does it again a moment later and falls gracefully into Windsor's outstretched arms.

Alice lets out a breath she didn't know she was holding, dropping her hands to her chest as if it would calm her racing heart. "Mother... of Tretanov," she closes her eyes and shakes her head. She sucks in a deep breath, turning to face the King and Queen before she opens her eyes. "Let's leave them to spend their time together and speak about our business before we discuss the ceremony."

Elenor and Gideon nod in agreement and take their places once more. Alice takes another deep breath, nodding to herself before starting back toward the chair. "I think we should discuss the treaty," Elenor murmurs hesitantly.

Alice nods, "of course."

Elenor blows out a sigh of relief. "We are... prepared for war, Your Majesty. They are aware of the events you have seen and have been instructed appropriately," she folds her hands together. "The essential Palace staff have directives to report the shifts within to Layne Renhart, who is to be Windsor's hand," she pauses for a moment. Alice can see the hesitation so she smiles reassuringly. She knew what was going to happen, she saw it, and she was more than okay with it. "He will prepare the borders immediately and Windsor will greet every Iverness citizen to get rid of their... *collars*," she spits the word out like poison.

"Those closest to the Palace have agreed to remain, so Tabot does not notice anything amiss, and fight beside Eowyn when the time comes." She squares her shoulders. "The treaty expires upon my death." Elenor avoids her gaze. "Ellie," she snaps her fingers. Elenor reluctantly looks up at her. "It is inevitable. But you will march with her and avenge me."

"I will," there is no hint of hesitation in her voice now. Gideon moves his hand to rest in his wife's. Tears spring to her eyes and she nods, wrapping her fingers around his. "She will not need me, but I will," she lifts her free hand to dab the tears brimming her eyelids.

Alice smiled sadly, watching her friend cry for her. But she was ready for Gragion. The afterlife would be peaceful, as a child who manifested two chosen lines. She could use some peace before jumping into the next life after this one.

14

THE SOULS- (KEEP UP)

The lion stalks through the trees. The firebird swirls above him, her happiness radiating the scent of cinnamon and fresh cream. He keeps his attention fixed on her. *Something is off.* Life is too still for this time of day. *Scan the area*, the Prince orders silently. His eyes blaze near white, glistening with gold accents of her lining the rings of his irises. One stays under him, two rush to the highest trees to follow Eowyn, a dozen scampering into the forest.

Palace grounds should be safe, the one under him whimpers. It breaks off into hundreds of pieces to search the bushes bordering the pathway.

He huffs with a slight shake to his head. *Nothing is safe when it comes to her*, the soul took it for what it was - the final word.

Safe, one soul skates up.

Safe, two. Four, five, six.

Windsor starts to relax and moves into a trot. *Seven, eight, nine, ten.* He nods to each one.

STOP.

He freezes, his ears twitching in every direction. He looks up at Eowyn while listening for any sound of intrusion. His eyes shift from white to blue and his breathing soul stretches as far as it can. He searches for any sign of life beyond the souls at his mercy. There is none.

LEFT.

He turns, something flying through the sky catching his cobalt flashing eyes. He roars and bolts toward it, running faster when he sees it is an arrow. A massive arrow. Headed for Eowyn. Another growl erupts from his chest.

Drop down, one soul whispers to the bird. *There is a threat.*

She listens to the warning and glances behind her. Her eyes widen when she sees a dragon hunting arrow hurtling toward where she was flying. *Find them,* she seethes out the quivering command. Both souls dart toward the source.

Up, the soul beneath Windsor warns.

He shifts and stumbles slightly. "Shift, Eowyn!" He shouts once he regains his balance. She does as he says and plummets into his arms. He drops to his knees, pulling her to his chest. Souls swirl around them, cocooning the pair in a tornado of shadows. "Did it hit you?" He whispers, bringing his hand up to run along the side of her face.

Her soul reaches out in the darkness as her body curls into his. "No, were they after you too?" Her breathing is ragged, yet it still soothes him.

His soul swirls around hers and dances happily. "No," he shakes his head.

TABOT.

Her soul retracts from his immediately when the soul shouts the name and she seals the path to her purest form. His soul cries out and claws at her. He's only met with red hot rage.

Two souls slip from the whirl surrounding them and slither down the path. They dance along the shadows, smoothing over the sides of the castle. They shift along the glass window, reflecting a vision into Queen Alice's eyes.

Tabot stands on the balcony of the room, arrow drawn all the way back and aiming for the firebird.

Alice shoots to her feet and starts toward the door. She ignores the King and Queen's calls of confusion as she follows the souls down the corridor. She reaches down and grabs the skirt of her dress, lifting it slightly off the ground as she picks up speed to stay with the souls. They lead her to the front doors of the Palace. She dashes down the steps, glancing up to see if she can find her husband on the balcony. She scoffs to herself and runs around the side of the castle. *Fuck him*, her thought makes the pair leading her sing in approval. The souls lead her to the path leading into the forest. She glances up to see a figure retreat into doors on the second floor of the West Wing.

A soul hisses, *Eowyn's room.* It follows him, staying close to the walls in the shadows.

The second darts down the path to Windsor.

Alice drops her gown from her fists and runs with the shadow. The soul leading her splits in two, one half continuing to lead her into the woods, the other follows closely behind her, ready to wrap around and *restrain* her. And it does when she approaches the clearing.

"I'm going to kill him," Eowyn growls, a whip of flames shooting from her palm at Windsor. Alice's eyes widen, the soul coiled around her *absorbing* her scream.

The Prince grabs the fire, turning into a stick of ice. She drops it with an irritated hiss. Alice relaxes in the shadow's grasp slightly. Another soul darts from behind his shoulder and sweeps over the shattered ice. The pieces vanish in a cloud of black smoke.

"Not yet, My Queen," Windsor says softly, as if talking to a child. He steps around her, wrapping his arms around her waist and pulling her back to his chest. "Is it too much for you?" He moves his left hand to grab hers. He flips it so her palm is facing toward the sky. Flames dance at her fingertips, lightning swirling around the small fires. "Is it overwhelming you?" He closes his hand around hers, the ice forming along his skin making her magic dissolve. His other hand slides up her stomach, between her breasts and settles over her heart. "Don't deny yourself, darling," he leans his forehead against the side of her head. "Let me hold some of it for you," he presses his lips to her ear. She nods against him, her breathing coming in tattered gasps. "Yes?" He presses another kiss just below her ear. She bows her head again, this time more frantically. "Just breathe, baby," he croons. She sucks in a sharp breath and five small icicles impale her chest. Her hand flies to his arm and she grabs his wrist with flaming fingers. "I've got you, sweet thing," he wraps his other arm, still holding her hand in his, around her waist. "I'm not going to let anything happen to you." She only nods again, not loosening her grip on him.

The soul tightens around Alice, accentuating the importance of this moment.

Flowing like blood, the rage slithers from her soul and into his fingertips. Alice watches as the red stream engulfs the blue running through him. Eowyn's hand tightens around his wrist and she shoves his hand away, but stays in his arms. "Enough." The icicles sink back into his hand obediently, leaving the blood dripping from his fingers. He keeps his head pressed against hers and lifts his arm across her chest to suck each finger clean. Eowyn lifts her free hand to his hair and pulls him forward. "Clean up your mess," her voice is low and commanding. Windsor leans over her shoulder, flattening his tongue against the bubbling blood of her chest. He slowly swipes his tongue over each mark. Souls dance around them as a *violet* light shines through each hole before the skin heals over again.

He makes her unbleeding, the soul coiled around Alice loosens when it hears her thought. Her eyes narrow as the Prince lifts his head. "Our treaty expires upon your Mother's death," his lips move along her jaw. Eowyn's muscles stiffen at the mention of the inevitable end to the sickness her Mother endures. "You will be Queen by then and may destroy him in the cruelest ways imaginable," his voice rumbles through the trees.

Alice's eyes widen again and she steps out of the soul's grip. *It isn't his voice, it's thunder.* The soul moves quickly, slithering along the ground and up Windsor's leg. It twines around both of their necks and forces their chins toward the sky. The rumbling grows louder and the sky starts to darken. Alice follows their gazes to the *Purple-Bellied Iradoc dragon with five small hatchlings perched on her back.* Windsor smirks as the Snow White Temra, twice the size of Zanna appears, beside her. The white dragon's eyes zero in on the Queen. "*Welcome home, Your Majesty,*" his sonorous voice rings through the clearing, "*we have much to discuss.*"

Tabot tosses the bow and quiver to the ground. He moves quickly, toward the chests lined against the wall. He zeros in on the ones decorated with the Azazé family crest. He crosses the distance, pulling on the lock. A low, frustrated growl courses through him when it doesn't budge. The soul perches itself in the shadows from the sunlight being blocked by the silk of the curtains. It snickers as the King of Iverness kicks the box like a frustrated child. It starts to move along the ceiling, sliding down a marble pillar to the floor. It slips under the crack below the door and skates along the baseboards of the West Wing halls.

The soul flips and swirls it's way down the steps, bolting for the North Wing. Gideon and Elenor rush, side by side, to find General Ancel Tidreda. Layne Renhart comes barreling past the soul with the General at his side. "The Prince has the Princess under control," Tidreda informs the pair. "Everys has successfully freed Zanna and both dragons are now on Exsarian ground." His spine is straight, hands crossed behind his back. "Alice Azazé's vision has begun to unravel."

"I must go," Gideon nods once. He kisses the side of his wife's head. "I will see you once I've handled this," he promises before starting toward his office.

One soul, utterly curious, dances in the shadows alongside him. It follows through the halls, around every corner and through the door. The King grunts as he yanks open a drawer of his desk. The soul slithers up the wall and along the ceiling, positioning itself above him. He pulls out a heavy leather pouch with a small scroll tied to it. He rushes out of the office, quickening his pace as he moves through the halls. He makes his way to the West Wing and pushes open the Princess's door. The soul hisses as it follows him. He tucks the pouch under the pillow before dashing through the door once more.

The soul waits, calls and coos for Eowyn. After a long few moments, the soul feels the pull of her magic grow stronger. The Queen of Iverness steps into the room before her daughter. "Under your pillow," Alice mumbles, "you will need it from this point on."

15

GIDEON

"The treaty will remain intact," The King of Exsar slowly paces back and forth behind his desk. "As long as you never step foot in Exsar again," he stops and turns to face Tabot Alnwick.

"Done," Tabot scoffs and starts toward the door. "I'll expect my wife along after your festivities." He waves one hand in the air almost *dismissively* while pulling the door open with the other. "Blaine Cromwell will stay as her babysitter."

The King's hands clench at his sides as he watches the pathetic excuse for a Ruler stalk out of his office. He'd just tried to *murder* his own daughter and he felt *nothing*. The only reason Gideon had not slain him where he stood was because of Alice's vision. *Alice*. Gragion, the wedding was tomorrow which meant her days were dwindling. She was to cross into Gragion within the year following the ceremony.

"Father," Windsor's voice drags the King from his drifting thoughts. He steps into the room and closes the door behind him. "The dragons rest."

Gideon nods, rubbing a hand over the side of his face. "The Princess?"

His son's nostrils flare. *He is angry*. "We've parted ways until the ceremony. She and Alice stay with Zanna and Everys and the hatchlings. Everys was eager to speak to Alice," he says lowly.

A grin spreads over the King's lips as he crosses his arms over his chest. "You do not wish to stay with the Princess until sunset?" Windsor shakes his head quickly. "You seemed to be enjoying your time with her. I'd thought you'd find a way to spend time with her, even after supper," he chuckles. Truth be told, Layne had told him that Windsor planned on *getting lost'* in the forest with his betrothed until the wee hours of the morning.

"I was planning on it," he grunts, "her Father had other plans." He moves across the room and sinks into the sofa against the wall to the right of the desk. "She allowed me to siphon from her today." Gideon's eyes widen, though he was even more confused as to why his son was so... *expressionless.* "Her anger when finding out it was Tabot was too much for her," he holds his Father's stare.

"She only let you siphon emotion? No power?" He walks around the desk to lean against the front of it. His hand grips the edge of the oak furniture.

"Rage is her power," he says dully, *"and she only gave me a drop of it."* Gideon's eyes narrow slightly. "Are you alright?" He asks slowly.

"No."

"No?"

"No."

They stand there in silence for a moment. He was unsure of what to do, his son wasn't elaborating on what was actually wrong. Windsor stares at him blankly, he didn't even know where to start if he just started to look for something wrong with him. He hesitates but inquires, "do you know why you are unwell?"

"I siphoned too much."

Gideon straightens, *what on Tretanov did that even mean?* "Too much in what sense?" He reaches his hands out to rest on his son's arms. "Are you in pain?"

"Yes."

The King's brow furrows. This is so unlike his son. There was no explanation for anything, only short, blunt answers and now it was concerning. "How can I ease the pain?" He looks over Windsor from head to toe.

"I need you to get *my fucking wife* in here," he snaps.

Gideon steps back, watching the lion fangs start to take form. His arms fall to this sides. "Windsor-"

The Prince cuts him off, "*now.*"

Unsure as to why, Gideon *obeys.* He steps around the Prince and starts down the hall. He shakes the confusion clear of his head, the only thing that matters is helping his son- regardless of whether or not he was thinking before he acted. Thankfully, Eowyn and Alice were walking into the Palace, arm-in-arm. Eowyn's eyes meet Gideon's and they glow bright red. Not a single word is uttered before she goes up into a burst of flames.

Alice gasps, her hands raising her hands to her chest. "I will never not be startled by that," she sighs, turning to look at Gideon. He stares at her, eyebrows raised and lips parted. She tilts her head to the side. "Your Majesty?" A look of concern washes over his features.

He blinks, shaking his head and bringing himself back to reality. "My apologies," he clears his throat. "It stuns me when she does that as well," he brings his hand up to rub the back of his neck. "Windsor taught her how to do that, they are exploring their opposing powers every day." Alice glances toward the wooden front doors, her eyes roaming over the intricate carvings as if she were trying to memorize the details. His smile falters slightly. "You will return after this, Alice. We will make sure of it," he steps forward and places a hand on her shoulder.

Her muscles relax under his touch. "I do not expect it, Gideon," she meets his eyes. "I only expect my daughter to return for her people." He purses his lips and blows out a breath, tilting his head and raising his eyebrows. "You doubt her?" She motions down the corridor.

They fall into step beside one another. "Absolutely not," he laughs, shaking his head. "I only doubt the son of Kanika who underestimates her, especially with him," he drawls.

Alice's eyes dance with amusement. "You know he makes her unbleeding?"

Gideon nods, "and she does the same for him."

Alice stops in her tracks. "You don't think..." she trails off, but he *does* think.

He sucks in a sharp breath. "I-"

"Queen Alice!" Blaine Cromwell yells as he runs toward the pair. "Your Majesty," he breathes heavily when he nears them. "The King has departed for Iverness," he gasps softly, a hand on his chest as he steadies his breathing.

"He was told the treaty remains intact upon the contingency that he does not ever return to Exsar," Gideon discloses near nonchalantly.

Alice is taken aback by Gideon's revelation, her eyes widening in surprise. "He was told the treaty remains intact as long as he never returns?" she repeats, still processing the information.

Gideon responds with a smile, his eyes twinkling slyly. "And I think I've just decided that the coronation should follow the festival, so you now need to stay even longer," he continues, his grin growing wider.

Alice can't help but notice the lopsided, boyish charm that has been a part of Gideon's demeanor her whole life, like an older brother up to his mischievous antics. Alice takes in Gideon's mischievous grin, realizing how his playfulness and brotherly demeanor have remained a constant throughout their lives.

She sighs, amused yet slightly exasperated by his behavior. "You are truly still the same, even after all these years," she comments, but there's a hint of affection in her voice.

They start down the hall again and Gideon shrugs, his smile unbothered. "I find joy in pissing the man off," he replies, his tone lighthearted and even despite his words. "To Elenor and I, he will only ever be the man who ripped an Azazé away from the territory they'd sworn to protect. He is no King," he belts out a laugh. "Not after the things he's done to his own daughter," the words hung between them heavily. Gideon knew Alice has left out details of things he'd done to her. He knew the collar wasn't the end all, be all of his abuse, just like it wasn't for the Princess. But he knew she'd never say. She was tired, she was ready to see Gragion and leave this behind.

"I am content leaving Eowyn and her blood in safety." Her voice is like a satisfied hum. He turns his head to look at her side profile. He takes in the way her eyes trail along every detail in the hallway, from the carpets to the light fixtures. "My death means something much greater, you understand that, don't you?" She pauses to swallow. "Elenor won't hear it, but it is *true*.:

"Elenor is struggling because she knows you've not seen events incorrectly before. She remains in denial because no seer is able to see their own death," he keeps his voice quiet. His eyes moved to follow hers and his gaze softened as he realized she was reliving her memories here, one last time.

Gideon had danced with many women the night he met Elenor. She and Alice were late to the (then) Prince's 18th birthday celebration as they had come straight from their graduation from Muddyvine Institute of Magic. The school was just over the border, the only part of Iverness outsiders were allowed to see since the fall of Kanika. They'd made the journey in less than six hours and Gideon was ready to retire for the night when they stepped in. He'd known who Alice was immediately, the Azazé's were the last remaining remnants of the House of Light. But next to her, stumbled in a breathtaking water manipulator, chosen by the line of the Planets. He was entranced immediately, they wed two weeks later. Alice had fallen for the Prince of Iverness, Tabot Alnwick and was betrothed within the year. Alice had made it a point to spend one week per month in the Palace in Exsar after her engagement. For seven years, she returned home to flourish once a moon. Then news broke of Tabot's ascent to the throne and all communications ceased.

Until four years ago.

Alice had found a way to get a message to Elenor, one of the upmost urgency.

My daughter is in danger and your son is her lifeline.

One single sentence on a scroll had turned into years of strategic planning. Elenor and Gideon had broken off Windsor's standing engagement to an Exsarian Noble immediately. He had begun his own exchange of secure letters with the Queen of Iverness when Tabot had imprisoned his Princess for burning down his temple.

"Your Majesties," the young girl with cream colored skin and ebony hair approaches Gideon and Alice. She curtsies in their wake. "Princess Eowyn wishes to say goodnight to Queen Alice of Iverness," she says quietly with her head bowed. Gideon smiles warmly at Olivette, the child having grown in the Palace alongside his son and Layne Renhart, as she straightens. "Queen Elenor waits with His Grace to prepare him for tomorrow," her eyes meet Gideon's.

Alice nods beside him. "Very well," she sighs. "Gideon, I suppose you will be very lonesome tonight as Elenor and I have plans to get drunk in the gardens to celebrate preemptively?" Her eyes swim with a playful glint and the King can't help but let a wave of nostalgia wash over him.

His lips spread into a wide playful grin as he starts toward the South Wing. "I'll see you in the gardens, Azazé," he chuckles.

"See you in the gardens, Exeter," she calls after him.

The King walks briskly, his feet carrying him almost unnaturally fast toward the Prince's chambers. He pushes open the door and steps in. Layne's rust colored irises meet his immediately and he straightens in his seat on the sofa, positioned at the end of Windsor's bed. Elenor sits beside him with Windsor pacing before the fireplace in front of them. Two things were for sure, it is frigid in this room and that meant his son was furious.

He takes a hesitant step forward. He'd only seen his son so angry very few times in the twenty five years he walked Tretanov. Each time his Unspoken power shone through, so brightly around the others, and iced everything over in his wake.

His wife's breath clouds in front of her as she speaks, "Windsor is unhappy with the Royal Tradition of not seeing his bride for the remainder of the day."

Layne nods his agreement, his attention moving back to the Prince. "He is doing well to follow code," he appraises, tiptoeing around the lion cautiously.

Gideon raises his chin and looks at Windsor. "Once the wedding festival has concluded, you will be crowned King." His head whips toward Gideon and his eyes darken. The eyes that shown nearly white in the past two months dimming to the oceanic blue, reminiscent of his Mother's irises. *That pleased him.* "Alice will stay longer, Eowyn will be happier," he continues, watching Windsor's muscles relax with every word. "As King, you will await Alice's decline and head to the border to greet the collared Ivernese people as planned. Then you will march with your Queen." *That* made him simmer immediately.

The temperature slowly rises back to normal and the Prince unclenches his jaw. The other three watch him intently as he sucks in a breath. "I'm going to see her," he runs a hand through his hair.

Gideon's eyes slide to Elenor as he nods. "That's fine."

Elenor stands from the sofa and shakes her head. "Windsor, you have just been told you will be *King*. You must abide by protocols," she steps toward him.

"You don't understand," Windsor snaps, catching everyone off guard. "She could've *died*." The words drip from his lips like venom. "The thought of that happening makes my skin crawl. It sucks the energy from me and suffocates me."

"So you love her," Layne shrugs, crossing his arms over his chest. "What's the big deal?"

"*Love* her?" Windsor growls. Elenor places a hand on his arm and strokes his skin with her thumb. "I don't *love her*, I live for her. I had no purpose before her and I'll have no purpose after her. And I can't even get close enough to her to figure out *why*." His chest heaves in ragged breaths and he shakes his head. "I'd encase half of Deteron in a glacier if she asked and I wouldn't think twice," he looks at Layne, almost desperately. "Saying I *love her* is an understatement."

16

EOWYN

The Princess sits at the desk in the den where Draven Idris had taught her since her arrival to Exsar. A book lay flat across the surface, her left elbow propped on the table with her head resting on her fist. Her silver curls coiled gently over her bare shoulders, the strapless dress style being her favorite of the Kingdom's. The door opens behind her but she doesn't look up, the familiar scent of crisp rain washing over her.

Windsor steps in and closes the door behind him. He stares at her silently for a moment, making the corners of her mouth twitch. She lifts her head, glancing over her shoulder at him. He takes a step forward, his voice hoarse as he whispers, "please."

She turns back toward the book. "Please?" She flips the page, sighing softly.

In the next breath, he's sitting in the chair next to her. He moves his hand to sprawl his fingers over the pages. She lifts her eyes to his unamusedly. "You let me touch you," he brings his other hand to the side of her face. "You let me kiss you," he leans his forehead against hers. "What do I have to do to *know* you, Eowyn?" His voice cracks desperately.

She raises an eyebrow. "You know me, Windsor," she murmurs dully. She knows what he's asking, knows what his soul so openly craves.

"*Stop*, Eowyn," he shifts in the seat, bringing his other hand up to cup her face between his palms. He gently tugs her closer. Her lips brush against his as she moves with him. "I want all of you," he nudges his nose against hers. "Even if I have to spend the rest of my life picking you apart piece by piece, I will. I'll do *anything*," his eyes flare white for a split second.

The Princess reaches out and wraps her power around his. His soul cries out, pushing between them and humming when hers strokes his. "Anything?" Her eyes glow softly, curiosity blooming in her red pools.

"Anything, darling," he breathes out instantly.

She pulls back, pushing his hands away from her. His face drops and he swallows loudly. She can feel him resisting the urge to lunge for her again and raises an eyebrow. "Grovel."

Windsor's eyebrows furrow together. "What?" She intertwines her fingers in her lap, blinking expectantly. "You want me to beg? For what?" His confusion smells like the Atraxian sea in the winter months and she inhales deeply.

"If you don't know what you are asking for then how shall I give it to you?"

His jaw clenches and a smirk pulls at her lips. Her eyes move with him while he slowly lowers himself to kneel beside her. "Eowyn," he grabs the legs of her chair and pulls her to face him completely. "Please," he wraps his hands around her ankles tightly. "Give me something. Give me a piece of you no one else has. Please, My Queen... I want nothing more than to drown in you." His words bleed honesty, raw vulnerability and she *loves* it.

Eowyn reaches down, cupping the side of his neck as she strokes her thumb along his cheek just below his eye. "Cry for me," she presses the pad of her thumb into his cheekbone, her nail biting into the thin flesh under his eye. "Show me just how badly you crave to know every part of me, show me how much it hurts to know you will only ever know what I allow you to," she demands in a hushed voice. As soon as she releases the pressure on his face, tears spring to the corners of his eyes. He blinks and one tear slips from his right eye. Gold flecks bloom within the red of her eyes, something that had only started once she crossed the border. "So eager to please me," she smiles faintly.

Another tear slips from the same eye as if it was a damn begging to be broken. "*Please*," he drags his tongue along the top row of his teeth.

She leans back, pulling her hand away from his face. He shakes his head frantically, gripping her hand in claw-drawn fingers and pressing her palm to his face. "What?" She pouts, stroking her thumb across his skin again. Her thumb runs softly across his skin, back and forth, a gentle gesture that both soothes and teases. His eyes flutter closed, his face turning into her touch, craving any bit of her he can get. The tears are still there, just barely clinging to his lashes, making her touch even more intense, more intimate. He looks at her, his face a mix of pain and desire, wanting nothing more than to succumb to her, give her everything she demands. She watches his thoughts swirl with each small change in his expression. "I *adore* our time together," she admits, his breath shallow and shaky as he blinks away the tears she urged.

"As do I," he mutters, almost inaudibly. His hands tighten around her ankles. He holds her gaze for another moment, his eyes pleading silently. "Eowyn, please," he moves his hands up to grip her calves. "Give me more, baby, give me something," he beseeches. His fingers dance up to the backs of her knees.

Something in him shifts slightly, his demeanor changing as his hands tighten possessively. "Windsor," she warns, lifting her chin. "We are not in one of our rooms." Memories of the past fourteen nights they've spent together flashing before her.

"Give me something," he says through gritted teeth. *He is getting angry,* her ears perk up at the revelation.

"You are playing with fire, cub," her voice hardens. His eyes shine white and she can feel him tugging at the fire within her. It rages, not against him, but with him. He unhurriedly ushers her legs open, his eyes never leaving hers. She quirks a brow but concedes. "I was confined to the Palace on my eighth birthday because I broke the collar off of my Mother," the only sign of any release of her restraint is the way her blinking slows. "Tabot had them altered to be completely magic resistant after that."

She watches the way his head tilts to his right, his fingers delicately massaging her muscles. "He began to mine Paronia," his eyes dim as they roam over her face.

Eowyn relaxes her features and nods. "Though as being chosen by the Infinite, he was unable to collar me," she discloses, cautiously.

The way his fingers occasionally brush against the outsides of her thighs makes goosebumps spread like a wildfire. "How did he get a collar on you for your birthday celebration?" He steadily pushes the skirt of the dress to sit just over her knees.

"I was to agree to it if I wished to attend the ball," her eyes drop to where his hands still massage the backs of her knees, his thumbs gently gliding over the sides of her joints. "It was to come off once I was in the dungeons again, but he instructed Blaine to leave it on," she lifts her eyes to his again.

He nods understandingly, bending to press his lips to her left knee. "The collar wasn't holding you, anyway," he mumbles into her skin before moving to do the same to the other leg. "You would've broken it eventually," he rests his chin in the dip between her legs. "I know you would've," his voice drops to a whisper as his fingers circle against her skin.

His touch and lips are like ice on her skin but it burns all the same. "I didn't have to," her eyes flash and he growls, pulling her legs further apart. "You saved me."

The Prince moves swiftly, pushing the skirt of the simplistic gown up to her mid thigh. "I would do it everyday for the rest of my life," his lips return to her skin, this time dancing along her inner thighs as he speaks. "I would save you every second of every day for the rest of eternity," his breath is cool against her skin. Eowyn watches him prudently, feeling the truth in his words but not being able to focus on anything other than the way his ice burned just as her fire did. It was nothing new, but it captivated her all the same - and he damn well knew it. "And then I would bring you back here," his hands slip up to hold her hips under the linen of the gown. He grips her roughly, his fingers digging into her flesh and pulling her forward. A small gasp escapes her lips, making a wicked grin spread across his face. "And I would do the most unspeakable things to you," he pushes the skirt an inch higher. "Then I would save you all over again," he nips at the skin of her thighs. "Just to bring you back *home* and worship you." His tongue tracing patterns across her flesh as he speaks, "I would save you, again and again, my love. Just so I could bring you here, to our sanctuary, and give you everything you desire. I would fight for you, I would die for you. And then I would spend every moment of every day making sure you feel nothing but pure bliss." His teeth sink into her flesh, leaving a mark, a memory of this moment on her skin. "No one else shall ever touch you, no one else shall ever see you like this." His hands grip tighter, as he starts moving up against her inner thigh, leaving a trail of hot, wet kisses. His teeth graze her skin, leaving behind red bite marks in his wake. His mouth moves almost frantically as he works his way up.

Eowyn lets out a shaky breath, reaching down and moving the gown even higher up her thighs. He groans against her and follows her hands. "No one will ever have me the way you do," she runs a hand through his hair, tugging gently. He holds her gaze as he lifts his head from her legs. His eyes flick between her face and her lap as she adjusts in the chair, leaning back and spreading her legs even wider.

"Mother of Tretanov," his eyes start to roll when she bunches the fabric around her waist. She watches his eyes shift from white to blue, the scent of her arousal making him fall victim to the predator inside of him. He wraps his arms around her thighs, pulling her to the edge of the seat. "I thought your happiness was the sweetest thing I've ever smelled," his eyes darken as he inhales deeply. "This is enough to send me to Gragion, right here, right now." He leans in and runs his nose along her slit, gathering her juices on the tip.

An involuntary shiver wracks through the Princess as he pulls away, letting the arousal drip off of his nose and onto his tongue. He yanks her forward again, this time his mouth widening to cover her from her clit to her core. She gasps and he dips his tongue into her. She grabs at the arms of the chair, focusing on the way her soul cradles his, rather than the way he leisurely trails his tongue up. He reaches the sensitive bundle of nerves, his tongue swirling around the throbbing bud. "Windsor," she breathes out as she jolts.

"No," he growls, moving a hand up her stomach and to her neck. He wraps his fingers around her throat, his claws slicing the skin on either side. The smell of her blood bubbling to the surface fills the space between them and he nips at her clit. She lurches forward, her hands flying to his shoulders as she whimpers. He retracts his claws and pushes her back against the chair. Her back collides with the wood on a soft thud. His tongue slithers down and back up again. He lifts his eyes to hers. An involuntary moan slips past the Princess's lips, her eyes drooping slightly. "Keep your eyes on me," he snarls into her. "Don't look away. Give me more, Eowyn," his other hand moves to lay flat on her lower abdomen.

Eowyn's chest heaves in sharp, ragged breaths. Her mind goes completely blank and all she can focus on is the way his tongue dips into her core. Her muscles contract around him as he carves his name into her walls, his hand sliding closer and closer to where his mouth moves against her. "I can feel you," she exhales shakily. "I can feel your jealousy when you have to leave me with Draven Idris everyday."

Before the Princess can comprehend what's happening, Windsor tightens his hand on her neck and moves the other to her hip. He yanks her off of the chair, pivoting to his left and slamming her down on the floor beside him. She feels a sharp pain rip through her head, followed by his elongated K9 tooth piercing through her clit. She lets out a sharp cry and lifts her hand to summon a flame. One hand on her neck, the other raises to put out the flame with iced over fingers as his tongue laps over the wound and seals it closed. Eowyn relaxes again, a breathy laugh escaping her as pleasure returns.

Windsor lifts his head, his nostrils flaring as his eyes land on her neck. She smirks when he starts toward the small cuts from his claws. "Don't you *ever*," he drags his tongue along the left side of her neck to her ear. "Say another man's name when I am *drinking* from you." He takes her earlobe between his teeth. She leans her head against his as he releases her neck. "Or just never again," he lays a soft kiss against her cheek. She lets out another low laugh, nudging her face against him. His hand dances across her stomach and her eyes flutter closed. He presses his body down onto hers, his hand moving between her legs. "I'm not going to be able to stop tonight," he admits in a gruff whisper. His lips continue to pepper tender kisses along the side of her face. She smiles and relaxes her legs, allowing her knees to fall open. He uses his middle finger to caress every inch of her silk flesh before dipping it into her.

For fourteen of the fifty-six nights she'd been in Exsar, one of them would sneak into the other's room. These were the only hours the Princess would allow herself to give in, to kiss and touch the Prince as much as she pleased, as he pleased.

Her hand slips between them and under the waistband of his linen night pants. "What if you didn't?" The words tumble from her lips as she wraps her hand around his hardened length. "Who would know?" She brushes her nose along his shoulder.

He laughs into the crook of her neck, his finger slowly thrusting in and out of her, his breath cold against her sizzling skin. Her soul tugs at his playfully, urging him to give in. She lifts her hips to meet his hand, licking her lips as she tauntingly strokes him. "Don't worry, My Queen," he presses a kiss to her neck before lifting his head to look at her. "You will be my wife in a few short hours and then you are free game," he pulls his hand away and presses a kiss to the corner of her mouth. She pouts, releasing him and pulling her hand from his pants. "Don't look so sad, sweet thing," his lips move along her jaw. "I have many plans for all of your free moments over the next few days," he nips at her pulse point on the right side of her neck. "Olivette slipped me a copy of your schedule during the festivities," he lifts his head and smiles down at her devilishly. "We will be starting with the ten minutes you have to change your gown between the ride through the capital after the ceremony and the feast."

17

WINDSOR

The Prince stares at himself in the mirror, his eyes narrowed impassively. "You're not going to wear it, are you?" His best friend and soon-to-be Hand chuckles from the bed.

Windsor turns to look at Layne, dressed in what his Mother had laid out for him this morning. "No," he shrugs off the black jacket. "I'd not hoped this to be the first Royal custom I change, but it shall be. I will be wearing my white suit," he scoffs and lays the black and red jacket on the bed next to Layne.

"Can I sill wear this?" He pinches the red stitches, black velvet lapels of his jacket between his fingers as he sits up.

Windsor lifts his eyes to meet the burnt orange orbs. "I don't care what you do, Lizard Boy, but I'm not wearing this shite," he says dully as he begins to unbutton the red cotton shirt.

Layne rolls his eyes and watches the fabric fall to the floor as the Prince starts toward the armoire that concealed the suit he had made behind his Mother's back. "I'm a salamander, not a lizard," he leans back against the headboard and folds his hands in his lap. Windsor swings open the doors of the wardrobe and smiles to himself. He begins undoing his belt, pulling it free of the black slacks and letting them fall to the ground. He reaches for the white pants, tugging them over his undergarments. "Mother dearest will make you change before the feast," Layne looks at Windsor pointedly.

"Mother dearest will need Kanika's help to find me before the feast," the Prince grabs the navy blue silk dress shirt and slides it over his arms, turning to face the bed as he fastens the buttons.

"I can't keep covering for you," the Noble lifts his finger to point at Windsor.

"You don't need to. In twenty minutes, she'll be my wife. What we do after that is between us," he flashes his teeth in a feral grin. He takes a moment to watch Layne shudder at the sight before turning to grab the suit jacket. "You ready to be hand of the King in a few days, Lizard boy?" He teases as he slips into the jacket. He moves back to the mirror and smiles at his reflection. He tucks the silk shirt into the waistband of the white cotton pants. He flips the collar, pausing for a moment to look at Layne in the mirror expectantly.

"Are you going to stop calling me Lizard boy once you're King?" He crosses his arms over his chest with a childlike huff.

"No," Windsor laughs and runs a hand through his hair. He nods once before turning to face Layne again. "Belt or no belt?"

Layne stays silent for a moment, his eyes roaming over the new suit. "I'm going to say belt because I know the belt is not for accessorizing," he meets the Prince's gaze.

Windsor grins, clicking his tongue with a wink. "Clever man," he swipes the belt from the platform inside of the wardrobe and snakes it around his waist again. "Oli said she was going to meet us here once Eowyn was finished getting ready," he glances at Layne.

"Oh," his muscles stiffen. "Olivette?"

Windsor smiles, focusing back on buckling his belt. He knew Layne had feelings for Olivette since they were teenagers and looked forward to seeing her whenever he could around the Palace. "Yes," he smirks when the door opens, as if on cue.

Olivette, flustered and disheveled, stumbles in and slams the door behind her. Her eyes move over the pair and she smiles, a light flush to her cheeks. "Happy wedding day, Cat man," she starts toward them. "She is vibrating with anticipation," she takes a seat on the edge of the bed, opposite Layne.

Windsor absorbs her words, the tension visibly leaving his shoulders. "Who's with her, bird brains?" He slips his feet into his shoes, holding her stare. His expression is still taut but he continues the playful banter.

"Her Majesties Alice of Iverness and Elenor, Sir Blaine Cromwell, and Amabel," she lists off the individuals effortlessly and turns toward Layne finally. "Hey," she swats at his leg light-heartedly. "You look nice," her fingers flick the cotton of his pants before she looks back at Windsor.

The Prince crosses his arms over his chest. "Why is Amabel with her? What does she need the Healer for?" He glances at the clock beside Layne.

His friend clears his throat and follows his gaze. Olivette, not oblivious to how awkward Layne felt now, retracts her hand as she rolls her eyes. "The Queen of Iverness felt faint. Amabel is going to walk with her to the front doors." She folds her hands in her lap. The trio falls into a tense silence. The Prince watches the clock tick. He still had five minutes before he had to leave. "Windsor?" Olivette's voice breaks the silence. He meets her stare, his eyes dropping briefly to watch her hand move to Layne's knee. "Everything changes for the three of us this week, starting today," she whispers. "You will be King, Lanye the Hand of the King, I will be the Lady of the Queen." He dips his chin in a single nod. "Eowyn will be Queen."

His nostrils flare at that, his power coiling. "We've come a long way from shifting in the parlor as children," he glances at the clock again. *Four minutes.* He moves his gaze to flick between his friends. "I can change the laws," he steps forward until he's standing at the edge of the bed. "I can change the laws and you two can be together and be *happy*."

Layne sighs, moving to stand from the bed. "Our first priority is Queen Alice's vision. We can talk about law changing once everything is said and done. But you need to focus on preparing Eowyn for what's to come," he runs a hand through his hair and looks at Oli.

She nods in agreement, holding his gaze just a tad *too* long before looking at Windsor. "Besides, I am perfectly content working for the Princess. She is an absolute delight," she smiles reassuringly. "I don't know that I'd want to be a noble's wife if it meant I had to spend less time with Her Grace." Windsor's features soften at that and Olivette takes notice. "She asks me to join her for breakfast each and every morning, she asked me to fly with her this morning…" Her voice is light and almost grateful.

"She flew this morning?" The unasked question hung in the air between them. *Without me?*

"She had a wonderful time, Win," she looks at the clock. Both men follow her gaze.

Three minutes.

"She has ten minutes to change between the festival and the feast. I need you to make sure we are undisturbed," he narrows his gaze on Olivette.

She raises her eyebrows and turns to look at Layne. He shrugs, tilting his head to the side. "She *is* about to be his wife. Nobody can really say anything," he walks past Windsor and stands in front of the mirror. "Not that I think anyone *will* say anything because your parent's pulled you out of one betrothal already," he picks a few pieces of lint off of his coat before turning back to look at the Prince. "And they won't start your wedding feast without you," he winks playfully.

Two minutes.

"Ellie might," Olivette snorts, pushing herself off of her bed. Layne falls to Windsor's side and she steps to stand in front of them. "But that won't matter, will it?" She looks between them. "You've got us, you've got Eowyn... who cares when the feast starts, right?"

"Right," Layne slings an arm over Windsor's shoulder. "Used to be the three of us against the world, now it's the four of us," he wraps his other arm around Olivette's waist and pulls her into his chest. She wraps one arm around Layne and the other around Windsor.

The Prince embraces his two closest friends with a smile. "And she will burn the fucking world down one day," Windsor whispers, pulling his friends closer. He leans his head against Oli's, exhaling deeply. A knock on the door pulls the three from their own little world.

Layne clears his throat, stepping back. Windsor lifts his head as Oli backs up as well. "It's time," Layne smiles brightly. "In ten minutes, she'll be your wife." He smacks Windsor's arm playfully.

The door opens and the King steps in. He looks over Windsor, his eyebrows rising. "I told your Mother you weren't going to wear black and red," he chuckles, shaking his head and motioning to the hallway. "Let's go, you three." Windsor follows his Father with Layne on one side and Olivette on the other. He hates that Oli would need to stay inside of the Palace for the ceremony and would not be able to be there with Layne. She falls off to the side as Gideon approaches the front doors. He pauses and turns to look at her. "The Princess has requested your presence by her side today, Olivette. You will do well to meet Elenor in the den. She waits with a gown for you and then Layne Renhart will accompany you to the appropriate position for the Ceremony."

"What?" All three ask in unison.

Gideon rolls his eyes, a grin spread across his lips. Olivette wastes no time taking off toward the den. "You two, come with me," he motions them to follow him as he starts toward the great hall. The pair follow him, almost confusedly and watch as he closes the doors behind them. "There is to be absolutely *no* funny business today," he looks at Windsor accusingly. "And you," he points at Layne, "will be held responsible if there is."

"Woah!" Layne raises his hands in mock surrender. "I've had nothing to do with his *funny business* in almost two months! He does what *he* wants!" He defends himself.

Gideon quirks a brow. "A King's Hand takes full responsibility for the King's lapses in judgment," he says plainly.

"What counts as a lapse in judgement?" Windsor crosses his arms over his chest defiantly.

The King belts out a laugh, shaking his head and wrapping his arm around his son's shoulders. "Whatever you think you're planning that you have to ask for, that's a lapse in judgement," he rubs his son's arm. "Stick to your schedule, let her stick to her schedule, make your Mother happy, and we'll all be fine," he glances between Layne and Windsor.

"Yes, Your Majesty," Layne nods and bows at the waist. "You have my word."

Gideon looks to Windsor and he just blinks. "I'm not giving you my word for anything, all common sense goes out the door when I look at her," he tugs away from his dad. "But I'll try."

"That's all I ask," Gideon mumbles, almost defeatedly. "I suppose that is all I needed to say. We should start heading outside before Elenor wipes the floor with me," he reaches for the doorknob, looking between both the Prince and the Noble. "You boys have all of my pride," he says just above a whisper before swinging open the door.

Olivette stands in a black gown with red stitching, matching Layne's suit, at the front doors. Layne wastes no time, rushing to her side and looping his arm through hers. Windsor can feel his power start to hum lowly. "She's coming," he murmurs.

Gideon nods and Windsor follows his gaze to see his Mother rushing down the hall. "Why can't you do anything I ask?" She scoffs as she approaches. She reaches for Windsor's collar and moves to fix it as he tilts his chin up to give her better access. "You look handsome, nonetheless," she lays her hands flat on his chest and looks up at him. "Are you ready for the rest of your life to begin?" She smiles.

He can't help but grin, leveling his stare to meet hers. "I've waited my whole life for this moment," he admits in a murmur.

Gideon steps forward and places his hand on the small of the Queen's back. "Let us walk, then."

And so they did.

Gideon and Elenor are the first to step out of the Palace. They wave to the thousands of people gathered outside of the Castle to witness the union, falling to the right of the doors where three large chairs sit. Gideon sits on the chair closest to the door, Elenor in the middle seat. Layne and Olivette step out next, one settling on either side of the High Priest set to marry the Prince and Princess. Then Windsor steps out. His subjects scream and applaud and chant louder than they did for the other four. He takes the time to soak it in, to glance around at the faces. His eyes flash cobalt, making them cheer even louder as he narrows his eyes on the crowd. He beams brightly, finally lifting his hand with a single wave before standing in front of the High Priest.

"I much prefer the white on you, Your Grace," the Priest whispers to Windsor.

The Prince chuckles softly. "Thank you, High Priest Xago."

The scent of warm sweet crème and cinnamon fills his nostrils and his head whips toward the door. Eowyn, much like he, did not abide by the Royal Dress Code. Instead of an eccentric, lace frilly, god's awful ball gown, she dons a tight white silk mermaid style dress. The fabric is simple, nothing more than a few flecks of glitter to accentuate her curves even more. She'd not kept it a secret since arriving in Exsar that she adored the style of strapless gowns, especially in the evenings, and today was no different. Even though it was barely high noon. His eyes roam over her, taking in the way the corset pushes her bust up slightly. Her makeup was just as pristine as ever, though a touch heavier than most days. Her silver locks lay curled around her, clearly left untouched after he sat in the tub and washed it for her last night.

Then she starts walking toward him and his knees nearly buckle under him.

The silk had a slit cut to her right hip, the fabric moving to reveal just one of the legs he couldn't get enough of the past fortnight. His tongue darts out to lick his lips as he remembers the first time he'd gotten to touch the smooth skin of her thighs. He'd been unable to sleep and ventured to the South Wing where the Princess temporarily resided until their wedding. She'd invited him in and they'd sat on the balcony together, watching the night sky fade into morning. As the sun broke the horizon, he'd knelt down in front of her and officially proposed to her. Eowyn had let her guard down slightly, joking that even if she didn't want to she couldn't say no, but divulged that she *did* wish to marry him. He'd wasted no time, lifting her from the chair and walking her to her bed. They'd promised each other that they'd not consummate their relationship until the wedding night, though they continued every night after that to sneak into one another's rooms and she'd worship him just as much as he did her, under the veil of night.

Now, she stood before him, ready to become his wife. He fights every urge within himself not to slam her onto the stone of the Palace steps and devour her whole, in front of his entire kingdom.

"You did not wish to wear the provided either," the mere observation is like the most beautiful harmony he'd ever heard.

"I'd have worn it if it did not look as old as it is," he mumbles, stepping forward. The High Priest clears his throat and Windsor halts. They both look to Xago. "Shall we begin?" He asks in a hushed tone. Windsor meets Eowyn's gaze and she nods without hesitation.

18

EOWYN

His hands slide past the curve of my waist and he presses his palms against my back. "Do it," he whispers as he pulls me into him, just before sealing our marriage with a kiss. "Show the world how beautiful my Vermilion is," he demands.

I smile, bringing my hands to cup his cheeks as I hum the melody to summon my wings. He presses his lips to mine which effectively silences the sound of bones cracking in my ears as the pinions take form behind my back. "Prince Windsor and Princess Eowyn of Exsar!" Gideon bellows over the roars from the sea of people gathered before us.

Windsor's arms tighten around me, his hands sliding to grip the opposite sides of my body. He presses me harder to him and his soul bleeds into mine. My fingernails bite into his cheeks, my soul happily wrapping around his and pulling for more. He breaks the kiss, sealing our marriage. His chest moves with ragged breaths. I watch his eyes flash white before he forces them to dim back to his usual electrifying blue, leaning my forehead against his. "My Queen," he slides a hand around and trails up to hold the side of my neck. The ice coursing through his veins bites against the fire burning through me, albeit delightfully. "I'm going to make the whole world bow to you," the corners of his lips lift to smile devilishly.

I stroke my thumb along his cheek, watching the red glow of my own irises reflect in his as I manipulate the life forces around us to drop to their knees. He pulls away at the sound of confused grunts, keeping one hand on my waist as the other drops to my shoulder. He surveys the scene before him. Thousands on their knees, bowing their heads, including the Royals and the Priest.

I pull harder on his soul and raise my chin. The purest form of him gives into me. He steps back, moving his hands to grip mine as he lowers onto his knees. His eyes glow white, the only apparent indication of my control. His eyes flutter closed, the twining of his magic with mine strengthening with each passing second, it's intensity growing. His mind, body and soul, obedient to my every whim. Power surges through me as he submits to my rule. I can *smell* the way his mind clears of every thought besides how to please me. A smirk tugs at my lips when he raises to his feet again. I release my grip on the forces within the atmosphere to allow them to follow my husband's motion.

Windsor's eyes dim when I loosen my hold on his eternal being and he drops one of my hands. He starts toward the Palace steps, leading me down the white herringbone stone steps. The people around us remain in a stunned silence as we descend. He stops at the bottom, just a few paces away from the carriages awaiting to parade us to the festival in the Capital. He glances over his shoulder and I follow his stare. Elenor, Gideon, and my Mother come down the steps, smiling as if nothing was amiss. Then he looks to his people - our people. They, too, returned to normal. His eyes move to me and he starts toward the carriage.

"I was making a point."

"It was unnecessary," he declares in a hushed whisper, "I know you do not *need* me to make them bow."

I smirk, willing flames to brush against the back of his hand. He tightens his fingers around mine, his hand icing over. "I know," I muse, "you did not resist."

The guards beside the chariot step toward us and move to either side of me. Windsor's hand tightens around mine, encasing both of them in ice as he lifts them, his teeth bared in a silent warning. They step back and the Prince helps me into the seat. He climbs in beside me and I decide to have the mercy to wait until he's seated to melt the ice.

Windsor watches his parents climb into the chariot behind ours, my Mother sitting with them. I take note of how many times I can pick out people saying her name. I scan the crowd, my eyes darting toward my husband's stiff form every few seconds. "What is it?" I mumble, tapping my foot for emphasis.

His eyes drop to my foot, then where our hands still sit intertwined between us. His thumb strokes along my knuckles. "This is going to be a long day for me," he turns his head away from me as we start down the road.

"I can..." I trail off, pulling my hand from his.

"Don't you dare," Windsor whips his attention back to me. I smile when he takes my hand again. "Just talk to me. Keep me distracted, maybe," he clears his throat.

I quirk an eyebrow, my interest piqued by every aspect of his behavior. "Is this a lion thing or something else?" I ask, referring to his rigid manner. I bring my other hand to rest on his forearm. *A question for a question.*

He nods once in understanding. The horse pulling our carriage starts into a trot, signaling we had twenty minutes until we are in the Capital. "It is a lion thing," he licks his lips and meets my gaze. He lets out a ghost of a laugh, moving to press a kiss to my forehead. He brings his other hand to the back of my head and tangles it in my hair to hold me to him. He turns, resting his cheek on top of my head. "Has Idris found out what the fuck is going on yet?" His touch was gentle despite his rough tone.

I can't lie to him. Those are the unspoken rules. If we choose to answer, it must be the truth. I nod against him. "He has," my answer is short and calculated. He wants to be distracted from the lion instincts, I'll make him get really specific for each question. "Why are you pushing for Layne and Olivette to wed?" He pulls back, his hand in my hair dropping back to his lap. I tilt my head to the side, keeping my features schooled to reveal nothing. I allow a small bit of amusement to shine through my pupils as I stare at him expectantly.

"Does Olivette not wish to wed Layne Renhart?"

I smile at his retort, only allowing it because it will encourage his keen eyes. "Olivette does not fancy him." Not only had I distracted him from his obsessive Lion mating need, I'd also distracted him from the situation Draven Idris was looking into. "What is your first act as King?" I brush my foot against his.

He shivers, leaning further into my side. "Ordering everyone out of the room so I can worship My Queen appropriately," he says nonchalantly. He lays his head on my shoulder, moving my hand to rest on his leg as his moves to wrap around me. He settles his palm on my hip, his thumb stroking against the soft silk. "Did she tell you if she does fancy someone?"

I hum, squeezing his leg in approval at his wording. "She fancies females. I thought you were her best friend, how did you not know?" I tease lightheartedly.

His movements pause and he sucks in a sharp breath. "Does Layne know?" He asks hesitantly.

I can't help but giggle, knowing what the sound does to the predator within him. "He does," I lean my head against his. "He knows she is meant for someone else, do not fret, cub," I pat his leg gently.

Much to my pleasure, he catches on. "*Knows*," he echoes. "Elaborate." His finger continues his ministrations.

"I've taken steps to prolong my Mother's life so she may return to Exsar at least once before she crosses into Gragion," I disclose gently.

He angles his head to press his lips against my throat. "You now harbor both Primary Abilities within two Houses," he says between kissing every inch of skin he can reach. "The collar no longer pulls from her life force." His lips move steadily. "And you've now seen who Olivette is destined to be with," he kisses up to my jaw.

"Precisely," I allow my eyes to flutter closed.

He moves across my cheek, bringing his free hand up to grip my face roughly. "Are you able to *see* if I'll get you alone for a moment during the festivities?" He forces my chin toward him and he starts down the other side of my neck.

I drape a leg between his. His hand falls from my face, almost instantly, to my thigh. He groans against my skin, gripping my leg possessively. "I'm sure we will be able to come up with some reason we need a moment alone," I whisper as his lips move to my shoulder. He sighs, lifting his head to look at me again. His fingers trails up and down my thigh, as if trying to sooth the way his soul cries for me by touching me. "Draven Idris wishes to speak with us alone after our coronation about what he found."

Windsor blinks, coming out of it partially. "About this?" He grips me tightly again, yanking me down in the seat.

I nod, placing a hand on top of his. "About why you get so defensive," I try to pull his hand off of my thigh but he growls.

"You've done it too," he snaps. My soul begins retreating immediately, making his eyes widen. "I'm sorry," his fingers loosen and he caresses my skin. "I'm sorry," he whispers, "I don't like when you do that." His hand moves up slightly as he presses his lips to my cheek again. "I don't want to stop touching you," he mumbles against my skin. He tugs on my soul again.

I smirk, his lips trailing down the side of my neck again. I release the grip on my own eternal being and let it twine with his again. I slide my hand along his leg. "What is truly going to be your first act as King?" I'm not done playing and he knows he'd be foolish to assume otherwise.

Not that it matters much, he's more than capable of doing two things at once. "Ask me something fun," he nips at the skin just under my ear, a soft groan vibrating against me. His hand drifts higher, his fingertips dancing against the thin fabric of my undergarments.

I press my lips to his ear, my lips searing against his cold skin. "Something fun," I repeat as he moves to grab my hip, tucked under the fabric above the slit in the gown. "What do you want me to ask you?" I move my hand to his chin to lift his attention to my eyes. Windsor shrugs, a lopsided grin spreading across his face. He glances forward to gauge how far we are from the capital before looking back at me. "What?" The laugh slips past my lips with ease.

He pulls me closer to his side, wrapping his other arm around my waist behind my back and releasing his grip on my hip. I drop my hand back to my lap as he turns his attention forward. "What about a new game?" His fingers gently squeeze the side of my thigh. "I'll tell you something I've yet to disclose to anyone else and then you do the same."

The curious glint to his eyes makes my tongue dart out to wet my lips. I take in the side of his face as if it's my first time seeing him. My lips tingle with the memory of grazing over his blade-sharp jawline, the way his stubble brushed against me in the moonlight. He glances at me from the corner of his eye. I lean up and nudge my nose against his face. "My gift to you today shall be doing as you please," I whisper.

A devious light flashes across his face. "I plan to meet with your Mother about the retrieval of Amethyst from the Dungeons in Iverness," his eyes follow the passing trees to avoid my stare.

"Amethyst Neverbelle? The Queen of the Pixies?" My eyes widen slightly. We'd only just found out we are to become King and Queen within the fortnight, he was already beginning negotiations to release my Father's prisoners. "And of Flare?" I can't help the desperate whisper amongst my roaring thoughts. Though I'd rarely show any sign of vulnerability, what was mine was... *mine*. I have no other way of explaining it than I wish to *keep* what is mine.

He dips his chin once. "We will discuss it with your Mother." **We.** *Right, I am to be Queen. That means something in Exsar.* My shoulders relax slightly and he strokes my thigh soothingly. "Lady Neverbelle will be easier to aid, let's start there."

I nod, concede and left stunned by his initiative for something so... *calculated*. "Zanna made a point to disclose that my happiness satisfies her hunger more than my rage," I feel his soul purr against mine.

It melts into me even more as he relaxes back in the plush seat. "Everys made a point to disclose he takes offense to the fact that you've not asked him to accompany you on a flight." We both let out bubbles of laughter. Though colossal in size and power, Windsor's dragon is a giant baby. "I'd told him once the hatchlings can be left alone for a few moments at a time you would ask him to fly with you and Zanna."

"I can do that," I run a hand through my hair. I spend a few moments wracking my brain for what I could divulge next. "I once manipulated my Father into allowing Flare Meadowglade a visit with his daughter," my tone is hushed, as if the man directing the horses on the front of the carriage had any interest in what I'd said.

Windsor furrows his eyebrows and slides his tongue along his top row of teeth. "Manipulated more than metaphorically." I nod, though it was more of a statement than a question. "Intriguing, why?" I arch a brow. He turns his head to me and looks at me knowingly. "Was it her?" I roll my lips together, noting the change in the sounds around us. I look up to see us starting down the road that leads into the heart of Exsar's Capital. "Eowyn," he squeezes my thigh roughly.

I whip my head toward him, smiling as I notice people gathering on either side of the road. I lean in to whisper into his ear. "It was her." He groans deep in his chest, pulling me into him even more possessively.

I let out a laugh, straightening my chin and schooling my features for public appearance. "Do not banjax your own mood because you *chose* to ask if she's the woman who once snuck into my bedchambers," I lightly scold as I reluctantly untwine my soul from his.

He scoffs, despite the cry his soul lets out as my walls go up. He keeps his hand firmly on my leg. "My mood is not *banjaxed*," he retorts, "not at all." I roll my eyes at the obvious lie. He can't disguise the slight edge to his voice. I watch him as he glares at the thickening crowd while we approach the center of the city. There's a moment of silence, the only sound is the clip-clop of the horse's hooves on the cobbled road. He huffs out a breath in an attempt to calm himself and straightens his shoulders. He forces a smile when his subjects begin to cheer toward the slowing carriages. His arm remains around me, his hand still possessively gripping my leg. We slow to a halt, yet he doesn't budge. "I'm going to have her mouth filled with rocks and sewn shut to burn it into your brain what will happen if you ever sit on anyone's face but mine again." His words knock the oxygen from my lungs. I watch him detach from me with a blank stare. "I can smell your satisfaction, Eowyn," he bends and grabs my hips, lifting me to my feet. "And I will devour it later, but for now, I need you to conceal it so I can behave myself." His hands fall to his sides.

"Yes, Your Grace," I watch as he climbs to the ground. He helps me, clasping both of my hands tenderly.

My eyes drift to where the King and Queen along with my Mother approach. Windsor drops my right hand and ushers my left arm to loop through his. "We've arranged for lunch in a private area before the festivities," Elenor's voice is laced with excitement.

They move around Windsor and I, starting down the street. The Royal Guard forms tight walls around us as I glance around them as much as possible. The light posts and buildings are decorated in all sorts of celebratory runes, flowers and other plants alike, and homemade signs to congratulate Windsor and I. I feel a soft tug behind my left ear. Windsor looks toward it at the same time as I and we both watch the soul scamper between the soldiers. He follows me as I push past them, his arm firmly holding mine. They break the formation and stop completely as we follow the shadow. It swirls in front of a small, red haired boy, no older than three years of age.

I pull my limb from my husband and squat down in front of the child. "Hello," I watch the glow of my eyes reflect off of his pale, freckled face. "I'm Eowyn." I glance around the confused looking child but none of the people staring at us move to claim the boy. I'd come to the capital with King Gideon for the past seven weeks and I'd never met a child or adult resembling him.

"Me Charlie," he jams his index finger into his chest for emphasis.

I let out a soft laugh, glancing back to Windsor. He stands behind me with his arms crossed over his chest, a satisfied smirk on his lips. Gideon comes to his side and scans the crowd. I look back to Charlie. "Are you lost, Charlie?" I ask with a slight tilt to my head. He nods with a deep frown. "Alright," I place my hands on my knees and push myself up. I extend a hand to him. "Why don't you walk with the Prince and I until we find your parents?" I offer.

Windsor's soul coos and brushes against me happily as the child takes my hand. The scent of clean and crisp ice fills my senses when I lead him to Windsor. "Me don't have daddy. Only mommy," Charlie mumbles when the Prince takes ahold of my other arm.

The crowd murmurs, astonished. No one says anything to me directly as we fall back into step within the order of the guard, though my Mother nods approvingly before resuming her conversation with Elenor. "Do you know your mommy's name, Charlie?" Windsor's voice grabs my attention.

I glance down to the boy. "Bry," he squeezes his little fist around my middle and ring finger tightly.

Windsor only nods, looking up as we approach the tent. Charlie steps closer to me when we step through the flaps. "Why don't you sit him down on the sofa and we can make him a plate?" He glances down at the child.

Something in me lurches and his eyes flash with acknowledgement. I turn to the boy, tugging my arm away from Windsor. "Let's go sit over here, Charlie," I keep my tone soft, a pitch higher. He nods happily and starts toward where my finger points. I help him onto the woven wool sofa and kneel in front of him. "Prince Windsor and I are going to get you something to eat. You just hang out here," I pat his small foot. He nods once, bringing his hand up and popping his thumb into his mouth. I stand and turn to face the massive tables in the middle of the tent.

I cross over, grabbing a small plate and scanning over the buffet. My Mother and Elenor approach the other side of the table and grab their own plates. "You are such a sweetheart," Elenor flicks her gaze to me as I use a set of tongs to place a few pieces of Brobosu and Omra on the plate for Charlie.

"Thank you, Your Majesty," I look between her and my Mother.

My Mother opens her mouth to say something but snaps it shut when a pair of arms close around me. I place the tongs in the fruit bowl and reach for the pair set beside the vegetables. "My wife, a natural caretaker," Windsor sets his chin on my shoulder. He steps with me as I shift toward the platter of meat.

I lift a piece of chicken onto the plate and step back. He tightens his arms around me briefly before releasing his hold. "A true lover," my Mother agrees with him.

I flash her a graceful smile before making my way back to Charlie. Windsor follows like a lost kitten and takes the plate from my hands. He places it in the child's lap. "Here you go, little man. Eat up so you can be big and strong like those guys," he points to the guards around the inside of the tent. Charlie follows his direction and his eyes widen almost comically. He lifts a veggie, red Joca, and pops the whole cut into his mouth. He chews it animatedly, making us both laugh. "Great job," Windsor pats his head affectionately, making my heart flutter. An involuntary shiver wracks through me and I shake my head to ground myself. "You stay here and eat for a few moments, I'm going to speak with Eowyn about finding your mommy, yeah?" Charlie nods happily.

Windsor straightens and starts toward me. His hand falls to the small of my back and he pushes me past the table of food. I allow him to lead me toward a hung red curtain. He pushes it aside and pulls me past it. The curtain falls back into place, the small makeshift room very obviously a medical station of sorts. Two small cots sit side by side, a table between them full of sharp metal tools. There's a sofa and two chairs beside the beds, blankets and pillows and another bag of supplies stacked neatly on one of the chairs.

Windsor's hand slides to my hip, the other falling onto the other side as he pulls me until my back is pressed against his chest. "So, Princess," his whisper is teasing. "What is your plan to find the child's Mother?" His hands move over my stomach, pulling me tighter to him.

"She's on her way," I say simply, leaning into him. I crane my neck to look up at him. "Which means that this is the moment alone you wanted."

He smiles down at me, leaning down to press his lips to mine. I turn in his arms and wrap mine around his neck. One of his hands stays around me, holding me against him as the other moves down my side. He grips the back of my right thigh, pushing the slit of the dress back. He deepens the kiss, his lips moving hungrily against mine. He slides his tongue along the seam of my lips before biting down on my bottom lip.

As if on its own volition, my leg lifts off the ground and hooks around his waist. He grips my thigh harder when I part my lips and his tongue invades my mouth. I let out a soft sigh into him, angling my head slightly as he explores my mouth. My fingers twirl the ends of his hair lining the nape of his neck. He pulls away abruptly, his jaw tense.

149

"What's wrong?" I tug at his hair lightly. The lion in him growls, clawing at his restraint.

He clenches his teeth together, silencing the predator within. "A moment alone is *not* the best idea," he blinks rapidly as if trying to keep himself grounded. His hand slides from my thigh to my backside and he grips it tightly, roughly pulling me even closer. "I might just shred you to ribbons right here," he growls.

19

ALICE

The Queen of Iverness watches intently as the Prince and Princess speak with the red haired woman called Bryanna. Eowyn seems to know the woman, happily rushing to her side with the child in her arms once the guards tell her that Bryanna was here to see her. Elenor stands to her right, Gideon on her other side. They continue to observe the scene before them, everyone's eyes following Windsor's hand to the small of Eowyn's back.

"Fifty gold marks that within the next two minutes his hand is moving lower," Gideon mumbles to the women.

Elenor and Alice laugh softly. "I'll give him a single minute," Elenor crosses her arms over her chest.

They wait with bated breath and within the next few seconds, Windsor moves his hand to Eowyn's backside and grips it roughly, jerking his hand slightly to pull her closer to him. She continues to speak with the Mother of the child as his fingers squeeze her through the dress.

"I'll take payment in the form of favors," Elenor snorts, looking at Gideon.

Alice can't help the chuckle that escapes her with her friend's banter. Eowyn turns, breaking away from the Prince's hold and starts toward them. The soldiers, Windsor, and Bryanna, with Charlie in her arms, follow her toward the tent. "I'd like Lady Bryanna and Charlie to accompany us today," Eowyn looks between Gideon and Elenor.

Alice's chest fills with an overwhelming sense of love and pride. The way Eowyn carries herself, demands what she wants and doesn't take *no* for an answer is nothing short of... well, *Queenly*. Windsor stands off to the side and watches in silence as Eowyn interacts with the other Royals. He's still bristling from earlier, but he does his best to hide it. He can't help but smile at the way she takes charge, the way she walks with purpose and demands attention. Alice notes the way he simply stands by admiring her. It is clear he loves the confidence and strength she exudes, the way she carries herself.

"Of course, darling," Elenor gives an approving nod.

Gideon glances between them, noting the way Windsor seems even more distracted now that Eowyn is directing her attention toward them. He takes mental inventory of his son's demeanor and shakes his head with a knowing smirk.

Windsor takes a step closer to Eowyn, his hand once again finding the curve of her spine. His touch is possessive, almost like he's marking her as his in front of the others. He leans in and whispers in her ear, his voice low enough for Alice to be unable to hear him. His eyes trail over her form, taking in the way the dress hugs her curves and dips so delicately along the soft lines of her skin. Alice can't help but stare as he admires Eowyn. She's radiant, a vision among a sea of people and she was eternally grateful that the Prince knew it. His fingers tracing light lines against the exposed skin of her back, as if they're drawn to her, unable to help but touch her.

Gideon and Elenor exchange a look, both noticing the way Windsor is watching Eowyn with an intensity that they haven't seen before. They can see the possessive gleam in his eyes, the way he can't keep his hands off her even in public. Elenor leans over and whispers to Alice, a sly smile on her face. "I'm going to bet on an heir within the year."

Gideon can't help but chuckle at the comment, knowing all too well how Windsor feels about the Princess. "Don't be so hasty, El. It takes time to build a relationship like that. You have to let the flame grow slowly. Too much fuel will burn it out before it's given the chance to become an inferno."

Alice scoffs playfully, "she is a living inferno."

Gideon laughs heartily at Alice's comment, picturing Eowyn's fire and spirit that he, too, has come to love since her arrival in his Kingdom. "You have a point there, Alice. But still, she's just like any other flame. Too much fuel too early on will snuff it out before it can become a roaring wildfire."

Elenor glances between the two. Alice lets a smirk tug at her lips. "She *is* roaring wildfire. Do not worry about her, Gideon."

Gideon raises an eyebrow at Elenor and Alice, his eyes narrowing in playful skepticism. "Are you challenging my judgment?" he asks, mock offense in his tone. "I know the Princess decently enough, I know how she is, and I know the kind of fire she holds within her. She might be roaring, but there's also a fierce fragility beneath it all." His tone is warning.

Alice crosses her arms over her chest. "There is nothing fragile about her," she looks over her daughter from head to toe. "And one day, you will eat those words."

Gideon gives a chuckle, clearly enjoying the banter. "Perhaps you're right, Alice," he concedes with a smirk. "The Princess certainly doesn't appear fragile on the surface. But I've seen that fire burn both hot and fast, leaving nothing but ash behind."

"Surely, you are not speaking of my wife," Windsor says, eerily lightheartedly as he steps to Gideon's side. Alice's eyes move to where Eowyn and Bryanna retreat with a fraction of the guards. "Because my wife is a firebird, born of the ash. She will burn and flourish even more powerful than the last time," he looks over his father with a warning glare. The King turns his head to look at the Prince, a mix of concern and caution in his expression.

"Your wife is spirited and passionate, Windsor, that much is clear," he nods, his tone measured. "But even a firebird needs to be handled with care. You can't simply let them fly wild without regard for the flames they might ignite." Alice's eyebrows raise slightly at the remark and her gaze flicks to Windsor.

The Prince's jaw tightens, ice grazing over his fingertips. "I think it best you keep your remarks about Eowyn to yourself from now on," he grits out.

Gideon raises an eyebrow at Windsor's sharp response. "Now, son, there's no need to get upset," he shakes his head, trying to keep the conversation civil, "I'm simply looking out for her well-being. I've seen the way she burns, and we do not know the risks as she is the first of her kind."

Though the King has a point, she understands the Prince's frustration. After all, they are two halves of one whole being and he'd know better than anyone what she was capable of. The Queen had visions of the things her daughter would do and she *knew* Eowyn would never burn out. But as Windsor had said, even if she does, she is a phoenix and will just rise even stronger.

She takes a step forward, Elenor following suit and stepping between her Husband and son. "Eowyn is very powerful and will do great things, this much we know," Elenor looks between the men. "We should put this conversation to rest and start toward the archery event."

Gideon sighs, stepping back and giving a nod. "You're right, Elenor. This isn't the place to discuss such matters. The archery tournament should be starting soon." He looks at Windsor, his expression a bit more calm than before. "Son, I know you care for the Princess, and I have no doubt that she holds her own, but please just remember, that fire, as powerful as it may be, needs a steady hand to tame it."

A growl rips from the Prince's chest and Alice watches his eyes flash *red*. All three of them step back, stunned looks on their faces. "Gideon, enough," Elenor whispers, placing her hand on her husband's arm. Windsor's eyes dim and his gaze shifts between them. He silently watches them for a moment before turning on his heels and stalking in the direction Eowyn had gone. They stand there, the tension hanging between them almost palpable. "What the hell was that?" Elenor looks at Alice.

Alice moves her eyes to her best friend and her husband. "I think he just siphoned her power without touching her," she glances at Windsor's retreating figure again.

Gideon watches his son walk away, eyes wide with concern. Elenor looks equally shaken, her hand clinging to her husband's arm. "He siphoned her power, without touching her," he repeats Alice's words, trying to comprehend what just happened. "That's... not supposed to be possible." He looks to Alice again. "Right?"

Alice shakes her head. "No..." she swallows and takes a step forward. "We should focus on the festivities today and consult Sir Idris tomorrow."

Elenor nods in agreement, though Gideon holds his brow still creased in concern. Elenor takes a breath, trying to compose herself. "Yes, you're right, Alice. Let's focus on the event. It's important to stay calm and assess the situation with a clear mind." She clears her throat, starting into a slow walk toward where the Prince and Princess went.

The trio walks with their soldiers, stopping periodically to socialize with Exsar's population. Most were elated to see Alice, the Azazè said to be destined to shine a light on the prophecy. Her heart clenches in her chest as they continue on. She'd been too focused on Eowyn for the past eighteen years to even think about The Mother's Prophecy. She shakes the thoughts of inadequacies away as they approach the field set for archery.

Gideon and Elenor lead her toward the platform, flanked with more guards. They climb up, sitting in the three thrones before them. Windsor comes up the steps a few short moments later, alone. "Where is Eowyn?" Elenor asks softly when he sits beside his Mother.

"Busy," he says shortly, his eyes meeting Alice's. He nods once, letting her know silently that her daughter is prepared.

"Attention, please!" Ezoklark Distren's, Gideon's Hand, voice booms over the sea of people gathered to watch the archery tournament. "The archers will now take the field!"

Dozens of people, men and women of all ages, start toward the field with quivers hanging from their back and their bows off of their shoulders. They line up perfectly, one target to each competitor. They shoot off their arrows one by one, until all contestants have shot all three. Alice leans forward in her chair as the crowd parts. Windsor rises to his feet and steps to the Queen's side. He lays a cold hand on her shoulder when their, shared, favorite silver haired woman walks through the crowd with ease.

Her wedding dress has been discarded for an intricate silver armor that molds to her every curve, the shoulder pads and gauntlets adding to her imposing presence. A bold, trailing red cloak billows out behind her, completing the striking image of a warrior ready for battle. Everyone falls silent, all eyes on her.

She slips out of her shoes, laying her bow and quiver on the ground in front of her. She places her palms flat on the grass and kicks her legs toward the sky. She balances on one hand, the other grabbing the bow. She bends her legs at the knees and situates the bow between her toes. Continuing to hold herself on one arm, she reaches for an arrow and loads it into the bow. They watch in silence as her other hand lowers to the ground and she pulls her foot back, her toes curling around the bowstring. She releases it, the first arrow hitting the target dead center. Gasps, oh's and aw's fill the air as she loads the second arrow. This one splits the first down the middle, the wood splintering into a million pieces. Then the third, shattering the second just as it did to the first. She bends her arms, pushing up with a grunt to launch herself into the air and land on her feet.

"Fucking phenomenal," Windsor laughs, clapping his hands together loudly. "That's my wife!" He yells over the roar of his people.

Alice glances back to see Elenor and Gideon laughing with their son, clapping along. She lets out a soft chuckle and turns toward her daughter as she sprints toward them. "I could hear you across the field," she scoffs, heading right for Windsor.

"That was the point," he wraps his arms around her in a bear hug and starts walking backward toward his seat. "I wanted everyone to hear just how proudly I claim you," he sinks into the chair, pulling her to stand between his legs. His hands move to her hips. Alice watches as he stares up at her, a grin spread across his lips. She takes note of how he doesn't pull her closer and tucks the information away to question Eowyn later.

"You did amazing, sweetheart," Elenor coos, placing a hand over her chest. "That was truly one of the sweetest surprises we've ever had at something like this," she reaches over and laces her fingers through Gideon's.

Alice's heart clenches slightly at the sight, her mind drifting to the prison she was to return to after her daughter is crowned. Her eyes move to Eowyn again to find her staring at her already. She smiles warmly at the Princess. "You've done well, little bird," she dips her chin in approval, crossing one knee over the other.

Eowyn looks back to Windsor when his hands slide down the sides of her legs. "You look tired, Princess. Would you like me to walk you back to the tent so you can rest before the next event?" His words are innocent but his tone is implying.

Eowyn shakes her head as his fingers wrap around the backs of her thighs, just above where the boots ended past her knees. "No, but I wish to change back into my gown if you are offering help," her voice is low and tender.

Alice swallows, turning her attention back to the crowd. Her thoughts swirl at a near overwhelming pace. This was her home. She was born into the House of Light, chosen by Planets later on. The blood of the chosen ones was rare, most are picked by The Mother upon the solidification of one's skull as a babe. Yet, she had been born with the Light and chosen by the Planets. She was to return to Iverness. The land of the caged, the broken and dying... The land that ultimately sealed her fate. Tabot had deceived her during their betrothal and nearly ripped her heart out when he had declared magic, of any kind, outlawed. She'd disregarded his law when Eowyn died inside of the birthing canal, harvesting power from Tretanov itself to breathe life back into her. Tabot slapped a collar on her immediately, subduing her power. The magic built for eight years, the pent up energy sucking the life from her as it reeled with the need to be released. Eowyn had destroyed the collar in a fit of rage after Tabot had her lashed for summoning magic she could not yet control. He confined her to the walls of the Palace for a decade as an extension to her punishment. Alice had released the pent up power before being collared again. The Paronia not only suppressed her power, but began pulling from the thread that connected her soul to this realm. Eowyn had worked with Flare Meadowglade in the dungeons tirelessly between the ages of fourteen and sixteen to learn to siphon the power from her veins. Eowyn pulled the electricity from her veins, only strengthening the teenager as she had gained the other Primary Ability within the House of Light. More recently, this morning, Eowyn had siphoned her seers abilities to ease the ache of the collar around her neck- now giving her Four Primary Abilities within *two* chosen Houses. And if Windsor *had* siphoned her power without touching her, that meant she would be able to summon *all* of the Chosen Gifts at once.

20

WINDSOR

They arrive back at the palace just before sunset. Eowyn heads toward the steps to change into her evening gown for the feast in their honor. Windsor follows closely with the train of her dress in his hands. He closes the door as soon as they enter her room. His wife stands in front of the mirror, her hair swept over one shoulder. He slowly unlaces the back of her dress and watches as it pools around her legs. His eyes drag to the mirror and up her body. Once his eyes connect with hers, he slides his arms around her waist. She places her hands on top of his and exhales deeply. He rests his chin on top of her head. She smiles at him in the reflection.

"You're absolutely stunning," he drags a thumb along her stomach. He holds her gaze and dips his head into her neck. "Divine," he whispers before gently nipping at her skin. Eowyn turns in her husband's arms. She wraps her own around his neck. "You're my *wife*," he leans in down, his nose brushing against hers.

Eowyn smiles, tightening her grip on him. "You're my *husband*." She barely gets the last word out before Windsor groans and presses his lips to hers. They both pour every emotion they'd felt earlier in the day into the kiss. Windsor devours her anxiety and she swallows his excitement eagerly. He holds her hips with a bruising grasp, walking her back toward the vanity.

He continues his assault on her mouth, his tongue dominating hers, his teeth nipping at her lower lip. He gently lifts her onto the surface of the vanity, his hands roaming across her body, leaving a trail of fire in his path. "You're so perfect," he whispers into her skin, biting and sucking at her neck. His hands roam her thighs, fingers teasingly tracing a path up toward the apex of her legs, before suddenly returning to her knees and gripping them firmly. "Tell me this is a piece of you only *I* have," he lifts his head to look into her eyes. "Tell me one will ever touch you, never like this," he pushes her thighs more open, stepping between them.

Eowyn's hands drop to his belt, her fingers working to undo the buckle quickly before she starts to unbutton his slacks. "No one will *ever* even *look* at me like this," she whispers, her fingers hooking into his waistband and forcing his pants down his thighs.

He kicks off his pants, the fabric falling to the floor. He captures her mouth in another desperate kiss, his hand gripping the underside of her thigh, pulling her closer to him and pressing their lower bodies together. He groans against her mouth. His hips moving against hers, the friction driving him wild. His hand comes up to grip her hair in a tight fist, yanking her head back. He grins and dips his head back to her neck. He kisses and nips at her skin, leaving a trail of red marks along her throat and shoulder. "My sweet thing," he mumbles into her as he kisses his way up to her jaw again. His hands drop to grip the backs of her knees, his mouth moving up to her ear. "My deliciously sweet, beautiful, *powerful wife.*" He grunts as he sinks himself into her throbbing heat. She grips his biceps tenaciously with a sharp hiss. His hands slide up the sides of her thighs and around her, holding her chest pressed to his. "I know, baby," he croons, kissing his way back to her mouth. He keeps his hips still, bringing a hand up to tuck her hair behind her ears. "Are you okay, baby?" His voice is soft, like a gentle caress. Eowyn holds his stare as she nods. He nods in acknowledgement. "Just focus on me, okay?" She nods again and he leans down, pressing his lips to hers.

Windsor kisses her deeply, unhurriedly, his mouth moving over hers. His tongue runs over her lips, his hands tenderly moving back to grip her thighs. He gently rocks into her as if they have all the time in the world. A soft moan pushes its way through Eowyn's throat and seeps into the Prince's bones. He grunts, his restraint faltering slightly. He grips her bottom lip between his teeth, tugging lightly, before releasing her and resting his forehead against hers. He breathes heavily, his chest rising and falling against hers.

"Shhh," he whispers, his eyes locked on hers. "Quiet, my love. Don't let anyone else hear those pretty noises you make for me." His hips pull back before rolling into her again, reveling in the feel of her stretching around him. Her head falls back and her lips part, a ghost of a moan coming out on her next breath. "Mmm, my good girl," her eyes flare at the appraisal, making something in him *snap*. "Is that it, baby?" He pulls back and shoves into her, harder this time. She gasps, her head whipping up to look at him again. "You want me to sing your praises while I take you?" He slams into her again, the force of the thrust sending the vanity thumping against the wall.

"Windsor," she gasps, her nails biting into the flesh of his arms.

He squeezes his arms around her, yanking her forward to meet him with a hard thrust. "What is it, baby?" He cocks his head to the side tauntingly. His hands drop back to her thighs, sliding down to clutch the back of her knees and lay her feet flat on either side of her. "Cat got your tongue?" He drives himself into her repeatedly.

Eowyn's hands fall to her sides, helplessly grabbing for something to hold onto as she lets out a sharp cry. He grabs her wrists and pushes them over her head, leaning forward until he has her head pressed against the glass of the vanity mirror. He continues to pound into her rapidly, guiding her hands to grip the polished ledge above her. Once her fingers wrap around the wood, his own dance down her arms. A shiver runs through her as his light touch contradicts his nearing belligerent pumps. She's a moaning, whimpering mess under him now, coaxing the predatory instincts to drive her to the edge. His hands move to her chest and latch onto her bust.

"That's it, angel" he husks, lowering his mouth to her collar bones as his hands kneed her breasts between his fingers. "I don't care who hears you. *Fucking deafen me.*" The demand rips through him on a growl.

She tightens around him and lets out an absolutely feral noise, a cross between her heavenly moans and her guttural screams. He pulses inside of her, the thick vein running along the length of him throbbing against her contracting walls. "Winnie, please," she whimpers, bucking into him.

Well, that's new.

In an instant, his claws are protruding from his fingertips and slicing across her chest. She arches into him as he lowers his head, flattening his tongue against her skin and lapping up the blood. "You taste so good," he groans, his movements never ceasing as he continues to swipe at her chest and lick the blood up, his saliva sealing the wounds. He lets out a moan, the taste of her blood on his tongue and skin almost driving him over the edge. "Perfect, so perfect, you're mine. All mine. Every inch of you. No one else gets to see you like this," he thrusts deep into her, his fingers digging harder as he tears into her skin.

"No one but you," she whines, lifting her hips off of the surface and holding herself up by her grasp on the mirror.

His tongue glides over each wound. "Don't you fucking dare let go without me," he bats at her ribcage, his claws slicing her skin to the *bone.* He leans down, listening to her cry out in pain as he *slurps* at the flowing blood before the violet light blinds him. She gasps, her cries turning back into moans. "Come on, baby," he lifts his head to look at her. "Give it to me. Let me feel it, sweet thing," he presses his lips to her jaw again. Windsor continues his assault on her body, biting and clawing at her skin, drawing more blood. The feeling of her hot blood sliding across his skin only makes him more greedy for her. "You like that, don't you?" he growls, his voice raw with lust. "You like when I mark you. You like knowing you're mine, like knowing my claws, my teeth, my tongue, are all over you." He grips Eowyn's sides, hard, but doesn't puncture her skin. He thrusts into her harder, his mind lost in a daze of pleasure and possessiveness. His eyes dart to the blood dripping down her chest, the red liquid like a drug to him. He leans in and runs his tongue across the trail, licking up every drop of blood. "Let me have you, Eowyn," he growls into her ear, "let me mark you, claim you, possess you. Give me *you*."

She nods frantically, her soul wrapping around his and yanking him over the edge with her. He wasn't prepared, he wasn't *that* close. His knees nearly buckle with the force of the unexpected orgasm ricocheting through him. Eowyn lifts her heals off of the polished wood, propped up on her toes, her knees spread as far as they would go and her hands hooked around the mirror. His thrusts slow to a halt as he admires the way she spreads herself for him. He trails his fingers along her torso to heal over the rest of the minuscule marks.

"I'm... sorry," she whispers, her legs trembling as she settles back onto the vanity.

Windsor immediately takes hold of the tops of her knees, his eyes scanning over every inch of her. "Sorry?" He strokes the backs of his fingers down the side of her face before wrapping them around the back of her neck and leaning down until he's eye level with her. "What in Gragion are *you* apologizing for?" His thumb strokes along the side of her throat.

Her delicate hands rest on her shoulders as his other arm moves to her waist and slides her off the surface. "I manipulated you to..." she trails off, her eyes meeting his.

He tugs her into his chest, his hand on the back of her neck cradling her to him. She hugs his torso back, her hold lazier than his. "I am yours to bend and break, mold and shift, whatever it may be... as long as it pleases you, my wife." Thunder rumbles above them as the words leave his lips, shaking the palace. They laugh together, Windsor rubbing his hands sliding up and down the length of her spine. "I should apologize to you for cutting you open so much," his voice is a hushed whisper, like he didn't even want the souls dancing in the shadows to know he was sorry.

"I liked it."

He presses his face into her, inhaling the lingering scent of her sweet arousal mixed with the overwhelming smell of *her*, a pathetic attempt to distract himself from her words. "My Queen," he kisses the top of her head gently. "We should get you ready for the feast."

The Prince slides the ivory shoe onto his wife's foot. He ties the ribbons around her ankle, dragging his gaze up to meet hers. She stares down at him with her hands braced on the cushions on either side of her. He slowly rises from his knelt position, cupping one hand around the back of her neck with the other on her hip and pulling her up with him. She presses her body against his and closed the gap between their lips. He slides his hand around her waist to secure her in place. She pulls back as a knock rang through the room.

"Eowyn?" Her Mother's voice called. "We have delayed dinner for thirty minutes. Is everything all right?"

The Princess smiles as Windsor kisses her forehead, muffling his laugh against her skin. "Coming now, Mother!" She calls back and listens for the retreating footsteps. "We are being summoned," she whispers, turning her attention up to him.

The Prince keeps a protective arm around his wife's waist as he leads her down the steps. "I am famished," Eowyn sighs when they hit the bottom.

"It's a good thing they've prepared our wedding feast," Windsor smiles cheekily before kissing the side of her head. She lets out a hearty laugh as they made their way to the Great Hall. He stares at the side of her face, admiring the way she'd grown in the past two months.

Eowyn now glows radiantly through the halls of their home, her skin tanned from all the time she spends outdoors. He'd been able to see immediately how the cage affected the bird in Iverness. But here, she was thriving. And that made him thrive. Though she'd only give him bits and pieces, he was *happy* with what he had of her. She allowed him to be possessive of her regardless of the fact that she'd never truly be his.

The Prince drags himself from his thoughts as they approach the Hall. Eowyn's arm rests in his. He pushes the door open and leads her into the room. Tables line the whole space and everyone awes when they stepped in. Every single person bowed as they walked to the small table for two at the head of the room. Windsor pulls out a chair and smiles at his wife as she takes her seat. He kisses the top of her head before grabbing his chalice of wine and raising it to the crowd. "To my wife, to a beautiful and happy marriage between us, and to the places we will take our Kingdom to."

Everyone cheers their agreement and raises their glasses. He takes his seat next to her and sips his wine. Eowyn shoots a small smile at him as she sets her glass down. He leans over and lays a gentle kiss to the corner of her mouth. "I much prefer aqua vitae and SuperNova to this sweet shit," he whispers, leaning back in his chair.

"I think it pleasant," the Princess hums quietly.

He follows her gaze to the chalice before her. His tongue darts out to wet his lips, her eyes moving to look over the Hall. "I will make sure that the kitchen is stocked with enough that you will never wish for it again," he can't help but look back at her face. *She's just so-*

"You don't have to do that," her tone is smooth, level, like he hadn't just cut her down to the bone and drank her blood like a flowing river. "Aqua vitae will suffice," her eyes flare once.

"No," he says, a little too quickly. He forces his eyes away from her. "If you enjoy it, it is yours, *forever.*" *But he wasn't talking about the wine.*

21

ALICE

Queen Alice gently pushes open the door to her daughter's room. She gasps, covering her mouth with one hand. Eowyn sits on the vanity with her legs wrapped around Windsor's waist as he slowly thrusts in and out of her, their lips never leaving one another. Alice pulls the door closed and laughs. "Mother of Tretanov, they wasted no time," she sighs as she turns toward the stairs once more. She walks down the steps, holding her friends' gaze, a knowing smile spread across her face. "It will probably be a little bit longer," she says to Elenor and Gideon once she has reached the bottom.

"Did you find them?" Gideon's eyes gleam with curiosity at her statement. Alice nods with another chuckle. "Yes, they are in Eowyn's room... *consummating*."

Elenor's eyes widen and she covers her mouth while her husband roars with laughter. "I will let the kitchen know we need another half of an hour or so," he turns and stalks off, down the hall.

Elenor grabs Alice's hands. "They did not waste *any* time," she jokes.

Alice nods with a grin. "My thoughts exactly." She squeezes her best friend's hands. "They truly are two of a kind, aren't they?"

Elenor nods, opening her mouth to reply but quickly snaps it shut. They can faintly hear Eowyn gasping and whining as Windsor continues to take her, their noises growing louder with each passing moment.

The sound of wood scraping against the floor and the sound of flesh crashing together echoes through the hallway. The other sounds of the castle become muffled and quiet, the noise of the couple taking up all the noise around them.

The Queen of Exsar clears her throat. "Perhaps we should make our way back to the main palace," she glances at the stairs. "I'd not like to witness my grandchild being conceived." She offers her arm to Alice.

Alice loops her arm through Elenor's. "Nor I," she laughs as they start into a leisurely stroll.

Their footsteps echo against the stone floor of the hallway, the sound being the only real noise one can hear outside of the couple still upstairs. Elenor tugs at Alice's arm, an almost giddy smile on her face. She giggles like a schoolgirl, covering her mouth as she does so. "You would think that their excitement could keep them at bay for one night, but clearly not." Her laughs echo through the corridor as they enter the main palace.

"Surely, you do not think they..." Alice trails off, a lopsided smile spread across her face.

Elenor shrugs, "only the Princes of Gragion know." She pats Alice's hand with another laugh. "However, Eowyn does well with keeping Windsor in line and I do not believe she would have allowed him to break their celibacy before they were wed."

Gideon emerges from a set of swinging doors. "Office," he mumbles, brushing past them and starting toward the North Wing.

The women exchanged a worried glance before trailing after the King. He does not slow, making the concern between the Queens grow. Gideon holds the door open for them and slams it behind them. "What happened?" Elenor moves from Alice to her husband.

Alice takes a seat in one of the chairs before the desk, watching closely as Gideon pulls away from Elenor. "Flare Meadowglade was executed this morning," he looks at Alice with sorrow filled eyes.

She feels her heart crack in her chest. She looks down to her lap, twisting her fingers together. *This is it.* She nods to herself and rises from the chair. "Right," she looks between them. "This does not change anything, everything moves forward as planned," she pauses. Eowyn would be prepared to kill Tabot the moment she found out of Flare's death. "This does not get shared with Eowyn. She is still to know **nothing** until my death."

—∞—

The Queen of Iverness watches the Prince and Princess enter the Hall. Eowyn's expression is blank, showing no emotion. Windsor's features match her own as he leads her to their table. She glances around, too consumed by the thoughts swirling through her head to pick up on the Prince's toast. She raises her glass of water and takes a swig with the rest of the crowd. Her eyes drop to Eowyn when Windsor settles next to her again. She smiles at him, the pair exchanging quiet words before the doors open again. Dozens of servants rush in, pushing carts full of food. Windsor's eyes remain on Eowyn as the food is placed on their table. He smiles at her when she says something, his eyes softening slightly.

"Alice?" She turns to look at Elenor to see both her and the King staring at her with raised eyebrows. "Are you feeling alright?" The words slowly drip from Elenor's lips.

She diverts her attention back toward Eowyn, sighing softly. She's tired, angry, sad... just too overwhelmed to be on this plane of existence any longer. Finally, she nods. "I shall retire after I speak with Eowyn," she glances down at the platter of food in front of her. Her fingers dance along the gold foiled edge before she pushes it away. She looks back to Elenor to see concern etched into her face. "I am simply tired, El," she reaches over and places her hand on top of her friend's.

"Eat something," Gideon motions to her plate with his chin. "Have a little bit of something to soak up all the alcohol from last night, eh?" He teases to lighten the mood.

Alice smiles, nodding in slight defeat and pats Elenor's hand gently. She takes a few grapes from her plate, popping them into her mouth. She chews absently, her mind racing. She turns back to look at the young couple. As she studies them, she begins to notice the subtle hints of stress and agitation on Windsor's features, while Eowyn looks like she usually does, blank and stoic. She notes the way that Eowyn avoids his gaze, her eyes glowing dimly as she looks around the room. On the other hand, Windsor seems to be unable to look away from his wife. The way his eyes move over her is almost possessive, like a dog guarding its territory. She can't help but feel a little bit guilty. She wishes that she had gotten her daughter out sooner, allowing her to prosper like this sooner.

"What are you thinking about?" Elenor's voice rips her from her thoughts once more.

"I wish I'd sent Eowyn with Blaine Cromwell when he crossed the border to leave his daughter in your care," the words fly from her lips on a hushed mutter before she can stop them. Her head whips back toward Eowyn to find her staring at her. Her eyes glowing a light, almost pink. "Elenor, what is that?" Elenor looks at Eowyn, catching the flash of her dimming her irises. "Why were her eyes pink?" Alice whispers demandingly.

"I-I don't know," Elenor shakes her head as Eowyn looks back to Windsor. "I've never seen her eyes anything other than Red or Gold."

"Gold?" Alice nearly chokes on her own saliva. "Her eyes shift to gold?"

Elenor looks taken aback by Alice's shock. "Her eyes have had gold in them since her arrival. I've only seen them fully gold once," she furrows her eyebrows. "Is that something you were unaware of, Your Majesty?" She places her hand over Alice's again.

She looks back to her daughter and pulls her hand from her friend's. She sits there, her mind racing. Had she really not known that Eowyn's eyes had a golden hue? How had she missed that? And if her eyes were able to glow pink for a few moments, what other abilities could she have? The possibilities are nearly endless. All she knows was that there was something different about her. She glances between Eowyn and Windsor once more to see that the Prince's hand had found its way to his wife's knee. It appears the two aren't speaking at the moment, instead just sitting in each other's presence. She shakes her head, trying to clear her thoughts. She doesn't know what was more interesting; the fact that there was something very different about Eowyn or the fact that she seems so attached to him.

She's pulled from her thoughts once again by Elenor's voice. "I believe there is something going on between them."

"What do you mean?"

"They are overly attached to each other. Windsor is overly protective of her, possessive even." Elenor shrugs, "he'd nearly ripped Layne's throat out last night for saying Windsor *loves her* and proceeding to explain why *love* is not a sufficient enough word."

"I have to agree with you," Gideon chimes in, leaning back in his chair. "It took them one day to be completely attached to each other. She was standoffish with us at first, over *him*, but it quickly changed to him becoming defensive of people coming close to *her.*"

Alice absorbs his words, knowing exactly what it had meant. Eowyn didn't like the feeling and merely passed it to Windsor, amplifying his own instincts. She swallows and nods, though staying silent as to not oust her daughter's scheme.

The King leans further back in his chair, his eyes glued to the Prince and Princess. Windsor still keeps his hand grasping her knee despite both of their expressions being completely void of emotion. "They're not even talking," Gideon mutters and crosses his arms over his chest. He drums his fingers on the table, completely dumbfounded by this weird behavior. "What the hell is wrong with them? I've never seen two people look so... *blank* in my life." He shakes his head with a scoff. "I get that they're in love, but to be completely blank... it's just odd." He looks over to Alice and Elenor, both of them watching the pair with confusion.

"It's almost like they can hear each other," Alice whispers, her eyes glued to Eowyn.

Elenor cocks her head as she watches the Princess. "Is that possible? Do you think they can actually read each other's thoughts without speaking?" Elenor murmurs back to Alice.

Alice shrugs, watching as Windsor's grip tightens on Eowyn's knee. "It's possible, I suppose. But to what extent?" She glances back up to their faces and notes how Eowyn's lip twitches slightly.

Gideon leans forward on the table at that. "Did you see that?" he mutters, his eyes narrowed as he stares at Eowyn's face. "She just twitched, almost like she was having an internal conversation."

"Or she was smirking because she could hear your loud mouth." Elenor deadpans.

Gideon shoots her a mock glare. "Oh, hardy har har, El. Very funny," he huffs.

Alice can't help but laugh at the King and Queen. She leans back in her own chair, her hands resting in her lap. "Perhaps we could just... ask them."

Gideon looks at her like she's crazy. "And say what? *Excuse me, do you two have the power to read each other's thoughts or are you both just psychos*"?"

Alice sighs, exasperated at this point. "I was going to say; ask them why they're being so silent and still. But we can go with your version if you'd like." She glances over her shoulder and flags down a serving girl who's carrying a pitcher of wine. Once the girl arrives at the table, Alice holds up her empty glass. The girl quickly fills it.

When she attempts to move the same toward Elenor, Elenor holds up her hand. "No, I'm okay-"

"Actually, you're not," Alice interrupts her, pushing the glass towards her. "Fill it"

Elenor turns to glare at their friend. "I just said-"

"This isn't a request." Alice raises an eyebrow at her. "Our children just married each other. We are celebrating."

Elenor sighs, rolling her eyes as she allows the girl to fill her glass. Gideon lets out a huff beside her, sipping on his own glass. "I just don't understand their lack of communication..." His eyes dart over to the couple, who are still completely silent.

Alice looks back to Windsor and Eowyn, her chin resting on her hand. "Perhaps they've had a disagreement," she looks over Eowyn's posture. She knew looking for some signal of anything was useless, her daughter would never show any sign of weakness.

Gideon shakes his head and leans forward. "They're not acting like two people who've just had a fight." His head quirks to the side and his eyes dart back and forth between both of them. "Honestly, they're acting like two people that are having a conversation solely through their brains."

Alice pushes herself from the seat, the sound of the wood scraping against the stone consumed by the bustling of the party around them. As soon as she stands, both the King and Queen turn their attention to Alice.

"Where are you going?" Elenor's expression is one of concern, worry seeping through the creases of her brow.

"I am going to talk to my daughter." Alice responds, her eyes drifting back to Eowyn. "And I have a feeling someone should speak with Windsor," Alice glances at the King, eyebrows raised.

Gideon leans back in his seat once more, a smirk on his face. "Good luck trying to get her away from him," he says mockingly.

Alice rolls her eyes and grabs her wine off of the table. She weaves her way through the sea of people gawking at the newlyweds. She approaches the table with a loving smile on her face, noting how Windsor's fingertips ice over as he pulls Eowyn's leg closer to press against his. "Hello, darling," she says softly.

Eowyn's eyes land on her mother's as she gives a nod to her. Windsor's head turns at the sound of her name, his hand still gripping Eowyn's knee. His fingers tighten slightly as his eyes dart from Alice, to Eowyn, and back to Alice once more. His eyes then scan her up and down once, a look that one can only describe as territorial lingering in the dark of his pupils. Alice quirks a brow at the Prince. "May I steal her for a moment?" She sets her chalice down on the table.

Windsor is silent for a few moments, his gaze flickering back and forth between Alice and Eowyn before a polite, blank, smile stretches across his face. "Of course." He gently pats her knee, reluctantly pulling his hand away.

Eowyn stands from her seat, following behind her mother. She looks over her shoulder at her husband one last time, a slight frown on her face. Alice follows her daughter's gaze to the Prince. He still has his eyes focused on them, but he's now taking sips of his wine. "He seems rather... possessive," Alice can't help but comment. Eowyn hums lowly, nodding to the guards as they push open the Hall doors for them. They bow deeply at the waist while the women pass by. A comfortable silence falls over them, Alice leading the Princess to the gardens until she's sure no one would be eavesdropping. "May I ask you something, my sweet bird?" She stops in her tracks, turning to face Eowyn.

Eowyn blinks, her chin dipping in a single nod. "Of course, Mother."

She looks her daughter up and down, searching for any sign of... well, anything. But, as per the usual, Eoywn's face remains completely blank. Alice sighs and gestures to a stone bench just a few feet away. "Sit down with me, please." The Princess does not hesitate to cross over to the bench, looking at her Mother expectantly. Alice folds her hands in her lap, deciding it best to be direct. "Are you a Windsor able to communicate... *non-traditionally?*"

"Yes." Eowyn's answer is short, clipped and just as forward.

The simplicity of her answer leaves Alice a little taken aback. She shakes her head, lightly pushing her own confusion away. "Why did you not say anything?" She pushes, "to Draven or Gideon or Elenor?" She questions.

The Princess turns her attention toward the garden. "It just happened."

Alice's eyebrows pinch together. "It just happened?" She repeats, attempting to wrap her mind around the disclosure. "Did it happen before the ceremony?" Eowyn simply shakes her head, still not meeting her Mother's stare. "When did it start? The... connection?"

Eowyn swallows thickly before finally meeting Alice's confused expression. "After," she states plainly, her stare still stoic.

"After," Alice nods, "can you be more specific? Perhaps tell me what was happening when you noticed?" Her eyes roam over Eowyn's face

"It happened after a moment of intimacy," she holds her Mother's stare. "Why?" Alice stares at her for a few moments, thinking about what she had just said.

After a few long and silent minutes, she puts all the pieces together and her mouth drops slightly. "Are you telling me that you were able to communicate... non-traditionally, after you had... consummated the marriage?" Eowyn nods once in confirmation. Alice lets out a loud sigh, her hands rubbing at her temples. "So, when you're..." she pauses, trying to pick her next words carefully. "Intimate with him, you can communicate through your mind?"

"No," Eowyn shakes her head. "We've been able to communicate nonverbally *since* consummating the marriage."

Alice's head spins. "You have been able to hear his thoughts since then?"

Eowyn lifts a brow. "Thoughts, no. Communicate, yes."

She lets out a sigh, but frowns. "Okay, then what exactly can you communicate through this *bond*?"

A feral grin spreads across her daughter's mouth and the sight makes her almost cower. "Everything," Eowyn whispers.

The thoughts bouncing around Alice's brain halt entirely. "Everything?" She echos, eyes widening as she processes the information.

The Princess nods. "Everything. All our sensations are heightened. The need for touch... a craving for one another, is almost completely unbearable when we're apart."

The heat rises to Alice's cheeks as the words flow from her daughter's mouth. "So... all of your, um emotions, is that something you can exchange as well? As in, you know what the other is feeling?" She clears her throat.

"If you are asking if I disposed of a certain feeling *into* His Grace because they were uncomfortable, I have no choice but to be offended, Mother."

She shakes her head. "That's not what I was implying, darling." She frowns again, trying her best to wrap her head around everything. "I just... I don't understand why you didn't tell me."

Eowyn turns her head, holding her chin high. "You are ill, not to be burdened with things I do not understand."

"I am your Mother, Eowyn," her voice cracks on a whisper. "I am here to help you, no matter what you do or do not understand."

"Alice." The Prince's voice startles her, causing her to jump up and spin to face the man who silently approached them. "You know when to leave well enough alone." His eyes flash pure white, then red, before dimming back to his natural cobalt color.

22

WINDSOR

The Queen of Inverness glances between the Prince and his wife, as if waiting for Eowyn to interject. She does not. Alice stands there, confused and hurt. Windsor watches Eowyn inhale sharply and feels her pull the emotions from her Mother. Zanna's markings sizzle against her skin. "*Get her to go to bed*," he says silently to Eowyn.

The Princess narrows her eyes, her irises shining red as she begins to manipulate Alice's life force. She silently turns and starts toward the Palace. A smirk settles across his face when she disappears through the doors. Eowyn's eyes dim and she cranes her neck to look back at Windsor. "She's keeping something from me," she says after a moment of holding his stare in quiet. She rises from the bench, smoothing her hands over the front of her gown. "Though she no longer has magic, I can sense it."

He steps forward and walks around the bench. "We'll speak with her in the morning," he assures. He stops a few feet away from her and lifts his hand between them, summoning a roll of SuperNova. "Join me?" He raises his eyebrows.

The Princess licks her lips. "Of course," she whispers. He lifts it to his lips and she lifts a flame tipped finger to light it. He inhales deeply, pinching it between his index finger and thumb. He pulls it back, passing it to Eowyn as he holds the smoke in his lungs. They start down the path leading away from the Palace. She draws in a breath around the roll.

"I'd like to take you somewhere," he exhales a gray cloud. "To watch the sunset." Eowyn nods, staring at the joint as she parts her lips. Windsor watches the smoke curl and swirl into her nostrils, passing it back to him. He takes a leisurely drag, holding the smoke in his lungs and brings it to her mouth again. She wraps her lips around it and pulls it from his hand. "What is it?" He tilts his head to the side with a curious glint to his eye while he watches her eyes scan the area around them.

She shakes her head, taking in a long, almost impressive pull of the drug. "Nothing," she says, her voice strained with the effort of holding in the smoke.

His eyes stay glued to her face while they continue into the hunting grounds. His gaze follows the billow of her exhaling through her nose. He doesn't wait for her to pass it, he plucks the drug from her fingers with a teasing smile. "I know when you're lying, sweet thing. Try again," he chuckles. Eowyn narrows her eyes, though keeping her gaze forward. He takes notice of the defiance in her eyes, how her gaze is set straight forward. He takes a large drag from the joint, noticing how she glances at him from the corner of her eyes. He blows the smoke into her face until her eyes dart towards him. He smirks as he takes in the redness that slowly spreads across her cheeks. "You don't usually get this tense when we enjoy such intoxicants, Princess. Is there something on your mind?" He keeps his tone low, still with a slight taunt. He blows another plume of smoke at her, watching her eyes darken to a deep maroon.

"I'm quite... intoxicated," she murmurs.

His lips form an amused smile at her admittance, slightly stilted from the drug as well. "I don't think I've ever seen you this relaxed before, My Queen," he slides his arm around her waist, tugging her until her hip is against his. The Princess doesn't resist, but rather steps with him. "We're almost there," he smiles down at her, "I'll sit with you until you're feeling less inebriated."

Her soul strokes his in reply, heating him from the inside out. She'd yet to let go of him completely since he'd taken her on the vanity and he was enjoying every second of it. Before today, she'd only wrap his soul with hers for brief moments, just to appease him. But now she was being greedy. She was acting like it was hers to hold and soothe, because it was hers. He'd said it once and he's sure he'd say it another thousand times before his time to cross into Gragion came, he'd give her anything.

The Prince finishes off the joint and flicks it to the ground, encasing it in ice before it shatters on the stone. A soul comes by, sweeping the remnants of the icicle away in a single breath. "Right down here, sweet thing," he shifts his hand from grasping her waist to the small of her back when he stops at a short but steep path, leading downward. She looks at him wearily, her eyes narrowed slightly. "I can carry you, if you'd like," his fingers dance lightly along her back as he speaks.

Eowyn scoffs, stepping forward and starting down the path on her own. He crosses his arms over his chest and summons a soul to slither between her ankles. Her head angles downward toward it before whipping back toward him. "Stop that," she scolds, standing in place. Windsor smirks, his fingers twitching along his biceps. The soul listens to his command and slithers up her left leg. She rolls her eyes and starts down the path again. He takes a step forward, lifting his hand and flicking it quickly.

Eowyn gasps, stumbling when she feels the soul caress the apex of her thighs.

The Prince lunges forward, grabbing her hips to stable her. "Careful," he pulls her until her back is against his chest. "Don't want you falling before we get to the best part," he whispers into her ear and walks her forward.

Eowyn steps with him, watching the soul slide down her leg and scamper away. "You just wanted to touch me," she mumbles.

Windsor chuckles quietly, his hands tightening to deliver a gentle squeeze. "Too bad for you that you are unable to lie to me now that I can feel you," he pulls her back, making her stop in her tracks. He maneuvers around her, stepping down in front of her and bringing his hands to her hips again. He lifts her off of the path and onto the ground. "Though, it does irk me how well you deal with such overwhelming feelings," he grimaces and shivers dramatically.

Eowyn smiles savagely up at him as he places her on her feet. "Feelings are the least overwhelming part of my being." She says nonchalantly.

"How so?" He keeps his hands on her sides. She hums, turning her attention to move around the heavily wooded area. The trees down here were mainly Blue Crolia, a few lilac colored Ofrows. Her eyes sparkle with wonder as they dance along the leaves. He already knew she wasn't going to answer because she would've by now, but he doesn't say anything. He stands there, cemented to the ground and openly gawking at her. He takes another step forward, drawing her gaze back to him. "Come here," he steps backward.

Her brows pinch together but she goes with him. His hands slip into hers and he continues back, watching her eyes widen as he leads her into a clearing. He smiles, slowing to a stop when she drops his hand. "What is this?" She breathes out.

Windsor's arms fall to his sides, watching Eowyn take in her surroundings. A tranquil and mystical setting nestled in the lush forest, where a small pavilion gracefully stands over a calm pond. The structure is lit from within, casting a warm glow that contrasts with the cool, ethereal atmosphere of the surrounding natural environment. A small waterfall cascades gently into the water, adding to the soothing ambiance. The pond's still surface perfectly mirrors the pavilion's reflection, creating a mesmerizing and magical sight. The dense forest around them is adorned with vibrant, luminescent plants, contributing to the dreamlike and otherworldly feel of this enchanted spot.

"This is your wedding gift," he whispers.

Thunder rumbles, loud and unending. A grin spreads across his face though Eowyn stares at him, blinking slowly and her face revealing nothing. He opens his mouth but she cuts him off. "Yes, it pleases me.

I adore it, thank you." Her expression cracks, her lips twitching. Her attention moves back toward the water behind him.

He steps aside and watches her eyes flick back and forth. *"Come on, baby,"* he bites his lip as he speaks to her silently. Her shoulders relax and she nods once. She meets his stare and nods again. He raises his eyebrows expectantly, lifting a single finger and moving it in a slow circle. She turns her back to him, reaching for her hair. He moves quickly to sweep it to one side before she can. Goosebumps form along her shoulder as his hand moves up the side of her neck then down to the lacing of her corset. He arches a brow, watching a coat of *ice* form along her skin. "Eowyn," he breathes out.

"I feel it." She doesn't move.

He doesn't either. It keeps growing, creeping up her shoulders. "How are you..." He trails off, his eyes dropping to his own fingers. He steps forward and presses his chest to her back. He extends his hand in front of them, both of their eyes widening as he summons a flame in his palm.

"Try lightning," she whispers.

Windsor's other arm comes around to press his palm to her stomach, holding her to him. Small bolts of lightning begin to crackle within the fire. She laughs and brings an ice covered hand to smother it out. "Eowyn," he looks at her, his mind swimming with questions. Or the mixture of wine and SuperNova, maybe both.

"It's from me not pulling away from you," she refers to the way her soul has cradled his for the better part of the evening. "It has to be." She looks so sure, so confident... so beautiful.

He drops his hand to wrap around her, now completely side tracked from their discovery. He leans his forehead against her shoulder and closes his eyes. "Does this mean you'll stay right where you are?" His tone is deep, raspy... *desperate.* He wanted to let the words slip out, wanted to let the insult fall off of his lips.

"You do not know how to cut *me* off from *you*, cub," her voice cuts through his darkening mind. He lifts his head. "You need to learn how to seal the way."

"I do not wish to learn," he steps back, a slight stumble in his step. She turns, her soul cooing softly to his. He shakes his head, feeling the tension slowly ease in his muscles. The dragon markings on the Princess's biceps flare. "I do not wish to close you out," he whispers. "I do not wish for you to feel the... the..." his eyes dart around.

He doesn't even know how to describe it.

"You need to learn." She grips his attention again. His mouth snaps shut as she reaches behind her. "We do not know why or how... whatever this is, is, so you must learn how to seal it as I do to you." Her arms move expertly and the gown falls to the ground. His mouth goes dry. No, he begins salivating. Perhaps both. Blue sparks dance around him, making Eowyn smirk. Gold and red sparkles flash around her now. "I am *not* prey, Windsor," she warns.

He licks his lips, slowly taking her in from her toes to her eyes. Her eyes flash a pale pink and he cocks his head to the side. "Do that again," his nostrils flare as if trying to pick up a scent of what she was actually doing.

"Do what," she says flatly.

"Your eyes," he steps forward, "They were pink." His eyes move over her again, taking in the way she held her chin straight, shoulders square and her hands by her sides. He looks back to her face before looking at her legs, knowing this was more important. She does it, briefly, but he catches it. "What is that?" His hands move on their own, working to strip him of his suit.

"It's a party trick," Eowyn laughs, stalking toward the pool of water. "It is merely something I can do, nothing more and nothing less."

The Prince watches her hips sway hungrily. He shoves his pants to his ankles, nearly tripping as he steps out of them. He doesn't care about what they were talking about anymore. Windsor wraps one arm around her stomach and yanks her back. "Don't walk away from me on our *wedding night*," his stubble grazes her ear as he hisses into it. He lifts a hand and points to the clearing above them where the sun begins to set. "You are officially mine until morning," he nips at her earlobe. "And I plan on *making* you prey by then." Her breath hitches with his words. He brings his other hand up to shove her head away from him, her neck now fully exposed. "Starting here." He yanks on her soul, beckoning her shifter's blood. She gasps at the sensation and abides, going up in one massive flame and emerging as the bird in the water. He grunts, following suit.

Eowyn flaps her wings a few times, just enough to lift her from the water and move to the paved edge. The lion huffs and charges across the pond at her. She caws and flies over him, dipping to skate along the surface of the water before landing on the other side. Windsor growls, turning to face her. She shakes her whole body to clear the water from the feathers coating her chest. He narrows his eyes at her and she waves a wing tauntingly. He leans back on his hind legs, releasing a tumultuous roar as he launches himself over the whole body of water. Eowyn lets out a cry and rolls to her left. Windsor hits the ground, head first. He pushes himself back onto all four of his legs and shakes the haziness away. She stands a few feet away, her own head tilted in concern as she blinks expectantly. He closes his eyes and nods once.

When he opens them again, she's gone. A red string illuminates along the ground. He lowers his head, sniffing her sweet scent of blood and cinnamon. She wouldn't leave a trail. *Unless...*

Windsor starts into a trot, following the glow around the water and to the pavilion steps. He shifts into the Prince again and starts up the stairs, a smirk on his face when he stops at the top. "I see you've found the best part," he whispers.

Eowyn jumps slightly with her back to him, still looking around the space. Her eyes dance along the bed, just big enough for two and to the small plate situated atop the fox fur blanket. He licks his lips as he approaches her and uses all of his willpower to step to her side instead of pushing her face down into the mattress. His hand finds its way to rest just above her backside, completely on its own, as if naturally. She turns to look up at him, then back down to the single slice of their wedding cake. Layne had brought it down here for them while he went in search of Eowyn in the gardens.

Her hand moves to the foot of the bed and runs along the fur. Keeping one hand on her, he leans forward and lifts the plate. "Sit down," he gently pushes her forward. She does as he says, sitting on the edge of the bed. He kneels in front of her and sets the plate down next to him. *"That can wait."* Eowyn lets out a breathy laugh at the scoff he sent down the mental pathway while his left hand dances along the shifter marking of a phoenix on her right calf. He smiles up at her, his control slipping the longer she holds his stare. She blinks, her hands moving to cup his face. He lifts himself to her lips and pushes her shoulders until she's flat against the bed. His lips move against hers slowly, his right forearm holding him up as his other hand guides her leg around his waist. There's a slight bend to her other leg and she lets it fall away from him. He presses his chest to hers and groans at the feel of her skin against his. He deepens the kiss as his hand moves from her thigh to her ribcage. Her lips part and her tongue eagerly meets his. He rolls his hips against her, biting her tongue when she moans. She kisses him desperately and it makes his head spin. "Don't move," he grunts into her, angling his hips perfectly between her thighs.

"I won't," she smiles against him as he slowly pushes into her.

184

23

EOWYN

The Princess shifts under the weight of the fur over her and Windsor. She lifts her arm from around his waist to shield her eyes from the morning sun. She blinks her eyes a few times before settling her palm against his chest. He stirs slightly, his arm around her shoulders tightening. He lifts his other hand to rub his eyes. "I know we said we would not skip our training today," he mumbles groggily, finally lifting his eyelids to look down at her. "So perhaps we can agree to double up another day this week." His fingers tighten on her upper arm and he shifts to face her, tangling their legs together.

She nods, allowing him to pull her close. "We can," she hesitates for a moment but tucks her head under his chin. Her forehead rests against his Adam's apple and her eyes fall closed again.

Windsor hooks his hand around the back of her knee and presses his thigh between hers. He kisses the top of her head a few times. She hums as his hand faintly skates along the skin from her thigh, to her ribs and back down. He kisses her hair again before settling his chin on the crown of her head. They lay there for a while, completely silent. She watches her fingertips tap his chest lightly, her head rising and falling with each of his breaths.

"Windsor?" She whispers, pausing her movements.

His arms seem to reflexively tense around her as if she jerked him from sleep.

"Yeah, baby?"

The new pet name made the hair on the back of her neck stand up every time he said it. But now, a shiver wracks through her. She bites down on her lip, disregarding how husky his voice is when he's balancing on the edge of consciousness. "I wish to keep the exchange of magic between us," her fingers resume their rhythmic tapping.

He exhales and nods, "of course." He kisses her head once more. "Are you hungry, My Queen?" He mumbles into her hair.

"No," she pulls back to look up at him, "are you?"

Windsor lifts his hand from her side to comb his fingers through her hair. "I'd rather starve than move right now," his eyes watch his motion. She can feel what he is thinking, he is unable to hide anything from her the longer her soul encases his. He knows they have another long day ahead and he is dreading returning to their duties. She almost pities the way the sadness consumes his thoughts. She closes her eyes and inhales sharply, stealing the emotion away and feeding it to Zanna. "Don't do that," he swipes a claw down the side of her face. She hisses in pain and recoils, though his arms hold her against him. "You let me feel everything when it comes to you, do you understand?" He pinches the cut between his thumb and index finger. She nods and he leans down to lick the wound closed. The Princess rubs against his hand as he uses his thumb to dry her face. "Cute," he mocks, forcing her head away from him. "Too bad you let me know a little *too* much to know you're not *that* innocent." She bares her teeth in a feral smile when his teeth dig into her flesh.

"Aye! Cat boy!" Layne whistles from the other side of the pond. The Prince sighs, releasing instantly and lifting his head. "Shows on, let's go!"

Eowyn tenses when he pulls back. She swallows and quickly relaxes. *Odd.* "Perhaps we can *watch the sunset* this evening." She blinks and focuses on his face. He props himself on his elbow. His electric blue eyes roam over her face. She feels something pull in her chest as his gaze snags on her lips. He leans down slowly. She reaches up and cups his face to pull him down until their lips are pressed together. He smiles into the kiss, shifting to slide one hand under her while his other holds him up.

Something reminiscent of rage flares inside of her, something just as intense but so... *new*, something so intoxicating and it only heightened as time went on. Every brush of his skin against hers, every kiss he's laid on her lips, every time he's touched her and she's touched him, it only feeds the unfamiliar feeling.

Windsor breaks the kiss first, his thumb soothingly stroking back and forth along her back. "My Mother will have my head if I make *you* late for your day," he whispers, pressing another tender kiss to her nose. "And I *will* make you late in a moment," his eyes move over her bare chest.

She watches him eye her hungrily before tugging him back down to her. "We can be late," she mumbles into the kiss. He groans and moves over her once more. His lips move against her desperately and she tugs on his soul. His light purrs, dancing within her. He presses himself down into her, grinding against her dripping heat.

"Let's go!" Layne's voice cuts through their moment again.

Windsor pulls back with a sigh. Despite his dramatics, she understands. It felt good to step away from... life. He sits back onto his knees. Eowyn jerks up, wrapping one arm around his back while the other hand grabs his neck tightly. He smirks and grabs the blanket in a tight fist. She flips them, but he holds the blanket around her tightly to force her to stay pressed against him. "Don't you dare," he pulls the cover taut. His eyes flash cobalt.

The Princess's smile feigns innocence. "Don't what?" She cocks her head to the side innocently.

Her eyes drop to where his tongue darts out to wet his lips. "Now, you're doing two things," he mumbles, laying his head back on the pillow. "Don't yell at him and just... don't look at me today," he sighs exasperatedly.

"WINDSOR!" Renhart bellows, clapping his hands.

"I'M FUCKING NAKED, LAYNE. I'LL BE UP IN TWO MINUTES!" The forest stills, even Eowyn flinches. "Sorry, baby," he leans up and kisses her forehead.

"Oh," Layne's footsteps slowly retreat. "See you up there."

Eowyn blinks, shaking her head slightly as the Prince moves them both to sit up. She feels almost as if she's in a daze. "Stay here," he climbs off of the bed. "I will retrieve your gown."

Her eyes drop to where his hand moves toward her face. She knows what's coming: he'll use his index finger to lift her chin, kiss her forehead, rub his nose against hers, then kiss her oh-so softly. Just as he'd done every time one of them had to go back to their room before someone noticed they were missing.

Only he doesn't. His hand drops. His fingers wrap around her throat and yanks her to her knees. She gasps, not knowing if she's scared or *really* aroused. He presses his lips to hers in a rough kiss. She places her hands on his shoulders to steady herself as she melts into him. He pulls back all too soon and a subdued sound pushes past her parted lips. He releases her neck and slides his hand up to cup her jaw. "You're just so *sweet*," he growls, his thumb presses into her cheek harshly before he steps back. "I could just rip you apart," he winks before shifting into the lion.

She exhales a short laugh, still feeling like she was in a cloud of fog. Her eyes follow him down the steps of the Gazebo and starting around the pond. Her body relaxes as she falls back onto the bed.

What on Tretanov is wrong with me? She brings her hands up to rub her eyes with the heels of her palms. She jumps slightly at the cold touch of her hands. *Right.* She wills the fire to roar louder than the ice she's pulling from him. *Is it him? Am I feeling what he's feeling?* She intertwines her fingers over her bare stomach. *No, I'm shielded.* Her eyes move along the ceiling as if looking for an answer. *It feels too good to be what he's feeling.*

The sound of shoes colliding with wood pulls her from her thoughts. Windsor steps into the enclosure, his pants buttoned but his belt not buckled. His shirt hangs over his chest but remains unbuttoned. He holds her dress in one hand, the other holds his suit jacket on a single finger over his shoulder. He pauses at the foot of the bed, pressing his lips into a flat line. He slowly lays the gown beside her and takes a single step back. "I want nothing more than to help you into your dress, My Queen." He swallows before snapping his mouth shut. *"But I am fucking addicted to you."* The words ring through her head and pull her lips into a smile. She smirks, feeling herself finally start to come to. She sits up and throws the material over her head. She pulls it down as she rises from the bed. *"Not a woman."* His eyes burn into her when she walks past him. *"A fucking goddess."*

"You are making it harder for yourself, Your Grace," she teases, starting down the steps with him hot on her heels.

"This is the best thing to happen to me since meeting you," his tone is just as taunting, though saying it into her head. The Princess rolls her eyes, smiling when he falls to her side and takes her arm in his. "Today is my favorite of the festival," he pulls her closer. "I get to parade my wife around the treasure she is." His lips press a firm kiss to her temple.

Eowyn hums, taking in the scenery once more as they walk by before starting toward the trail. "You have quite the sweet tongue, Your Grace. No wonder you were set to marry before I." His soul squirms in her embrace at the mention. Oh, interesting.

"You never divulged what happened with that." She glances over to see his stare ahead and jaw clenched.

"I cannot speak of it because of the bargain I have with your Mother," he grits out, "I'm... sorry." Another hum, closer to a growl, vibrates through her chest. Her own jaw ticks, her soul starting to untangle from his. "You cannot be upset with me for a bargain," it's pathetic, somewhere between snapping at her and desperately pleading. She keeps her arm in his but fully retracts from him. "Eowyn, please," he helps her up the steep path. He pulls her up, onto level ground and grabs her hips. "Don't do this, Eowyn. You can't hold it against me, please," he whispers, stepping closer to her. She stares at him, not moving. He can get as close as he wants, nothing is going to soothe the emptiness he feels in his soul now. "Eowyn," his fingers tighten.

She cocks an eyebrow and crosses her arms over her chest. "I am not stupid, Windsor, and I will not be treated as such." His hands fall to his sides and he steps back. Her fire begins to erupt, rage consuming her again for the first time since their ceremony. "I know you are well aware of the fact that my Mother's bargain means *nothing* anymore," she bites out.

His features fall. "Baby, I-" Eowyn raises a hand and silences him. She starts toward the Palace. He follows behind her silently, despite how loudly his soul cries for her. They approach the open glass doors of the rose garden when he finally speaks. "Eowyn, wait." He doesn't reach for her, keeps his distance. She takes note, appreciating the space. She turns on her heels to face him. "If you are going to be this upset about it, I will take the chance that part of the bargain remains and break it to tell you," he scans her face and takes a slow step forward. His words echo through her brain. He would die to please her.

"No," she whispers.

She watches Windsor's eyebrows lift. "No," he repeats.

The Princess runs a hand through her hair and shakes her head. "The fact that you would break an oath to a seer just to appease me is more than what I need." The words are honest, raw in vulnerability. It's the first time she's spoken of any kind of feelings toward the Prince other than saying she enjoys his company.

She can see the words swirling around his brain, hear the way his soul chants the last word like a prayer. *Need, need, need, need me*, it sings happily. Another silence engulfs them as they make their way through the Castle. Windsor's arm found its way around her waist once more somewhere between the main Palace and the South Wing. His soul continues singing while it tugs at her helplessly. Eowyn keeps herself shielded from him, not quite sure why but more than happy with keeping him at an arm's length until she could figure out why she's felt so off today. As if something has shifted.

Windsor pushes open the door to her bedroom, revealing Layne Renhart and her lady Olivette. He places his hand on the small of her back and ushers her in. "Out," he demands lowly. Eowyn looks over both of his friends before glancing at him. His attention stays locked on them. "My wife and I need to bathe. Get out," he growls.

Need, need, need, need me.

They look stunned, shocked, completely caught off guard. "Out," he snarls sharply.

Silently, they start toward the door. The Princess watches Windsor intently as his own eyes follow them, narrowing them on the door once it's closed behind them. She places a hand on his bare chest in the opening of the unbuttoned shirt. His gaze drops to her hand then to her face. His features soften and he laces his fingers through hers. He leads her to the bathroom tucked into the guest suite.

Need, need, need, need me.

Windsor reaches for the glass of the standing shower, dropping her hand and slamming it open. *Oh.* She leans back on her heels, interest piqued. He grabs the nozzle with white knuckles and flicks it to the left, turning on the hot water. He straightens and there's a shift in the air with the movement. His normal clean and crisp scent of ice is replaced with something more intoxicating, the same scent she picked up on the second they entered her room after their ceremony yesterday. Then she feels a pull and her eyes widen.

His soul slips past her borders and seeps into hers again. He keeps his back to her as he lets the silk fall to the floor. Steam wafts from the glass enclosure around them as she feels his soul coiling into hers. She isn't sure if she's angry at the invasion or if she's impressed by the way he managed to slither in, though definitely pleased by the fact that his form still cowers at the sight of hers and allows it to consume him. She watches his muscles flex as he pushes the pants off of his waist before turning to her. She blinks, her eyes flaring red at him.

"I told you not to do it," he shrugs and steps into the shower. Eowyn tilts her head to the side but strips the gown from her body. She steps in front of him, her eyes boating into his being.

Need, need, need, need me.

"Why is it still doing that?" She snaps, stepping closer to him.

Windsor lifts his head from leaning into the stream of water. "I don't know," he says shortly. He goes back to running his hands through his wet hair. "But it won't fucking shut up."

"I know," she barks back at him.

He lifts his head again, this time with a smirk. "It bothers you that my soul sings for you?" He narrows his eyes predatorily.

Eowyn's jaw clenches at the sight of his *feigned* dominance. "It bothers me that it does so obnoxiously," her eyes blaze in warning.

He bares his teeth, those damned K9's sliding over his bottom lip slowly. "Then maybe you should give it what it wants," his tone drops an octave, catching her off guard. His smirk returns at the slight hitch in her breath. He takes a step forward. "Maybe you should just let it live in you," he takes another step toward her. He grabs her hips and jerks her to him, his claws ripping open her flesh. "Maybe you should just let *me* live *inside of you.*"

24

ALICE

The Queen of Inverness feels the way her blood moves slower than the day before, her breathing weaker with each passing second. The carriage approaches the Castle in Iverness as tears well in her eyes. She's quick to blink them away when it comes to a stop. Blaine looks over at her with sorrow filled eyes. "I'm... sorry, Your Majesty," he whispers, rising from the bench across from her. She shakes her head dismissively. He nods once and opens the door, stepping down before offering her a hand.

King Tabot waits at the stop of the steps for her, his jaw tensed with his arms over his chest. His fingers twitch against his biceps. She walks toward him slowly, behind Blaine Cromwell. He doesn't acknowledge her when she passes but follows closely behind her. Alice makes no move to look back at him, her body protesting with every step toward the Queen's suite. "Alice," Tabot's voice is worse than sitting in the blacksmith's shop for the entire day. She halts her steps, noting the way Blaine slowly turns to watch the exchange. Tabot steps in front of her. "You have yet to acknowledge your King," he growls, grabbing her by the hair and shoving her to her knees.

"Your Majesty," Blaine steps forward. "The Queen is ill. Please allow me to escort her to her chambers," he looks between Alice and Tabot.

Alice does not move, does not resist. Tabot bares his teeth down at her. "You are too unwell to greet your husband?" He hisses. She does not reply, her muscles weakening the longer she sits on the floor. He jerks her head, yanking on her hair roughly. "Answer me, bitch," he bends his right knee and slams her face into it.

"Your Majesty!" Blaine grabs his arm and yanks it away from the Queen. She still does not move, does not make a single noise, even as blood drips down her face and Tabot rips a fistful of her hair from her scalp. Blood drips down the back of her head, from her nose over her mouth, her eyes hooded as she watches the King stumble back. He lets out a grunt and Alice sees the clump of her hair fall to the ground.

Without another word, he turns and stalks down the hall. "Alice," Blaine drops to his knees in front of her, bringing a handkerchief to her face. He holds it there, shifting to look at the back of her head. "Let's get you to your chambers. I've a healing potion from Exsar," he whispers to her. She just nods, allowing him to pull her to her feet.

The Queen's exhausted body slumps against the Noble. He leads her through the dim Palace keeping his pace slow for her. Her eyes take in every detail of her surroundings, just as she had done before leaving Exsar. "Blaine," she croaks as he helps her onto her bed.

He sighs, sitting on the edge of the bed beside her. "Yes, Alice?" He pulls the duvet over her trembling body, knowing full well that she wasn't cold.

She wraps a hand around his wrist. "I need you to make an oath," she whispers. "An unbreakable one. Before I die."

His eyes roam over her face before he sighs. "Of course, my love," he brushes her golden hair away from her face and rests his palm against her cheek. She brings a hand up to cover his and leans into it. "Anything, for *you*," he leans his forehead against hers.

She wraps her fingers around his hand as tears slide down her cheeks, her eyes falling closed. "Blaine Cromwell," she sucks in a sharp breath. "I ask you to pledge your life to the Queen Exsar in every way possible, including when she marches against Inverness."

"I vow my life to the Queen of Exsar and I will stand by *our* daughter in every way possible, *especially* when she marches on Iverness."

A glimmer of gold shines in both of their eyes, locking the bond in place and sealing his vow. Tears stream down both of their faces now, Blaine staring at the Queen. "Blaine," her voice is rough and strained.

"Shhh," he soothes, pulling back slightly and ushering her to lie back. "Just rest now, my love," the tears continue down his face as she stares up at him.

She keeps her hand on his, holding it to her face. "Don't leave," she pleads, "don't let me die alone, Blaine."

He lies down next to her and wraps his arms around her. "You won't, my love," he tucks her head into the crook of his neck. He rests his head against her and inhales deeply. "I'm here," one hand runs through her hair while the other moves up and down her back. The Queen listens to his voice as he continues to fill the silence, his heart of gold knowing that if they sat in silence, she would crumble. "I remember the first time I saw you teaching Eowyn how to control her magic," his voice cracks on her name. "I'd found you both in the old slave pits behind the Palace." She can't help but smile at the memory. "I'd stood off to the side for a while, watching you speak to her so softly, telling her all about the House of Light and how to control the fire in her." His hands tremble around her. "And her eyes flashed when she saw me," he laughs. "Then a shadow crept up her neck to let her know I could be trusted." Alice knew it wasn't a shadow that day just as well as she knew now. "And everyday until her imprisonment, I watched you." His voice breaks on an involuntary sob. Alice lifts her head to look up at him. She gently wipes his tears as he continues. "I watched you and our daughter every damn day, Alice. *Everyday.*" He shakes his head.

"I love you," she strokes her frail hand down the side of his face. "And I'm going to wait at the other end of the path to Gragion everyday until you come running to me," her hand falls flat against his cheek. Blaine pulls her closer, sniffling as he kisses her forehead tenderly. She closes her eyes and lets out a sob. "You are the greatest love I've ever known, Blaine Cromwell."

He continues to kiss the same spot on her forehead. "I've loved every second of loving you." He pulls her flush against him. "Every blessed moment of being able to witness you put Eowyn to bed, every glance across the ball room, every stolen kiss in passing, I'll never forget any of it." She sucks in a shaky breath as his hands move aimlessly over her. "I'll forever cherish every night I've spent with you, every single second I've even been in your presence." He kisses down to her lips. Her chest sputters but she kisses him back weakly. "Don't leave me, Ali," he sobs into her mouth. "She needs to come home. She needs to rescue you and we'll tell her the *truth*."

She pulls away, shaking her head with quivering hands now holding both sides of his face. "Trust in the seer's vision," she recites. "Do not bend, do not break, do not yield, Blaine." Her thumbs move along his cheeks.

"Please," he pulls her even closer to him desperately.

"Coordinate with Windsor," she goes on. "Plan with him, contact her... whatever it takes, Blaine." The Queen can feel it in her bones. Her toes are slowly relaxing, growing heavier.

He exhales his defeat, burying his face into her neck. "On Eowyn's third birthday, I'd spent the morning in Vredo looking for the weaver that crafted the blanket we wrapped her in when she was born," he recalls. "Every three years from then on, I made sure to get her a blanket from Elaine," his muscles tense. "She still has them all. All seven of her blankets. I sent her one for her eighteenth birthday." Alice breathes out, feeling the heaviness creep up her feet. "I remember how proud I was of her for the temple," his voice drops to a whisper. "How good it felt for her to stand up to him, how much it felt *right*." He shakes his head again. "I'd have killed him a thousand times over by now just for the things he'd done in the first year of his reign." Below her knees fall limp. He senses the impending end, his body trembling around hers.

The door pushes open and Charlotte enters the room. She pauses, taking in the sight before her as she shuts it behind her. "Your Majesty," she mumbles as she approaches the bed.

"Blaine," Alice ignores her. He lifts his head at the sound of her voice. "It's time, my love," it comes out a near whimper.

He shakes his head, a sob wracking his body as he leans his forehead against hers. "I remember escorting you and Eowyn down to the dungeons day after day so she could study under Flare Meadowglade. I remember the way you would laugh when she would throw fireballs at me for teasing her during her lessons," he rambles on. "I remember the way it felt to walk a few paces behind you both through the Palace, how grateful I always was to just be here with you and with her. I remember how it felt to fall in love with you, how it felt to look at you every day since then and cherish every moment I was able to just be in your presence. I remember how it felt when you told me you were pregnant, how you knew she was mine, how you wouldn't *let* her be his." His grip on her approaches bruising. "I remember the way it felt to watch her shift for the first time," he sniffles and laughs. "I remember how much it terrified you, the way you jumped into my arms." Alice smiles weakly, her eyes becoming heavy as the weakness moves up her thighs and through her hips. "I remember the day she siphoned the electricity from you. I remember the way she summoned lightning so naturally," he swallows loudly. "I remember the first time you let her have her way after that and thunder shook the entire country."

Alice feels her body go cold beneath her waist and he reaches up to tuck a piece of her hair behind her ear. "Keep going," her eyes are glassed over now. All she wanted to hear about was Eowyn now.

"I remember when you asked me to contact Elenor," he kisses the side of her face repeatedly. "I remember you telling me about the vision, about how our daughter was going to destroy the entire world. I remember seeing her in a new light after that." The coldness starts inching up to her chest. "I remember the way your lips part when you're taken off guard," he chokes out. "I remember the way you hiccup every time you drink Norang Juice, I remember the way your toes curl when you have to do something you don't want to." He sucks in a deep intake of breath. "I remember the way Eowyn only showed you anything other than boredom. I remember the way you'd kiss both of her temples before the center of her forehead and her nose before you tucked her in every night. I remember the way you'd sit beside the window for hours each night, just waiting to see her fly under the blanket of darkness." Her shoulders drop and her breathing shallows. "I remember all of it, Alice," he sobs as her eyes fall closed. "I remember every single moment and I will cherish it all until my dying breath," he kisses her lips desperately.

"I love you, my Raven," her breath comes out cold and quiet.

"I love you," he continues kissing her lips, as if attempting to transfer his remaining years to her. The Queen's chest sputters and she lets out a strangled breath, her soul breaking free of the chains and starting toward Gragion.

25

WINDSOR

I open my eyes. I sigh when I see, for the fifteenth morning since the day after our wedding ceremony, I slept alone. I glance at the door to the Queen's chambers as if I can see her on the other side. I push myself up and before I know it, I'm pushing open the door. She's not in here. I walk to the door leading to the corridor. I pull it open and glance around the hallway. I furrow my eyebrows before making my way back into her bedroom, then our shared one. I'm sure to shower and dress before moving to the only other exit from our shared room. I step into my private room, glancing at everything that has remained where it is since we wed. I cross the distance to the door and start down the hall.

I catch a glimpse of flowing silver locks by her office. I quicken my pace, jamming my foot in the door just before it closes. She pulls it open and blinks up at me. "Eowyn," I whisper, making no move to push her more than I already have. She sighs and pulls open the door before stepping aside. I smile gratefully at her as I cross the threshold. "May I close it?" I curl my fingers around the doorknob. She holds my stare for a moment. My eyes wander over every inch of her face. I take in the way her lips sit in a perfect pout, the way her cute nose stares at me, her eyes gleaming pure blood red. She nods once, bringing my gaze back to hers. I kick the door shut, watching her walk toward her desk. I follow closely. She sits in the chair behind the oak and I lean against it in front of her.

Come on, baby, play with me. I cross my arms over my chest. She quirks a brow. Her soul sits still around mine, no matter how much it dances or sings or cries for her. Her expression is just as blank. My eyes drop

200

to my feet and I nudge her foot with my own. This is what my life has become, constantly begging. I just want her, I want that piece of her I had. I hit the tip of my shoe against hers again, this time looking up at her face while I do.

"I miss you," I whisper down the mental bond.

"I'm right here," she says bluntly.

I sigh, running a hand through my hair. Her eyes follow the motion, the black rings around her irises turning gold. I drop my hand and tilt my head to the side. "Did you fly this morning?" I reach for her hand.

She doesn't retract. I lace my fingers with hers, pulling her hand to rest against my chest. "I did not have time," she admits.

My eyebrows jump to my hairline. "You slept in?" She nods once. "You went to bed early last night." I note, but she doesn't respond. "Are you feeling unwell?" I bring my other hand to caress the side of her face.

I track the hesitation as it passes over her features. "I had limited social interactions in Iverness. I have been seeing hundreds of people everyday since becoming Queen." Her eyes dim.

I feel my shoulders relax slightly. I move my fingers down the side of her neck and over her shoulder. "Clear your day to rest," I trail my fingertips over her skin.

She shakes her head lightly. "Your Mother wishes for me to add to my ladies. I have tea with eleven Nobel women this afternoon." Her hand tightens around mine and ice dances along her fingertips. *She's attempting to soothe me.* "I am not angry with you, Windsor," she whispers.

I move my hand back to her neck and pull her up. She rises to her feet and I shift to pull her to stand between my knees. "Yet you are not pleased with me," I slide my arms around her waist. "That hurts just as much," I pout. My hands cautiously travel down to her backside. She doesn't push me away, rather places her hands on my chest.

"I just want to please you, My Queen," I pull her closer to me. Her fingers curve around the collar of my shirt, a gesture of reluctant surrender. The tension is still palpable between us, yet a hint of vulnerability flashes through her eyes. "Tell me what I have to do, Eowyn," I lean my forehead against hers.

"You know what I want you to do, Windsor," the heaviness in her tone nearly makes my eyes roll. I know what she wants from me, but she knows what I want before I give it to her. Her hands shift her grip to my shoulders and she pushes me gently. I hold her stare, my own hands tightening on her hips as I lower myself to my knees in front of her.

I watch her eyes flare when my hands start to slide down the sides of her legs. "My Queen," I whisper, hooking my hands around her ankles. I yank her forward, causing her to fall back into the chair. "You want me to beg," I push the skirt of her gown to sit on her thighs. "You want me to grovel," I press my lips to the inside of her right knee. "Cry for forgiveness," then her left.

"No," she threads her fingers through my hair and forces me to look up at her. Her eyes gleam as she releases a small amount of her power to wrap around me.

Even if I ever wanted to, I could never fight against her. Everything in me cowers before her and wants nothing more than to satisfy her every desire.

My neck arches back, my lips parting as I stare up at her. My tongue darts out to wet my lips. "No?" I echo. "You do not wish for me to beg your forgiveness for pushing past your... boundaries?" My voice feels like sand rubbing between my vocal cords.

She shakes her head lightly, loosening her grip on the roots of my hair. "You could not control what your soul did out of desperation, cub," she runs her fingertips down the side of my face. Her fingers are burning hot again, sizzling down the path as she drags them against my skin. "I have since been able to keep you at bay," she pinches my chin tauntingly.

I dip my head to kiss her hand, almost despairingly. She relaxes her fingers and I kiss her palm, bringing my hand up to hold her wrist in place. "Please, Eowyn," I kiss up to her wrist, my lips lingering over her pulse point. I close my eyes and swallow a groan at the feel of her blood racing against my mouth. "Just a taste, baby," I mumble against her skin. I don't wait for her to answer, she'd pull away if she didn't want me to, so I sink my teeth into her flesh. I open my eyes, immediately locking my gaze with hers while her saccharine blood fills my mouth. I groan at the taste and swipe my tongue over the wound once to seal it. I pull away and rest my forehead against her still-wet skin. "Have dinner with me," I trail my lips back down to her palm again. "At the pond. I'll have Layne and Oli clear your morning so you can rest," I finally lift my head but leave my fingers around her wrist.

Eowyn nods once, "okay," she concedes.

A grin spreads across my face and I jump to my feet. "Wonderful," I lean down to kiss her forehead. "I shall see you tonight."

There's a knock on my office door. I glance up as it opens. "Your Majesty," my Father steps in with a grave expression. "It is time."

I drop the quill onto the treaty I was correcting with red ink. "Alice," is all I manage to whisper. He only nods. "Very well," I clear my throat and rise from the chair. "I shall make preparations to head to the border," I step around the dark oak desk.

"What of the Queen?" He asks, stepping forward as if I'd not thought of her first.

I scoff, moving past him. "I've made the necessary preparations for her as well. Please inform Renhart of our departure. I will say goodbye to my wife and meet him in front of the Palace in one hour," I leave no room for argument as I exit the office.

I move briskly through the halls, toward the courtyard. Eowyn sits at the long table amongst the eleven noble women, suggested to her by my Mother to add to her personal cabinet. There's a variety of beverage filled pitchers along the table with even more types of pastries and fruits. Her eyes meet mine instantly. "My Queen," I stop several feet away from the women.

They all look between us, almost awkwardly. She rises from her seat at the head of the table. I can't help the ways my eyes rake over her form. Those damned collarbones are on display above the white lace lined sweetheart neckline and her utterly perfect tits. I blink, forcing my eyes to take in the rest of her gown. The lace peaks above the red silk corset and over the bubbled silk starting at her mid bicep, flowing to her delicate wrists. The skirt flares out dramatically, the crimson coated in black appliqués peaking from beneath white tulle ruffles. "Excuse me, Ladies," she says softly. She folds her hands in front of her as she approaches me, seemingly floating on air. "Your Majesty," she raises her eyebrows expectantly at me.

I reach out and grab one of her hands. Kneeling before her, I press my lips to the back of her hand. I keep them there for a moment as I glance over to see the other women staring with parted lips. I bring my gaze back to Eowyn when I pull away and rise to my feet. "Come here, sweet Vermilion," I wrap an arm around her and press my palm to the small of her back. She walks a few paces away with me. "There is an urgent matter I must attend to," I say quietly, "on one of the isles of Chaka." I nearly wince at the bitter taste of the lie on my tongue.

"Oh," she leans into me. Our steps slow the farther we walk and I move my hand to hold her hip securely. "When do you leave?" She keeps her gaze forward.

I lean over to press a kiss to her shimmering, silver braided up do. "Immediately," I mumble into her hair.

She stops and treads back. "Immediately," she repeats, her eyes gleaming as her fire rages.

I feel her soul huff, nothing more. I drop my arm to my side with a frown. *"I leave in one hour. Spend it with me,"* I say into the bond that formed in the midst of our wedding feast two weeks ago.

"How long will you be gone for?" My shoulders sag at the coldness. Ever since my soul had slipped past her barriers, she'd reverted to the way she was before I'd kissed her the first time. She'd even robbed me of our special coronation day plans.

"I'll only be away for a few days," I clear my throat. She stares at me blankly. "Oli will be here with you and Mildy will aid you with my duties," I offer a reassuring smile. She just blinks, making me nod and step back. I hold her vacant expression for what feels like an eternity. "Goodbye, Eowyn," I sigh. I step around her and start toward the Palace.

"You will return." Her voice makes my head whip toward her faster than how I chase after her each morning through the forest in our predator forms. She never lets me catch her anymore. "Windsor," she snaps. I shake my head and focus on her face. "You will return," she repeats.

I cock my head to the side and slowly nod, "I will return." She nods once and turns on her heels, going back to the table like nothing happened. I stand there for a few minutes, watching her talk and move. The way her chest rises and falls with every breath, the way her hands wrap around her teacup, the way her lips brush against her pastry, the way her eyelashes flutter against her cheeks as she blinks... I shake my thoughts back to reality and make my way into the Castle.

My fingertips itch with the need to walk back out there and slam her down onto the table to slice her open, just to lick her closed again, in front of every single one of them. I roll my neck as I start up the stairs toward our shared chambers. The tension in my neck keeps building with each passing second. I shove open the door to the King's suite, growling deep in my chest as it hits the wall behind it. *My own fucking wife.* I storm past the untouched bed and sofa at the foot of it. I go right past the armoire, to the door conjoining it to our shared bedchambers. I feel ice start to form along my toes and fingertips when my eyes narrow on the only other way out of the room, to the Queen's suite.

Truth be told, I'm not entirely sure what bothers me more. The way she acts so coldly awake, or the way she sleeps in here instead of beside me in *our* bed.

I summon my claws and swing both hands at her bed, one after the other. I let out an animalistic snarl as I grip the blanket, reeking with a mixture of cinnamon, blood, and burning hair, in tight fists. I tear it into hundreds of pieces, moving to push everything off of the night table beside the bed. I spin around, looking for something else to destroy.

I stop when my eyes fall on Eowyn, knelt beside the bed with the tattered purple quilt in her hands. Tears drip onto her white knuckles and my eyes widen.

*She came to spend time with me before my departure and I made her cry. Cry. **I've never seen her cry.** She's been here for almost four months and the first time I've seen tears from her are my doing.* I step back. *Sure, I want her to cry for me, but not like this. I want her to cry because of how good I make her feel, not how bad.*

"Get out," she whispers, the smell of burning hair flooding my nostrils. A wave of heat engulfs the room, nearly snuffing out the power coursing through me.

My heart cracks at the despair lacing her tone. "Eowyn," I retract my claws and step toward her.

My wife lifts her head to look at me. She brings the pieces of the blanket to her chest as my eyes move over the tears flowing down her cheeks before. *Fuck, I've never seen her cry before.* "Get. Out." She grits her teeth. "Before I fucking kill you."

I step backward until I'm in the shared room again. I blink, jumping when the door slams in my face. "Windsor?" I spin around at the sound of Layne's voice. "Woah, what's wrong?" He looks at me with furrowed eyebrows.

"Nothing," I say too quickly and move away from the door. "Are you prepared?" I don't need him knowing that I destroyed her room and the blanket. The blanket, she is so upset about the blanket...

"Yes, Your Majesty." He looks me over once more. "Are you sure everything is alright?" He takes a hesitant step forward.

"Drop it, Renhart," I growl, my shoulder hitting his as I pass by.

He grabs the back of the collar on my jacket and yanks me back. "The fuck is your problem, Windsor?" He lets go of me and shoves me forward.

I whirl on my feet, acting before thinking and pinning him against the wall. I bare my teeth at him. "Find Olivette and send her into the Queen's chambers. Tell her I need every last bit of that purple blanket she can find," I order before releasing him.

"Windsor-" he starts.

But I cut him off. "Get the fuck out of my face." Layne knows not to question, not to resist or refuse. He just leaves. I watch the door close before turning back to the one connecting our shared room to Eowyn's. I reach for the doorknob but hesitate. I can still feel the heat radiating from the metal of the handle so I retreat. "I love you." I whisper to the door before heading back toward my unused private room. I grab the small satchel tucked under the bed on my way out.

"Your Majesty," General Ancel Tidreda falls into step with me as I walk into the main Palace. "I have troops at the border."

I nod, squaring my shoulders while we continue. "Where's Everys?" I push open the door leading the main corridor of the Castle.

"Everys will meet you at the border. He wishes to fly with the hatchlings before his departure." My lips turn down. *I wish to run with Eowyn before my departure.* "Sir Renhart is preparing the horses," he pushes open the doors and we start down the Palace steps.

"I want you to let Olivette know to send word everyday to let me know Eowyn is okay," I ordered in a hushed whisper when we hit the bottom stones. I start toward the stables.

"Windsor!" I turn to see Olivette dashing toward me. "Here," she pants, thrusting a handful of purple fabric into my satchel.

"Thanks," I glance between her and Tidreda. He takes the hint and takes a step back. "Is she still upset?" I whisper.

Oli crosses her arms over her chest, her black her swaying dramatically. "I don't know what you did or why you needed this, but she is hysterical up there." My heart sinks into my stomach and my shoulders sag. "On the floor, sobbing, Windsor." She snaps.

I glance to the stables. "I should talk to her," I start to make my way back to the Palace but she stops me.

"I wouldn't." I take in the seriousness of her tone, the concern in her features. "As sad as she is, I think she'd *love* a lion skin rug under her toes right now," she looks at me warningly. I pull my arm away from her and glance back at our home. "Leave it alone, Windsor. She might destroy you."

I sigh and nod, stepping back. "Layne and I shouldn't be gone long. Send word if anything happens," I look her over once. "And Oli, as much as I love you, I love my wife more and will not hesitate to end your life, if hers is in danger."

The corners of her mouth lift into a smile and her eyes move to where Layne approaches us, my mare and his stallion led behind him by their reins. "I knew you loved me," she crosses her arms over her chest.

I roll my eyes and mount Beatrix as Layne mounts Gruff. "We'll be back in a few days," I say before digging my heels into Bea's side and making her start into a sprint. Layne and Gruff come up to our side, half a minute later. "When we get to the border, once I've unlatched their collars, have the weavers of Iverness step off to the side," I grit out.

"Why?" Layne cocks his head. "We have weavers in Exsar."

I whip my head to the right and narrow my eyes at my best friend. "Because I asked you to," I snap.

"Does this have anything to do with the shredded blanket in the Queen's room?" I turn my head forward. Even if I did lie, he'd see it all over my face. I sigh and nod in confirmation. "Oli told me that they were gifts from someone in Iverness but that's all Eowyn would say..."

I shrug, my eyes following the winding path before us. "She will only say as much as she wants to say." I clench my jaw. She hasn't spoken to me much the past few weeks. She doesn't sleep in bed with me. She locks her door so I can't go ask why. She doesn't play with me when she flies in the mornings anymore, she just flies in circles unless Zanna or Everys accompanies them.

The ride to the border was nothing short of brutal. I sat there festering in the saddle, thinking of all the things I could do to make it up to my wife. I even tried calling to her through our bond, only to be met with silence. I could still feel her though. Simmering, stewing... She was sending every tear down that bond like a punch in the face. She was letting me know I fucked up.

"Your Majesty," the Royal Guard bows behind Ezolark Dristren as I dismount Bea. "We are prepared." He steps forward.

"Start them in, then. I don't have all the time in the world," I bark out. He turns and starts toward the Exsarian soldiers protecting the border to Iverness.

I follow him with Layne next to me. "Perhaps we should call the Queen to assist-"

I growl and turn toward him, lunging at him and tackling him to the ground. "That's my fucking wife, you idiot." I wrap both hands around his throat. "If I ever hear you speak of putting her in danger again, I will fucking end you, am I clear?" I ask as I thump his head against the ground before releasing his neck.

"Understood," he coughs, "understood, Your Majesty."

I clench my jaw as I climb off of his waist. "Go get me the fucking weavers, Renhart." I toss over my shoulder before making my way to the border. I roll my neck and nod to Dristren. He ushers the collared beings over the border, five at a time, while I break the chains that subdue their abilities.

Once I was unable to stand on my own, I retired to the tent Ancel had set up for me not far from the line. I didn't even make it to the cot before collapsing onto the ground and giving into the exhaustion. I'd go on to do this for the next *twenty three days* until Blaine Cromwell marched on us, the only thing he could spew was an apology.

26

EOWYN

"Your Majesty?" Olivette's voice punctures the peaceful silence. The Queen grinds her teeth and looks over at Oli. "Are you hungry?" She smiles, holding a plate of food. Eowyn looks away, sitting on the top step of the Palace like she had for the past *sixteen days*.

He said he'd be back in a few days. We are bordering on a month. Twenty nine days to be exact.

"May I sit, at least?" She places the food down beside Eowyn. She just nods, making Olivette sigh. "He will return, Your Majesty," she nudges Eowyn's bicep with her shoulder. The Queen has not spoken in sixteen days, though continuously proving she is in fact listening. "Would you like to fly?" Eowyn shakes her head. "I can draw you a bath?" Again, no. "Is there something that I *can* do?" Olivette sighs when the Queen doesn't even bother answering.

Eowyn jolts upright. Oli does the same and follows her gaze. Layne Renhart comes mounted on Gruff, the black stallion she'd ridden into Exsar, Windsor's white mare beside him. But no Windsor. She starts down the palace steps, holding her gown in both hands as she runs. "Your Majesty," Layne dismounts the horse. She looks at him with bright red eyes, coaxing the truth to spill out of him. "We were at the border aiding Ivernese citizens to cross into Exsar. He was shattering the collars off of them all. Then Blaine Cromwell came and said he was very sorry for this and then Windsor shifted and took off into the woods. Is he here?" He looks past Eowyn to Olivette. She shakes her head slowly.

A snarl pushes past Eowyn's lips and she shifts into the firebird. She wastes no time darting for the sky. She wills ice into her veins, her eyes glowing blue as she releases a stream of power to find him. She lets out a loud squawk every few moments as she gets farther and farther from the Castle. A white dove coos next to her, Olivette, before dipping closer to the ground. Eowyn lets out a huff and feels Zanna tug at their mental bond. She opens the pathway, allowing her to find the bird. The sound of dragon beats behind her follows a moment later.

"He lied," she seethes to Zanna.

The dragon dips her head in acknowledgment. *"It was your Mother's wish. He was not to let you know that he was aiding those who have been chained."* She flies underneath Eowyn, concealing her from sight of those below them. *"He is missing, Eowyn.*

"I know," the Queen snaps back too quickly. *"Why can't his power find him? Why can't I feel his soul?"* She drops down to rest on Zanna's back.

"You would feel it if he died. He probably recalled his power to destroy the Paronia." She slows down, confusing Eowyn slightly as she half shifts back.

She spreads her wings as the Queen, turning to face Everys. *"You reek of him."* She flaps her wings to move closer to the King's dragon. *"Where is he? How come the bit of his power I hold can't find him?"* She soars beside his face to keep his attention.

"I told you," Everys scoffs audaciously.

"You did miss me!" Windsor jumps up on the White Temra's back.

Eowyn nearly vomits, her movements ceasing. Zanna dives below her, allowing her to fall flat on her backside. The dragon beats her wings harder to rise to her mate's side. Eowyn watches, wide eyed as Windsor hops from Everys' back to Zanna's. He drops to one knee and braces both hands on two of her spikes when she turns back toward the Palace. Relief came and went so quickly, now all she felt was rage. She stands in her spot, fully ready to push him off of her dragon.

"Good feed," Zanna huffs.

"I'm just getting started," Eowyn grunts aloud, stepping toward Windsor.

"Eowyn, wait," he stands up, wobbling slightly. "Baby, listen to me. Everys just-" She cuts him off, sending a massive ball of fire toward him. He side steps and shoots a stream of ice toward it. The flame ceases and the ice disappears on a gust of wind. "He just found me!" He tries to step closer to her but she gathers another blaze in her hands.

"You can't talk to her right now," Zanna taunts Windsor.

Eowyn lets out a bitter laugh when he takes a cautious step back again. "What do I do, Zanna?" He asks impotently. The dragon just huffs in response. He rolls his neck and steps forward. "Guess it's just us, pretty girl," he smiles cheekily.

She growls, shooting a bolt of lightning toward him. His eyes widen, not in horror, *but in awe.* Eowyn hesitates, her breath catching at the gleam in his eye. She blinks to compose herself and thrusts another flash in his direction. He drops to all fours to evade her strike. He jumps back up, grinning at her outburst. He tackles her onto her back, falling onto Zanna's scales. *"I did just find him in the woods,"* Everys finally chimes in.

She shoves him off of her and he climbs back, raising his hands in surrender as he stands. "I was on my way back to *you, My Queen.* I was coming *home* when Everys came up behind me," he takes one step back to allow her to rise with him.

She stands with a grunt. "You lied," she reaches a hand out and a string of lightning wraps around him, bringing him to his knees. "You *begged* me to trust you with *me* and you turned around and *lied* to me," her rage seeps through her voice like venom. The fire thrums through her veins the more her anger builds. He looks at her helplessly, enraging her even further. *He did this. He put himself here.* "You have been gone for twenty nine days," she wills the lightning to squeeze him tighter, biting into his flesh now.

"I'm sorry," he doesn't even bother thrashing against her power. "Eowyn, I... I was in trouble. Tabot sent Hagan," he looks at her helplessly, pleadingly.

She narrows her eyes at him. "Layne said it was Blaine," she deadpans. She'd manipulated his soul to tell her the truth, there was no way *he* was lying.

He nods frantically. "Yes, yeah, baby. Okay, okay so you know.. Yeah, Blaine came from the front, Hagan snuck in at some point or something..." He shakes his head. "I don't know. I heard his voice behind me right after Blaine said he was sorry. I shifted and ran," he rambles, his chest heaving with every ragged breath. "Come on, sweet thing," he sinks back onto his heels and looks up at her like *that*. "Manipulate me, make me tell you the truth. Because it's the same damn thing," he breathes out, tears brimming his lower lash line.

The words ring through the Queen and she stares at the helpless look in his eyes. She releases him from the twine of electricity, dropping to her knees in front of him. "That means you've been missing for six days, Windsor," she cups his face. "Where in Gragion have you been?" She nearly sobs.

He belts out a hoarse laugh, pushing his forehead to lean against hers. "I was with Blaine Cromwell," he presses a soft kiss to her lips. "I was safe, baby," he says between kisses. "You were safe." He brings his hands up to tangle in the back of her hair. She relaxes into his touch and meets his lips desperately. *He was safe. He is safe. He's coming home.* Her lips move in rhythm with his, her legs parting as he shoves one of his between them to get closer. He pulls her onto him so she's straddling his thigh. "I'm here," he mumbles into her. Her nails bite into cheeks as she grips him tighter. Neither of them is sure who he is reminding, but both were relieved to hear it all the same.

Windsor drops his hands, one wrapping around her and the other falling behind him to hold them in place as Zanna dives toward the ground. Eowyn doesn't pull away, she presses further into him. Her soul screams and yells, rages, toward his. He releases the hold he's had on it since being gone, allowing it to flow into hers and become one with her. She engulfs him, absorbs him, threads through him and checks every inch of his purest being.

Zanna lands in the Palace hunting grounds with a thud and Eowyn finally pulls away. Her hands slide down the sides of his neck, to his shoulders and down his arms. "I have so much to tell you, My Queen," his hands find her hips again. "So much time to make up for," he smiles mischievously as he lifts her off of him.

Eowyn quirks a brow. "Yes, well," she smooths her palms down the front of her gown. "Much has happened in your absence." His features drop slightly. She wasn't pushing him away, like he thought, she was merely reminding him there are more important matters at hand. She moves to dismount Zanna but he grabs her wrist. She turns to face him.

Windsor stares at her, almost helplessly. She cocks her head to the side curiously. "I'm sorry," his voice cracks. "I'm sorry, *Eowyn*." She blinks, completely confused by the broken apology. His soul cries out, gripping at hers and trying to pull her tighter around him like a cocoon.

"Windsor, I-"

His hand tightens around her wrist and he steps closer, cutting her off. "I'm sorry, My Queen," he lifts his hands to her face. He cups her jaw with trembling hands, his skin ghosting along hers as if he was afraid to touch her. "I'm sorry for *everything*. For destroying your private room, for lying to you about where I was going, for scaring you," his right hand slides to hook his fingers around the back of her neck.

She lets out a deep exhale, stepping into him. "Windsor," she leans her forehead against his. "I've never felt anything other than rage. Being scared for your life was a nice, *brief,* change of pace."

His breath hitches in his chest when her head meets his. He closes his eyes, pulling her closer. "Mother of Tretanov, I have so much to tell you," he breathes out, shaking his head slightly. "So, so much, Eowyn."

"You were ushering people over the border," she drags a single finger along his jaw.

He swallows thickly and nods. "I was, My Queen. I was breaking the collars," he admits quietly.

"My Mother?" She focuses on the micro expressions, the changes in his features when she inquires about the Queen of Iverness. He tenses, his jaw clenching under her touch. "Where is my Mother, Windsor?" She grabs his chin roughly and squeezes his cheeks, her nails pricking into his skin again.

His eyes fly open and he looks at her pleadingly. "I'm sorry, baby," he whispers, shaking his head again. Eowyn's hands drop to her sides and she tries to step back. He tightens his arms around her. *"No,"* he growls lowly. "You stay right here, with me. You let me hold the pain with you, Eowyn. Don't you fucking dare hide from *me,"* his eyes move over her face as if he's searching for something.

"Windsor."

"No."

Her power reels at his refusal to let her go. Her soul rages inside of her, feeling like it's bouncing off of the inside of her while kicking and screaming. Uncontrollable flames ignite at each of her fingertips. "Let go," her tone is quiet, warning.

"Eowyn," he presses her even further into him.

The anger inside of her starts to swell. "Let. Go." She repeats, now through clenched teeth. Her control is slipping and soon the fire would be uncontrollable.

"Stop, Eowyn," he near whimpers, his claws now threatening to pierce her skin. Instinctively, her fire starts to nip at his fingertips. He hisses in pain, pulling his hands back quickly. He looks at her, desperation etched across his face. "Baby-"

Flame erupts between them, keeping him away. "Stay there," she barks out, unable to control it any longer. He furrows his eyebrows and takes a step forward. The fire spreads, almost like an arm reaching out to him. He jumps back and looks at her between the dancing flames with wild eyes. "I can't control it," she admits, watching her rage manifest physically.

"You have to let go of my power so I can help you," Windsor runs a hand through his hair, taking another step back. He watches helplessly as she struggles to control her power, the fire raging around them like a living, breathing thing. Her heart aches as she sees the pain and desperation in his eyes, the way he's fighting a battle with intervening or not. "Eowyn, look at me," he says firmly, his voice cutting through the crackling of the flames. "You have to let go, sweetheart. You have to let it out, or it will consume you. Let me help you, let me take some of it from you."

"I'm going to hurt you," her chest sputters on a ragged breath.

Windsor takes a step closer, his eyes locked on hers. He doesn't flinch back as the flames start to leap closer to him. "I don't care," he insists. "I'm not going anywhere, sweetheart. I'm not afraid of your power." He takes another step toward her, his gaze never leaving hers. "You won't hurt me," he breathes out. "I trust you. I know you can control this."

He holds out his hand, his palm facing the ceiling. "Let go, baby. I'm here. I'll help you."

The Queen clenches her jaw and moves back. "No." She can feel the magic in her *seething*, it was striking to kill right now and he couldn't be *here*.

"Yes," he says instantly, his voice unyielding. He takes another step forward, not allowing her to retreat any farther without fearing he'd be consumed by the physical manifestation of her anger."You're not doing this alone, Eowyn. I'm not leaving you to face this by yourself." He looks into her eyes, his gaze steady and unafraid. He holds out his hand again, my palm facing her. Flames lick at his skin but he doesn't flinch. "I'm staying right here with you. I'm not letting you push me away. We're doing this together."

A single tear slides down her right cheek. "I don't want to hurt you," she whispers. She can hear the way his heart clenches as his eyes follow the tear.

He takes another step closer, his hand still held out to her. "You won't hurt me," his eyes don't waiver from hers, even as the flames part for him. "I trust you, sweetheart. I know you can control this. Let me help you. Let me in, baby. Let me share this burden with you. You don't have to carry it alone." He finally takes note of the opening and lunges for her, jumping over the fire, one foot before the other.

"WINDSOR, NO!" She screams when the flames reach for him, wrapping around him and yanking him down.

27

WINDSOR

The King feels the flames as they lick at him, but he welcomes the pain, for her. "Baby, it's okay—"

Her screams drown out his words when the fire wraps around him and pulls him to the ground. He struggles to get up, her power keeping him pinned to the floor. The flames press down harder and his body struggles against them. He can hear her voice, but can't make out the words through the roaring in his ears. The heat is growing more intense, searing against his icy skin as it envelopes his body. He tries to push back against it, but it's too strong. He takes a deep breath, trying to stay calm and focused. It's clear that he can't break free on his own. *I need to reach out to her, to get through to her. I need her to hear me.*

"Come on, sweet thing," he calls into the abyss of her raging soul. *"You can do it, baby. I know you can."* The fire burns brighter around him. He squeezes his eyes shut and searches for his favorite part of her, the most beautiful, purest form of her that was taking care of him... The part of her that cared for him. *"My pretty girl, I **need** you."* His eyes snap open again. The flames roar over him as ice slowly encases his frame. He pulls his eyebrows together in confusion when the fire retreats from him. Eowyn steps forward, blowing out the ring around him in a single breath. A sheet of ice forms under him as the melting ice over his limbs begins to melt. He pushes himself to sit up.

Her eyes shine bright *blue. His* ice grazing over her fingertips as her own fire rages behind her... *controlled.* Her eyes are intense, the light shining behind flickering over her features. But it's not the fire that holds his attention, it's *her*. She's controlling the rage, wielding it like a weapon. He watches her with a new sense of reverent awe.

"You did it," he breathes out, "you controlled it." His gaze travels over her entire form, taking in the curves of each muscle. He'd not expected her to halt her workouts in his absence, but she was definitely doing *more* now.

"I did not," she says bluntly, extending a hand to him. His eyes move to hers confusedly. "You did."

He slowly takes her hand and wraps his fingers around it. "I was unable to wield, my love. That was *you*," he tugs her down to the ground with him. He pulls her back flush against his chest and grips her chin roughly. He forces her head back onto his shoulder. "That *is* you," he growls possessively as they stare at the dying blaze. Her muscles start to relax against him. He turns his head, his lips brushing against the side of her neck. He inhales deeply, breathing in her scent. "You were incredible." He tilts his head to press his lips to her temple, eyes never leaving the shrinking flames that dance before them. "You were so powerful, so strong," he praises, bringing his attention back to her. She relaxes back into him as he releases her face, bringing his hand up to tuck a piece of hair behind her ear. The fire dies out and the ice ceases, her eyes dimming. "Gragion, I've missed you," he trails his fingers down the side of her face. Eowyn's eyes fall closed, allowing his voice to soothe her frayed nerves.

Despite her best efforts to remain composed, Eowyn gives into the comfort of Windsor's touch. His words wash over her like a soothing balm, easing the raw emotions that had been coursing through her veins. She leans into him, her head falling back against his shoulder once more. "I've missed you too," she admits, her voice barely above a whisper. The simple confession is a crack in her armor, a chink in the wall she had erected between them.

Windsor's hand continues its path down the side of her face, his thumb gently tracing over her cheek. He watches as her features soften. The tension leaves her body like a deflating balloon. He can feel her guard unraveling, her defenses slipping while she slackens into him. He takes the opportunity to continue his gentle motions, his hands moving over her arms, tracing small circles on her skin. The silence between them is not uncomfortable, but rather filled with a deep understanding and a yearning for intimacy. "You were made for power," he murmurs, his voice barely more than a breath. He draws her even closer to him. Her back is flush against his chest now and he can feel the heat radiating from her. He continues to explore her body, his fingers trailing over her, as if mapping out every contour and curve. Eowyn's breath hitches in her throat. He feels the way his touch ignites something within her, awakening a deep-seated hunger that she has been fighting to suppress. A flame much... *colder* than her anger. "And I was made to worship you," he whispers, his lips brushing over her earlobe. He feels her shiver against him. The tiny movement sends a thrill through him. She lets out a soft gasp, the sound so faint it almost goes unnoticed. His hands move down to her thighs, massaging the tense muscles he finds there. He knows she's exhausted, he can feel it. But he also knows that she needs this, needs him, as much as he needs her. "Let me take care of you, My Queen," he pleads, pressing his forehead against her shoulder. His heart stills when he feels Eowyn's defenses crumble further. Windsor's words and touch chip away at her resolve like an axe to stone. He revels in the way she *allows* him to feel her need to give in, how overwhelming it is in this moment. She nods slightly, a small gesture of surrender. She shifts against him, her body seeking closer proximity as the space between them dwindles. Windsor takes notice and pulls her even closer, his arms wrapping around her like a vice and turning her to straddle his waist. He runs his nose along the side of her neck, inhaling deeply.

Her scent drives him wild, making him fight the urge to take her right there on the floor. But he knows that she is vulnerable now. He needs to be gentle, show her that he's *sorry* and *proud*. He starts to trail soft kisses down her neck, everything else can wait while he holds her there.

Nothing is more important than her, ever, especially right now. "I've missed this," he whispers against her skin, "I've missed you."

Eowyn's breath catches in her throat as his lips dance across her skin. His words, soft and sincere, sink deep into her soul. The weight of his emotions pours over her, soothing her bruised heart. She tilts her head to give him unrestricted access to her neck, her fingers wrapping around his forearms. She is both vulnerable and powerful at this moment, and only for him. He closes his eyes to absorb the feeling of her soul slowly starting to let his bleed into it. "Windsor," her hushed voice pulls him from his thoughts. He lifts his head to meet her gaze. He only hums his response, bringing a hand up to rest along the side of her neck with his thumb resting just behind her ear. "I..." her eyes move between both of his like she's searching for something. "Where were you?" His ears perk at the desperation in her voice.

The vulnerability in her tone nearly pushes him to the brink of consuming her then and there. His jaw tightens as the lion claws within him at the faintest scent of the firebird. She's crumbling before him and he's utterly obsessed with it. The way her pulse hammers against her skin, beating against his palm while her breath sputters in her chest.Her eyes stare at him with a sort of calmness he'd never dreamed he'd see in her. "I went to the border," he admits, even though she knew that. "Alice was to send word when she was declining. I would then go to the border to usher in the collared people of Iverness and break them off." He swallows thickly. "So I did. I went and I welcomed over two thousand Ivernese citizens," he strokes his thumb along the side of her neck. "My Mother and Father have been preparing housing for them since our Mother's spoke of our betrothal."

"You knew my Mother was declining," she whispers, almost brokenly.

His heart clenches, but his soul sings at the rawness she's giving him right now. The pure, unfiltered version of herself, and it only took him disappearing for one whole moon. "I did not," he shakes his head lightly. "My love, I would have told you. I would have brought you with me. I..."

he blows out a breath, leaning his forehead against hers. "There was no warning, baby. Blaine Cromwell sent word that she was already gone." Eowyn's pain radiates off of her in waves, hitting him like a lightning bolt to the heart. Her shoulders begin to shake with the settling grief. Windsor pulls her closer, tucking her head under his chin and holding her tightly. He nuzzles against the top of her head. His heart aches as her silent tears soak his shirt. He combs his fingers through her hair, an attempt to soothe her. He feels helpless, useless. He wants nothing more than to take her pain away, to protect her from everything that causes her hurt but he knows he can't. "I'm here," he whispers, his voice thick with emotion. "I'm here, my love. I've got you."

Eowyn clings to him like a lifeline. Her fingers grip the fabric of his shirt on either side of his waist. He wraps himself around her, surrounding her with his coolness and strength. He doesn't know how long they stay like that, huddled together on the floor at the end of the bed. He just holds her, letting her silently cry until there are no more tears left. He can feel the tension slowly leaving her body while he rubs circles over her back. He carefully maneuvers her so that they're lying on the floor with her head resting on his chest. He wraps his arms around her, cocooning her in his embrace. The silence blankets them like a heavy fog, the only sound their synced heartbeats.

"Draven Idris is still missing," she whispers, bringing a hand up to lay on his chest.

He moves his own to rest on top of hers, tucking his thumb under her palm. He smiles as her fingers wrap around it. "Draven Idris is the least of my concerns right now," he admits. He watches a soul dance along the far wall where it meets the ceiling. It stills momentarily before sliding down the wall and scampering toward the window. "I am concerned with nothing other than my wife." He looks down at her.

The Queen lifts her gaze to his. He feels her soul purr and something in her heart settles. She squeezes his thumb tightly, sighing as she absorbs the comfort in the solid warmth of his body beneath her. He revels in the way her emotions wash over him, the way she *allows* him to feel it with her. She takes a shaky breath, the grief and turmoil still swarming inside of her. Windsor continues to cradle her against him. His hand strokes up and down her back, feeling the way her muscles tense and relax with each of her breaths. She's holding back, she has more that she wants to say, but he keeps quiet and waits for her to speak. A small smile graces his lips when she lays her head back down on his chest and gives his thumb another squeeze. The gesture, so small and subtle, speaks volumes to him. It's almost as if he has learned to listen to her when she is not speaking.

Windsor continues to hold her close, his hand still stroking her back in a soothing motion. He can feel her exhaustion, her grief weighing heavily in a swarm of fury. He wants nothing more than to take it all away. He wants to make her feel safe and loved, to shield her from all the pain and hurt the world has thrown at her. The connection between them, the way he can feel her emotions like they were his own, is something he has come to cherish deeply and will protect at all costs.

"My sweet girl," he lifts his hand to comb his fingers through her hair. Eowyn leans into his touch, her eyes closing as she melts under his fingertips. He can feel her unraveling in his arms, the walls she put up around her emotions crumbling down one by one. "Let go," he nearly begs. "You don't have to hold it all in. I'm here, sweetheart." He continues stroking her hair gently. Her breath hitches in her throat and she buries her face deeper into him. "It's okay," he murmurs, pressing a kiss to the top of her head. His hand moves to her shoulder, rubbing gentle circles into her tense muscles. He can feel the emotions swirling in her, the way she is fighting against them to remain composed. She takes in a deep breath and her fingers curl around the fabric of his shirt. The words she wants to say are right there, but she will never say them, never admit that she has a weakness.

28

THE SOULS- (KEEP UP)

Lady Bryanna watches with her arms crossed as the Queen effortlessly tosses her daggers into the center of the target. Her eyes follow Eowyn's every move, studying her technique with a careful eye. Bryanna had always considered herself skilled with daggers, she'd been trained by Exsar's military before Charlie was born, but she can't shake the pang of jealousy that wracks through her while watching the Queen wield them with such deadly grace. Nonetheless, she smiles, always impressed by her talent. She watches in awe as Eowyn's next dagger whizzes through the air and pierces the target right between the other two. It's a flawless aim and Bryanna can't help but let out a breath. "Impressive," she smiles when Eowyn turns to face her.

Eowyn's eyes move past her to the young, blonde haired girl approaching her, followed by two royal guards. *How peculiar,* one swirls around her neck. The girl's brown eyes meet the Queen's and her face lights up. She dashes toward her, making Bryanna step in front of Eowyn. She keeps her posture stiff and alert, as if ready to protect the Queen at a moment's notice. Her hand drifts to the dagger strapped to her hip. The young girl's gaze stays fixed on Eowyn and she tries to push past Bryanna but she grabs the girl's arm.

"You are approaching the Queen of Exsar," she says lowly, "you will act as such."

The girl looks up at Bryanna. "I just want to talk to her," she snaps defiantly, trying to push past the Queen's maiden again.

Bryanna narrows her eyes and grips the hilt of the dagger tighter. "You do not approach the Queen without her permission," she shoves the girl back.

Another soul curves around Eowyn's neck as she raises her chin. *She is harmless*, it whispers into her ear. "She may approach," she says softly. The girl's features brighten with her widening grin. Lady Bryanna wordlessly steps aside. "What is your name?" Eowyn keeps her chin high and tone even. Her eyes drift to where a soul dances in the shadows behind the soldiers a few paces beyond the girl.

"Elizabeth Croux," she raises a hand toward the Queen.

Bryanna steps behind her, raising the dagger to the side of her neck. "You *kneel* before your Queen," she grits out, pressing the tip of the blade into Elizabeth's skin. Eowyn's eyes shine blood red as she forces the girl to her knees. "Why is she here?" Bryanna snaps at the guards. "Her Majesty is not to be disturbed during her personal hours."

"I was brought here upon the King's request," her eyes don't show any sign of magic. "He asked me to be his Royal Mistress."

The souls around Eowyn hiss while the one dancing in the shadows darts toward the Palace. The Queen lifts her left leg, drawing Meteor from her heeled boot. Gideon had given her the red blade, held by an intricately carved stone hilt the day Tabot attempted to shoot her out of the sky. He'd tucked it under her pillow with a note, the only words on the parchment reading: *Talk to Alice*. She always kept it with her, per her Mother's *only* instructions of course, but this was the first time she wielded it. She slides her tongue along her top row of teeth, her gaze flicking to the soldiers.

Her eyes flash in warning before she focuses on the girl knelt in front her. "My husband will not take a lover," she keeps her tone steady, nearly bored. Her slender fingers grip the dagger, her knuckles white as she raises it. The blade glimmers in the light, nearly translucent in the light, and the girl on the grass watches in pure horror. In one swift motion, she drags the tip of the dagger across her neck followed by a trickle of blood spilling from the wound. The dagger lets out a low hum, rumbling against the Queen's palm. She just grips it tighter and allows her soul manipulation powers to overtake her.

Calling out to those around it, the soul skating along the Palace walls sings its praises out to the Queen before slipping into the King's office. Windsor sits behind his desk with a quill dipped in ink grasped between his fingers. He draws on the blank parchment, skillfully mapping out a patch of land not too far from the border. The souls dance around the room, almost ecstatically, grabbing his attention. He lifts his head just as the door opens. His wife stands in the doorway, Meteor gripped in her right hand, blood dripping from the blade.

"Eowyn?" He stands up and quickly walks around the desk. She drops the dagger to the ground and grabs him by the throat. His eyes widen as she walks him back into the room, kicking the door closed behind her. "What are you-" she cuts him off by shoving him against the wall.

He hisses in pain when her fingertips ignite into small flames. The fire licks at his skin and sizzles against the coolness of the ice thrumming through him. "You will *not* take a mistress," she snarls, her face only an inch away from his.

"No, I *will not*," he snaps back. He doesn't fight against her despite his utter confusion.

"There was a girl," her nails dig into his skin. A single drop of blood bubbles beneath her index finger, just below his ear.

His hands move to her hips, his grip gentle and loving. Her fingers tighten even further around his neck. "Baby, you're going to have to give me more than that," he chuckles, making her eyes narrow and hand squeeze harder.

She's hurt, angry...*jealous*. The flames at her fingertips dance and spark, reflecting against the eerie dimness in her eyes. Her body is pressed against his with the heat from her skin approaching the same scorching temperature as the flames she struggles to contain. She can feel his fingers on her, so familiar and tender. It only fuels her rage. "There was a girl," she repeats, her voice sharp and cold. "Young, blonde, speaking of you like she... like..." She can't bring herself to say it, but Windsor already knows, he can see it in her eyes, feel it down their soul bond. She's letting something consume her, something... possessive.

He's almost buzzing with excitement. The knowledge that she's feeling this way, that he's the one stirring this deep, dark part of her nearly sends him to his knees. He tries to fight the smirk growing on his face when a soul curls around her wrist, slithering up her hand to close her fingers around him even tighter. "Eowyn," he whispers as his fingers trail along the curve of her waist and he notes how she tenses even more. "I am not taking a mistress," he keeps his voice firm but gentle enough to not spark an explosive response. She's jealous and he's nothing short of *loving* it. He leans in, bringing his lips to her ear. "You are the only one who drives me insane," his lips ghost over her skin. She lets out a sharp exhale, the sound nearly a hiss. She ever so slightly leans into him, the fire at her fingers slowly flickering out. Her grip loosens, no longer applying pressure to his airways. She knows he's being sincere, knows that he is obsessed with her. But jealousy and possessiveness still thrum through her and she can't quite let the anger die out. "I would never betray you like that," he pulls back to look at her again, his tone low and earnest. "You are my Queen, my love, *everything* I live and breathe for. I have no desire for anyone else." His gaze locks with hers, his eyes holding all the love and loyalty he feels for her.

Eowyn inhales deeply, letting the scent of him envelope her senses. The familiarity of his crisp coolness brings a sense of warm comfort. Despite the anger coursing through her, she grasps onto one fact: he is hers. She pulls her hand away from his neck, her fingers leaving agitated imprints on his skin. "I killed her, Windsor," she clears her throat and shakes her head. "I forced her to her knees and slit her throat."

The King blinks in surprise. "You... what?" He sputters, his mind struggling to process the information. He grabs her chin and forces her to look at him. "You killed her? Because she *said* she was my lover?" He feels his fangs start to take shape. He knows Eowyn, he knows her temper, but this? This is something entirely different.

A soul wraps around Windsor's wrist and forces his hand away from the Queen. It wraps around his waist, looping around both arms and holding him tighter. Eowyn snickers, "she was speaking so... so matter of fact." Her fingers curl into fists as she stumbles over her words. "I couldn't... I can't... You're mine, Windsor. You belong to **me**."

His eyes widen and the soul tightens around him even more. He's never seen Eowyn like this. She's usually so composed, so in control. But right now, she's embracing the animal, so ready to attack. "Baby," he croaks, trying to calm the brewing storm he can feel swirling inside of her. "You have to understand, it doesn't matter who says what. I am yours, sweetheart," he breathes out, "I will always be **yours**." He glances down to the shadow restraining him. *"Get off,"* he commands silently.

You left once, it hisses back at him.

His wife narrows her eyes at his words, watching him attempt to free himself. She wants to believe him, she does. But the possessiveness coursing through her is like an untamed horse. "It does matter," she snaps. "I will not tolerate anyone even *thinking* about you like there is a chance." She flicks her hand and the soul releases him. "No one else will ever have you the way I do," she steps closer to him. *A threat.*

He swallows hard. He wants to soothe her, to make her feel more secure within herself, but her territorial behavior is too distracting. He looks down at her, his eyes studying her face. "I understand," he concedes, bringing a hand up to cup her cheek. "I *only* belong to you and no one else." He leans his forehead against hers. His thumb brushes along her cheek, stroking her skin softly. "You don't have to fret, my love. I am yours and *only* yours." He could not judge her, for he had also done something terrible for something *so much* simpler.

The Queen brings her right hand back to his neck and grips him tightly. His breath hitches at the way she stares back at him. "Mine," she growls, shoving him back until his knees hit the chair behind his desk.

He collapses into the seat, watching her climb into his lap. "Yours," he breathes out, completely in awe of the way she effortlessly overpowers his senses. Cautiously, his hands drift to the back of her thighs. "Go ahead," he pulls her closer, "prove it. Show me I'm yours." Her eyes flash at the challenge. His fingers dance up to the clasps holding her armor to her body. He slowly undoes the first clip, the metal clanking with the motion.

Eowyn's other hand moves between them and she holds his stare while she pulls his belt from its buckle. Her hand remains clamped around his throat, not tightly, just... *territorially*. He flicks open the second clasp, leaving only one left. Her thumb slips into his waistband while she unbuttons his pants before pulling the zipper down. Windsor slides his hands down to the backs of her thighs and gently lifts her. He brings one hand around to push his pants past his knees before settling her back on his thighs, undoing the last clasp in the process. He peels the metal armor from her body and sets it beside them.

The King doesn't move as his Queen, bare in all her glory on top of him, grazes the tip of his arousal against hers. A feral growl rips through him and he sinks his claws into her thighs. She lowers herself onto him, her nails biting into his neck when she stops after the first inch. She sucks in a sharp breath and he doesn't miss the whimper that she tries to hide while she lowers herself onto him completely. Without retracting his talons, he slides his hands up to her backside. She lifts herself again, her grip on him loosening minutely.

He grins when she rolls her hips on him, establishing a steady rhythm. "That's it," he purrs, "look at you. You're doing such a good job." Eowyn pulls her hand away from his neck and flicks her wrist at the souls in dismissal.

The souls scatter, three out the window while another seven slip under the door. One scampers faster than the others, heading for the throne room. Layne Renhart walks beside General Ancel Tidreda, preparing the rows of chairs per the King's command. The souls scatter sticks to the shadows.

"I believe him to be preparing for war," Renhart adjusts a chair to line up with the others on either side. "I do not think Blaine Cromwell aiding the King in escaping Hagan was a coincidence," he scoffs as he straightens.

Tidreda smirks, shaking his head. He crosses his arms behind his back and shifts back onto his heels. "You would be correct," he says shortly.

It slips between the rows of chairs, moving through three columns to sit just between the men. The King's hand rolls his neck and sighs. "Blaine Cromwell is... an ally?" Tidreda nods once. "Does... this have anything to do with the disappearance of Draven Idris?" He hesitantly asks.

The General's smirk widens into a grin. "No."

The boy's brows furrow together with his deepening confusion. "You have knowledge of Sir Idris' whereabouts," he concludes. "Yet, it has nothing to do with an ally close to the King of the lost lands," he looks down to the ground. The soul recognizes the thoughts flashing across his irises and wills him to speak them. "Windsor has not said anything about Draven's disappearance since the Queen mentioned it the day after their wedding. He is also aware of the Headmaster's location?" The words tumble from his lips against his will. The soul purrs as Eowyn's magic coos in approval, despite the distance between her and her commandeer.

"He is, Sir Renhart," Ancel steps forward and places a hand on Layne's shoulder. He dips his chin to look at the General's touch before looking back up, even more confusion gracing his features. "King Windsor Exeter of Exsar, the ruler who did all in the name of the eternal flame," Tidreda glances over Layne's head to the clock across the room. "Come, we must attend to a few more things before the King addresses the army. He will explain all then, young Renhart."

29

EOWYN

The Queen stands at the foot of the dais with her hands crossed in front of her. She keeps still, adorned in a masterpiece of a gown. The dress, a canvas of artistry, bears intricate and ornate patterns of shimmering gold wrapped around rubies and sapphires, cascading down the bodice like a regal waterfall. The skirt, a simple but elegant white, billows gracefully around her like a cloud of purity below the masterpiece of a bodice. Her shoulders are wrapped in a resplendent white fur cape that drips power, the fabric soft and luxurious against her skin. The ruby and sapphire encrusted crown sits atop her head, drawing no attention away from the matching jewelry she dons.

"Your Majesty," Layne Renhart bows deeply. "May I have a word?" He meets her intimidating gaze briefly.

She watches his eyes dart around the room to avoid her stare for longer than a moment. "You may," she glances over him from head to toe once. "Unless you plan on whisking my husband away for another month. Then you will meet the same fate as Elizabeth Croux." His face pales and he gulps. He hesitantly brings his eyes back to hers and she can't help but snort out a laugh. "What do you need, Renhart?"

Layne sucks in a quick breath, trying to compose himself. He can't help the sweat that drips down the back of his neck as he stands in front of the Queen. Her gaze is intense, and he can feel the weight of her authority bearing down on him. "I apologize for my reaction to your words, Majesty." He dips his head in a swift bow. "I bring to you news regarding the border."

"Oh?" She quirks a brow. "You are bringing *me* information regarding the border? *Not* Windsor?"

Layne hesitates for a moment, his gaze flickering to the ground before returning to her. "This piece of information is not for the King," he replies bluntly.

That piques her interest. "Pray tell, Layne."

Another moment of hesitation and she scoffs. She flicks a finger, dangling in front of her, using her magic to force the information out of him. Layne feels a sudden pressure in his mind, like someone is trying to pry open his thoughts without permission. He lets out a grunt of pain, his body instinctively trying to resist the intrusion. But the Queen's magic is strong, and her will is unyielding. His thoughts and memories start to come loose, spilling out from the depths of his mind. He sees flashes of information, bits and pieces of conversations and observations that he has gathered over the past few weeks.

"Queen Alice of Iverness sent word five years ago that she had a vision of you and the King taking over the continent." His eyes widen as he tries to hold back, to keep some of his thoughts and memories hidden, but the power of the Queen's magic is too strong. "Elenor ended Windsor's engagement immediately and they began to plan your betrothal. Then Tabot sentenced you to a year in the warded dungeons. Alice had bargained with him to allow you to have your eighteenth birthday ball." Suddenly, it stops and he gasps, stumbling back as he tries to regain his bearings. "Your Majesty-" he starts to say, but she shoots him a sharp look, silencing him with a few words.

"Continue," she commands.

He swallows hard, his mind racing to put together coherent thoughts. "When the week came, His Majesty departed for Iverness to retrieve you."

Eowyn's eyes flash and her jaw tenses. "Renhart," she warns tacitly.

His eyes dart to the doors and she scoffs. As if she hadn't been watching the other side of the door through one of her souls. He clears his throat and looks back to the ground. He squeezes his eyes shut. "Windsor and Alice had been planning your retrieval for a year. She had sent a letter each day which held three pieces of information. One piece of information about Tabot, an update on your progress with Flare Meadowglade, and a drawing of a part of a map."

"A map?" She didn't care about anything else, she would just ask Windsor to see the letters. But a map of what?

Layne nods and lifts his attention back to the Queen. "Alice did not disclose as far as my knowledge goes. Unless it was spoken between them, I am unsure." A soul slips from under her throne and twines around him threateningly. "It was something she siphoned from to resurrect you. She hid it and swore never to speak of it again," he rushes out as the soul squeezes him tightly.

"My Mother siphoned from Tretanov's life force to drag my soul back from Gragion," she hisses, keeping her posture squared.

He shakes his head quickly. "No, Your Majesty. It was something that is hidden in Exsar now."

The King approaches, the soul outside the door seethes. Eowyn waves her hand and the one holding Layne releases him. The doors push open and the Queen turns her head to see Windsor walking over the threshold with Mildy Bewyn and Ancel Tidreda following closely. The Royal Advisor steps around the men, rushing toward her.

"Olivette says you spoke this morning when she entered your chambers," Mildy's black eyes bore into Eowyn's red irises.

"Mildy," Windsor starts.

She turns on her heels, whirling to face him. "My Queen had done nothing but sit on the front steps *completely silent* for sixteen days," she snaps.

Eowyn reaches out and grabs her hands. "All will be explained in just a few moments," she assures the advisor. Her head whips back to the Queen. "Do not fret, Mildy. Windsor and I spent the entire night discussing everything," she pauses to glance back at the King's hand. "As soon as the forces and nobles alike are seated, we will discuss Windsor's absence and our next steps as a country." Her tone is laced with finality. Mildy's expression softens and her tangerine colored hair bobs with her gentle nod. Her hands relax in Eowyn's grasp. She turns to face Windsor and Ancel, her eyes flitting between the two men.

The Queen looks over the stout older woman's head to meet her husband's gaze. Windsor stands stoically, his icy azure eyes locked on hers. He doesn't look away as the others exchange muttered words. *"You are exuding power, My Empress,"* he blinks as he speaks into her soul. She feels the words reverberate through her mind, the connection between them strong. She resists the urge to react, keeping her face impassive as Windsor's voice echoes through her consciousness. *"You are the most powerful being in this Palace,"* his voice continues. *"No one can bring you to your knees."*

Her chest constricts with the power of his words. His head turns to his right and she follows his line of sight. "Are you prepared?" General Tidreda asks with his eyes flicking between the Royals.

Windsor rolls his neck and starts toward his wife. "Let them in," he says curtly. He loops his arm around Eowyn's waist and tugs her up toward the thrones. She walks backward up the steps to watch Ancel make his way through the hall. "Why does Layne look like he's getting his portrait painted?" He pushes her down into her throne. She smiles up at him and he brings a hand under her chin, his thumb resting just below her bottom lip. "What are you up to, my gorgeous bird?" He runs the tip of his thumb along her bottom lip. She scoffs and gently pushes his hand away from her face. He nods once and takes his seat beside her. "My apologies, I forgot that I am yours but you are not mine," he mumbles.

She rolls her eyes before watching the seats before them fill. The high class nobles fill the first half of rows before the troops start filling in the back rows. The rest of the army takes up the empty spaces between the columns and along the walls. The General approaches the dais. "Your Majesties," he bows.

They both rise and look at each other. Windsor exhales loudly and offers her his hand. She takes it, stepping forward with him as he raises their joined hands to the crowd. The room falls silent, every pair of eyes staring at the King and Queen. "Lords and Ladies of Exsar," Windsor's voice bounces off of the walls. "Thank you all for arriving so swiftly upon such a short notice. I am sure many of you are wondering why we have called you here today," his deep voice commands attention.

Eowyn's souls skate along the shadows casted by every person in the room. She pulls her hand from his and takes another step forward. "I would like to preface by saying your King has done unbelievably remarkable things, even as the Crown Prince. He is nothing short of astounding," she glances over her shoulder at him. "And I will proudly call him *mine* until we cross into Gragion *together.*" He bristles at her deliberate comment but smiles at her.

"Thank you, my love," Windsor steps to her side. His eyes flash as his voice echoes in her mind. *"I'm going to show you just how much you are mine the next free moment you have."* He clears his throat. "The former King and Queen," he gestures to the front row of the second of three sections of chairs. Elenor and Gideon rise to their feet and bow to Eowyn and Windsor. They turn to the crowd and wave before taking their seats. "They have been in contact with Queen Alice of Iverness for nearly five years." The crowd begins to murmur but Windsor silences them by raising a single hand. "Alice Azazé of Exsar, the seer with the pure blood of the light, had a vision that ended with King Tabot's death." He doesn't pause for their gasps. "She contacted my Mother immediately. As many of you know, Iverness is the Lost Land. Tabot is the worst thing to happen to the country since the *War of the Chanceless*. I speak first hand when I say, as Her Majesty can also attest, even the land in Iverness is starved. He collared and abused Alice Azazé, he tossed *my wife*," he glanced at Eowyn before looking back to the crowd. "In the dungeons for wielding her power after threatening her bonded animal's life."

Her eyes widen as he starts down the steps. She doesn't move, not yet.

Windsor laughs humorlessly, crossing his arms behind his back as he shakes his head slightly. "I won't even speak to what he attempted to do while my Vermilion was soaring just before our wedding." He pauses at the foot of the stairs. He looks up and scans the crowd. "My apologies, I digress," he runs a hand through his hair. "My Mother and Father took action immediately. They ended my betrothal to Skyla Bishop and began planning how to approach the subject of mine and Eowyn's marriage with the King." He starts forward again, walking between the first and second sections of seats. "They exchanged letters secretly, once a month, for three years." He halts and scans the room again. "Your Queen," he turns to face Eowyn and smiles lovingly, "*My Queen*." He lifts his hand to his heart. "She defended what was hers. Just three weeks after her sixteenth birthday, her Father had ordered the execution of Zanna." His hand falls to his back again and he turns on his heels to start toward the back again. "When she learned of this, she marched- *alone*- on his temple and burned it to the ground around them."

Small gasps erupt within the room. Windsor nods, bringing one hand up to rub against the stubble on his chin. His eyes flick to Eowyn's and she flares them in approval. He winks, turning left to walk along the back row of the second section. He pats a few soldiers on the shoulders as he passes and they stiffen slightly.

"Her Majesty was sentenced to one year in the warded dungeons- no, they are not a myth, I saw them myself but we will circle back to this- for committing High Treason." He sucks in a sharp breath. "Alice pleaded with Tabot to allow Eowyn to attend her own eighteenth birthday ball to choose her own suitor. He agreed, she then began to contact me," he discloses. "She would feed me information, things to prepare me for an interaction with him." He turns left again, starting up the aisle between the second and third sections. He weaves through the standing soldiers as he goes on. "She had taught me how to word certain phrases so I could bring the blood of the light home." He pauses all movement, looking up to Eowyn again. "Anything to get *her* home." She smiles at him, keeping her stance as still as a statue. "All while communicating with my Mother and Father about Eowyn's magic, how powerful she is, and how she was working day and night with Flare Meadowglade," he continues walking. "As Eowyn's birthday approached, Alice and I struck a bargain. A seers bargain." The Queen's soul strokes his, not for his comfort, but for hers. "Tabot grew angrier by the day. My wife," he chuckles, shaking his head again. "*Your Queen* is so powerful that she was wielding in the dungeons. Warded, bars made of Paronia, and her magic was *still* reeling. Alice feared he would kill her." He rolls his neck and turns right, walking along the front row of the third section. "If I had seen Eowyn's power first hand, I would vow to protect her with my life in exchange for marching on Iverness beside her after Alice's death." The King looks over the room before slowly dropping to one knee. He bows his head silently.

Eowyn takes a step forward. "Their bargain was sealed with a faux peace treaty, one that expires upon my Mother's death. One of the seers' terms being Windsor would not speak of any of this until she crossed into Gragion." She looks to Elenor with tears in her eyes.

"*I know, sweetheart,*" Elenor mouths as she dabs her own tears away with a handkerchief.

"Queen Alice of Iverness is... Dead?" A soldier by the door asks hesitantly.

Windsor rises to his feet and nods solemnly. "Yes," he says shortly. "It was very sudden. Her health was declining, but we had initially planned on *her* sending word when she began to get worse."

"Why?" The soldier pushes on.

Eowyn starts down the steps. "Once Windsor had signed the treaty with my Mother, she had led him down to the dungeons. He was to get me out that night. Your King shattered a collar made of Paronia with his bare hands," she walks toward Windsor. "When she felt she could no longer complete daily duties, she was to send word to Exsar and the King would then head to the border. And he did, though she'd already passed." Windsor meets her halfway, wrapping an arm around her waist. "He ushered over two thousand Ivernese citizens, safely." She gestures toward Elenor and Gideon. "The former King and Queen have been building extra housing and creating more employment opportunities to ease the transition for them, for almost two *years*. Windsor broke off their collars and General Ancel Tidreda alongside Sir Layne Renhart ushered them to their new homes." She's caught off guard by the eruption of applause and cheers.

Windsor laughs softly in her ear, kissing the side of her head as he raises his freehand to silence the crowd. He looks over the room with an eerie sense of calmness. "Now, we follow our Queen into battle to reclaim the Lost Lands."

30

WINDSOR

"What do we do if we invade and he slaps us in the face with Paronia?"

"Tabot's General is said to wield Nightfall!"

"We have been at war for seven hundred and sixty-eight years! We cannot simply reclaim the Lost Lands!"

The King raises his hand and the voices cease at once. He guides Eowyn back up the steps of the dais in silence. They turn, so elegantly that anyone in the room would have sworn it was rehearsed, opposite ways and face the crowd before their hands fall into one another's between them. Windsor laces their fingers together and holds her hand tightly. "I can destroy Paronia. Tabot's General does wield Nightfall, that means nothing. Lastly, we *can* and we **will** reclaim the Lost Lands," his words drip with finality. "Now, if you would be so kind, please ask questions one at a time. We know this is both a lot and a little information. My Mother and Father will answer any questions you have for them, Eowyn and I are encouraging you to ask *us* questions." The room falls silent. Eowyn squeezes his hand, her only indication of unease. He releases her hand and shrugs. "Nothing is more important to me than your understanding. I will sit," he takes a seat on the top step, leaning his elbows against his knees. "Right here, until you all stop looking at me like you're ready to revolt against me."

The silence is tense as the nobles and soldiers alike digest the King's words. It's clear they are not entirely satisfied with the information they've been given. Windsor sits casually on the step, his hands interlocked in front of him as he waits for someone to speak up.

Eowyn steps forward and rests a hand on his shoulder. He looks up at her, his brow furrowing as she walks past him and starts down the steps. "When I was eight years old, I siphoned the power of the Light from my Mother's veins," she looks over the crowd. "We'd just found out that the Paronia was not only suppressing her magic, but had begun to drain her life force. I begged," she pauses at the foot of the stairs. "I pleaded with her to let me do something. The only thing that I could do was pull her magic and hope that the Paronia would adjust accordingly... Not pull so hard, if you will," she sucks in a sharp breath. "I repeated this again on the morning of my wedding to His Majesty," she keeps her gaze forward as she gestures back to Windsor.

His heart swells with a sense of pride at the way she speaks so freely. *"Alice would be so proud to see her firebird flying so high,"* he whispers into her.

Her shoulders relax and she continues. "I filtered the power of the Planets from her just an hour before my wedding. She left Exsar, powerless." He can feel the sadness in her soul while it holds his tightly. The flame deep within her rages with her bubbling grief. He slowly pulls it from her, feeling her soul coo gratefully as he takes some of the weight from her. "She died the night she returned to Iverness." Tears stream down her face when she turns to face her husband.

He moves so quickly, he stumbles over the steps and down to her. He wraps his arms around her and hugs her tightly. "I'm here," he whispers. He slides his hand up her back and cradles his head against his shoulder. He presses a soft kiss to the top of her head, his eyes moving to his Mother as he breaks royal protocol. She shrugs back at him, a smile on her face.

"That was almost six months ago," someone says into the silence. The King lifts his head to glance at the noble a few rows back from them. "He did not even let his daughter, the Queen of the country he holds a peace treaty with, know her Mother had passed for *six months?*" He stares at them in disbelief.

Windsor looks down to Eowyn. She pulls back slightly, not stepping out of his arms just yet. "Precisely," she nods once. "He did not send word. His Secretary of the State sent word when it was safe for him to do so," she holds the man's stare.

Another noble, a woman in the same row but in the first section in the hall, stands up. "Alice Azazé of Exsar was a lightning wielder, you were born a fire wielder," she swallows thickly. "Does that mean you now hold two primary abilities within the House of Light?"

"Yes," she does not hesitate. "Electricity was my secondary from birth. That is why I was able to take it from her," she holds the woman's stare. "I also..." She hesitates. Windsor rubs his hand along her spine. "I was also born of the Planets. It was more difficult because I did not hold a secondary ability within the blood but I managed to relieve my Mother of her Seeing ability." He watches in awe as she continues to speak so freely, something he'd only seen once before.

Six hours ago, the soul skating by him hisses.

The King does not acknowledge the reminder. He didn't need it. He'd been home for less than two full days and had not managed to sleep at all. After Eowyn's meltdown when he first returned home, he'd only fallen asleep for an hour. He couldn't rest, he had to prepare for *this*. And after Eowyn *killed* that girl yesterday? He told her right then and there. He stood in the middle of his office and told her everything from start to finish. Then he showed her each of Alice's letters. Then he answered all of her questions, all while Layne, Ancel, Bryanna, and Olivette set up the meeting. Oli and Bryanna wrote all of the summons as the General briefed the army and Layne prepared the hall. He'd planned to tell her everything today and hold this meeting tomorrow, but he couldn't hold back anymore. Not when she was so openly allowing him to love her.

"I have a question, My Queen," Tidreda steps forward. Windsor blinks himself back to the present as Eowyn steps away from him. She turns to face the General. "I suppose 'tis more of a suggestion, but perhaps it would make everyone feel better..." He gestures around the room. "If we opened the Palace to them for the week."

Good. According to plan. Bring it home, Ancel.

He turns to look at the room. "Come and speak with the King and Queen at your own leisure. Ask questions, get to know them as I have," he brings both of his hands up to cover his heart. "Because this is happening. We will be moving quickly, so educate yourselves now. In the words of the departed, but *astounding* nonetheless, Flare Meadowglade; *Knowledge can only make you stronger.*"

The mention of Flare Meadowglade's words, the ones that used to be inscribed on the doors of Muddyvine Institute of Magic, seem to resonate with the crowd. The late, legendary Mage had been a beloved figure amongst the people of Deteron before his imprisonment, and many held his words of wisdom in high regard. The suggestion put forward by Tidreda seems to be well-received, and even before he finished speaking, the soldiers had begun to move toward the front door. Their boots thunder across the marble floors.

Windsor looks to Eowyn, finding her already staring at him. A small, smug smirk tugs at his lips. He crosses his arms over his chest. The soldier's rhythmic marching echoes through the room while he takes in her *soft* expression. "What now, My Queen?" He drawls, bowing at the waist with one arm along his front and the other draped behind his back. He holds his position, his eyes glued to his wife.

The entire room follows suit. Even the soldiers, not quite out of the room yet, stop in their tracks to bow to their Queen. "For the next seven days," her voice does not waiver, "from dusk until dawn, you will have both Mine and Windsor's undivided attention. You may come and go as you please, ask whatever you like, learn what you must to protect yourselves to the fullest extent in the event that Windsor and I fail, because it is a possibility." She pauses for a heartbeat. "It is a very small possibility as my Mother had a vision of our success, but nonetheless, we only want to protect you." She starts down the aisles. Windsor straightens, watching her wings take form. "We want you to be happy." Her wings bristle and he feels her start to manipulate everyone in the room. The nobles relax, their spines straightening before they take their seats again. "We want you to *thrive*," she continues. "We wish we had more time to spend with each and every one of you, but unfortunately, we must act now. One of *our* own *died* at my Father's hands." Her words soothe the souls around her even further. "Enough is enough. We must reclaim the Lost Lands." The King's eyes widen slightly. That was the first time she'd referred to her homeland as an Exsarian. "There is no room in a world of peace for suppression." She halts her steps.

Windsor feels the tension in the air lessen as she releases her grasp on the life forces in the room. Clapping and cheering fills the air, thickening it with a palpable energy. Their voices raise in approval while the applause thunders with a deafening roar, drowning out any other possible noise seeping through the Palace walls. The ground beneath feels like it trembles, whether it was from the sound or the raw power thrumming between the King and Queen would remain unknown, but it shakes the very foundations of Tretanov. The cheering grows into a vibrant symphony. It's impossible to mistake it for anything other than it is: a testament to the power of collective enthusiasm.

His wife is thriving. Her soul is singing for the first time since he'd known her. Its melody is so entrancing he can't do anything but stare at her. He's nearly overwhelmed with awe and pride, marveling in the way she absorbs the energy of the crowd from the air. The power rippling between them is tangible and he can feel his bones vibrating. His wife is thriving, glowing, something about her so new and captivating.

His feet move quicker than he thought he was going, closing the distance between them. "We're done here," he huffs out when he steps to her side. "I need to run."

She nods once and motions him toward the door. Windsor glances back at General Tidreda, who nods. He hooks his arm around Eowyn's and leads her out of the hall. The sound of her heartbeat drowns out all of the noise around them as they step into the hallway. He barely crosses into the hallway before giving into the lion.

"Windsor-" Eowyn calls, but he's already headed for the garden doors. He nudges the glass doors open with his head and takes off through his Mother's rose garden. He glances back, seeing his Queen step out of the doors with her wings still sprawling from her back. He huffs before taking off toward the hunting grounds. He pulls her, his hold on her soul tight as he moves further and further. The only signal of her following him being the way her power moves with him, still engulfs him instead of straining. His paws carry him to the clearing where Everys, Zanna, and their hatchlings feed on their third meal of the day. He glances back, digging his nails into the ground when he sees Eowyn isn't behind him.

She does not need to move for you to feel her, cub, Everys lifts his head as he speaks into the King's mind. His white face is covered in the poor lamb's blood and the scent of it makes Windsor's pupils dilate. *Hungry?* Everys lifts a paw and swats at the carcass in front of him. *I'll cook it for you as your keeper does,* he taunts.

"I am *not* his keeper," Eowyn's voice makes the lion's head snap in the other direction. "And I do not cook it, I merely char it so I do not have to hear its soul crying for release." She takes a few steps and stops at Windor's side.

A sound too close to home? Everys taunts the Queen.

Windsor lets out a low growl, shifting on his feet and baring his teeth at his Dragon. "Yes," Eowyn admits, "it is a sound I used to hear everyday. I do not wish to hear it any longer."

That makes him shift back.

"You don't hear it anymore?" He stumbles on his two legs, not waiting for himself to regain his balance before he tries to approach her. "You do not hear your own soul crying out?" His eyes are wide.

"I do not," she says bluntly. He rolls his neck and attempts to sort through the billions of questions circling his mind.

Since when? Zanna cuts in, stepping toward Eowyn. *Your soul has cried since the moment it was torn from a Prince of Gragion's arms by your Mother.*

"It stopped the moment Windsor said *I love you* through the door."

His eyes widen and his knees nearly buckle. "What?" He breathes out, stepping back.

You've satisfied her soul enough to be at peace in this realm, Everys looks between them. His attention moves to the hatchlings, still feeding behind them. He looks at Eowyn. *Your soul has found its purpose outside of Gragion.*

31

EOWYN

The Queen walks beside the near exhausted King toward the pond and pavilion he'd gifted her for their wedding. "You have hardly slept since returning home," she slides her hand into his.

Windsor's fingers slip between hers and lock around her hand tightly. "I have hardly slept since I've last caught the bird," he admits, helping her down the slope toward the clearing. He reaches for her other hand while walking backward, guiding her down a few steps before gripping her waist and lifting her off her feet. He holds her stare as he sets her down on level ground, his fingers still lightly tapping along her sides.

She takes a moment to regain her balance, her hands coming to rest on his forearms. She can feel the tension in his muscles, the way he's wound up tight. "You should sleep, Your Majesty," she chides gently, her fingers tracing along the skin of his wrists. "The strain of lack of sleep is starting to show on your face."

He cocks an eyebrow, a sly smirk playing at the corners of his mouth. "Are you telling me I look old?" He teases while his hands shift to pull her closer.

She shakes her head lightly. "I am merely pointing out that the dark circles under your eyes are... *unattractive*."

His eyebrows jump to his hairline. "Unattractive?" He leans in, their faces only inches apart. "You're saying I'm unattractive now?"

She lifts her chin defensively, willing her eyes to flash challengingly. "I'm saying you look like you need to get some sleep," she counters, her voice firm but amused.

"And are you going to help me with that, My Queen?" He asks playfully, his hands shifting to intertwine behind her back, pulling her flush against him so their bodies are pressed tightly together. "Are you going to hide away down here with me, away from our responsibilities and make sure I am getting the rest you feel so strongly that I *need*?" He leans down to nudge his nose against hers.

"Perhaps," her eyes flutter as his nose bumps against hers, his arms wrapped securely around her waist. "Maybe I want to make sure that my tired, *old* husband gets a proper rest."

"Old, huh?" He muses, his voice a soft and low rumble that resonates through his chest. "I'm only a few years older than you, sweetheart."

The Queen's hands slide up his arms to his shoulders. "*Older*," she corrects, rolling her eyes. She can feel his excitement, the way he felt content with the banter. "I will stay with you," she whispers, "and make sure you are getting the rest that I *know* you need."

He can't keep the smirk off his face. He squeezes her hips and draws her impossibly closer. "Are you sure you're up to the task, sweet girl? It's quite a monumental responsibility." He snorts out a laugh.

Eowyn rolls her eyes again, but smiles nonetheless. She moves her hand to rest along the base of his neck. Her fingers twirl the hair at the nape of his neck. "I do not wish to be away from you anymore, not after a full moon of not knowing where you were and if you were alive or safe," she shakes her head again, her expression dropping to a more serious display. His soul bleeds even more into hers at her words. She can feel the tingle in her bones, his power latching onto hers. A wave of guilt washes over him and she quickly pulls it from him, shaking her head once. "I did not say that to hurt you. I simply stated a fact."

His gaze drops to the crook of her neck and his muscles tense beneath her as if he was trying to pull her closer, even though in order for *that* to happen, she'd need to crawl inside of his skin. *"Forgive me,"* the words are barely a whisper. His own insecurities start to creep between their souls, manifesting and screaming at him to pull away.

She slides one hand through his hair, tilting his head forward until his forehead is resting against hers. His eyes flutter shut at her touch. He relishes in the comfort that her simple action provides. "Don't you dare," she says in response to his urge to untwine. "You begged me for this. You will not untangle us," her words are harsh but it's probably the softest voice she'd ever used with him. He takes a shaky breath, nodding as his grip on her hips loosens, the tension draining from his body. He brings his own hands up to frame her face when his eyes slowly open again. His thumbs stroke featherlight lines along her cheekbones.

She stands still, absorbing all of his emotions, all of his guilt and insecurities. She can feel them flowing through her as if they are her own. She takes a deep breath, bringing her own hands up to cover his and applies a gentle pressure. He meets her eyes to find her watching him intently, her expression less... *unreadable* than before he left. She shows him a slight vulnerability. He lets out a shaky breath, his body relaxing completely beneath her touch. "Forgive me," he repeats, "I wasn't thinking clearly. I should have come to you and told you everything before leaving. I should have taken you with me, I should have done so many things differently, My Empress."

"You should have," she agrees simply. "Yet, you did not and here we are." Her hand in his hair gently massages his scalp. He lets out a soft purr and leans back into her fingers, his eyelids falling closed again. "And I am glad we are here."

He nods his head in agreement, a sigh of contentment leaving his lips as her fingers continue. "I am also *very* glad we are here." His thumbs continue to trace circles on her cheeks, relishing the touch of her soft skin beneath his fingertips. He cracks his eyes open to look at her. Once he meets her gaze, he realizes he can't look away. She gently tugs on his soul. He studies her, his eyes flickering back and forth between hers, tracing every curve and contour of her face. "Eowyn," he drops his arms to his sides. She mirrors the motion.

The King watches confusedly as his wife turns her back to him. She starts toward the pond and reaches around, unlacing her dress. Windsor's attention drops with the gown. He blinks, never looking away as she starts into the pond. Eowyn turns to look at him, tossing a beckoning glance over her shoulder. He swallows thickly, greedily taking in the sight of her bare form. The warm glow of the now setting sun reflects on the water, highlighting every curve of her body as she walks further away from him. He's completely mesmerized, watching every small move she makes. Eowyn turns to face him and the lion within him whimpers, cooing a song of longing for her blood. She notes the way his fists clench at his sides. She watches his eyes take in every piece of her while his soul claws at her to give more. She releases a bit more to him and his attention snaps back to her face.

"Are you coming, *my* King?" She smiles, almost sweetly, at Windsor. He stands as still as a boulder, staring at her.

She can almost feel how dry his throat is. He hesitates, his gaze unyielding. She feels the guilt lingering, swirling within him. She watches flashes of his days spent away, at the border and escaping Perceval Hagan, in his eyes.

The Queen spreads her fingers, dragging her hands along the surface of the water as she wades further into it. Windsor blinks, seemingly snapping back to the present. He hastily pulls off his clothes, dropping them into a pile atop her gown. He steps into the water. Eowyn barks out a laugh as he tries to step forward, but he'd riled himself up enough to freeze the water around him the second he touched it. He lets out a sharp growl and summons a flame from her line of power coursing through him. His eyes turn bright red as he melts the ice. He puts the flame out, his eyes still glowing red. His fangs start to take form and he strides forward, stalking like a predator closing in on its prey. Eowyn stands, unmoving, as her husband stops just in front of her. She tilts her chin up to look at him and smirks. His need to be close to her nearly consumes both of them.

Good, he needed to need her.

Windsor reaches for her. His fingers grip her hips gently. "Your grief of your Mother's death is something I wish you would let me share with you," he murmurs.

"No," she retorts almost immediately, "I need it."

His brows furrow together. "You... need it?" He echoes. Eowyn simply hums, her delicate fingers grazing up his torso until she wraps her arms around his neck. "And I thought we were past this," he huffs out, tugging her forward until their chests are pressed flush against one another.

"I cried in your arms for countless hours since you have been home. You feel every emotion of mine, my power encases yours and you can wield it. Yet, that is not enough for you. You want to take an emotion away from me." She is not scolding, not criticizing, merely observing.

"Nothing," he breathes out, "nothing will ever be enough when it comes to you." His words drip with equal parts honesty and sweetness. "I will never be able to get enough of you. Not until I've picked you apart bit by bit and memorized every piece of you." He sucks in a sharp breath. "But even then," he reaches up to tuck a piece of hair behind her ear. "Even then, baby, I'm going to want more, *need* more." His hand settles on her cheek.

Eowyn subconsciously leans into his touch. "I will not share my grief with you," she whispers, "it is all I have left of her."

His other hand comes up to cup the other side of her face. "You have her power," he nods for emphasis. "You have her heart, you have every good quality she possessed. You have so much more than just... *sadness*," he says the last word with so much pain, not only in his voice but in his soul. Like it hurts his soul to know she carries anything more than the rage that will destroy everything in her path.

She brings her hands up to cradle his elbows. "The grief is the fuel I-we," she corrects quickly, "need for this all to work. Zanna needs to be fed and I need that rage *hot*."

"I want to know what happens when we make it *cold*," his nails bite into her skin. His hands tremble with restraint, the lion *still* begging to slice into her. "I want to know what happens when we take that anger and we-we... we flip it upside down," he shrugs desperately.

Eowyn's eyes flash in defiance. "Windsor, I will not-"

He doesn't let her finish. He presses his lips to hers. She can feel the tension coiled like a spring inside of him start to ease. She sighs and kisses him back. He hums against her, his hands sliding down her body and resting on the backs of her thighs. His tongue gently parts her lips as he starts to bend at the knees. Eowyn lowers with him, her arms locking around his neck. He pulls her down until her legs are around his waist and the water is lapping at their shoulders. Her lips move against his slowly, following his every move.

She almost groans in protest when Windsor pulls away. "I meant what I said before I left," he whispers. His hands slide down to cup the backs of her knees. "And I mean it even more now," his eyes glitter with red specks amongst his cobalt blue irises. "Now that I have you, here, like this."

Eowyn leans her forehead against his, her eyes fluttering closed. "I like it here, like this," she admits. He lets out a breath, reminiscent of a sigh, but does not say anything. She allows her arms to fall lax around his neck, extending them behind him and crossing them lazily at her wrists. She opens her eyes to see his closed, an almost pained expression on his face.

The Queen brings a delicate hand around, cupping his jaw and tilting his head up until their lips meet once more. His fingers dig into her thighs and he yanks her down. One of his hands moves to the back of her head, threading his fingers through her silver strands. She parts her lips, smirking into the kiss as he hungrily accepts her invitation. His fingers shift from gripping her hair to holding her head in place, his claws peeking out from his fingertips. His tongue continues to lap at every inch of her mouth, desperately tasting every piece that she allows him to.

Eowyn shifts, the water around them rippling with her movement. Windsor lets out a sharp hiss, pulling away from her mouth when she slides down onto his arousal. His eyes snap open and lock on hers. He pulls her head back, exposing the column of her throat to him. "My impatient little bird," he growls, grazing his teeth along her neck. "Yet, if *I* were to do something like that, you would untether me and leave me to the abyss." His nose brushes against her shoulder as he angles his jaws right over her trapezius.

His hand on her knee tightens and he bites down on the muscle. Eowyn belts out a sharp cry, shoving against him, but he doesn't release her. Her blood fills his mouth, drips down her arm and chest, down his chin. "Windsor!" She shoves him even harder but his grip on her tightens, his fangs taking form and tearing into the tissue. "Enough," she snaps, tears running down her face.

The King's gaze meets hers, his irises a deep shade of maroon mirroring hers. His jaw tenses again and forces more blood to spurt from the wound. Her body relaxes slightly, making him grin against her skin. He sucks on her shoulder, harshly for a moment, before lapping his tongue over her skin to seal the wound and pulling away. He lifts his head, blood smeared across his chin, cheeks, and nose. He wipes his face with the back of his hand, eyes still locked on hers as he brings it to his mouth and licks it clean. "Go get in that bed," he jerks his chin toward the pavilion as he lifts her hips, pulling out of her and setting her down on her feet. "*Now.*"

32

WINDSOR

The King holds his Queen's chin in his hand, his thumb holding her bottom lip folded over as she sits on her knees in front of him. His gaze drops to where her hands sit folded atop her thighs. "You kill a girl in cold blood for attempting to claim me as hers but you do not allow me to call you mine," he uses his thumb to apply more pressure to her lip and drags his eyes from her lap to her teeth. "You are my wife, Eowyn." He locks eyes with her. "Why does that bother you so badly?" He releases her face, his hand falling to his side.

"I am not *just* your wife." Her tongue darts out to wet her lips.

He scoffs, lowering himself to sit before her. "You are much more than just my wife," he agrees, reaching for her hands. He smiles as her fingers sizzle against his. "You are the Queen of Exsar, you are the *only* firebird shifter in the *history* of Tretanov, you are the daughter of Alice Azazè; holder of *both* primary abilities in Two Chosen houses. You are a manipulator of life. And the smallest bit of you, baby," he gently squeezes her hands, "is my wife." He brings her knuckles to his lips and kisses each one. "And for the next ten hours or so, you are..." He lifts his head once more, brows raised. "...mine." The final word hangs in the air but a taught rope, one he knows is about to snap.

She wants to keep her grief, to hide from him? He'll make her uncontrollable.

Windsor's right hand lowers to her thigh, his left hand shifting to clamp around both of hers. "Don't worry, *My Empress,*" he leans forward and lifts her hands over her head, his other hand coming around to rest against the small of her back. He guides her to lie down on the wooden floor at the foot of the bed. *"Belonging* to me isn't so bad," his voice is low, almost amused as he studies her quickening pulse thrumming against her neck. "As soon as I'm through with you, I'll take care of you." He presses a soft kiss to the spot he'd been eyeing. She pushes against his hands when his lips linger a little *too* long. He chuckles and leans his forehead against her cheek. "I won't bite you again, sweet thing," he presses another kiss to her jaw. His right hand moves from her back, to her hip and over her stomach. "Just don't move," he lifts his head to look down at her. She blinks but nods slowly. He smirks, releasing her hands and sitting up on his knees.

"Win-" He shifts into the beast, the one that's been scratching for her since this morning. "What are you doing?" She props herself up on her elbows. He huffs, using one paw to swat her knees apart. He growls at the sight of the candy apple red blood dripping from her. That's what he'd been after. "Windsor, you can't be serious," she tries to close her thighs but he positions his head on her stomach, her legs hitting either side of his neck. He sighs, rubbing his chin along her skin. "You want to..." She runs a hand through his dark mane. He nods slightly before nuzzling his nose along the underside of her breast. "The blood?" Her questions force a *red* glow from his eyes.

It is a hunger for her he cannot control since she'd allowed his soul to fully submerge in hers.

Windsor steps back and her legs fall open. He keeps his head straight, inhaling deeply. She is both rich and delicate, the sweetness enough to stop his heart then and there. He inches closer and the scent of her blood only intensifies. His gaze flicks to her face one more time, holding her stare as his head dips down and-

"Wait," she sits up. He growls, but takes a step back and sits on his hind legs. "You still haven't told me everything," she points an accusatory finger at him. He huffs and uses his paw to push her back down, quickly pushing her thighs open with his head and dragging his tongue from her knee to the juncture at the top of her thighs on her right leg. She swats at his head. "I'm serious, Windsor," she tries to close her legs but only clamps them on either side of his head.

He smirks internally. *"I know you are, sweet thing,"* he coos into her soul. *"But I need this."* She yanks on his stream of Shifter blood and forces him to shift back. He chuckles, shaking his head as his hands move to hook her legs over his shoulders. "You can force me to shift all you want, baby. I'm not moving until I've had every last drop of your fertile sweetness," he drags his index finger along her slit, gathering more blood before sucking it clean.

"Where is Draven Idris?"

The words go in one ear and out the other. They had to, or else he'd have used his teeth to pierce *her* again and *not* heal it. He hums, lowering his head and nuzzling her sensitive skin between her folds with his nose. "My pretty girl," he murmurs, gripping her hips and pulling her core closer to him. "My sweet, delicious wife," he groans. He glances up as his tongue darts out, circling the hole blessed by Kanika herself, collecting the near intoxicating nectar dripping with fertility. He groans, dropping his forehead to rest against her stomach, just above her sex. He shudders as her scent fills his nostrils. "Two minutes," he lifts his head enough to meet her gaze. "I can control myself, *for you*... for two minutes. Ask whatever you want."

The second the words leave his lips, she repeats the question. "Where is Draven Idris?"

Without a thought, his hand darts around her leg and to her neck. He grabs her roughly, pulling her to sit up with him. "What *the fuck* did I tell you about saying another man's name when I have you splayed out like this for myself?" He snaps. "Draven is no concern of yours any longer, *My Queen*." He presses a soft kiss to her lips, a stark contrast to the grip he has on her.

"Where is he?" She whispers, her eyelashes fluttering almost innocently against her cheeks.

Windsor stood on the balcony of his room the morning of his wedding to the Princess of Iverness. He patiently awaited Layne's arrival with their suits for the ceremony. He held a cup of tea in one hand, a lit roll of SuperNova in the other. His ears perked up when he heard footsteps below the platform. He inhales another deep drag of the drug, shifting his inner ears to that of a lion, just to hear a bit clearer. "Flare Meadowglade and the Azazè girl failed to mention she was a firebird," Draven Idris, but he sounded... angry, *about that fact.*

"The first in the written history of Tretanov." Another, less important and undistinguishable, voice replied.

Windsor set the teacup down on the chair behind him, taking another long drag of the roll between his fingers. "And the power she wields on top of that? The girl is blessed by Kanika herself," Idris scoffed. Windsor rolled his neck and put out the roll. He placed it by the teacup on the chair, rolling his shoulders back as if he knew what was coming next. "I'd give anything to cage her and study her every breath."

Windsor turned back toward the railing, placing one hand on it before jumping over it. He shifted into the lion midair, landing on all fours in front of the headmaster of Drexreth school of Magic.

"Your Grace," Idris almost shouted in surprise. The nameless man by his side scampered off, **good.** *Windsor shifts back into his humanoid form, a silent snarl on his face. "You should be preparing for your wedding." Windsor said nothing, simply grabbed the back of his head and dragged him into the Palace.*

"He is none of your concern, my love," he sighs, loosening his grip on her neck slightly.

"Windsor," she pries, pushing against his wrist.

He groans, sitting back on his heels and running a hand through his hair. "Eowyn, I do not wish to-to..." he shakes his head to clear his thoughts. "I filled his mouth with stones and had his mouth sewn shut." He admits. Her jaw slackens, her muscles tensing as her rage blazes. He studies her face for a moment. "He wanted to cage you," he mutters, "I heard him speaking of caging you to '*study her every breath*', Eowyn. He's lucky I did not do to him as you did to the girl in the gardens."

Her eyes glimmer, blue specks forming in her blood red irises. "You..." the unspoken words hang in the air between them.

Windsor shifts closer, his palms gravitating toward her hips and pulls her onto his lap until she's straddling his thighs. "I will *die* before I see you in another cage," his hands slide down the sides of her legs. "I will burn Tretanov, I will encase the entire continent in a glacier before I see you in another cage or with another collar." He slides his hands, slowly, up her body, until he cups her jaw with gentle hands. "Because you are mine, whether you want to be or not, Eowyn. You are mine to love, to protect and defend, even when you don't need it." He leans forward, nudging her nose with his. She stares at him, parted lips and wide eyed. "I'll take you to see him if you wish. He's still alive." Her eyes widen even more, completely stunned to her purest being. He shifts one hand to hold the side of her neck, his thumb pushing her chin up so her stare is level with his. "He can easily be... *unalive*... if you prefer," he whispers nonchalantly, his eyes roaming over her every feature.

She blinks, cocking her head to the side. Windsor lets out a shaky breath at the pure innocence in the motion. "Why have you never told me about your brother?"

Ah, she wanted to look innocent. He smirks, "you've not asked about my family beyond my parents." He tightens his fingers around her neck and pushes her head all the way back with his thumb. "Have you?" He croons, playfully nipping at her chin.

Her lips tug up into a smile. "You failed to mention your brother is a King on Euclus," her side eye makes his smirk lift into a smile.

Windsor lifts his thumb, releasing her chin to stroke her bottom lip. "Do not fret, My Queen," he laughs lightheartedly. "Waryam and Evangeline will be here soon to meet you," he assures her, his lips moving toward hers. "But do not call him a King, he is the Emperor of Euclus. Just as you will be the Empress of Deteron," he promises.

"Exsar," she whispers.

His smile widens and he nods once. "The Empress of Exsar," he looks from her eyes to her lips. He moves his other hand around her back, sliding it down her spine. "Waryam is much older than I," his palm glides over her backside. "He has a son, Oscar, who is eight years old now." Her soul thrums with satisfaction the more he divulges. "They protect the artifacts of the Shifters," he confesses.

Her hands rest against his bare chest. "What are the artifacts of the Shifters?" She looks up at him, almost innocently.

He hums, his chest rumbling against her palms. His hands move to rest on her ass and he pushes her forward. The curious side of her had always gotten to him. He'd cherished the nights she would knock on his bedroom door to ask for clarification of some tidbit of Exsarian history. He'd give her every answer her heart desired, especially when it came to her wanting to understand the blood that courses through her. "There are a few, less than the Weapons Catalog left by that of the Planets." She nods, urging him to continue. "There is the Judgement Hide, the Feather of Faith, and the Stones of Malice," he presses a kiss to her forehead.

She leans into him, her forehead resting on his shoulder. "What do they do?" Eowyn's voice is quiet, her soul settling around him.

Windsor tightens his grip on her and rises from the floor. "Well," he lets out a heavy breath, moving toward the bed. He lifts one knee, swinging his leg onto the mattress. He sits in the middle and positions her between his legs, her knees bent over his thighs. He smiles as she leans forward and rests her head on his chest again. He brings one hand up, cupping the back of her head. He leans back, pulling her to lay down with him. "The Judgement Hide was the hide of the first Bear Shifter. He was skinned by Rubur and Kiwi of Tunate as punishment for a crime."

"Did Kanika preserve the Hide?" Her question makes his heart swell with pride.

"Yes, sweet girl," he brushes a loose curl away from her face. "Kanika preserved the hide. He was executed the day she claimed her power." He watches her pull the duvet around them, a slight shiver skating through her. "I forgot you do not enjoy being cold," he chuckles faintly. He wills the fire streaming from her soul to heat his skin for her. She hums contently. "The Feather of Faith is a grey feather, said to be the first feather to fall from the first Shifter offspring of the Aves. Legend says that if you write your heart's desire with the feather and your own blood as the ink, it will manifest before your very eyes," he absentmindedly drags his fingertips along her spine.

She lifts her head, resting her chin on his chest. "That's a very... powerful object," she notes. "Is that why it is kept on Euclus?"

He tucks one hand under his head. "Yes and no," he replies, glancing up to the ceiling of the pavilion. "Euclus was the House of Shifters territory, as Deteron was the House of the Infinite before the Light broke from the Unbleeding to build Exsar." He shrugs and allows his eyes to fall closed. "It is best to keep some of the relics left by the chosen ones away from the ones that reside in Exsar. It would be catastrophic if someone, say, wielded Skyfall while harvesting from a Stone of Malice."

He feels her head settle back down, just above his heart. "Skyfall is the sword with a blade of pure Paronia, carved with a bird?" He nods in response. "And what does a Stone of Malice do? How many are there?" Her curiosity washes over him like a wave from the Atraxian.

"There are fifty-four Stones of Malice," he mumbles, carding his fingers through her hair. "The Stones of Malice were placed all over Tretanov by Kanika. They were uncovered over the past several hundred years. They are said to contain the power of her anguish." His muscles slowly start to relax and he lets out a yawn. "We'll take a trip to the Trove of the Unbleeding within the next few days. I'd like you to be armed with those weapons before anything else. I will, hopefully, find a way to arm you with all seven of them."

33

EOWYN

Windsor's fingertips run along her spine lazily. "Why are you fighting sleep so hard?" Her hand moves up and down his bare torso.

His palm falls flat atop her ribcage. "I am doing *no* such thing," his tone is laced with exhaustion. She laughs quietly and lifts her head just enough to rest her chin on his chest. He cracks his eyes open to look at her. "What? I'm not," his index finger moves along the indents of her skin between her ribs.

Eowyn lays her head back down and hums. "Just because you are fighting *more* than sleep does not mean you are not fighting it," she retorts to his blatant lie.

She can feel the exhaustion in his bones, hear it in the way his soul purrs lazily. It is almost funny to her how he could not remain silent since she'd allowed him back into her.

"I am fighting the scent of your blood, Eowyn. I cannot sleep because I am too focused on ignoring *you.*" He brings his other arm around her again and pulls her closer. His power reels away from her and his skin begins to heat up as he summons her magic.

She continues to drag her fingertips along his skin lightly. "Would it be easier for you to rest if I was not here?" She does not need him to be tired for the week ahead, he needs to be as healthy as he has ever been, for as soon as the week ended they would start briefing the Exsarian Army.

"Absolutely not," he huffs out a laugh. He shifts onto his side, pulling her so that their chests are pressed together. "I do not intend to spend another sleep without *My Empress*," he reaches up to comb his fingers through her hair. His hand falls onto her backside, just below her where the ends of her silver locks curl.

Eowyn hesitates, but tucks her head under his chin and slings a leg over his waist. His hand slides along the back of her thigh before resting behind her knee. "What does a Stone of Malice do?" She smiles as his heart rate increases at the same time his chest rumbles with a low hum.

"The Stones of Malice were said to be placed all over Tretanov by Kanika herself," he informs her. "Much like you, Kanika was said to hold power in her rage. According to *all* of the texts in the Archives of the Light, she had stored her power in pockets in the ground," his muscles relax even further.

She shifts closer to him. "All of the texts?" He wraps his arms around her uncompromisingly as he nods. "Is it possible that my Mother siphoned from a Stone of Malice and not the Planet?"

"Mhm," he slides closer to the edge of unconsciousness. Eowyn stays quiet, her palms flattening on his bare back. He lets out a deep breath, leaving her unsure of who fell asleep first.

...

The Queen's eyes open before the sun has breached the horizon. She smiles sleepily against Windsor's chest and nudges her nose against him. Her soul wraps tighter around his as do her arms. She finds herself tucking her right hand under his side, between his ribcage and the mattress. He mumbles incoherently and nuzzles his face into the crook of her neck. His hand clasps around the back of her knee and pulls her impossibly closer, as if trying to be absorbed by her. Then his hand slides between them.

"Insatiable," she rolls her eyes.

He breathes out a sleep laced laugh. "Always," he slides his finger along the inside of her thigh. "It will be worse every time you are bleeding," his husky voice skates along her skin like a sheet of ice. Her eyes follow his hand as he brings his finger to his lips and sucks it into his mouth. "Not to mention," he releases his digit with a *pop*. "I am just utterly obsessed with you," he whispers before placing a soft kiss against her neck. He angles his head down, pressing his forehead against the spot he'd just had his lips on. Her gaze drops to his hand as it travels down her right side. "I could just stay right here," he makes his way back up to her shoulder, "like this." His hand slides down her arm and he interlocks their fingers. He brings her hand to his face, but instead of kissing it, he rests the back of her hand on his cheek "Forever," he sighs contently.

She watches his eyes fall closed again. "May I ask you something?" She spoke softly but she was only asking to let him know it wasn't going to be an easy question. He nods against her, his nose brushing against her collarbone as he does so. "What does it feel like?" She could feel everything he did, he wasn't able to block her like she was him. Yet, she felt nothing different in him and she'd felt nothing new.

He finally lifts his head to look at her. Eowyn can't help but let out a soft laugh at his tousled hair falling over his face. He keeps her hand against his face while pouting down at her. "What does *what* feel like?" His eyelids flutter when she leans closer to him.

"To love me," her lips brush against his.

Windsor drops her hand and grabs her face, his thumb on one side of her face with his fingers digging into her opposite cheek. She grins up at him. He smirks back before pressing his lips to hers. He kisses her as if it is a promise, firm and unwavering. Her hand loosely rests along the base of his neck. His thumb moves under her jaw, pressing into her pulse point while his tongue forces her lips apart. She doesn't fight him, simply existing at the moment for him to show her *exactly* what he felt. He pulls away abruptly.

Eowyn furrows her eyebrows as he completely detaches from her and stands up from the bed. She rolls onto her back and props herself up on her elbows. He walks to the end of the bed and points an accusatory finger at her. Her muscles stiffen slightly as she holds his stare. "That's what loving you feels like, Eowyn," he whispers, brokenly. "Thinking you know what's coming next, looking forward to something *so much* and it just walks out the door before you get a chance to openly consume every last bit of it." His words leave her stunned. Her lips part, her shoulders drop and her toes uncurl under the blanket. He sighs and lifts his outstretched hand to run his fingers through his hair. "I don't understand it, Eowyn," he brings his other hand up and rests both on his neck. He cranes his head back to stretch at the ceiling as he shakes his head. "I don't understand how you can be so-so..."

"Needy?" She mumbles, pushing herself to sit up fully.

"Needy," he nods, dropping his arms to his sides. His eyes roam over her for a moment before he drags them to her face. "I don't understand how you can be so needy one moment and just..." he trails off again.

She pouts up at him before leaning forward and crawling toward him on her hands and knees. She sits back on her heels at the edge of the mattress and grabs his hands. A soft breath pushes past his lips and he steps closer to her, his knees pressed against the bed. He pulls one of his hands from hers and combs it through her hair. "Just...?" She urges on.

"It doesn't matter," he swallows tightly. Eowyn's eyes fall with him as he kneels in front of her. His hands flutter up and down the sides of her thighs. "I live for these moments." He watches his hands move over her skin. She quirks a brow, raising her chin slightly. "If this was the last piece of you, right now, that I was honored to hold, I would be able to die happy."

His soul is weeping, she can feel his heart start to fall apart at his own words. Wordlessly, her hands move to his wrists. Her palms glide over his forearms, dragging his attention back to her face. "Yesterday," she grips his biceps softly as he continues, "when you were speaking about your Mother and you turned to *me* with tears in your eyes. You let me *hold* you. You let me *love* you, openly and wholly."

She notes the way he seems to study her, as if he was never going to see her again. "Win-"

He shakes his head and cuts her off. "That's all I want, Eowyn," he leans forward and wraps his arms loosely around her waist. "I just want this. Not just here, or in the gardens, or in our bedroom... I want this all the- no, I **need** this all the time, baby."

"Windsor, I... I have no intention of... Retreating from you." Her throat feels tight as she forces out the words, but tight in a satisfactory restrain. Almost like her body was fighting against the reluctance of her mind and soul.

His ears perk up at the combination of her words and delicate tone. "Eowyn-"

She smirks, cutting him off this time. "I will Seer's Bargain it."

Windsor grabs her hips roughly and shoves her back on the bed. She stares at him, wide-eyed as he stays knelt on the ground. "That was not funny, it was cruel." He bites out sharply, his words stinging her to her core. His spine snaps straight like he felt the pain too. "You..." she nods, reaching toward him almost instinctively. He lunges forward, grabbing her wrist and pulling her to meet him near the end of the bed. "Say it," he pleads, begs. His soul yearns, tugs, screams and cries.

She holds his stare, unsure of what he expects of her. He knows she won't admit a vulnerability. But she knows that he can feel the change inside of her. She knows, since the wedding ceremony, the flame inside of her flicked to the beat of the thrumming coldness in his blood. While she could manipulate his entire life force, he was able to change the way she burned- at her core. He'd learned to control the temperature of the flame inside of her- flicking the flame from red-hot anger to icy... whatever this is.

"I don't have to," she shakes her head. He growls, confusing her even more as he shifts into the lion. "What are you-"

He lifts a paw and shoves her back onto the mattress. She gasps as the same paw comes down on her chest and pins her to the bed. He huffs down at her, sitting between her parted legs. She blinks but opens her legs even wider. She could swear a smirk passes over the cat's face but before she can say anything, the papillae of his tongue scrapes against her inner thigh like sandpaper. Then he bites into her, his teeth sinking beneath all of her layers of flesh.

She lets out a sharp cry, her fingers clawing at the sheets below her. His tongue runs over the wound, now spewing blood, and the pain subsides completely. His mouth vibrates against her with another, more satisfied growl. He lifts his head and just stares at her for a moment. She stares back, wide eyed and chest heaving, legs trembling with a mix of pain and adrenaline. He nods once, to himself, dipping his head back down to lick the other thigh. Not only was he licking her blood off of her, he needed to bite her to get more from her.

He licks up the blood from her other thigh, his tongue soothing the injury with each pass before going back to the beginning and starting over again. He moves slowly up her leg, leaving a trail of saliva and blood behind. Eowyn's heart beats faster as he starts to lap up and down the length of her thigh. She lets a soft moan slip as his tongue moves over an untouched spot just below her hip. Before she could stop them, her hips buck upward, as if trying to increase the pressure while her legs twitch on either side of his massive body. He forces more of his weight on her, pinning her in place with his own body as his tongue continues to trace a slow, tortuous path along her thigh. A soft whimper escapes her as she closes her eyes again, her body shivering with anticipation. He pauses, his nose pressing into the junction of her hip and her thigh as he breathes in. Her fingers twist in the sheets again, her body starting to writhe beneath his. She knows he can smell the desire dripping from her, she can feel how crazy the scents of her were making him. Every muscle in her body clenches as he continues to hold her in place with

267

her teeth grinding together. He lifts his head, his jaw scraping along her skin. His cobalt blue eyes flicker and turn darker as she shifts beneath him, his gaze drinking in every inch of her quivering body. He drags his tongue up her skin. His eyes move between her face and her exposed body. He stops, his nose nuzzling into the sensitive flesh he'd been clawing to get out for.

He flattens his tongue on her, dragging his sand-paper like tongue along her slit. Her hips jolt, involuntarily, at the onslaught of new sensations shooting up her spine. Her hands on the sheets tense while she tries to close her thighs around his head. A strangled, desperate noise slithers past her lips.

He, on the other hand, means business. He growls into her, earning a breathy moan from his wife, his claws stabbing into her chest. She bucks against him again and he purrs, dragging his paw down the front of her. She belts out a cry, watching her own skin split beneath him. He flicks his paw once he gets down to her hip, digging in even harder before he retracts the large claws.

His eyes connect with hers and she could swear he smiles up at her when tears slip from her eyes. He lifts his head from between her legs. He slides his tongue over her mound, to her hip. His tongue slides back and forth, slowly, lapping up the blood and coaxing her skin to heal over. He drags it out for quite a few minutes before the wound is entirely healed. He nudges her chin with his nose.

"Stop," she swats his face gently. "That was uncalled for," she brings her hand up to wipe the few stray tears away.

He growls again, lying down on the bed between her legs. She watches him look back down to the apex of her thighs, watching a small amount of blood trickle from it. He only lifts his eyes as his head lowers down to her core again. He nuzzles his nose against her, coating his snout in her blood and arousal.

Eowyn gasps when he flattens his tongue against her, pushing her folds apart as he swipes from her core to her clit. He applies more pressure, the tiny backward facing spikes poking into the sensitive bud. She bites down on her lower lip when his eyes blaze a bright purple. She feels a deep satisfaction settle in his chest. He moves his front legs under her thighs, his paws resting on either hip to hold her still. He repeats the motion with his tongue, this time slower, as if savoring every last drop of the mixture seeping from her. He drags out the movement making her back bow off the mattress with a groan. His possessive snarl reverberates through her and her fingers curl around the sheets. His eyes darken as she lets out a soft moan. His claws bury themselves in her skin.

"Winnie," she whines, pushing against his paws. He just growls into her, rolling his massive tongue before dipping it into her core and *slurping* the juices flowing from her.

34

MILDY

The Royal Advisor stands to the left of the King's office door, the former King and Queen waiting to the right. Dawn will break in less than ten minutes and the King and Queen are nowhere to be found. The Palace doors will open, allowing in hundreds of citizens who are here to see them.

"Have you checked the Dragon's Quarters? Or the hunting grounds?" Elenor steps forward, her fingers twisting together in front of her. "Perhaps Windsor is hunting with the hatchlings?" Her throat bobs with an anxious swallow.

"I checked the Dragon's Quarters, my love," Gideon places a hand on Elenor's back.

Mildy nods, glancing toward the windows. "We've checked everywhere either of them would be. Layne, Ancel, Bryanna, and Olivette are still looking," she assures the former Queen.

"Lady Bewyn." The three of them turn toward the voice, finding a single soldier standing at the end of the hall. "It is time."

"They're not here," Elenor starts toward the soldier. "We cannot start without the King and Queen." She scoffs incredulously.

Mildy looks toward the soldier, dipping her chin in a slight nod. "The Palace doors are to open at dawn and close at dusk, those are the Queen's orders." He says as he bows at the waist to Elenor.

Five.

Mildy's gaze shifts from Elenor's horrified expression to Gideon's concern twisted face.

Four.

Ancel Tidreda comes walking down the hall behind the Exeter's, Layne Renhart a single step behind him. Right in formation.

Three.

The clacking of heels echoes from Mildy's back. Olivette and Bryanna flank either side of the Royal Advisor.

Two.

"My apologies," the soldier straightens and locks eyes with Elenor. Gideon steps to her side and wraps his arm around her protectively. "But the doors will open in two minutes as instructed." He looks at Mildy and she flashes a tight lipped, dismissive smile. He turns on his heels and walks down the hall once more.

One.

The office door opens and the King steps out, the Queen's hand threaded through his. *"It's time,"* he sings, walking around his parents. "Mildy, you will catch them up?" He raises his dark brows at her, his eyes flashing cobalt.

"Of course, Your Majesty," she nods. Her eyes follow the pair as they start toward the Main Palace. She takes a moment to admire how perfect they look. The way her silver locks flowed, complemented by his dark hair that gets longer by the day; how she looks so dainty but powerful next to him. The way she stands nearly a head shorter than him but the way she carried herself, the way *he* seems to force one's attention to *her*. It's quite odd the more she thinks about it. She blinks, turning toward Elenor and Gideon. Ancel and Layne silently follow the King and Queen, Olivette and Bryanna behind them.

"They are wearing Royal clothing," Elenor snaps, her eyes glued to the four main pawns in the King and Queen's game.

Mildy nods, a smile taking form on her face. "Yes, they are," she folds her hands in front of herself. "As of one hour ago, the four of them *are* Royalty in Exsar."

Elenor's horrified expression returns, leaving Mildy unsure of whether it was because she realized she was no longer the Queen and now in the dark, or because her son had not informed that he was making such a monumental decision before a war. Gideon stands there, just as confused as his wife is horriffied.

"The King and Queen have hand picked their own... for lack of a better term, legion to accompany them throughout the next few weeks," Mildy discloses, motioning down the hall. She starts forward, Elenor and Gideon following quickly. "Bryanna Grisel and Olivette Lincoln were graced with the titles of Ladies during Windsor's absence. Her Majesty has pulled back their Palace duties so they may work with both her and His Majesty to harness their power in the event theirs fails."

"Bryanna Grisel does not possess magic," Elenor bites out.

Mildy chuckles as their footsteps echo throughout the hallway. "Lady Bryanna has been *gifted* power by His Majesty. He has passed on his gift of Temperature manipulation."

Their eyes widen at the declaration. "He no longer holds the blood of the Planets?" Gideon pipes up after a silent moment.

Mildy's eyes glitter with amusement. "His Majesty now holds the blood of *all* four Chosen Ones," she clips.

Their confusion only grows, Elenor scoffing out a breath as they descend the grand staircase. "That is impossible. He only harbored three bloods, he does not hold *more* after *gifting* some." Her tone is bordering condescending.

Layne Renhart waits at the bottom of the steps, his eyes locked on the former Queen. "There is much you have missed," he says, an eyebrow cocked. "You'd think it wise to not speak of things you are not knowledgeable of in the Queen's presence."

Elenor stops in her tracks, two steps from the ground where Gideon and Mildy now stand with the King's hand. "You are... threatening *me*?" Mildy could feel Elenor's hurt. She'd practically feel the pain radiating off of her.

"It is not a threat," he whispers, lifting the right side of his coat to expose a sheathed katana. One with a blade of a precious metal known as Esnil, *only two in existence.*

Gideon steps in front of Elenor at the sight of *Warmonger, The Katana of the Wretched.* The blade was last secured with the rest of the weapons left behind in the Trove of the Unbleeding. It was the only thing left by those born of the Light when they broke away from the Infinite. "You wield an Unspoken," the ground rumbles with Gideon's anger, the stone beneath the Palace shifting. "Why?" He grits out.

"Father." Gideon and Elenor spin around to face their eldest son, Waryam, and his wife, Evangeline. "Eowyn will be starting now."

"When did you arrive?" Elenor nearly sobs.

The Emperor and Empress of Euclus silently, as planned, walk past his parents. She looks to Mildy helplessly, then to Layne and her husband. "It is time," Renhart says after a moment of silence. "All will be disclosed very shortly," he gestures down the long corridor. Mildy studies the former Queen, her eyes briefly taking in her husband as well. They *are* helpless. So they nod and follow Layne into the Throne Room.

Mildy follows a few paces behind them. It is quite odd to see Elenor so hurt, but she is no longer Queen and Windsor needn't ask her permission anymore.

Eowyn and Windsor sit atop the dais. Eowyn sits on her throne, her husband sitting on the ground with his back against her legs, his head tilted back onto her thighs as she runs her fingers through his hair. Her eyes lock on Mildy's and she sends an affirming nod to the Queen. Eowyn pulls her hands from Windsor and he lifts his head to look at Mildy. He grins and she smiles back as she watches him rise to his feet. The room goes silent, all chatter ceasing as the hundreds of people gathered stare at their King.

He paces the width of the dais for a moment, bringing a hand up to rub the stubble on his chin. The only sound is the padding of his shoes against the marble beneath him. "I've unsealed the Trove of The Unbleeding," he drops his hand and crosses his arms behind his back, continuing to move back and forth. "Waryam wields The Unyielding, Eve holds Twisted Silence, Layne Renhart; Warmonger, Olivette; Vindictive Slicer, Bryanna Grisel; Blazefury... I hold Thundersoul while my wife will wield HeartSeeker." He starts down the steps.

He pushes his jacket aside to reveal Thundersoul. He unsheathes the haladie, pulling the cover off of both curved blades. Waryam steps to his right. He pulls Unyielding, the blade of the Oracle who initiated the split between the House of the Infinite and the House of Light. Layne Renhart moves to Windsor's left and reveals Warmonger; The Katana of the Wretched. It is made of Ensil, a now extinct metal on Tretanov. There are only two known blades still in existence made of Ensil. The Katana of The Wretched was the only thing those who left with the House of Light had forgotten. Evangeline of Euclus stands on her husband's other side. She bends at the waist and lifts the skirt of her lavender colored gown. She pulls a small, carving knife from a strap around her ankle. Twisted Silence; a carving blade whose power is in that of who wields it, the power being driven by desire. Bryanna, on Layne's left side, lifts Blazefury: The Katana of the Forest from its spot on her back. The Paronia blade gleams in the

Palace lights among the murmurs and gasps. She immediately sheethes it again, as instructed by Eowyn this morning when they opened the Trove. Next to Lady Grisel, Olivette pulls a thin, gold blade from her hip. Vindictive Slicer, a gift to the House of the Infinite from Kanika herself.

"Your Majesty," a noble woman by the name of Amina, from the house of Mannillo, stands from her seat in the front row.

Mildy watches as Windsor's eyes move to her before her gaze flicks to Eowyn. The Queen sits stiffly while Windsor approaches the noble. "Lady Mannillo," he dips his chin in acknowledgment.

She curtsies before looking between the Royals. "The Infinite are still hunted through the World. Wielding a weapon of the Unbleeding is almost asking to be infiltrated," her concerns are valid, to an extent.

"Mm," Windsor brings his hand back to his chin and nods. "While that may be true, Lady Mannillo," he starts to walk back toward the dais. The rest of those who hold the most powerful weapons on Tretanov move to stand against the wall beside the thrones. "My wife and I will handle anyone trying to *hunt* one of the Infinite." He slowly walks up the steps. "Not that it will matter once Tabot has been killed for his crimes during his reign, but we are not in fear of our lives," he positions himself at the Queen's feet again and leans back against her.

Mildy crosses her arms over her chest with a smirk. "Why are you not sitting on *your* throne?" Elenor barks out as she steps forward. "You are the King. You sit on your throne." She points at him accusingly.

The corners of Eowyn's lips twitch upward, a slight smile tugging at her features. Windsor leans his head back against his wife's thighs and grins up at her. She hums lowly, her hand returning to his hair. He lifts his head to look at his Mother. "I am not sitting on my throne for the simple fact that I do not wish to," he shrugs nonchalantly.

"It is-" Elenor tries to retort but Gideon silences her with a hand on her back. She snaps her mouth shut and looks up at her husband.

A palpable silence settles over the room, the air heavy with tension. Mildy turns toward the rest of the room, glancing over the hesitant faces. A man, toward the back, rises to his feet. Mildy's eyes gleam as she reads his mind before the words tumble out.

"If I may, Your Majesty?" His anxiety nearly makes him crumble before everyone.

"Of course, young Trecca," Windsor's voice, rather Eowyn's power, soothes over the *entire* hall and pulls the unease from the oxygen.

The youngest of the Trecca house squares his shoulders and stands taller. Mildy looks back to her Queen, a gentle shine of admiration gracing her features at the tame, yet eccentric display of power. "As a citizen below two of the most powerful rulers Exsar has seen, it is... *nice*... to see such casualty between you," he gestures toward them, bowing his head.

A feral grin spreads across Windsor's face. "Thank you, Jonathan," Eowyn finally speaks.

From the corner of her eye, Mildy glances at Windsor's parents. Elenor's face is such a dark shade of red, it would be mistaken for purple in a lower lit room. "I live and breathe for my wife," Windsor leans his head back again as he speaks.

Mildy's eyes widen. *That is not part of the plan. You do not admit to weakness.*

His left hand rises, his index finger brushing against her cheek softly. "A child chosen by all four Houses," he sighs, as if under some sort of trance. "A child of suppression, freed and soaring... capable of so much more than anyone knows," he stares up at her.

Mildy squints, leaning forward. *Both of their eyes are **pink**.*

"Her power knows no bounds," he continues. Her toes curl in her shoes when he lifts his head with a wicked smile, his hand dropping back down to his lap. "Her Majesty cannot only siphon power from others," he pushes himself off of the ground once more. Mildy watches with still narrowed eyes as he walks down the steps once more. "She can also temporarily... *gift,* copies of her abilities to others." Windsor lifts a hand and summons a massive ball of fire. His eyes dim, back to cobalt. Mildy's head whips toward Eowyn. Crimson.

Mildy rolls her shoulders and clears her throat. *Not how we wanted to get there, but at least we got there.* Layne Renhart steps to Windsor's right, Bryanna Grisel to his left. Renhart extends a hand, palm facing the ground, and five icicles start to protrude from his fingertips. Bryanna flicks a wrist, the ball of fire blowing out on a gust of hot air that melts the icicles instantly.

Eowyn rises from her throne. "To be Chosen by a House as a babe is cruel," she intertwines her fingers in front of her. "When the bones of your skull solidify, you are either chosen by a magical blood or none at all." She pauses and takes a moment to look at everyone in the room. "I can change that," she smiles sweetly. She takes the first step down. "I give you power, I can show you how to use it, to protect yourself in the event that I fail you." Windsor walks to the edge of steps and reaches for her hand. "Thank you," she says softly as he helps her down the last two. "Windsor and I are not asking you to trust us. We are asking you to trust yourselves. We are asking you to trust yourselves to learn from us and have your own backs. I do not know what my Father is capable of, but I know he must pay for what he has done," her eyes continue to roam over the room. "I know I will not let another soul cross into Gragion because of him. I know I will do everything, including *die,* to save you all from ever feeling the effects of his reign." She snaps her mouth shut before taking a deep breath. Windsor pulls his hand from hers and slides it around her waist, resting on the other hip before pulling her flush against his side. "Our continent has suffered too much in the past seven hundred and sixty eight years since The Mother's disappearance. It is time to end this war once and for all and reclaim the Lost Lands from a Tyrant."

35

E O W Y N

"My Lady," another couple approaches the Queen where she stands at the bottom of the dais.

She smiles and stretches out both of her hands. "Come, come," she motions them closer. Her power swirls through the room, pulling the woes and anxiety from everyone gathered while feeding it to Zanna and the hatchlings. "It is very nice to be meeting so many new faces today. What may I call you?" Her eyes dance between the young couple.

She notes the bits of jewelry on the dark haired woman, not as extravagant as some of the arrogant nobles in the room. She dons a sky blue cotton, off the shoulder gown that ends just before the white cuffs around ankles stemming from her sandals. The man wears a matching button up shirt, and white... army trousers?

"I am Tarbus Tidreda," his voice snaps Eowyn from her revelation. General Tidreda's son. "This is my wife Irina." He gestures to the woman beside him.

Eowyn blinks, the resemblance so astounding. "Tarbus and Irina," she crosses her hands in front of her. "It is so lovely to meet you. Ancel speaks very highly of you both," she looks between them. Her power passed on from her Mother, that of the Planets, reels with the need to manipulate them to what she needs. Windsor's power gently strokes hers, allowing her room to breathe and them the option.

Irina looks from Eowyn, to Windsor who converses with another man beside them, then up at Tarbus. He sucks in a sharp breath as he meets his wife's gaze and nods. He turns back to Eowyn and she gives him a reassuring smile. "We would like to... offer our services," he says with another nod.

"On the front lines," Irina quickly adds.

The Queen laughs, reaching for each of their hands. "We would absolutely love your assistance," she gushes, giving them both a gentle squeeze. "Why don't you find your Father, Tarbus, and ask him to take you to have some breakfast? Windsor and I will be along shortly to discuss how much you wish to be involved and how we can use your aid."

The couple relaxes and they both nod. "Thank you, Your Majesty," they bow to her before starting toward the doors of the hall.

Windsor steps back and places a hand on her back. "Would you like to take a break, my love?" He asks before planting a kiss on her forehead. He pulls back with a sly smile and leans down to her ear. "I've asked Oli to arrange for our breakfast to be in your cove so you could have a few moments of silence," he kisses the side of her face.

Her eyes flutter closed. "That sounds lovely," she whispers, "but..." He straightens and pouts down at her. She opens her eyes and smiles. "I am not ready for a few moments away. Perhaps in a short while," she grabs his free hand and intertwines their fingers.

His fingers gently stroke her back, his other thumb moving across her knuckles. "We have been awake for several hours already, My Empress, and it is only just now nine in the morning," he deepens his pout. "Surely you are ready to sit down briefly?" His eyes dart toward the thrones.

Eowyn leans into him, glancing at the crowd staring at them impatiently. She nods slowly and looks up at him. "I will sit with you for a moment." Her power settles in him, a slight ease washing over the King. "I will sit with you for as long as you need," she whispers, tucking a piece of his shoulder length, black hair behind his ear.

He blows out a relieved breath. "I feel like I'm buzzing right now," he mumbles, his hand on her back gently pushing her toward their thrones. She starts up the stairs. "It's like I can't sit still because you're not," he wraps his arm around her waist and pulls her into his side with a slight roughness she almost melts for. "Right here," he tightens his hand on her hip.

"Well, it's a good thing I'm *right here*," she lays her hand on his and her fingers dance in featherlight strokes on his skin.

"It's not good enough," he grumbles, stretching his fingers to trap her between them.

She can't help but let out a small laugh, leaning further into him once they're in front of the massive chairs. "You are quite needy today," she whispers before lowering herself into her throne. He stands in front of her, staring down at her with the saddest eyes she has ever seen. "What is it?" She frowns back at him. Windsor's shoulders drop and he shakes his head. She arches a brow, an amused smile tugging at her lips. "You're not going to accept this, are you?"

He shakes his head again. "I need more than to sit with my head in your lap," he clears his throat, "please."

"More?" She taps her right index finger on the arm of the chair.

He steps forward, his legs pressed against hers. He stares down at her, eyes wide and pleading. "Please," he repeats, "I just need to be close to you." His voice is the softest she's ever heard, no trace of the King left, just a man desperate for his wife's attention. He swallows thickly, reaching for her hand. "Five minutes, please," he kneels in front of her and presses his lips to her knuckles. "Even if it's just in the corridor, sitting on the floor, me holding you... I need something, Eowyn. I'm...

I feel like I'm going... I feel like I'm going to tear everyone apart if one more person holds your attention longer than I do," he rambles.

"Your Majesties," Ancel Tidreda calls out from the bottom of the dais.

Windsor's eyes fall closed and he sucks in a sharp breath. Eowyn peers over him, bringing her hands up to cup his cheeks. He leans into her touch and sighs. "Yes, Ancel?" She strokes her thumbs across his stubble.

"May I approach?" He looks between the King and Queen. "It is a pressing matter." Eowyn only nods and he skips over the steps. "My King and Queen," he kneels beside Windsor and bows his head. "Perceval Hagan is riding for the border."

Windsor's head snaps up and his eyes shoot open. Eowyn drops her hands to her lap. "How do you know?" She asks quickly, pushing Windsor back as she rises to her feet.

Both men follow suit. "Blaine Cromwell sent word," he discloses.

Eowyn pushes past them both, bounding straight for the doors. The Queen barrels through the crowd and does not look back. Once emerged from the Throne Room, she shifts into the Firebird. She flaps her wings once and lets out a sharp cry. Everyone in the corridor pauses in place and stares at her, wide eyed and open mouthed. She flaps her wings harder, rising over the few lingering citizens before darting out of the Palace doors. A loud roar shakes the ground below her as the Lion emerges a moment later. She unleashes a small line of cobalt magic, a line of his ice stretching from her to him, a way for him to follow.

She shoots higher, flapping faster, positioning herself in the clouds. She glances down at the capital, briefly taking in the bustle of life along the streets. She soars over the lake between Leogar and Shimmerfall, feeling the line pull taught as Windsor goes around the lake, toward Shimmerfall. She lets out a shriek, an ear piercing call to the lion. His returning roar shakes the trees free of birds above him, one dove in particular moving a little too fast toward the Queen. She huffs when she realizes it's Olivette.

Olivette soars just above her, concealed from view as they dive through the mountains. Windsor lets out another ground trembling roar, one to let her know he was right behind her. Her wings beat faster, pushing her closer and closer to the border. Olivette falls back, dipping toward the valley between two of the mountains. Eowyn moves faster, completely disregarding the feeling of the line between her and Windsor snapping as she crosses over the border into Iverness. She doesn't slow, she doesn't drop, she continues to soar over her prison with a purpose.

She lands in the middle of the old Slave Pit behind the castle. The bird lets out a screech, a ring of fire erecting around her. Her form shifts, the bird retracts into herself, a flame engulfing her until she stands in her human form, her hair whipping around her face in the brisk wind. She takes a deep breath, her eyes glowing bright red as she scans the area around her. A dark figure stands atop the highest row of seats, one reserved for the Royal family when the pits were used for fighting before Kanika's takeover. Her eyes blaze knowingly, the fire around her dying out. She takes a step forward.

"You come into my territory as a bird and use your magic to become a Queen," Tabot does not step out of the shadows, merely speaks from the darkness like the coward he is. "Your Mother is dead, Eowyn. Nobody here will protect you anymore, and you came alone." He laughs bitterly.

Eowyn clenches her jaw but doubles down on the grip of her lashing power. "I do not need protection," she says evenly. "I am here to offer you a truce."

He leans over the railing, bracing his hands on the steel bar before him. "A truce?" He snorts out. "You wish me to call a truce with you? If it was up to me, you would've stayed dead when you emerged from the womb, just like your sister." His words strike her in the chest, leaving her almost completely stricken.

She had a sister? One that died during childbirth too? But why does she care when she's never cared about anything. Not besides her Mother, until Windsor.

A sharp pain shoots through the Queen's neck as something clamps around her. She gasps, turning to see Blaine Cromwell behind her, his hands falling to his sides. "I'm... sorry, Your Majesty," he whispers as he steps back.

Eowyn whips her head back toward Tabot. "You have one chance to remove the collar," she seethes, her power beating against the restraint of the Paronia. "Or I will decimate you where you stand," she takes another step closer.

Blaine Cromwell catches her by the arm. "Stay still," he mutters under his breath. "There are a hundred and fifty arrows aimed at you right now."

She rips her arm from him, her stare still on her father. He chortles, "a bird brain *for sure.*" He jerks his chin toward her. "Put her back in her cage," he flicks a hand dismissively.

Blaine grabs her biceps quickly and pulls her back. "You have to trust me, Eowyn. I made a bargain with your Mother," he grips her arms tightly. "Act like the Paronia is working and walk away." Eowyn holds her Father's stare for another long, drawn out moment before nodding. "Come on," he starts backward, pulling her with him.

She turns and allows him to push her toward the Palace. He leads her toward the tunnel entrance, the one that deposits them straight into the dungeons. Her breath catches in her throat when he pushes open the door. He looks back at her, his brown eyes flashing maroon. "You..." she stumbles back, her chest tightening.

"It's okay, Eowyn," he takes a cautious step toward her. "We just have to get you in there and I'll get Windsor," he curls his hand in a *come here* motion.

Her eyes widen. "Windsor?" She blinks, shaking her head frantically. "No, he went to the border. He went to take on Hagan and I... I left him behind," she manages to breathe out beyond the burning in her lungs.

"You need to breathe, sweetheart," Blaine whispers, taking another step closer. Her eyes dart around, almost like she would find Olivette hiding somewhere in the open sky. "Eowyn," he grabs her shoulders. Her gaze moves back to his, eyes wide. "You're okay, you're going to be okay. We just have to get you inside so you're safe until I can get Windsor here."

Her throat tightens even further, "But what if-" she stops short, biting back her tears. She shakes her head again, her hands clenching into fists at her sides. "I... I can't leave him-" she starts.

Blaine drops his hands to his sides and his eyes turn black. "You... Eowyn, do you... feel something for him?" He looks at her, completely shocked by her emotions concerning her husband.

She swallows thickly, her cheeks growing red despite her best efforts to keep her emotions reigned in. Her power is spiraling, swirling, jumping and thrashing at the mention of Windsor. She doesn't quite meet Blaine's eyes, her fingers clenching and unclenching again and again at her sides. "I... I don't know what I feel." She admits, her voice shaky and uneven. "I don't... things feel better with him around," her attention turns to his feet. "And I... don't want... *anything* to happen to him."

Blaine's shoulders sag at her declaration. "Do you..."

Eowyn blocks out the rest of his question, disregarding his words entirely when a sudden realization settles over her. *She has a purpose beyond revenge to live in this realm. Her soul was pulled back to Tretanov to find the missing piece of it. She wouldn't have known peace in Gragion until she'd found a reason to breathe beyond her rage.*

36

WINDSOR

Olivette lands right in front of the lion. He shifts, immediately snapping at her. "Where is she? Why did the line break?" They'd tested it early this morning, Eowyn soaring to the East Coast of Exsar while he ran toward the West. When it didn't break, they'd both deposited themselves into their bedchambers to dress and then into his office. "Oli, why did it break?!" He nearly yells.

She shifts into her human form and brings her hand to her lips to shush him. "She must've broken it," she huffs out. "We tested it. Unless she... went to the Palace," she looks up to Windsor.

He stares back at her, his eyes a simmering icy blue. He feels so empty, feels no trace of her. "She promised she wouldn't break it, promised we'd march together," he turns in a small circle. "She doesn't have HeartSeeker yet. What if she's in danger, Oli?" He stops his pacing and unsheathes ThunderSoul. The haladie vibrates, humming against his fingers. A branch snaps behind him and he whirls with a snarl.

"Well, well... well," Perceval Hagan steps from beyond a line of trees, entering into Exsar. "Look at what the cat brought us, boys," he starts toward Olivette.

"Careful, Percy," Windsor taunts, stepping in front of her. She shifts, the dove immediately darting into the trees. "Touch one of mine and you're going to make me break a promise to my wife." He rolls his neck, ThunderSoul still gripped tightly in his fingers.

He barks out a humorless laugh, starting to circle the King, *in his own territory.* A thin sheet of ice slowly starts to creep along the ground beneath their boots, but Windsor pulls his magic back when Tabot Alnwick steps over the invisible line, marking the border. "You think your promises to your breeder matter?" His colorless eyes pierce straight into Windsor's soul and he has to dig his heels into the ground to keep from shifting and tearing both men to shreds. "You think your breeder is even worth promises?" He snorts out.

"She is not a breeder," Windsor snaps. "She is the Queen of Exsar, regardless of whether or not she bears an heir. And she will be the Empress of the Continent once you are dead." He steps forward, the ice returning around him.

"She is collared in my dungeons and she will be used for the only thing she is good for," Tabot hisses.

Windsor lifts ThunderSoul, only for Perceval to step behind him and grab his wrist. He kicks out one foot, swinging it into Tabot's stomach before turning and uppercutting Perceval's chin. He drops the King's wrist and he takes the opportunity to return to the lion. He grabs the haladie in his jaws before taking off into Iverness. Unsure of what he's going to do, he just runs.

His paws carry him down the same route he'd come down with Eowyn when he'd gotten her out of the dungeons the first time. His claws shred the ground below him. *Gragion, she's probably panicking.* He can only hope that Blaine Cromwell, her *real* Father, has intervened and is keeping her safe. His legs move even faster. *The only thing she's good for? He wasn't going to... no, he had to be speaking of her power. Surely, he wasn't **that** evil.*

A small flutter of lightning appears in front of the lion and he skids to a halt. Ryoko, the bright yellow hatchling from Zanna and Everys, appears before him. He hums out a low growl. Ryoko's small wings flutter and he nods his head the opposite direction, signaling he knows where to go. Windsor huffs again. Ryoko starts to fly through the trees with the lion following closely. He leads the King around the side of the Castle, showing him to a worn dirt and gravel path leading to a rusted door. He slowly trots behind the small dragon while his eyes skate over every inch of their surroundings.

Windsor shifts, dropping ThunderSoul from his mouth and picking it up before sheathing it again. "Go home, Ryoko," he says, reaching for the steel handle of the door before them. The small Dragon nods his head and disappears in another bolt of lightning. Windsor can't help but chuckle softly. "At least you listen better than your Father," he mutters under his breath as he pulls open the door.

A dark, never ending, tunnel stares back at him. His nostrils flare at the scent of burning hair. That's the only confirmation he needs before blindly bolting into the hall, leaving the door to slam behind him. He ignores the sound, ignores every instinct in him that screams to turn around and wait for someone else to be here. But he continues on, following the intoxicating scent of *her*. He comes to an abrupt stop as the tunnel mouth opens into the dungeons. The stench of burning hair is much stronger now, the air thick and acrid with the scent of dying magic. He squints into the darkness, his heart racing with every beat as he tries to spot any movement. No sound. "Eowyn?" He calls out in a shaky voice.

Please please please…

He squints, willing his eyes to flare only once. Unlike the last time he was down here, there is *no* light.

Prince of Gragion, please let me find her. I need to find her. Please let me find her.

He continues to chant the words in his head like a prayer as he continues on. His hands move over the Paronia bars, his rings clanking against the metal. He stops abruptly and wraps his fingers around the bar his hand paused on. It's hot to the touch, like something inside was having a hard time keeping a fire away from prying eyes. "Eowyn?" He swallows thickly, bringing his other hand up to grip the bar next to it. He squints, trying to look into the cell. Her eyes flutter open to reveal those gleaming red irises he'd come to love so dearly. "Baby," he breathes out, instantly icing over the bars before pulling out ThunderSoul and shattering them. Eowyn chokes out a sob when he falls to his knees in front of her. His hands come up and cup the sides of her face. "Are you hurt?" His fingers slide down, pausing on the collar. She shakes her head, her chest heaving with each panicked breath. "It's okay, sweet girl, I'm here," he leans forward and presses his lips to her forehead. "Don't move," he mumbles, stroking her skin before freezing the Paronia necklace. His fingers wrap around it and he pulls it off of her, watching the cobalt line of power sweep the pieces of it away before it hits the ground. He finally pulls back, removing his lips from her head. "We have to get you home," he whispers, bringing his hands back to her face.

Her hands cover his. "We have to kill him, Windsor," she slides her hands down his arms.

He shakes his head. "Absolutely not. We are going to get you *home* and *then* we will march on Iverness. You are not doing this alone," he speaks with finality lacing his tone.

Her fingers wrap around his biceps and she gives him a firm squeeze. "I'm not alone." She leans her forehead against his. "You're here."

He nearly groans at her words, but he kills it deep in his gut before it can bubble up. "Let me get you home, baby. Let me get you to safety and then we can do this like we planned." He pleads with her, to her *soul*. "I know you feel that you need to do it now, but he tried to trap us, baby. He tried and he failed and now we can go home and show him *exactly* how a predator kills its prey." Her jaw clenches and unclenches under his hands, her fingers biting into the fabric of his jacket. "We have to do this right, Eowyn. Not for you or me, not to spare him... For your Mother." Another soft cry pushes past her lips and he nods. "Not for anyone but Alice Azazé of Exsar, a *direct descendant* of the original Infinite bloodline. We need to restore order to Tretanov, Eowyn. You cannot do that if you do not *use* what is at your disposal." He watches her squeeze her eyes shut. She sucks in a deep breath and he presses another kiss to her head. "Come on,"' he pulls away and takes a single step back. She leaps toward him, latching onto the front of his jacket with white knuckles.

Good girl.

He wraps his arms around her tightly. "I'm going to feed you my power, you need to focus enough to use it to get us home. It's going to hurt to Gragion and back, you're going to be extremely exhausted. But the second we are in our territory, I will take care of the rest. Can you do that?" He gives her a reassuring squeeze. She nods, leaning further into him. "I need you to say it for me, sweet thing. Just let me know you're not lost in the trauma," he lifts a hand to tuck a piece of hair behind her ear.

His Queen flashes across the scared features and her chin raises. "I can do it," her grip loosens.

Windsor doesn't waste another moment, his irises glazing into a pearlescent white. She gasps when his magic shoots through her back, immediately finding the shrinking flame within her. It flares, consuming them both in a violet firestorm. Eowyn screams as his ice courses through her veins. He grabs the back of her head and pushes her face into his shoulder. She cries out against him, falling limp as the fire around them dies out.

"I've got you," he grunts, scooping her into his arms. She slings a heavy arm over his shoulder and he nods to himself. He lifts his head to see them at the bottom of their bed, in the pavilion, situated over the pond, in the cove hidden within the Dragon's Quarters, behind their Palace. He breathes out a laugh and sits on the edge of the mattress. He cradles her in his lap. "You did it," he mutters as his arms tense around her. "Are you alright?"

Her eyes remain closed, her arm slung over him. "Mm," she hums in acknowledgment.

Windsor chuckles again and falls back onto the bed, taking her with him. "You are incredible," he exhales while one hand moves to comb through her tousled hair. "All you had to do was get us over the border." He shakes his head with a grin. "I bet you just wanted to be alone with me," he pulls his hand from her hair as he whispers to her.

"I felt like I was dying." His features drop. "You said you live for these moments. Right here. The least I could do was give you one more."

That was it. She needn't say it flat out, that was enough for him.

"Not just getting us here, but the whole time I was Iverness," her voice cracks and he finally looks down at her. Her eyes flash blue before they turn back to red. "When Blaine Cromwell locked me in that cell, I lost all sense of my known reality." His eyebrows shoot to his hairline at her declaration. "I thought rage was the only thing keeping me, keeping Zanna, alive. It was quite odd that Zanna preferred my joy as her lifeline while I still held rage as mine, once she was in Exsar." She clears her throat, tucking her face into the crook of his neck. He leans his cheek on top of her head. "I had just failed to realize how much brighter I burn when the flame is cold," her arm shifts and she strokes the backs of her fingers across his cheek. He allows his eyes to fall closed, utterly unaware of her manipulating his force into a deep slumber.

37

ALICE

I step into the stone Palace, my bare feet cold against the floors. I furrow my eyebrows as I glance around the empty corridors. I turn to my right and start down the long hallway. I take in the simple walls with simple art, paintings of landscapes and such. I make note of the absence of a rug beneath my toes. I walk past several closed doors on either side of me before stopping at the only open door. The last door on the left, just like Eowyn's cell in the dungeons of Iverness. My gaze falls upon a familiar pair of blue irises. "Alice," Prince Ri-Zahn, guardian of the Infinite, smiles broadly. "Welcome to Gragion," he bows deeply at the waist.

Gragion, right. I just crossed the path into the next realm.

"Prince Ri-Zahn," I curtsy as my voice rips through my throat.

Loud footsteps thud down the hallway before three other men rush in. "It is true," the one with emerald gleaming eyes gasps. "Alice Azazè has made the journey," Prince Sihon rushes toward her. Their brothers, Uhzana and Nox, dip their chins in acknowledgement.

"The prophecy is beginning to unravel," Ri-Zahn stands in front of me now.

I furrow my eyebrows. "Kanika's Prophecy?" I shift on my feet. Prince Uhzana steps in front of Ri-Zahn and places a hand on my hip. "Eowyn mentioned something in the Palace in Exsar. That it was crying to get out." I look between the Princes of Gragion, the resting place for souls who have completed their journeys through time.

Uhzana walks me back a few paces and guides me to a comfortable chair. I slump down, looking between my brothers. "Mother's body rests below the drawing room of the Palace our niece resides in." He kneels down in front of me. I look up at Ri-Zahn, Nox, and Sihon. I blink, my soul shedding the amnesia of the last life I lived to recover all those before. "Kataya?" Uhzana draws my attention back to his face. "You are home, yes?"

I nod slowly, "yes." I roll my shoulders and glance around the room. I take in the carvings in the stone, the walls of the Palace we'd carved at the tip of Mount Kiwi, the mountain erected in our grandmother's honor.

"Eowyn and Windsor, they will restore Tunate." I look over at Sihon. "I saw it."

His thin, pale lips spread into a wicked smile. "It is truly a shame, dear sister," he turns on his heels and starts toward the door. "That you did not tell your daughter she and her sister are the only living beings on Tretanov who were born to the Lost Ones." He crosses the threshold into the hallway and closes the door behind him.

I rise from the chair. "I must see Eowyn. How long was my journey?" I look between my other three brothers.

Uhzana's eyes flash brightly and Nox nudges his shoulder. Ri-Zahn scoffs and steps forward. "Too long, sister," he pauses to stare at me for a moment. I take in his near luminescent features, the way his irises almost blend in with the whites of his eyes, if it weren't for the gold rings between them."We have been keeping up with her movements on Tretanov. She and Windsor have unsealed my Trove," he smiles proudly.

"She has been using her manipulation abilities to bend the citizens to her will," Nox mentions. "Sihon finds it amusing that she thinks she is doing the same to Windsor."

I furrow my eyebrows. "She is not?"

He chuckles and shakes his head. "He was waiting for her, he will do whatever she wishes without a thought," his smile broadens. "It is quite entertaining to watch a grown man cry when asked to." My eyebrows jump to my hairline. "Oh yes, his soul jumped to Tretanov too early and now he cannot deny something his other half wants. He has been in pain waiting for her," he moves to place a hand on the small of my back. "Come, let us show you what she is up to now." He pushes me toward the door.

I glance back at my other two brothers to see them falling into step behind us. "Does Ri-Zahn think I should have told her about the House of Shadows?" I ask Nox when we start down the wide walkway, the granite cold against my feet.

"It is your House to do with as you please. The Lost ones are chosen by you and you have not chosen any since Mother died. Until you had children of your own," Uhzana chimes in from behind us. "Though your first daughter does not know she is yours," he clears his throat. "But Eowyn's soul recognizes hers so she is safe."

"Safe?" The word echoes off the walls, the implication that my daughter would leave anyone unsafe causing a wave of heat to brush past us.

"Eowyn's rage will kill many, as Mother's did, as yours did. She, too, will destroy anything in her path to resurrection." Ri-Zahn says nonchalantly. I scoff in return and he laughs. "Dear Katya" he wraps an arm around my waist and leads me into the room of Planets.

Nox closes the door behind us, darkness settling in the room. I look up, watching the universes swirl along the spherical ceiling. I point to a bright star to my right. "I am Katya, Daughter of Kanika, Keeper of the Lost Shadows. Show me Tretanov," I command the stars.

The star enlarges, nearly blinding all of us as it displays the Castle in Inverness. The black granite sucked the light from everything else in sight. I squint, narrowing my attention on Tabot Alnwick, the suppressor in Mother's Prophecy. He sits in his throne, Blaine Cromwell to his left and Perceval Hagan kneels before him. His gravelly voice makes my teeth grind together. "They are setting up a camp in my territory?" He snarls out, his fingers digging into the decorated granite.

"Eowyn's Legion destroyed your base last night. Windsor led the army this morning to set up less than a ten minute ride from Muddyvine," Hagan informs the King of Iverness.

"How many does Eowyn's Legion include?" Blaine steps forward.

Hagan lifts his head. "The bitch and her keeper, plus five," he grits out.

Tabot shoots to his feet, his long, coarse hair swaying behind him in the dim candle light. "Seven took on a hundred and fifty?" He bends his right leg at the knee and shoves it into the General's chest.

"They wield the dead legends, My Lord," he coughs. "She holds the Orb in her hand, she manipulates the lion. I saw his eyes change from blue to red, just like hers, when he ran into Iverness before she disappeared two days ago," he rambles on.

Blaine smirks before rolling his lips and schooling his features. "Legends are dead for a reason, Perceval. Do not *lie* to our King," he bites out.

I feel a sense of pride swell deep in my chest, the way he does his best to put a divide between Tabot and his General. *Soon, his soul will make the journey to live out eternity in Gragion. Soon, I will be with him again.*

The pudgy man rises to his feet, his round face red with anger. "I do not *lie*, Cromwell," he steps up to the Secretary of the State. He looks Blaine up and down once. "The bitch holds HeartSeeker. She is wielding the Orb of life, you must believe me." Hagan whips his head toward Tabot. "Her eyes are changing. I saw her behind a row of soldiers."

That's a trait of the Lost Ones. In order for me to keep my own protected, they were ever changing, never to be one thing. She and her sister are the only two on Tretanov with the blood of all Five Houses, leaving her to be only one of two who can gift her powers from all other houses- completely untamed and unlimited. She knew it, Olivette didn't.

"Is there a way to siphon her power from her as she did to Alice?" Tabot's question makes my skin crawl, my teeth clench together so hard I feel them start to crack.

Hagan smiles wickedly. "It seems her Legion draws their power from her," he lifts his left hand to his heart. "I did my research on those who march with her. Two of them were born only as shifters, one with no magic at all, yet they all seemingly possess the power of all Four Dead Ones.

I flick my wrist almost violently. "Show me Eowyn Exeter of Exsar," I snap at the stars.

Sihon chuckles beside me. "Still as hot headed as ever, Dear Katya," he croons.

I roll my eyes at him, my eyes focused on the whirling landscape as the commanded star starts to swirl through Iverness. Just West of the Iverenese border sprawls hundreds of tents, stretching over ten miles, covering all the land between the border and the villages of Whitbell and Tourfort. Exsarian soldiers move through the villages and the abandoned building, Muddyvine Institute of Magic, scrawled onto the doors. "Why can I not see Eowyn?" I mumble as the star continues to follow the Exsarian Army.

"She does not wish to be seen," Sihon steps to my side. "She has learned how to use her ability to manipulate one's life force to..." He trails off.

I turn my head to look at him, feeling the shadows begin to creep closer. "To what?" A shadow hisses as it curls around my brother's neck.

"Careful, baby sister," he drawls, "your anger is getting the best of you again."

Uhzana steps forward, the display of Ancel Tidreda directing his Troops toward the border behind him. "Eowyn has learned how to manipulate the Planets. She grows stronger by the day. Tabot will never be able to siphon her power, she simply has too much," he lifts his hand and plucks the shadow away from Sihon. "You've done what you needed to on Tretanov. The prophecy will unfold as it should. There is no need for you to be angry with us." Uhzana turns back to me.

"She is my daughter," I snap at him.

All four of my brothers laugh. "No," Uhzana shakes his head, pointing toward the ceiling. Eowyn in front of Windsor, her body clad in a metal dress- war gear fit for a Queen- while he kneels before her. "That," Uhzana points between Eowyn and Windsor. "That is our Mother, come to restore order to Tretanov," he whispers. "Together, they are Kanika, Mother of Tretanov, guardian of *all*."

38

EOWYN

The Queen stands at the entrance of the camp, her heels dug into the dirt on Exsar's side of the border. She stands with her arms crossed over her chest, the iron dress sculpted to her every curve hugs her tightly. "Perceval Hagan stole NightFall," she says to the thousands gathered in the camp on Iverness grounds. "NightBane has been missing for five hundred years," she starts to walk along the edge of the border. "For those of you unaware of what those two things mean, NightFall is a sword made out of Paronia. NightBane was its twin blade, both were left by the last of the pure Blood Planets." She turns and starts the other way, crossing her arms behind her back. "I advise you to steer clear of the General and leave him for me." She pauses exactly where she started. "Am I clear?"

In one swift motion, the *entire* military lowers to one knee. "Yes, Your Majesty!" They chant as one.

She raises her chin, watching as one man rises to his feet among the crowd. Windsor grins lopsidedly, already strutting toward her. "Get up," he commands coldly as he strides through the rows of soldiers. "Get food, get drunk, get rest." He quickly closes the distance between them. He wraps one arm around her waist and pulls her roughly against him. "Tomorrow your Queen gives you orders," he holds her stare as he speaks to the crowd behind him. They take the dismissal as it is, dispersing into the camp. Eowyn tears her gaze from his to watch them retreat. A few started toward the fire pit at the entrance of the camp, gathering around the cold chests containing meat. Her eyes find

Windsor, staring at her again. "Why are you guarded right now?" He grumbles, the lion's claws scratching at her armor.

"Something is trying to manipulate me," she admits. "I can feel it tugging at my... I don't even know what power is what anymore," she scoffs and shakes her head "I can't tell what is crying for release and what needs to be-"

"It's okay, sweet thing. Come with me," he cuts her off, grabbing her wrist and starting further into Exsar. Eowyn glances back at the camp as they retreat with furrowed brows. "Flare Meadowglade was executed while your Mother was still in Exsar. No one in Iverness is capable of even attempting to manipulate you."

She stops, yanking her wrist from him "When?" It comes out almost as a plea. She can feel the way his heart ached at the way the word dripped from her lips, but she doesn't care. He'd been executed half a year ago? Windsor *and* her Mother did not tell her?

"While Alice was here," he turns to face her again. "She did not tell you?" His face scrunches with confusion.

Her rage burns over his ice trying to quell the fire within her. "*You* did not tell me," she grits out, stepping forward. "*You* have been here with me, *she* has not. You did not think it wise to tell me of a significant death before waging a war?" Flames ignite on either side of her, lapping at her legs.

"Eowyn," he steps closer to her, his left hand outstretched. She can feel his magic gathering, can feel him straining as he tries to smother the fire. "Surely, she would've told you if she thought it was important," he flashes her a smile but she can feel the anxiety creeping up his spine.

"*You should have told me.*" Her voice comes out, tasting foreign on her tongue. "*You* are my husband, *you* are the King. *You* should have told me." She feels her skin start to sizzle. She glances down to see his ice start to creep along her skin.

Windsor reaches forward and uses a single finger to tilt her chin so her gaze is aligned with his. She lets out a breath, the flames around her dying out. "There's my girl," he rests his thumb just below her bottom lip. "*I am sorry* I did not tell you of Flare Medowglade's fate. I was under the impression that Alice would tell you and console you," he drags the pad of his thumb along the soft skin of her lip, pulling his ice away from her skin. He leans down and presses his forehead to hers, his hands coming up to cup her face. "I should have told you," he agrees, "please forgive me."

Eowyn clenches and unclenches her jaw under his palms before pulling back. His hands fall to his sides and he stares at her, his irises flaring as he searches her soul, expecting her to sever their tie again. He blinks, his eyes dimming and he looks back to her eyes.

"Your Majesty," Bryanna calls behind the pair. Eowyn turns to glance at her over her shoulder. "Your Legion is gathered in your tent." She says, bowing her head.

"I'll be there in a moment," she quips dismissively. Bryanna simply nods before retreating. Eowyn looks back up at Windsor. She holds his stare for a moment.

He takes a hesitant step forward and places his hands on her hips. He opens his mouth, the plea for her not to shut him out again dancing on his tongue. He shakes his head and sucks in a sharp breath, his forehead falling to rest on top of her head. "Please speak to me. Yell at me. Anything besides silence," he begs, "please."

She wraps her fingers around his wrists, pulling his arms to lock around her waist. "We have a Legion to brief," her fingers trail a wake of blue flames as they dance up to his shoulders.

He nods, an incredulous look taking over his face. Eowyn cocks her head to the side. Within the next heartbeat, his right hand is wrapped around her throat and he's pinning her against the nearest tree. She can't stop the smirk that tugs at the corners of her lips. "Not good enough," he drags his thumb along the length of her neck.

She smiles up at him, tauntingly. He rasps out a chuckle and leans his forehead against hers. "What do you need?" Her palms slither under his tunic, resting on his abdomen. "I can't give it to you if you don't tell me what it is, cub," she whispers. Her flames dance along his cold skin under his garments.

His hand tightens around her neck and he licks his lips. "I don't know, my sweet, *sweet* girl," he grinds his teeth together and inhales deeply. "Gragion, you smell fucking sensational," he groans. Her eyes flutter closed and his jaw clenches at the first sign of her submission. "Are you angry with me?" It comes out as a rough demand rather than a question.

Nonetheless, she gives him a breathless answer, her smile faltering, "yes."

A growl tears through his chest and he squeezes her neck. Her eyes shoot open when he cuts off her oxygen and he snarls at her while his fangs start to form. "Well, I guess *your* Legion will have to wait," he thumps her head back against the tree. "Won't they, baby?" He presses a gentle kiss to her jaw. Her throat bobs against his palm but she doesn't reply. *"Won't. They. Baby?"* He accentuates each word with another jerk of her head. Her eyes close again with a throaty grunt, her second slip up. Windsor relaxes his grip, only slightly. "I've got you now, sweet Vermillion, don't I?" He drags his hand down the front of her, slipping it behind her back and unlatching the first hook of her armor.

"Yes," she concedes, "you've got me." She opens her eyes and looks up at him.

His tongue glides along his top row of teeth in a feral display as he unclips the last two fasteners. "I know," he lifts the steel dress off of her shoulders and places it on the ground next to them. "I just like hearing you say it," he chuckles, skidding his hands along the outside of her legs while slowly straightening. Eowyn's eyes drop to his fangs before jumping back to his. "Don't worry," he wraps a hand around her thigh. "After..." he yanks her leg up to rest on his hip. "Forty-four days and nights without you, every single piece, down to the rawest part of you, I'll be bleeding you dry for a good few months."

Eowyn smirks, moving to start unbuckling his belt. "I thought you were too preoccupied running through the forest and plotting with Blaine Cromwell where to set up our camp to count the days," she teases, unfastening the belt and reaching for the button of his trousers.

"Yes," he unleashes his claws and digs them into the skin of her backside. "I was," he watches the Queen tighten her legs around his waist and reach under her thighs to shove his pants toward the ground. "That doesn't mean I didn't count all one thousand and sixty two hours I was away from you," he drops her slightly, flawlessly sinking himself into her. She whines, her hands flying to his shoulders and tearing at the skin of his traps. "Doesn't mean I didn't count every single second I could've been with you," he shoves her back against the tree again, his grip moving up to her hips.

Eowyn leans back, her gaze dropping to where he sits inside of her. Her power coils around his happily, making him grit his teeth and hiss at her. She cocks her head to the side again, tauntingly. She clenches her thighs around him, her arms moving to grip the tree branch above her. She locks her fingers on top of the branch and lifts herself slightly before sinking back down onto him. "Got you now, don't I?" She repeats the motion once, then twice, then a third time.

He leans up and captures her lips with his. Her arms fall from the tree limb and it takes him all of thirty seconds to drop to the ground, sitting on his knees with her riding his lap. "I don't need to be caught," he mumbles against her while he guides her hips. "But what I do need..." he slides one hand to the small of her back and pushes her until her chest is against his. He doesn't continue, just stares up at her with parted lips and ragged breaths as she circles her hips.

"What do you need?" She threads her fingers through his hair and repeats the motion, tilting his head back even more so she could see his entire face.

He groans, his eyes fluttering closed. "More," ice bites into the skin of her back as he holds her in an attempt to fuse their bodies together. "I need everything from you, Eowyn," he drops his head to her shoulder. The Queen shifts her right leg, untucking it from under her and laying her foot flat in front of her with her bent knee pressed to her chest. She lifts her hips up, holding herself there for a long moment. Windsor hooks his fingers under her knee and pulls her leg onto his shoulder. She huffs out a laugh when she collapses onto him. Her hands tighten in his hair. "I need..."

Eowyn gasps as he thrusts up, one hand holding her leg on him and the other holding her waist tightly. "Winnie," she moans quietly. "I can't give it to you if I don't tell me what it is," she pulls his lips back to hers. He grunts, digging his claws into her skin. His fangs slice open the thin skin of her bottom lip. He sucks it into his mouth, pushing into her even harder. She whimpers and he lets out another feral sound before releasing her lip.

"I need to watch you fucking burn Iverness to nothing," he pants, using his grasp to move her with him. His eyes meet hers, effectively pulling all of the oxygen from her lungs once more. "And then I'm going to need to bring you home," he kisses her chin. "And tie you to the bed until you're swollen with my child." Her eyes flare crimson before flashing violet. She watches his blaze in acknowledgement and he grins before their irises dim to their normal colors. "What part of that excited you, pretty girl?" He dips his head back down to nip at her collarbone.

She lets out a shaky breath as he slows his rhythm. "All of it," the admission pushing past her lips, as if instinctually, makes her physically relax.

Windsor straightens his neck, sliding his hand up her spine to grip the base of her neck. She leans back into his grip and stares up at the branches above them. His other hand retracts his claws before sliding down the outside of her thigh, the rocking of his hips slowing by the second. "All of it?" He whispers, drawing another low whine from his wife. "Tying you down and keeping you there until I say otherwise?" He uses his index finger and thumb to massage the base of her skull. "The thought of me claiming you in such a... a *primal* way?" She belts out a cry of pleasure when the words tumble so sweetly from his mouth. "Or is it the idea of you having absolutely no responsibility and knowing I'll take care of you?"

"All of it," she reaffirms earnestly, clenching around him while he moves in and out of her.

"That's my girl," he holds her tighter, the pace of his thrusts increasing with each breath once again. "You let go for me, okay, sweet thing? Let go, baby." He coaxes her climax straight from the heat pooling in the pit of her stomach.

Her fingers clench and unclench in his hair as her core pulsates around him, a string of hushed moans and whines falling from her lips. He lets out a sharp, animalistic growl before she feels his seed seep into her. Another soft sound escapes her as she completely relaxes against him. He slows to a stop but never lets go. She clenches and unclenches her jaw while he smirks, feeling her jaw move against his hand. Her own movements steady on his lap and once they stop, he lowers her leg back to the ground.

Eowyn hums as he circles his hips gently, an attempt to feed the hunger blazing within her. "I'm so proud of you," he tucks a piece of hair behind her ear. "So much blood," he rubs his hands along the backs of her thighs and gathers the red trickles before bringing them to his lips and sucking them clean. "So many wounds that wouldn't kill you if I refused to close," he runs his fingers over the marks he'd made.

Eowyn huffs out a response, her head dropping to his shoulder. The saliva on his fingers seals the cuts while he uses one arm to hold her to him by her waist, the other reaching for her armored dress. He pulls it to his side before wrapping his other arm around her, their panting breaths the only sound between them.

"Your Majesty?" Layne Renhart's voice echoes through the trees.

"Fuck off, Renhart," Windsor calls back, shifting to sit with his back against the tree. "We'll be there in a moment." Eowyn repositions on his lap, sliding him out of her and settling back down on his thighs. "Careful, baby," he kisses her forehead. "Move too much and you'll drip our children onto my legs."

39

EOWYN

The King and Queen step into the massive tent. Waryam, Evangeline, Olivette, Layne, Bryanna, and Ancel stand stiffly in front of a long table with eight chairs positioned around it. As one, they lower to one knee and bow their heads. "Our Empress," Bryanna lifts her head while the others stay where they are. Eowyn lifts her chin slightly in acknowledgment. "HeartSeeker has been uncovered."

Eowyn rolls her neck, clicking her tongue. "Where is it?" She watches the six of them rise to their feet.

Ancel Tidreda steps forward. The Queen watches him walk past her and Windsor. He stops in front of the flaps of the entrance to the tent. She smirks as he balls his hands into fists and uses his power to manipulate the terrain below him. The ground shifts slightly and rocks of all shapes and sizes emerge from the dirt, perfectly arranging themselves to create a stone wall before him. He turns back to face his King and Queen. He gestures toward the table. Eowyn diverts her gaze to the long wooden surface where the rest of the Legion now sits. Windsor steps behind her and grabs both of her hips, pushing her toward the head of the table. Layne snickers as they walk by, earning an elbow into his shoulder. He sits up straighter and everyone watches their Queen sit down.

Waryam places a sheathed sword, the blade nearly as long as Eowyn's arm, with a hilt made of what could only be Vosmium- an ashen metal not mined since Kanika's children disappeared seven hundred and sixty seven years ago. Her eyes move over the white metal, taking in the intricate spirals carved into it. Her skin grows hot and she starts to blink rapidly, gripping the arms of the chair tightly. Something inside of that needs her and it's coiling around her.

"Eowyn," Windsor snaps his fingers in front of her face.

She sucks in a sharp breath, exhaling shakily. When she looks up at him, the jewel in the hilt catches her eye. She shoots up from the chair and lunges onto the table. She grabs the hilt, yanking it closer to her face. *Not a jewel.* A small, gold, iridescent shard lays in the center of the cross-guard just before the blade begins. She runs her thumb over it and it glows gently. "Windsor," she whispers, her attention glued to the sliver of the Gold Pearl. It purrs to life, a soft shimmering purple flowing under the surface of the glitter. Windsor wraps his hand around the sheathe and pulls it off of the pure gold blade. Her breath hitches when a string of violet sparkles emerges from the shard of the Pearl that gave Kanika her power. It wraps around her and Windsor, whispering a soft *watch out* between them.

Eowyn opens her mouth to respond, but a male's voice shouts through the camp, "INVASION!" Both of their attention whips toward the crumbling stone barrier. General Tidreda pushes past them with Layne and Bryanna hot on his heels. Windsor fights against the violet thread binding him to his wife when Waryam, Eve, and Oli take off behind them.

Finally, the power dissipates. They both drop the sword and look at each other with wide eyes and parted lips. Windsor blinks, a deep growl rumbling in his chest. He pushes past Eowyn and walks toward where ThunderSoul lays on a velvet bench. She watches him grab it and latch it onto his belt in one swift motion before scooping *Desolation of the Cosmos* off the ground.

Waryam had presented his younger brother with the most powerful weapon left behind in the Weapons Catalog of the House of the Planets. The white steel handle stretched into three glass looking icicles protruding from an Ice Crystal, a stolen artifact of the Infinite. Waryam and Eve were the only two, like Eowyn, not surprised to find that new icicles start to form- extending the weapon- when in Windsor's hands. Layne, Olivette and Bryanna had been stunned.

Eowyn shakes herself back to reality as she watches her husband leave the tent.

Grab me, child. She glances back at HeartSeeker and snatches it off the table. *Don't forget little meteor,* it sings when she slides it onto her back. She clenches her jaw and grabs the dagger Gideon had left for her the day Tabot tried to shoot her out of the sky.

She pushes out of the flaps of the tent and glances toward the hilltop behind the camp where a line of soldiers stand with binoculars.

Windsor staggers out of the soldiers' temporary barracks and meets the Queen's eyes. He turns, bolting toward the front of the camp. Eowyn dashes after him, summoning her wings. "Stay back," Windsor growls when she falls into step beside him.

She wills her legs to move faster, keeping up with him, even through the protest of her burning muscles. "I will do no such thing," she snaps. Her blood begins to simmer when her eyes land on who leads the Invernese army toward them. *Perceval fucking Hagan.* Rage courses through her and ignites her entire hands with large flames.

"That is an *order*," Windsor barks, his voice cutting through the ringing in her ears while he raises a cage of ice around her.

Eowyn slams into the bars, falling onto her backside. She grumbles lowly and lights the ground around the enclosure on fire. She watches angrily as Windsor charges for the opposing infantry, alone. The heat melts the ice enough for her to shoot to the sky, flapping her wings as hard as she can.

"Fall back!" The King orders his approaching militia behind him. He continues running as fast as he can toward General Hagan and Tidreda falls into pace with the King, half shifted into the centaur that the blood of the Shifters had chosen when he was gifted with Eowyn's power. "Stay with me, Ancel." The General beside Windsor nods as they charge on.

"Kill them all!" Hagan shouts. "But save the bitch Queen for me!" The opposing army cheers animalistically and starts forward, swords drawn and aimed toward the moon.

Windsor sucks in a sharp breath and halts. Tidreda skids on his hooves, shifting back into his full humanoid form. He falls onto the grass and looks back at Windsor. The ground below them rattles and Iverness' army pauses when a feral scream erupts from Windsor's chest. His eyes begin to shimmer before glowing white, his pupils reduced to pinholes. Tidreda drops his gaze from the King's face as the light from his eyes shines even brighter. He slowly raises his arms from his sides until they are stretched over his head.

Eowyn hovers above, watching the ground split below her husband. An army of *dead* soldiers rise from the cracks in the surface of Tretanov, most of them nothing but half degraded bones. "No one makes it out alive," Windsor's voice booms, a low command rumbling through the atmosphere.

General Tidreda's hands rise toward Eowyn. His power pulls rocks from the dirt almost magnetically and he manipulates the formation into a platform above the enemy. The army of dead soldiers hobble toward the Ivernese troops, bones clacking on their way. Eowyn watches them move as she lands on the platform. She poises herself perfectly before diving into the heart of her Father's drunken, brainless, good for nothing, pathetic excuse of an army. She lands on her feet and unsheathes Heartseeker, expanding her wings as far as they would stretch. She lets out a feral snarl when she steps behind Perceval.

He turns slowly with a laugh. "And the bitch came to me," he raises his eyebrows at her, looking her up and down. "My, my, don't you look confident with a blade." His eyes fall to the hilt and widen. "Is that...?" He takes a half step backward.

Eowyn wastes no time, using his shock against him and starting toward him. He quickly recovers, pulling the black steel sword from his own sheathe at his side. Eowyn lets out a grunt and swings toward him. He uses his blade to block her attack and jabs it toward her. She jumps back, hissing as the tip of the blade grazes her partly exposed thigh. He lunges forward accompanied by a frustrated show of his teeth.

Eowyn flaps her wings once, laughing bitterly as he misses her entirely. "Getting soft, old man?" She taunts through gritted teeth. She takes another swing from the air, clenching her jaw even tighter when he drops to the ground. She glances around, noticing the absolute havoc the dead soldiers are wreaking on Iverness' army.

"Just warming up," he scoffs, jumping up from the ground as she lands on the grass once more, her attention back on the arrogant prick in front of her. He swings at her shins. She holds Heartseeker tighter, jumping into the air and bringing her knees to her chest. She extends both of her legs mid air and both boots collide with Hagan's face. She shifts mid-air, landing on her knees with the sword still in her hand. She rises and lunges for the black sword, fallen beside Hagan's delirious head.

She stands over him, a foot on either side of his shoulders. "Say hello to Kanika for me," she snarls before plunging his own sword into his eye. She breathes heavily, gasping for breath as she looks around. Half of the Ivernese Army is torn to ribbons, their intestines sprawled all over the field. The frost bitten glass is now painted the same color as her irises, a sight that made the fire in her flare once more. General Tidreda lunges toward his King. Windsor's pupils dilate slightly as he focuses on Ancel. "What?" He snaps, his tone still low and guttural.

"Queen Eowyn is in there."

Windsor immediately drops his arms, his eyes simmering before the glow dies completely. He blinks and his eyes shift to blue as he scans the scene before him. The dead soldiers fall to the ground, leaving a quarter of Iverness' Troops standing between him and Eowyn. He drops to one knee, punching his fist into the ground. Tidreda takes several steps back as the ground encasing the battle starts to freeze over under a sheet of ice.

Eowyn glances down to see the ground ice over. She sucks in a breath and sheaths Hagan's sword, NightFall, where HeartSeeker once sat. She clutches Heartseeker in her hand, closes her eyes and demands the ice below her to erupt into flames. The entire battlefield goes up in flames and the remaining soldier's screams make her... *laugh.*

"Your Majesty," a group of soldiers comes running toward Windsor. "The Queen..." the man in the front stares at the flames, watching his ruler go up in flames.

Windsor stares at the fire with a smirk. "I know," he says smoothly.

An ear piercing shriek makes everyone wince... *Everyone besides Windsor.* His eyes follow the Phoenix from the bright red flames to the night sky. The soldiers eyes widen and they all crane their necks to see the bird soar through the sky triumphantly. Eowyn lands beside Windsor, chirping her melody to shift back. The soldiers cheer loudly, whether it was for the victory or the King and Queen sparing their lives so effortlessly, no one knew.

"We invade tomorrow," Eowyn says, silencing the crowd. "Get as much rest as you can, tomorrow, Tabot dies," she seethes out.

The troops before them start to disperse immediately at her command. Eowyn turns to Windsor, her arms crossed over her chest while it heaves with ragged breaths. "Any other secrets you wish to tell me?" She raises her eyebrows expectantly.

"You're one to talk," The King snorts and starts toward the massacre. She follows him through the bodies. "Besides," he kicks the decapitated head of an Ivernese soldier. "What's the fun in that?" He nudges her shoulder with his. Eowyn breathes a soft laugh from her nose. She stops walking when she sees one of the dead Windsor rose to defend the camp. He falls to her side. "What's wrong?" He inquires, watching as she squats to the corpse.

She lifts a small, copper badge from the tattered suit. She studies the badge and rises to her feet. Windsor places his hand on the small of her back, coming up behind her to pear over her shoulder. "I think it's some sort of... identification badge," she lifts it to his face.

He keeps his hand on her back while raising the other to grab the copper. His fingers burn on her skin, so cold that his skin sizzled when it touched her sparking fingertips. He drops his hand to his side, clutching the medal in his fist. "You're angry," he flicks his thumb along the burned skin of his index finger.

"So are you," she steps back.

His eyes roam her face, taking in every detail and clenching his fist tighter. "Are you angry with me?" He cocks an eyebrow. She nods once, holding her chin higher. "For telling you to stay back?" He takes half a step forward. His eyes drop to the growing line of ice behind her. She turns to glance a moment too late. He shoots up a frozen wall, ten feet high. He presses his chest to hers and pins her against it. Her eyes morph from blood red to gold when they meet his. He brings a hand up to her neck and wraps it around her throat. "I gave you an order," he bares his teeth, staring at her lips. "I will *never* order you to do *anything* unless your life is in danger." He glances back to her eyes, a wicked smile spreading across his face as he sees pools of gold blossoming in her irises. "*You alluring... Little... Minx.*" He tightens his fingers around the sides of her neck, careful not to put too much pressure on her windpipe. Eowyn holds a blank facial expression as he leans in, his nose brushing against hers. "Are you enjoying this?" An involuntary shiver wracks through her. He laughs and she successfully suppresses another shiver when his hot breath fans her lips. "You are," his eyes gleam with curiosity. "You like being angry with me, like making me defend myself," he presses a soft kiss to the tip of her nose.

"Why are you angry with me?" She breathes out, laying her palms flat against the wall of ice. Water begins to coat her hands while she melts the structure behind her, dripping into her boots.

He pulls back slightly. "I gave you an order," his eyes drop to her mouth again. "You went against the King's order." His gaze flicks back to hers. Eowyn tenses under his intense stare, a muscle in her jaw ticking. "You almost died." She shoves his chest. He chuckles as he steps back, raising his hands in mock surrender. "Do you want to spar over it, darling?" He taunts.

Eowyn rolls her eyes. "I killed Hagan," she snaps. "I wouldn't say that's *almost* dying."

"The attitude says you want to spar," he drawls, lowering himself into an attack stance. She hesitates, really not wanting to prove him right, but leans back in her own stance. "There's my fiery girl," he smiles broadly. She lunges toward him and he grabs her wrist, twisting it behind her back and pulling her to his chest. "You know the rules," he says into her ear. "No one swings until they say something on their mind." He gently shoves her away.

Eowyn spins to face him, dropping back into her pose. "Why do you assume I can't handle myself?" She asks, dropping to the ground and sweeping under his legs.

He jumps, laughing as he avoids her leg. "I do not assume anything about you, My Empress," he laughs. He lunges toward her, wrapping his arms around her waist and tackling her to the ground. He pins her wrists above her head, kneeling beside her. "The only thing I saw when you ran up beside me was Hagan holding your head with your blood still steaming," he stares into her eyes. "That's why I did not want you going."

"You put me in a cage," she pushes against his grip.

He lets go and she sits up. He lays his left hand on the ground on the other side of her legs. "I..." He swallows thickly before nodding. "I did."

She stares at him, completely unsure of what to say now. She's hurt and angry and... *betrayed*. But surely, she cannot be betrayed by someone she does not-

"I'm sorry," he moves to kneel over her legs, straddling her shins. He places a palm on each of her thighs. She lifts her head to look at him. "I did not want to cage you. I wanted to keep you *safe*." She can feel the honesty dripping from his pores. "I'm sorry, Eowyn. I'm so sorry," he whispers. "My caging you was not my fear of *you*, it was my fear of **losing** *you*."

40

WINDSOR

"I forgive you."

The three words continue to burn themselves into the King's brain as he helps his wife off of the ground.

"I forgive you."

He'd done something so unspeakable, something so impulsive, and risked his wife's *mind*. She would've been rendered useless during the battle, had his actions pushed her into the panicked state he'd seen her in when she flew into Iverness, only to be collared and thrown back in the dungeons. But she *forgave* him.

"Your Majesties." The way Eowyn stops and goes rigid before stepping closer to him, makes his arm slide around her back and grip her opposite hip. "It seems I am... too late," Blaine Cromwell says behind them.

Windsor turns, dropping his arm from around her. She doesn't move with him so he uses the other arm to do the same thing as before, only across the front of her. He tugs her into his side and smiles when her arm wraps around him in return, holding him the same way. Except, she seems to grip him to keep herself grounded. His thumb rubs gentle circles over her armor. "It appears so," Windsor muses. "Perceval Hagan is dead."

Cromwell's eyes widen. "He's... *dead*?" His tone is laced with shock and disbelief.

Before he knows what's happening, Eowyn whirls to face her *actual* Father and presses the tip of HeartSeeker into the side of his neck. Cromwell's eyes widen and dart to Windsor. "Don't look at him," she snaps, withdrawing NightFall from her back and stabbing it into the ground between them. "He does not control me. He cannot help you." Blaine flinches at her tone.

The King smiles proudly and crosses his arms over his chest, widening his stance. Blaine gulps, shifting his attention back to Eowyn. "Your Majesty," he raises his hands over his head. "Please, I only wish to speak with you. We can speak here, you may take my weapons... Gragion, strip me down to my undergarments. But I must speak with you." Windsor can feel the man's desperate tone chipping away at the Queen's resolve. "Please, Eowyn," his shoulders slump, almost defeatedly.

Windsor studies the side of his wife's face. *"Do not hurt him,"* the sword coos to her.

She slowly lowers HeartSeeker, her eyes still narrowed on Cromwell. "Speak," it's more than a verbal command, her magic wrapping around his soul and forcing his words out.

"Alice and I met the same day her and Tabot did," he rushes out. "He courted her, she was truly in love with him. After they wed and were crowned, he outlawed magic."

Windsor watched Eowyn carefully, his power tugging at hers. She doesn't budge, not physically or otherwise.

"He became... violent toward your Mother." He continues, "I intervened once. He cut off my wings." Eowyn stiffens and Blaine nods. "I am a raven shifter. He clipped my wings and Alice made me strike a bargain to never do it again."

"Why did you take it?" Eowyn snaps. "I would've had my wings clipped ten times over for her." Her face remains blank but the fire in her fights against Windsor's ice that holds it.

His eyes widen as Eowyn forces Cromwell to his knees. He belts out a pained groan when he collapses onto the ground. "I did it because the woman I loved asked me to," he looks up at Windsor. "I put my life on the line for the woman I loved because she simply asked." Windsor dips his chin in a nod and the man looks back to Eowyn. "Trust me, Eowyn, I wouldn't have made the bargain if I knew she was pregnant with your sister."

Windsor tenses, feeling Eowyn's power take a dip. He looks over at her and she stares at Blaine blankly, but her power retreats into her. "Eowyn," Windsor steps forward and reaches a hand out.

"I don't have a sister," she raises HeartSeeker and levels it in front of his right eye.

"You do," he whispers desperately, tears streaming down his face. "Alice and I welcomed a baby girl seven years before we knew she was pregnant with you," he wipes his cheeks, unflinching when the back of his hand scrapes against the tip of the blade. "I... brought her over the border when she was born. No one knew Alice was pregnant besides myself and Charlotte." Windsor clenches his jaw when he realizes Eowyn is shutting her emotions down before they can bubble up. "I savored every moment I had with your Mother, Eowyn," he chokes on a soft cry. "Every kiss in the empty hallways, every night I was able to spend with her in her chambers, every moment I got to spend with *you*."

Eowyn's spine snaps straight, his words striking the memories they needed to. Windsor watches her drop the sword to the ground and take a trembling step backward. He steps behind her, his hands on either hip. "You..." she breathes out.

Cromwell looks up at her, new tears replacing the streaks on his face. "I am so grateful for every moment she allowed me to be a part of, with you, Eowyn." He smiles sadly. The Queen shakes her head slowly. "Did you read the journals your Mother left you? She details every moment the three of us shared as a family."

"I... can't read them," she grits out. "I'm not ready."

"And you don't have to," Blaine steadily rises to his feet, his eyes flicking to Windsor over her shoulder. He nods once, letting him know he may proceed. "You don't have to do anything you don't want to." He bends at the waist, holding Eowyn's gaze as he grabs HeartSeeker by the blade and holds the handle to her. She leans back into Windsor's chest and wraps her hand around it. "You invade Iverness tomorrow," he pulls his hand from the metal. "You are not alone, Eowyn."

She blinks, doesn't move or even breathe for a moment. She holds his stare as she sheaths HeartSeeker. He smiles, reaching for NightFall. He pulls it free and turns to hand it to his daughter. Windsor gasps when she drops to the ground, outstretching her leg to sweep Cromwell's feet out from under him. He lands on his backside with a grunt. Eowyn jumps up and brings her left foot up to knock his shoulder back. Her foot pins him to the ground and she holds NightFall to his throat. "If Tabot flees or prepares for my invasion in any way, I will personally tear you limb from limb." She slides the tip of the blade down the length of his neck, not cutting deep enough to kill but enough to hurt and bleed like a river. "Consider that your only warning." She steps back and wipes his blood off of the blade.

He brings his hand up to his neck, dropping his eyes to the ground and nodding. "Thank you, Your Majesty," he mumbles.

Windsor watches Eowyn turn and walk back toward their camp. He waits a moment, just following her with his eyes to see if she would look back, but she doesn't. He sighs and extends a hand to Blaine. "She would not have spared you if she truly did not believe you," he helps him to his feet. "Here," he touches the man's neck with an iced over index finger, sealing the wound with a combination of his and Eowyn's magic.

"Thank you," he clears his throat. "She will do well, I know it. I can feel it. I can feel her-her power. It's radiating off of her, almost toxically," he rambles, staring in the direction she disappeared into moments ago. "I pray to the Mother and the Princes of Gragion that she can feel that too." He looks back to Windsor.

Windsor grins, "she likes to be told how powerful she is." He crosses his arms over his chest, the sentence being spoken both aloud and down their mental bond.

Thunder rumbles in the distance, making Blaine bark out a chortle. "Alice had spoken of a new form of communication sprouting between you two," he grins, "I truly hope to hold the honor of witnessing it flourish."

"You spoke of journals Alice left my wife," Windsor circles back, kicking his heels against the grass. "How important is the information in them to her calling?" His eyes meet Cromwell's again, flashing a deep purple.

Blaine leans forward, his eyes narrowing slightly. "You are shifting your power back and forth?" He looks over the King. "Your magic is twining?" He stares at Windsor, almost in awe.

"The journals. How important are they?" He demands, pushing aside a limp body and sitting down in front of the other man. He was not going to tell anyone outside of their Legion that she *could see through* his eyes.

He clears his throat, gesturing to the ground next to Windsor. He nods once. Blaine kneels beside him, his hands folded in his lap. "The journals are not pertinent to her success. They are a tool to help her cope with her Mother's departure toward the path to Gragion," he discloses.

The King nods, leaning back on his palms. A short, tense silence falls between them. Windsor glances over when he senses the male's heartache. *Thank you, Eowyn.* "Do you think Alice has made it to Gragion yet?" He nudged Cromwell with his elbow.

"One can only hope," he looks to the stars. "I truly hope that her soul may now rest and she does not need to live another life." He clenches and unclenches his jaw as he speaks. Windsor studies the man by his side. He knew of everything he'd told Eowyn, Alice had told Windsor long ago. "Would you check on Eowyn?" Blaine looks at him again.

Windsor meets his eyes and nods. "Of course," he turns and starts to walk away. "We'll see you tomorrow, Raven!" He calls over his shoulder before bursting into a sprint, weaving through the massacre to get back to the camp.

I wonder where my pretty little bird ran off too. She probably went to spar with Bryanna to clear her thoughts.

He smiles when he sees small groups of soldiers scattered throughout their temporary living quarters. He takes in the sight of a group sitting by a fire, no more than ten of them gathered with mugs of *aqua vitae* between their hands. His eyes drift to the posts where the horses are tied. He furrows his eyebrows when he sees Layne and Bryanna sitting in front of the trough full of hay. His feet start toward them on their own volition, drawing their attention.

"Your Majesty?" Bryanna straightens while Layne remains slack by her side.

Windsor takes a seat on the other side of her. "Lady Bryanna," he nods in greeting, "Layne."

His best friend leans forward and shoots him a quick smile before settling back against the trough again. "I can't believe you raised an army of dead," Layne huffs out. "You said you'd never use that magic." His tone holds accusations and animosity.

"This is war," Bryanna cuts in. "We do things we never thought we would." Windsor's eyes widen slightly. He quirks a brow, pulling from a string of Eowyn's magic to manipulate a *living* being this time. "I was content running my saloon, Charlie and I were perfectly fine. But then...

Her Majesty crossed the border," she shrugs, looking at Windsor now. "It's like she calls us to something higher, calls us to a greater place. I'd sworn I didn't want to be a mage, didn't want to learn or wield... but Her Majesty is..." she trails off, looking down at her lap where her fingers twist nervously.

No matter how much of her power I summon, the King thinks to himself, *I will never be able to take on the burden of another's emotions the way she can.*

Layne slips his hand between Bryanna's and locks his fingers around hers. She looks over at him and he smiles at her, his eyes then moving to Windsor. "Her Majesty calls us to a higher standard," he finishes her sentence. "She pushes us to be better, to be worthy of serving her, without even knowing she's doing so."

Windsor's heart pounds in his chest, the lion clawing to get out and bask in the way they praise his wife.

"She *loves* so fearlessly," Bryanna nods to herself, looking down to her and Layne's intertwined hands.

"She believes herself to be incapable of love," Windsor says bluntly, running a hand through his hair.

Bryanna breathes out a laugh and shakes her head. "I know," she meets the King's gaze once more. "That does not mean that she *is* incapable of it. While you were here, planning with Blaine Cromwell and she believed you to be missing..." she shakes her head again. "She cried, she screamed, she destroyed things, and then she went silent. She was grieving *you.* You cannot grieve the absence of something you do not love."

41

EOWYN

Eowyn stares upward in the darkness, her mind nearly crumbling.

Tabot is not my Father. No, his Secretary of The State- now General of his Army- Blaine Cromwell is. No wonder Tabot hates me, technically I'm not even royalty. That would mean Windsor and I should not be married. I'm sure High Priest Xago will grant him an annulment, seeing as though I did commit fraud.

Windsor shifts behind her, moving closer and wrapping his body around hers. His large hand flattens against her stomach and he presses his lips to the back of her neck. "Why are you still awake?" He tugs her so that she is snuggly pressed against his chest. She just shrugs against him, the silent tears having already soaked her pillow. He sighs and presses his face into the crook of her neck. "You've not said a word since you've spoken to Blaine. I'm starting to worry about what's going on in that phenomenon of a mind you have." His lips move along her skin as he speaks. The Queen squeezes her eyes shut, her features pulling with the force of her scrunched face.

*I'm going to war with a man who downright hates magic, hates **me**. That's probably why he hates me, because he knows I'm not his. That's probably why his only goal from the moment I was born is to end me.*

"Eowyn," Windsor momentarily pulls her from her trampling thoughts again, propping himself up on one arm to look down at her. She doesn't acknowledge him, doesn't even open her eyes.

I was never even technically a Princess. Gragion, am I even actually a Queen?

Eowyn gasps as she's shoved roughly onto her back. Her eyes shoot open and she sucks in a burning breath.

Was I not breathing?

Windsor is holding himself above her, his eyes glowing dimly as they scan over her face. "You're spiraling right now," he says so matter-of-factly, she belts out a sob. "Oh, baby," he breathes out and positions himself on his knees between her thighs. He gently grasps both of her shoulders and pulls her to sit up. Her body feels excruciatingly heavy, each breath searing a path up her windpipe. "Sweet girl, I need you to breathe for me," his palms glide over the skin of her shoulders, then the sides of her neck, and up to her cheeks. "One big breath, all right? That's it, just one." He holds her face in place. "Can you do that, baby? Can you breathe?" She nods in his hands and sucks in another shallow breath. "There she is," he sighs, sitting back on his heels and dropping his hands to rest on her knees. "One more for me? Just to let me know you're here with me," his whisper is like a desperate plea to her soul. She closes her eyes and takes another breath, then another. Windsor sits there silently for a moment, his hands lazily massaging over the soft skin of her thighs. Eowyn drops her chin to her chest and her eyes fall closed again.

*My own Mother didn't even tell me. Why would she? She didn't even tell me Head Master Meadowglade was executed and I was **married** when that happened. Why would she tell me that I'm a bastard child if she couldn't even tell me the only friend I'd known in Iverness was dead?*

"Eowyn, please," she can hear his voice, can feel his hands tensing on her legs like he's trying to pull her out of her mind.

*Had she even known? She had to have known, he said they'd been lovers since she married Tabot. But how can I trust anything Blaine says? It's not like my Mother is here to confirm, nor deny **any** of it.*

322

"Fuck it." Windsor's voice echoes in her ears before his magic starts to pull at hers.

*And I had a sister that was sent over the border before me? That **nobody** else knew about? Who was seven years older than me? Was that who Windsor was betrothed to before me? Is that why no one spoke of it? People probably found out that she was a bastard and shunned her or... worse.*

Windsor's power pulls and cries. He holds her trembling body against him tightly. He'd pulled her in between his legs and she curled into herself, hugging her knees to her chest. She's completely silent, save for a few sputtering breaths every so often, and she keeps her face buried against her knees. "Give me something," he beseeches. "Fucking Gragion, Eowyn, let me know you're in there."

*It doesn't matter. He is mine. Mine is **mine**. I don't let go of mine... right? It seems I've never truly had anything that is mine. My Mother was mine, but she... she wasn't mine because I have a sister. Or had a sister. I don't even know if she's alive. And Blaine Cromwell says she was his. She never truly belonged to Tabot. But she couldn't have been mine if she was others. But Windsor...*

"Baby... my sweet, beautiful, powerful Vermillion... *please*," his voice cracks. His tears drip into her hair and he kisses the top of her head repeatedly.

*Why does it... **hurt** when I think about Windsor? Well, the thought of him not being mine is what hurts. Does that mean he is mine? I don't even know what mine means anymore. I don't even know what anything means anymore.*

Windsor lifts his head and tilts it all the way back. He blows out a breath, his grip on his wife never loosening.

It hurts worse than when he was missing. Even though he was able to account for every second the night he returned home, I'll never forget the excruciating pain I felt every cursed second he wasn't there. Olivette and Bryanna had sat there with me for over two weeks, just trying to get me to speak to them, to let them know what I was feeling. But how could I look at the only people

I trusted, besides Windsor, and tell them that it felt like I was being torn to shreds just by not knowing that he was breathing?

"I'm right here, Eowyn," Windsor leans down to kiss her head again. "I'm waiting for you, pretty girl. I need you to get out of that magnificent head of yours, please." His soul continues to poke and prod at her, but to no avail.

An annulment would fucking kill me. I wouldn't let him go, I'd destroy all of Deteron, maybe even Euclus, just so he couldn't escape to his brother's territory. No. He's mine, he knows it, he's not going anywhere. But is he mine? What truly makes him mine? Just because it hurts to be away from him?

"I love you so much, baby. Please just... just let me help." His hands trace lazy patterns on her small frame, tucked up against his chest. "I love you, Eowyn."

*He's proven he's mine, he **wants** to be mine. He wouldn't have come to my room, every night for the fortnight before our wedding if he didn't want to be mine. He wouldn't have begged me to let his soul twine with mine, wouldn't have let his power flow freely through mine if he wasn't mine... right?*

Windsor lets out a helpless breath when he notices the sun slowly starting to rise outside of their tent, the morning coming all too quickly just as her shallow breaths have been for more than four hours now.

*But what makes him mine? What makes it so that he is mine and he stays mine? Me? What if he **was** betrothed to my sister before me and she **is** alive? What if she knows about me and seeks vengeance for stealing what was supposed to be hers? Would I have to kill my own blood?*

"My Empress," the tent flaps push open just as Lady Bryanna Grisel calls for the Queen. She stops just inside of the makeshift door, her eyes darting between Windsor and Eowyn's trembling frame. Windsor looks up at Bryanna, his own face covered in tear streaks as his eyes silently plead for her to help.

I wouldn't hesitate. I'd completely destroy the world for him, I'd do whatever I could to keep him here with me. Here, happy and safe, content just being mine. No one has ever been content being near me.

"I will retrieve Oli and Amabel," Bryanna swallows thickly. Windsor just nods and tightens his arms around the Queen.

*But I don't even know who or what I am anymore. My entire life has been a lie, suffering that I didn't **need** to endure. How can he be so content being mine if I don't even know what I am?*

Windsor shifts her limp, shaking body so she's straddling his legs, the top of her head falling to press against the middle of his chest. He locks his hands around the small of her back. "I can't take this, Eowyn," he sighs heavily, more tears rolling down his cheeks. "You're mine to protect and I'm fucking losing my mind here because I can't protect you from yourself."

*No, he can't, can he? He can't protect me from myself but neither can I. Am I my own enemy? Does that make **me** evil for dragging him down with me? He feels everything I feel, when I allow it. Am I hurting him now? As much as I'm hurting myself?*

Windsor grabs her chin and forces her head up to look at her face. She stares blankly at him, her eyes nearly black. "Eowyn," he breathes out, "give me something. Even just a blink."

*He quells my fire, he soothes me, and I'm sitting here, **hurting** him. His soul, his power, his eyes... he's crying and pleading. I used to **make** him cry and beg for me. Now, I hate the sight of it. I want to lick all of the tears off of his face and gut myself clean for making him feel like this. I want him to see anyone and everyone who has ever made him feel anything other than happiness, myself included, reduced to ash.*

He brings his palms up to cup her face. "What is this, baby? Come on, come back to me," he clenches and unclenches his jaw. "You're my wife, you're not supposed to be holding it on your own. Give it to me, Eowyn.

Let me take it from you. Let me in, just-just a crack in your armor, baby. I'll do the rest of the work, just let me in so I can pull you back."

Take it from me? I'd rather die here than give this to him. I'd rather rot into nothing in this pit of inadequacy than allow him to feel a sliver of this.

He leans in, his nose pressing against hers. "You're my wife," he whispers again, "mine. I'm just as responsible for carrying this as you are." He tries to reason with her blunt silence.

I wasn't worthy of the truth, wasn't worthy of being told the secrets of my own life. I wasn't worthy of being spared of the pain and suffering. I'm not worthy of being his wife, nor the Queen of the Free Lands. I should be in that dungeon with my collar still clamped around me. I should be having my power, my life force, sucked from me by Paronia- just like my Mother.

"I'll do anything," he nearly whimpers. "Anything, I'll give you anything... Fuck, Eowyn, please." He digs his fingers into the skin of her cheeks, trying to physically snap her out of it. Her chest heaves with another stuttering breath, making him close his eyes and shake his head. "Come back to me, baby. Bring my girl back to me, please." She blinks once, then twice. Her eyes lighten slightly.

His girl.

Windsor opens his eyes, his eyebrows raising when he sees her eye shifting from black to maroon. "I'm here, sweet girl," he pulls her closer. "Look at you," he tucks a stray curl behind her ear. *"My good girl,* coming back to me." He smiles sadly.

*His. That's what I am. I am Windsor's and he is mine. I don't need to care about anything else because **I. Am. His**.*

He presses another kiss to her forehead, his hands sliding down to her biceps. "I'm right here. Take your time, sweet thing, I'm going to be right here until you just let me know you're in there." He gives her arms a gentle squeeze.

*Anything that came before this doesn't matter. It doesn't matter because I'm here now. I shouldn't care about who or what I was before because it got me **here**. To him. Right where I'm supposed to be. I don't need my anger, I don't need my pain, because that doesn't make me who I am. He is mine and I am his.*

"I love you," Eowyn whispers.

42

THE SOULS - (KEEP UP)

The entire Exsarian Army is in disarray. Thousands of soldiers frantically search the grounds, dashing between both Kingdoms. Inside of the First Legion's tent, Eowyn sheaths HeartSeeker, then NightFall. Waryam and Eve sit at the table, quietly watching her every move. She'd not spoken a word this morning, she silently made her way into their makeshift armory and began preparing for their invasion of the capital of Iverness.

"Your Majesty," Trabus Tidreda bursts into the enclosure, his face red and sweat beading along his forehead. "King Windsor is missing," he pants.

Waryam's jaw tightens when Eowyn's face doesn't budge. "I know," she says bluntly, keeping her back to him.

"You know?" Tarbus nearly stumbles backwards. "What are we going to do? We cannot-"

Eowyn turns, her expression cold enough to silence the Light Manipulator. "We are not going to do anything. Ancel is leading the army into the invasion as planned and Windsor and I will meet you when we need to," her tone stays enigmatic.

Waryam rises from his seat, both palms planted on the table. "If you know where my brother is, say so now before I kill you where you stand," he snaps. "You may be the Queen of Exsar but he is my blood. If you have double crossed him, I will end you," he seethes.

The souls gathered at the Queen's feet hiss in retaliation, unbeknownst to the Emperor of Euclus. Her eyes slide, eerily, to Waryam. "Do *not*," her eyes shift from red to violet, showing Windsor what is happening from a distance. "Threaten me in my own territory." She feels a hum of approval from her husband's end in response.

"It is not a threat," he moves around the table. He steps directly in front of Eowyn. "I am promising that I will send you straight to the pits of Gragion to live out eternity in pain if he suffers by your hand, whether it be directly or indirectly."

Windsor's magic shoots through her veins and gathers under her skin. "I've lived without Windsor," she steps forward, drawing Meteor from a divot in her armor under her left arm. "I know pain." Waryam's eyes drop to the blade matching her true eye color. When he looks up, he shivers at the way her eyes have shifted back and gleam at him threateningly. The Queen unleashes her magic, gifted to her by the House of the Planets, manipulating his soul into dropping the subject entirely. "*My Legion*," her eyes move between the Emperor and Empress. "Aside from General Tidreda, will accompany me. Ancel will lead the Army into Iverness, Zanna and Everys will fly us to the pits behind the Castle."

Tarbus looks between her and Waryam, baffled. He'd just been so angry a moment ago and now he was taking orders from her. "Do you know where Windsor is?" Evangeline breaks the silence.

Eowyn slides Meteor back into place with a short, "yes." She steps back from Waryam, diverting her attention back to the young Tidreda. "Leave," she commands, rocking him to his soul. His feet move a little too quickly for his liking, but he's quick to dismiss it as the heat of the moment. Eowyn grabs *Desolation of the Cosmos* and holds it out to Waryam. "You may return it to him when *I* retrieve my husband," she offers coldly.

He grabs the handle, his other hand coming to grip her wrist so she can't pull away. Eowyn's eyes flash purple again. "Restoring order to Deteron, then conquering Croaka," he squeezes her tightly.

Her pulse thrums against his fingertips, sizzling against his skin in defense. She brings her other hand to rest on top of his, around the handle of *Desolation of the Cosmos*. "Restoring order to Tretanov," she corrects him.

Windsor chuckles to himself as his wife shows him the exchange through her eyes. His bones scream and ache at the sudden movement in his diaphragm, the Paronia collar locked around his neck pulling his power from his pores. Seventy-six chain links connect the collar to the shackles on both of his wrists and ankles. A single link between his wrists is hooked on a peg to hold his arms above his head. "Stop," Blaine Crowell snaps from beside him.

The King of Exsar lifts his head, groaning as his muscles strain. "Is something funny?" Tabot snaps from above the old slave pit.

Windsor looks up, the sun burning his eyes as he tries to narrow his gaze on the man sitting in the Throne that Kanika herself built. "Yes," he grunts out, "I'm thinking of all the ways my wife is going to torture you when she arrives." A soul curls around his neck, cooing at his sleeping threat.

Tabot belts out a dark, bitter laugh. The souls around Windsor hiss in retaliation. "Your wife?" He chuckles, "you think your breeder will save you? She couldn't even save her own Mother."

Windsor's muscles go taut at the insult. He bites his tongue, holding back his retort that Alice didn't *want* to be saved. She wanted Eowyn to have a calling to *kill*.

"Your Majesty," Blaine Cromwell steps forward, dragging Windsor from his thoughts. "We must make it known that we have the King before the invasion."

As if on cue, a loud horn blares through the Palace grounds. Windsor lifts his head to meet Tabot's gaze. He watches a muscle tick in the man's jaw as the horn continues to signal Exsar's approach. "Bring him up here," he orders Cromwell, "and light the pit."

Windsor feels a surge of Eowyn's power, the order falling from Tabot's lips calling to it to protect him from the impending flames. Blaine unhooks Windsor's wrists and he groans as his arms drop. The three soldiers behind him begin ushering the other prisoners, those caught using magic to create an uprising to aid him and Eowyn, toward the steps leading to Tabot's platform. His feet drag heavily beneath him, his muscles screaming with every step. The Paronia eats away at the magic within him, not much, but enough to hurt every damned second. Blaine holds his arm loosely as they approach Tabot. He wastes no time laying another wallop to Windsor's face, sending him stumbling backward. Cromwell tightens his grip to steady him before the second blow connects with his abdomen. He doubles over, his eyes catching the ring in the center of the pit below them igniting into what could only be described as a portal to Gragion.

The three soldiers begin to shove the other prisoners, two at a time, toward the edge of the balcony. Windsor watches in absolute horror as they toss the magic born off of the platform, like they were flicking lint off of their coats. But the screams burned into his soul. He'd never seen anyone die, he'd only been able to command the dead.

This was horrendous and painful, absolutely devastating.

His eyes dart around frantically while the souls break free of their bodies. They slither along the walls, deep within the shadows of the pit. He hears their whispers rise with the flames. *"Tell her he is here,"* they murmur to the other souls approaching. His eyes widen, *she saw them living through his eyes and now she manipulates them in death.* Drowned out by the screams of each prisoner being sent to their death, Windsor laughs at the revelation.

Lady Bryanna kneels beside Zanna, her hands intertwined as she boosts Eowyn onto her back. Olivette sits on the dragon's neck, gripping one of her spikes tightly. Eowyn climbs next to her. "Hi," she grabs Oli's hand.

She meets the Queen's gaze and squeezes her hand tightly . "My Empress," she smiles weakly.

Eowyn's features soften. She lays her other hand on top of her Lady-in-waiting — no, her *friend's* hand. She gently pulls the anxiety and woes from her life force, watching her visibly relax. "I'm next," Bryanna laughs nervously.

Eowyn can't help but snicker and Olivette just looks confused.The Queen pats her hand before turning to the fiery haired woman she adored. "You may be next," she sighs, *almost* jokingly. She simply taps Bryanna's nose, ingesting her consternation.

She blinks, her eyes glazing over briefly before focusing back on the Queen. Eowyn giggles and shakes her head, glancing over to Everys. Waryam holds Evangeline close to him, his hands braced on either side of Everys' neck. He meets Eowyn's gaze and nods once. Bryanna moves to position herself above Oli and Eowyn. "Ready?" Eowyn looks between Zanna and Everys.

Both look to their younglings. Shenron and Ryoko flutter their wings, Camolus disappears entirely, depositing himself above the clouds over Windsor's head. Saphira nestles on her Mother's back while Eirami perches on Everys' head.

"I still cannot believe you did not tell me you had a *mate*," Eowyn grumbles to the dragon bound to her soul.

Zanna huffs as her and Everys slowly start to lift them off of the ground. "You needn't bear the weight of my life on top of your own at that time," she replies simply.

Olivette bristles out a short laugh, grabbing the Queen's attention. "Oli?" She cocks her head to the side in question.

"Zanna has been flying back and forth since the three of us were thirteen years old," she implores with no further questions.

Eowyn's eyebrows furrow together and she looks over at Everys. "The chains never held her, Child," he nonchalantly responds as they begin to pick up their speed. "She found me on your eighth birthday."

A soul wraps around Eowyn's neck. *"Your magic needed his to manifest fully. Once they mated, his magic was trickling into you through Zanna,"* it hisses into her ear.

She grunts, swatting the soul away before summoning her wings. "I'll meet you there," she darts into the sky, leaving the rest of the Legion with the dragons.

Eowyn's wings flap almost frantically as she nears Iverness. She spots the Exsarian army at the gates of the capital, waiting for her as instructed. She fully shifts midair and dips into the heart of the army. They part slightly as Ancel pushes through to get to her. She lets out a chirp of acknowledgement when he bows his head to her.

A shadow slithers between her feathers along her back, creeping up around her torso with five others swirling along with it. *"He is in the pits,"* the souls cry.

The firebird growls, pushing off of the ground and flapping her wings once. She thrusts one wing toward the Paronia gates, a violet ray springing from a stray feather and shattering the metal. The soldiers cover their ears and duck while their Queen takes off toward the sky. *Tabot* grips Windsor by the hair gathered at the nape of his neck. He yanks him back, watching with cockeyed smirk when Windsor winced at the motion. "Oh, is the poor cub in pain?" He mocks, shoving him forward. "Do you have any last words, Windsor Exeter?" He snarls, crossing his arms over his chest.

The Ivernese soldiers grab Windsor, one on each of his arms. They walk him closer to the edge and he can't help but look down. He watches more of Tabot's minions douse some sort of flammable substance all over the ground, making the fire blaze even higher, as if reaching for him. He diverts his gaze to the sky, feeling a sudden yank on his soul.

He turns to look at Tabot over his shoulder, a feral grin spreading over his lips. "I do, actually," he clears his throat and turns to face Tabot. The old man raises his eyebrows unamusedly. "Don't play with **fire**."

An ear piercing shriek comes from above the clouds.

The fire below him goes out, nothing but smoke rising toward the sky.

Tabot's eyes go wide and he takes a step back. "No," he whispers, shaking his head.

Eowyn swoops down as the Phoenix, her eyes flashing bright red- matching her feathers, Windsor notes- as she effortlessly ignites guards surrounding him. They scream, stumbling before dropping to the ground in a pile of char. Windsor lifts his bound wrists, Eowyn hooks her neck through them and darts toward the sky. Tabot rushes down the steps of the Slave Pits, hurriedly making his way back into his palace. Windsor swings himself around to straddle the firebird's back.

"I was afraid you weren't coming," he strokes the back of her neck. Eowyn huffs through her nose, ceasing the flap of her wings to scare him with a gut wrenching drop. He only laughs in response, shaking his head when she starts upwards again.

43

ANCEL T IDREDA

"Form six!" I yell to the sea of soldiers before me. They shift, soft grunts emitting from each and every one of them as they start forward. "Legion Two, push forward!" They march faster, harder, positioning themselves in the front of the army. "Legion Two, move!" The 150 men and women move swiftly, calculatedly.

An earth-shattering growl, followed by a high pitched squawk ring through the air. My forces continue forward, all seven hundred and sixty seven of them marching into Iverness. I narrow my eyes as I begin to manipulate the terrain behind my army. I part the trees, the rocks, the ground itself moves for the King of Exsar as he barrels toward me in his lion form.

She got him, I let out a breath I didn't know I was holding. *She really went and saved him.*

Eowyn shifts halfway, dropping down onto Windsor's back. He runs past me and I follow the Queen's lead, summoning my hooves to run after them. "First Legion!" Eowyn bellows, leaning forward on Windsor's back. She presses her chest to his neck. I follow her gaze upward, watching Zanna and Everys dip below the clouds.

Waryam Exeter jumps from Everys' back, stabbing *The Unyielding* into the ground as he lands with a grunt, down on both knees. The Empress of Euclus follows behind him, a pair of white feathered wings lowering her to his side. Olivette, completely shifted into the dove, swoops down and flits her wings beside my head as I chase after the lion and firebird.

"Where is Bryanna?" Eowyn's wings bristle as Waryam shifts into the bear, pulling the Queen's magic from his weapon. A ground shaking roar rings out and the tiger falls into step with the jet black lion. "Ah," Eowyn reaches out and pats her head. "Good girl. Go get 'em," she commands. Bryanna growls and moves faster, bounding for the Pit behind the Castle. Zanna and Everys follow above her, their babes launching off their backs to flutter beside Oli. "I want every person who defends Tabot torn to bloodied ribbons," Eowyn calls over the roar of the wind as we approach the Palace of Iverness. "But you leave him for *me*."

"Yes, Your Majesty," I say with a grunt. Eve and Waryam push forward, the bear running with purpose toward the three soldiers stationed at the foot of the steps.

He grabs the first one by his neck and holds him tightly as he whips his legs toward the other two. Eve flinches when the first soldier's neck cracks and he falls limp in Waryam's paw. We continue forward as the Emperor of Euclus tears their bodies to pieces. "Oli, stay with Ancel. Eve, wait for Waryam. Windsor..." Eowyn tilts her head down and strokes the lion's mane. "You know what to do."

Windsor skids to a halt, letting out a rumbling roar. The ground beneath the lion begins to shift, making the rest of us stumble to a stop as well. Eowyn stands on his back, her feet one in front of the other. "Olivette," I mutter, jerking my chin toward the back of the Palace where Bryanna disappeared. She chirps in response and follows me around the back as our King raises an army of dead, *Kanika's army*. The soldiers behind us groan to life while their bones clack while coming back together, each piece of their decomposed bodies being pulled from the ground by Eowyn. "Bryanna will have cleared the rest of the guards by now. I need you to help me get everyone out of the collars." I grip the Torch of the House of Light tighter, summoning the Queen's power from the relic. I feel it trickle into the pores of my fingertips and warm the blood coursing through me. I slow to a trot as we approach the gates. Olivette sings a three note melody, shifting back into her humanoid form. I pause my steps to look over her. My eyes take in her black hair and pale skin, making sure she wasn't hit by an arrow.

Tabot had shot at his own daughter, I'm sure he has no issue sending his men out to try to kill us.

Oli rolls her neck, her wings still rustling behind her. She reaches into the chest plate of her armor, pulling out a long, thin blade. The gold gleams in the sunlight and she looks down at it. "Not that Her Majesty is unjustified in her rage," she meets my eyes again, "but I like the... irony... of this blade being called *Vindictive Slicer.*"

I chuckle lightly, despite the gravity of the current situation. "None of ours is left behind. All of his die." I turn toward the gates. "You know what to do if you are cornered," I swallow thickly.

"Her Majesty will not fail me," she scoffs as she brushes past me.

I focus on the soft clacking of my hooves against the stone as I enter the pits, my eyes trained on Olivette. She keeps her head straight while stepping over half charred remains of Tabot's victims. Her jaw ticks every time a soft hiss erupts from the carcasses. Those of us in the First Legion, siphoning the King and Queen's power, could only hear the presence of the souls- not hear their exact words. My eyes follow them along the pathway, retreating back toward Eowyn.

I turn back to see Olivette approaching the unnaturally large tiger. I quicken my pace to close the distance just as Bryanna shifts back into her humanoid form. "There's no guards out here," she breathes out, keeping the razor sharp claws protruding from her fingertips. "They all retreated with Tabot." She pulls back the claws and glances around again. "It *reeks* in here, what is that smell?" Her face scrunches with distain.

"There's over a thousand bodies that were burned today alone. I'm assuming that," Oli retorts sarcastically.

I clear my throat and shake my head. "No, she's talking about the smell of dying magic. She's never smelled it, Olivette, not until she started siphoning from Eowyn."

"I can taste it," Bryanna rubs a hand over her chest. "I can *feel* it."

"That's because she's feeding off of it," a grating voice calls behind the three of us.

I turn, drawing my sword at the same time Bryanna pulls Blazefury; The Katana of the Forest and Olivette raises Vindictive Slicer when we find Tabot behind us.

He chuckles darkly, waving his hand at us dismissively. "Please, do not defend her. She would sacrifice all of you to get what she wants," he takes a step forward. "These people?" He gestures over the ashes piled in the center of the pit. "Their magic is going to *her*. She's summoning their still breathing souls and draining the last bits of magic they have," he shrugs nonchalantly. "I wouldn't trust her if she was on my side, doing that and not... *aiding me*," he smirks eerily and takes another step forward. "Because that's what happened here, isn't it? She left her *kitten*," he points at Bryanna. "Her *dove*," his finger moved to Oli, then me. "And her *centaur*. She left you all behind, for what? To try and kill *little old me*?" Another gravelly laugh escapes him, making a shiver run up my spine.

I turn to look at the girls, stepping in front of them. "Her Majesty has not *left* us," I say simply.

"She hasn't?" He takes another step forward before turning in a circle. "Because I see three, poorly armed, members of what *these* people..." he gestures to the pit again, once he's facing us. "... Called *Kanika's Resurrected Legion*."

My eyes widen slightly. Bryanna steps forward. "Just because she is not *here* does not mean she is *not* here." She seethes, her eyes shimmering a dusty purple. I feel a pull, my blood reeling as my King requests to watch through my eyes. I blink, feeling the physical shift in my own eyes as I abide by his request.

"Speaking in tongues will get you nowhere," Tabot lets loose another sardonic breath of a laugh. "I would know if she was still in my territory," he glances toward the pit again. "She grabbed the King and left to Exsar. Leaving her precious legion behind," he fake pouts.

"Keep him there," Windsor's voice rumbles through the three of our minds.

"She's on her way."

I blink, my eyes shifting back to normal. Olivette moves in front of both of us. "Your Highness," she keeps her tone pleading, almost broken. "Surely, you are mistaken. Our Queen cares deeply for us. She would never abandon her hand chosen legion," she laughs nervously, glancing toward Bryanna and I. "Right?"

"Of course," Bryanna scoffs, crossing her arms over her chest. "She would never *leave*."

I stay silent, my eyes darting between the two. Olivette looks to me, her eyes glazing over sadly. "Ancel?" She croaks.

I clear my throat, my gaze shifting back to Tabot. "Come on, General," he chortles, "tell her the truth."

I swallow thickly, squeezing my eyes shut. "The First Legion is Her Majesty's sacrifice."

44

WINDSOR

The King of Exsar stands behind Eowyn on the Royal balcony of the pits. She stares down at Bryanna, Olivette, Ancel, and Tabot. Windsor stares at her back, feeling her walls fall back into place, brick-by-brick with every word they speak.

"The First Legion is Her Majesty's sacrifice," Tidreda says to Oli, a blatant lie, but distracting nonetheless.

"That can't be," she breathes out, shaking her head.

Windsor steps closer to Eowyn, her magic steadying to strike. "She doesn't care about anyone or anything," Tabot snaps. "She is incapable. She feels nothing more than anger, *at best*."

Windsor stands beside Eowyn. He can feel the way the words are slowly chipping away at her, the reality she's come to know, the way the venomous words are pulling her back from the woman she's become. He slides a hand to the small of her back, drawing her attention briefly. She glances at him out of the corner of her eye and her jaw slackens before she looks back to the four under them.

"She is here for one reason: revenge. She doesn't care about these people," Tabot gestures behind himself dramatically. "She didn't care about her Mother."

Eowyn steps forward at that. Windsor moves with her, his power coiling around hers. "You know it's not true, *stop*," he commands lowly. She nods once, her focus unyielding.

"She doesn't care about you," he motions to half of Eowyn's legion. "She doesn't care about Windsor." Before he knows what's happening, Eowyn jumps off of the balcony, flapping her wings quietly to lower herself to the ground. Windsor bites his tongue as to not give her away while Tabot continues. "She's only ever known pain, that's all she'll inflict. She'll never love, never care for or cherish. You're all pawns in her game."

Windsor watches Eowyn summon the souls gathered amongst the ash. They swirl around her, tugging her into the shadows as she begins to stalk Tabot like her *prey*. A satisfied noise rumbles from the lion within him. *"Good girl,"* he praises down their mental bond. *"Show him how much you care about everyone. His victims, your people, your legion... your husband. Prove him **wrong**, baby."*

He crosses his arms over his chest and widens his stance. Eowyn tugs at him and his eyes shift. She stands directly behind the King of Iverness, a few feet away. Bryanna's eyes trail along the shadows and she flutters her eyelashes, a signal. A soul slips away from his Queen and curls around her ankle. Bryanna's lips twitch, her eyes darting up to Windsor.

"She is a pathetic girl who should have stayed dead." Tabot spits.

Eowyn steps out of the shadows just as a figure steps through the gates of the pits. Windsor's eyes widen when Blaine Cromwell halts in his tracks and watches his daughter.

"Say that to my face," Eowyn's voice echos through the old arena. Tabot whirls on his heels. Eowyn pulls at his soul forcing him to his knees as she approaches. "Say it *to my face*," she grits out.

Her power swirls around the entire arena, gold and red and blue rays zip and churn around them. "You are a pathetic girl who should have stayed-"

He's cut off by a strangled growl. Windsor whips his head toward the tiger charging at Tabot. Olivette shifts into the dove, squawking loudly as she ascends to the clouds. "Fuck yes," Windsor mumbles before shifting into the lion and running toward the edge of the balcony.

Eowyn's eyes meet his, her tongue sliding along her top row of teeth. In the next breath, the fire bird is coming right toward him. He tucks his back legs in and outstretches his front paws. She swoops under him, turning at the last second, allowing him to fall perfectly on her back. She lets out a deep grunt, her wings fluttering almost in a panic with the sudden weight. Windsor adjusts, snarling over her head at Tabot.

Bryanna catches him by the arm and clamps her jaw around it. He howls with pain. She growls, sinking her pearlescent teeth deeper into his skin before slowly starting to trot in a circle. Eowyn dips back toward the ground and Windsor pushes off of her, running to grab Tabot's *other* arm. Eowyn darts toward the sky with Olivette. Tidreda shifts fully, letting out a gruff neigh before barreling straight into Tabot's chest. Windsor releases him, but Bryanna rips his arm off at his elbow. He watches with wide eyes, Tabot's screams drowned out by the scene in front of him.

Bryanna, the tiger, holds the King of Iverness' gaze as she lashes her head back. She widens her jaw and his arm *disappears* into her throat.

The Firebird above them lets out a shriek and Windsor's breath stutters when she pulls his power from him. She gathers the death from his veins and mixes it with the life in hers, swooping down and shooting a stream of fire at Tabot. She swings upward again and Tabot lifts the regenerated arm. Waryam, as the massive black bear, comes barreling into the slave pits, Everys screeching out above them. Windsor's eyes dart around, looking for any sign of the Firebird. Eve jumps from the clouds, assumedly from Zanna's back, onto Everys'. She flips off of Everys, landing on Tidreda's back.

"Where the fuck is she?" Windsor snaps at the souls around him.

Bryanna lunges for Tabot again, pinning him to the ground and snarling in his face. Eve unsheathes *Twisted Silence* and holds it to his neck. Waryam *digs* at his legs, shredding the skin to ribbons.

Windsor jolts when he feels a sharp pull inside of his chest and Eowyn lets out another ear-piercing shriek as she swoops down. Waryam jumps back and she lights Tabot's legs on fire, healing the wounds *again*. Windsor's eyes widen and he steps forward hesitantly.

"She's playing with him," the souls cheer into the ashes below his paws. *"And so are they."*

His eyes move along the scene, now unable to miss the way Eve holds the Carver to his throat, the way Bryanna uses a single claw on her right paw to slice thousands of cuts into her skin, the way Waryam continues to shred his legs, all while Tabot thrashes and screams in pain- just for Eowyn to swoop down and heal him to do it all over again.

He cranes his neck toward the sky, watching his wife retreat again. This time, she perches just above the awning over the Royal balcony. Windsor's nostrils flare with the scent of magicless beings approaching. Tabot's soldiers.

"Protect your Queen," Windsor snarls into the abyss of power leant to the Legion before him. Tidreda immediately looks to the gates, then Eve. They nod at each other before dashing toward the approaching army. Tabot laughs bitterly as Waryam takes off after his wife, leaving Bryanna and Windsor with the King of Iverness.

Windsor shifts back into the King, raising his hand in the air to summon *ThunderSoul* and a *Stone of Malice* on a breeze of cobalt colored magic zipping around the arena. A guttural scream draws his attention back to the gates.

Eve.

She falls, a Paronia sword blade impaling straight through her abdomen. Waryam shifts and falls to her side, leaving Tidreda to attempt to hold off the army. His eyes travel over the men, some armed with more blades made of Paronia while the others had... bear hunting arrows. Aimed at the balcony. Windsor follows their aim with his eyes and grunts when he sees Eowyn just sitting there.

"Lower your weapons," Tabot calls out from behind Windsor. Before he can turn, Tabot is snapping something around his neck.

"Fuck sake, again?" He grumbles quietly. "If it didn't work once, what makes you think it's going to work *now*?" He taunts.

Tabot grates out another laugh, grabbing the haladie and *Desolation of the Cosmos* from Windsor. "Don't worry," he snorts, "she's not saving you this time." He shoves Windsor to the ground.

He catches himself with his knees and palms, glancing over to Waryam, holding his bleeding Empress. Tidreda grunts, his breathing heavy as he continues to slice and jab at the soldiers... *passing him?* His eyes follow them, though he keeps himself planted on the ground. They line up, one at a time, aiming their crossbows at Eowyn. Tabot stands in front of them, obviously scared to meet her on the balcony. "Shift and talk to me like a human," Tabot demands.

The bird chirps defiantly before shifting back into her. She stands on the awning, her arms crossed over her armored chest. Her wings sprawl from her back, looking menacingly *darker* than usual. A glowing white strand of light circles her for a brief moment before evaporating entirely. Windsor's eyes rake over the white gown made of feathers. A metal belt holds her waist tightly, a thick plate of ruby encrusted metal running up to her neck where the biggest ruby sits, holding the feathered cape to her. He squints. "Paronia?" He whispers to himself. "You put it on yourself?"

Eowyn looks past the line of soldiers and nods, like she *heard him*. "Eowyn," Tabot shouts, "this is your last chance for a peaceful surrender!"

She blinks, extending her wings. Windsor's lips part as they slowly start to shift from red to black. "Come down here and I'll let you and your husband spend the rest of your days in the dungeon. Then we can make good use of you."

"My husband will never see the inside of those dungeons as I have," she calls out bluntly. "And I do not plan on returning."

He grinds his teeth together. "I had high hopes that your keeper would hold your leash tighter," he snaps, "I suppose I was wrong."

She quirks an unamused eyebrow. "My keeper? I belong to no one."

Tabot nods, combing a hand through his beard. He turns on his heels and grins mercilessly at the sight of Windsor, still on the ground. "*Your* wife," he clicks his tongue. "*Your* breeder, *your* whore... you let her speak to another man like that?" He kicks Windsor's left shoulder, stomping him down to the ground.

"I belong to *no one*." Her voice echoes, bouncing off the walls of the arena. "I am no one's *woman*."

Tabot's foot lifts and Windsor is on his feet in an instant, his anger fueling him more than his adrenaline. "Keep him away from her," Tabot scoffs.

Two soldiers grab Windsor by his arms, yanking him back to their King's side. "You are my woman!" He yells, thrashing against the guards. "You're mine to fight beside, mine to hold and kiss and mark," his voice breaks. "You're mine to love and obey. You own me, Eowyn. And I *own* that fact, that is what makes you mine. That I'm the one who has the fucking *honor* of putting the world at your feet." He holds her stare as he whispers, "you are mine because I am *nothing* without you."

Thunder crackles above them, loud and never ending. Lightning bolts hit the two guards who hold his arms, leaving them to go up in flames. Eowyn runs toward the edge of the awning. She jumps, flapping her wings to propel her toward him, shooting exploding balls of flame at the soldiers rushing toward him and Tabot. Tabot stares at Eowyn with wide eyes as he drops ThunderSoul and Desolation of the Cosmos. Their screams are nearly silent, Eowyn's souls rising from the ashes to suffocate them as they burn. He watches in utter *awe*, the way she proves Tabot *wrong*- wrong about *everything*. She pulls the pain, pulls the anguish and despair from them as they die. Zanna roars above them, her own fire aimed right toward Tabot's **precious chapel**. Eowyn drops to the ground and taps a single finger on Windsor's neck, shattering the Paronia secured around them both. She turns back to Tabot, moving one arm behind her to pull Windsor into her. He places his hands on her shoulders and kisses the top of her head. Tabot grabs the nearest weapon, a pathetic dagger left behind by one of his own.

A huff of warning draws Windsor's attention. Tidreda rushes toward them, half shifted, holding SkyFall out to his Queen. Eowyn snatches it from his hand, the gift of the last Serpent Shifter glowing to life in her grip. The intricate swirls within the pure Paronia blade gleam crimson red. Windsor steps back and Eowyn lunges for Tabot immediately. He dodges her swing, narrowly, but snatches the sword out of her hand. Eowyn bites out a laugh, unsheathing HeartSeeker at the same time he hands her ThunderSoul.

Windsor knows how this ends, watching with crossed arms.

"You think..." Tabot grunts, lowering his shoulder and charging at the Queen of Exsar like a bull.

She breathes out another sarcastic sound, effortlessly side stepping him. "I think?" She twirls the haladie in her hand.

He turns to face her once more. "You think you will win this?" He raises both swords over his head and thrusting them down as hard as he can, stumbling like a drunken fool.

"He is a drunken fool," Eowyn sings down their silent pathway. "Haven't I already?" She tilts her head to the side, tauntingly. "Or do you need

to see one last trick?" She smiles viciously. Windsor's eyes drop to the tiger stalking closer to his wife. She bares her teeth, though silent as a mouse. A soft hum rings through the air and suddenly, everything was still. Tabot reaches one hand up, slicing along Eowyn's neck with a sharp hiss.

45

Everything stills. Her blood bubbles to the surface, gushing out of her like her skin was a broken damn. Tabot hit her. He slit her throat. She was going down, *fast*. Windsor doesn't even blink. Bryanna tackles Tabot to the ground and Windsor runs. He pushes himself to move as fast as possible. The blade of ThunderSoul shines from under the metal coating, the pearl in the hilt of HeartSeeker crying out in response. Windsor drops to one knee and skids along the ashes. He cranes his neck to the side, thrusting his tongue out as far as he can. He drags his tongue along the seam of the entire wound in one fluid motion. His salvia glitters against her blood, small violet sparks closing the gash.

Eowyn gasps, straightening and bringing HeartSeeker and ThunderSoul to her chest. The blades clink against each other. The ground beneath them rumbles when Windsor's eyes turn white. He drops to his knees. ThunderSoul's blades *explode*, leaving scattered pieces of shimmering *power* behind. Bones clack and rise from the ashes, Windsor's hands silently commanding the dead life matter to morph back together. The hilt of HeartSeeker magnetically gathers the pieces of ThunderSoul. Eowyn lifts a hand, allowing each and every piece to fall into her palm as she meets Tabot's gaze once more.

"No," he shakes his head, thrashing against the tiger.

Tidreda looks on as Windsor raises all of Tabot's victims from the ashen pits. The charred bones and melted skin mesh together, groaning soldiers now at his every beck and call. They start moving, heading for the walls of the arena. Eowyn stares down at Tabot, where Bryanna holds him down. Her paws pin his shoulders to the ground, claws piercing the skin just below his collar bone. Her drool drips onto his face with every silent snarl she releases following each of his movements.

Eowyn moves her head, glancing at Windsor over her shoulder. "Seize him," Windsor growls to the army of the dead.

Eowyn turns back to face Tabot. "You had your chance," her eyes flash bright red. "Though, I'm glad you didn't take it because I've been waiting for this for nineteen years." She shrugs, almost nonchalantly.

Bryanna releases him, allowing the dead to grapple haphazardly at the King of Iverness. He thrusts a hand upward as if he were grasping at someone to help him. Bryanna snaps at his hand, chomping his pinky clean off. Windsor chuckles darkly, thrusting one hand toward Tabot. A river of violet magic skitters toward the pinky, generating a whole other hand off of the pinky stub. Bryanna purrs and clasps her jaw around the new hand. Blood spurts from Tabot and he screams, yelps and whimpers. Eowyn hums lowly when they hoist him off of the ground. He cradles his arm to his chest, sobbing pathetically.

"Take him to the square," she grits out. "He's going to admit to each and every one of his crimes before he's hanged."

Bones clank and rattle as they obey their commander. Windsor shoves his power down their mental bond, making her eyes shift to white. Her pupils shrink to the size of pinholes and she lets out a guttural scream. One dead man shoves a fist full of ashes into Tabot's mouth, silencing his scream. They march out of the arena, Eowyn spreading her wings and flying after them. Bryanna books it, her head angled up to follow Eowyn from the ground.

Windsor glances to where Waryam sits on the ground, his hands gently working over Eve's wound. He steps forward and his brother looks up. "I'm going to be fine," Eve croaks, reaching a hand up to cup her husband's cheek. Waryam looks back down at her and she smiles tiredly.

"I've got the best healer on Tretanov," she whispers before turning her attention back to Windsor.

Waryam smiles down at his wife, his grin turning feral when he meets Windsor's eyes again. "Go kill that son of a bitch." The King doesn't need any more persuading before he shifts into the lion, bounding after his wife.

As he approaches the town square, at the center of the capitol, he slows to a trot. Thousands, those who Windsor hadn't seen across the border months ago, stomp their feet and clap their hands above their heads. "Long live Queen Eowyn!" They chant.

Windsor halts in his steps, Eowyn appearing in the sky above the marching army of death. Her wings, now fully *black*, hold her high above everyone else. Tabot is disposed in the dead center of the square, still quietly crying and holding his mangled hand. Bryanna huffs beside Windsor and he can't help but snicker in response. The lion turns to the tiger who stares at Tabot like she's using all of her self control not to eat him whole.

Bryanna shifts back first, Windsor following right behind her. Tidreda appears beside Tabot, manifesting from a single flame- assumingely summoned by Eowyn. He doesn't spare a single breath before manipulating the stones under his feet to form a gallows atop a small platform used to spread news. The dead soldiers march forward, yanking the King of Iverness to his feet and tossing him onto the wooden surface. He lands with a thud, another pitiful whimper falling from his lips. Eowyn drops to the platform and Windsor grins at her. He moves toward her, but before he knew it, gold light was flashing through her palms and striking Tabot's chest.

He watches in awe as the man falls backwards, down the steps. He attempts to stand when she blasts him again with a grunt. He fallsdown another step and lands at the bottom where the crowd parts. "You will die at my hands!" Eowyn screams as she hits him with a violet surge of power. "You've disgraced the title of '*King*' too many times," she lunges toward him.

Zanna lands next to Windsor. *"I hope she saves part of him for the babes to feast on,"* she grunts as her younglings land next to them.

Windsor strokes the Dragon's scales. "Me too, Zanna," he whispers. "Long live Queen Eowyn!"

Eowyn yelps as she continues to throw him around like a rag doll with the power thrumming from her veins. "Spare me," Tabot cries out, grabbing at his chest. "Spare me, daughter. I will atone for my wrongdoings."

"Long live Queen Eowyn!"

Eowyn bends down and wraps her hands around his throat. "You've suppressed my people, killed my mother, and attempted to marry me off to become a breeder while you ruled, feeding off of my people's power," she grits out. "You will die by my hands. And I will rise to the status of *Empress* by loving and caring for *my* people."

Tabot tilts his head down and spits at her feet. "You are not fit to be Queen, let alone an Empress."

Windsor sends a thrum of magic to her in an attempt to soothe the power coursing through her veins, aching to end the man before her. "I will rule by love. I will rule with love by my side," she gesturs to Windsor. "I will rule by loving my people and nursing My Empire. Not as you have, by fear." She spits back, the saliva landing in his eye. "Sir Blaine Cromwell," she turns her head and directed her hand at Tabot. He winces, bracing for another impact of her power to his bones. The King's hand, Tabot's new General since Hagan had *died*, steps forward. "Your sword," she demands.

Tabot yelps from the ground, "I will end you, Cromwell!"

The General looks at him, then to Windsor, and back to Eowyn. He pulls the sword from the holster and kneels before her. He bows his head and raises the sword balancing on his palms. The crowd around them silences. Eowyn grabs the blade, blood instantly dripping from her palms. She tosses it in the air and catches it by the handle.

"I think you've said enough," Eowyn snarls. "You will die by a sword that was sworn to you, one that has my blood still dripping from it." She shoves the blade into his gut and retracts it quickly.

Tabot begins choking on his own blood as he attempts to rise to his knees. Windsor rushes down the steps and stalks up behind him. He grabs Tabot by the hair, without a second thought. "Y-You don't know what you're unleashing inside of her," Tabot looks up to Windsor with pleading eyes. Eowyn slashes his throat. Blood sprays over both of them, soaking her armor and bare skin that peaked out beneath the joints. Windsor steps toward Eowyn with Tabot's head in his hand. He grabs her wrist and raises it to the sky, the other hand raising the head to the crowd.

They cheer, screaming and clapping, some even dropping to their knees. "Long live Empress Eowyn and Emperor Windsor!" They chant over and over and over.

Eowyn raises her other hand to silence her subjects. "I am to return to Exsar and deliver the news of *Tabot the Terrible's* death, our victory. I will return in a month's time. Please focus on rebuilding your towns." She turns to Blaine Cromwell. "I'd like you to see to it that no more wrongdoings are forced upon my people in my absence." He nods his head once in understanding. "And seal off that fucking dungeon." She drops the sword, the metal clanging against the cobblestone.

She walks away from Windsor, moving toward Tidreda. He glances down to Tabot's decapitated head in his hand and tosses it to the ground. He kicks it with the toe of his boots. Ryoko, the yellow babe from Zanna and Everys, flutters forward with Saphira behind him. They land beside the head and lick the dripping blood off of the stones. The other three younglings trot over timidly.

"I'm sorry your gallows went to waste," Eowyn says quietly to Tidreda as her husband stalks forward.

Tidreda shakes his head, his eyes dimming as Eowyn calls back her power from the legion. "There is no need to apologize, Your Majesty. I am simply glad to see him no longer breathing," he crosses his arms over his chest, his gaze sliding to Windsor.

Eowyn turns, slowly. "Your wings," Windsor whispers, reaching out to drag his fingers along the feathers. Tidreda retreats quietly. Eowyn looks to where Windsor strokes her right wing, his fingertips gripping a single feather and plucking it off of her. She cocks a brow, meeting his eyes once more. "They're... black," he lifts the feather between them as if he is beginning to inspect it.

She hums lowly, stepping back a few paces. Zanna turns and looks between the pair. Eowyn's wings bristle in silent command and in a single breath from her Dragon, Eowyn goes up in flames. Windsor sucks in a sharp breath, attempting to steady his nerves.

She is made of fire, he reminds himself silently.

He groans out, "Zanna, please." She doesn't stop, keeps breathing out a never ending blue flame. He clenches his jaw before summoning his ice and shooting a line of it directly into the fire consuming his wife. Zanna straightens her neck, a puff of smoke coming out as she ceases fire. Eowyn kneels on the ground, her chin pressed against her chest, her wings gone. "Eowyn," Windsor snaps, a little too harshly. Her head snaps up and her eyes flare. She lets out a soft hum. He flinches when he hears the familiar sound of bones cracking as she summons her wings once more. He furrows his eyebrows, noting the way her feathers were back to red and orange and yellow. "You..." he trails off, stepping forward with a hand stretched out. She blinks up at him and he frowns, his arm falling back to his side.

"The rage within had to die out before she could restore her natural form," Everys implores, nudging Windsor with a paw. "Her rage was *killing* her."

The King, no... *Emperor* of Exsar drops to his knees in front of his wife. "Eowyn," he whispers.

She leans forward, cupping his cheeks and wrapping her wings around him. "I love you," she breathes out. "I love you and I love our people. I love our country and I..."

He nods eagerly, wanting nothing more than to hear her keep talking, keep that softness and gratitude in her voice. "And you what, baby?" He pulls her onto his lap. "Tell me, tell me what else, baby, please," he nips at her chin almost playfully.

She breathes out a soft laugh, pulling away slightly. "I'm... *excited*... for... *our future*," she admits.

46

ONE MONTH LATER

Windsor sits at his desk, his pen tucked between his teeth as he leans back in the chair. Eowyn stands by the door with her arms crossed over her chest. The magical markings on her biceps glow dimly, the light shifting every few seconds as she taps her fingers on her flesh impatiently. The long, strapless red gown did nothing to hide the blazing Phoenix marking on her right calf. The silk skirt stops just below her knees, a subtle yet obvious way of showing her husband how badly she needs to release her power, now.

Bryanna and Olivette sit across from the Emperor. His eyes dart between the three of them for a long moment "Alright," Windsor sighs, leaning forward and setting the pen down on the surface. He folds his hands in front of him, his gaze flicking to Eowyn briefly before he focuses on the women in front of him. Her only two ladies-in-waiting since she'd arrived, her two friends. "You two want *me*," he points to himself dramatically. "To let *you*," he gestures to the two of them, "take *her*," then to Eowyn, "*my wife*... to Euclus to see Evangeline? My own brother's territory, you want to take my wife to my brother's territory, without me?"

Bryanna clicks her tongue and winks at him. "Precisely." She crosses one leg over the other, still in her Puzzled Monkey uniform.

Windsor levels a short lived glare at the fiery haired woman. "No." He leans back in his chair.

Her spirit matching her hair, she immediately shoots out, "she's going."

Eowyn pushes off the wall. "I'm going," she snaps.

Windsor cocks an eyebrow. She flinches slightly, a hint of a flush creeping onto her cheeks as a pang of guilt runs through her. "Are you?" He tilts his head to the side. "I said *no*."

"You cannot tell her she cannot go to an ally's territory," Olivette laughs, shaking her head. "Mama would kill you if she knew you're trying to," she points at him accusingly.

Windsor knew that, but he never said he would stop her from going. He smirks, focusing on Eowyn while she approaches the desk. She stops between Bry and Oli, an Empress standing between her two favorite ladies. "No, I cannot. But you asked my permission and I said no," he shrugs, his eyes boring into Eowyn's. "You may do as you please, but you don't have my agreeance on the matter," he shrugs.

"Leave us."

Neither of the women protest Eowyn's order, they simply rise to their feet and shuffle toward the door. Once the faint *click* of the door closing rings through the room, Eowyn flicks her hand, a small *clank* of the lock snapping into place. Windsor reaches out, tapping the desk in front of him with his index finger. She steps around the desk and hoists herself onto the surface. The leather chair groans as Windsor pulls himself closer, folding his hands in his lap. "What is it, my love?" He smiles up at her.

A muscle in her jaw tickles when she clenches and unclenches her jaw. "Why?" She picks at her nails, almost nervously.

He brings his left hand to her right calf and flattens his palm over the glowing mark. He ices over her skin, just enough to dull the ache. "Why, what, baby?" He moves both of his hands to her knees, gently massaging up and down her thighs.

"Why did you say no?" She whispers, "I'm just going to Euclus, it's not like I'm walking into enemy territory."

He slides his hands to her hips and grips her possessively. "*Everywhere is enemy territory*," he retorts, "I don't care who's running the goddamn country, I'm not in agreeance with you traveling across *this* continent just to get on a ship and cross an *ocean* without me... I can't lie to you and say I agree. You may do as you please, I know you can keep yourself and your... *little girls* safe, but that doesn't mean I have to agree with you." He gently pulls her closer.

She lifts her feet and plants them on his knees, her bare shins now pressed against his chest. "Euclus is safe," she crosses her arms again.

He rolls his eyes and slides his palms down the sides of her legs. He takes his time, soaking in the feel of the bright red silk that clings to her, then the warmth of her skin. He wraps his fingers around her ankles, jerking her forward and down onto his lap in one motion. His hands move back to their place on her hips. "*No where*," he snarls, baring his teeth just inches from her face, "is safe *for my vermillion*." Her eyes flash defiantly. "Do as you please, Eowyn," he releases her waist.

She stares at him, blinking vacuously. "You do not wish to know how your Brother's wife has healed?" Her power swirls and rages with her emotions. "You do not care to know how she is doing after almost dying for me?" Despite the accusatory words themselves, she manages to keep her tone level.

He quirks a brow, mainly surprised that she's still sitting here with him, even after he'd not said what she'd wanted him to. "I know the Empress of Euclus is in good health. That is about the extent of how much I care," he divulges simply.

Her own eyebrows furrow in confusion at his nonchalance. "The extent of how much you care? For your sister by law?" She asks quietly, as if she couldn't believe what he was saying.

He reaches up, tucking a single silver curl behind her ear. "I care *nothing* about *anyone* but *you*." His hand drifts down to cup the side of her face.

"I do not wish to go without your approval," she admits, turning her head and kissing his palm.

He hums lowly, "you do not need my approval to do anything, my love." He smiles when she leans her cheek against his hand again. "Though, I must admit, I am enjoying your… *need*… to be near me since being home," his other arm locks around her waist. With a roll of her eyes, she relaxes against him. "One might think you are–"

"I am not," she snaps quickly, pushing his hand away from her face.

Windsor smiles when she climbs off of his waist. "Eowyn, do not throw a tantrum. You may go to Euclus with your friends whenever you please. I will not stop you," he can't help the way his eyes drift over her as she *stomps* toward the door.

"I do not wish to go without your accord. I will not be going until you have time to accompany me, if that is your only qualm. And I am not having that… *other* conversation again," she calls over her shoulder, irritation lacing every word.

His grin only broadens as she reaches for the doorknob. "What other conversation?" He teases.

Eowyn scoffs, rolling her eyes and pulling open the door. Windsor watches as the crimson strapless gown, matching her irises, sways with her dramatic steps. She slams the door behind her, rattling the frame. She sucks in a sharp breath and smooths her hands down the front of her dress. She glances down at herself before shaking her head. Her feet start to carry her toward the Empress' chambers, the shoes on her feet pinching her toes. She scoffs at the soft pain, *just before high noon, peculiar.* She drags her feet through the halls toward her bedroom. Once in the sanctity of her own space, she blows out an exasperated breath. She closes the door and leans her forehead against the wood.

"Eowyn."

Her body tenses, even her breathing ceasing. She slowly turns on her heels and summons her magic silently, turning to face the unnamed male. "Who are you?" She looks him up and down.

He stands, unnaturally tall and pale. His eyes, icy blue, just like Windsor's the night they met. "I am Ri-Zahn. I am one of the four Princes of Gragion."

Flames gather at her hands defensively. "You expect me to believe a Prince of Gragion, one of the Prince's who sees over the afterlife, has come to Exsar and entered my chambers to... what? Chat?" She grits out, her eyes flashing violet as she sends a glimpse of the scene to her husband.

He chuckles, rocking on his heels and crossing his arms behind his back. "Technically, I am here as the original Infinite, but I thought it best to greet you as a Prince who welcomed your Mother home, *safely*." Her eyes widen and she stumbles back. He takes a step forward, then another, grabbing her arms to steady her. "Careful, falling could be detrimental to the-"

The sound of the door opening behind them cuts him short. "Get your hands off of my wife," Windsor's voice rumbles through the room.

Ri-Zahn glances at Eowyn's face before nodding and stepping back. "Emperor Windsor, I came to tell the Empress that her Mother has safely crossed into Gragion," he sketches a quick bow.

Windsor moves around Eowyn and steps in front of her. "I don't care who you are or why you're here. It is unjustifiable for you to show up in my wife's *private* chambers and put your hands on her," he snaps, reaching a hand behind him.

Eowyn slides her trembling fingers between his and holds onto his hand tightly. He gently pulls her forward and she rests her chin on his shoulder, watching the exchange. "My apologies," Ri-Zahn frowns deeply, "to both of you. I mean no harm. I come with urgent information." He looks between them and takes a step back to emphasize he is not here to harm anyone. "I am Ri-Zahn, breather of life into the Unbleeding, Prince of Gragion. I come, *peacefully*," he pauses briefly, "as the *first* of Kanika's children, **freed** from the Gates of Gragion, as you have begun to unravel *my Mother's Prophecy.*"

EPILOGUE

EOWYN

Windsor marches through the swinging doors, leading into the kitchen. He pushes past Davilina, the head baker, and Nathaly, her assistant. He stops abruptly, taking in the scene before him and clicks his tongue. "Leave us," he demands. The command is cold, calculated. He crosses his arms over his chest and watches them leave the kitchen. "What are you doing?" He asks on a breath of laughter.

"I am slicing and frying potatoes," I say with a nonchalant shrug. I make another paper thin slice and dangle it in front of him before dropping it into the pan of bubbling beef fat.

His eyes shift to the potato, watching it sizzle before looking up at me again. "Why?" He drops his arms to his sides and crosses the distance between us. He leans back against the counter next to me, one arm sliding between my waist and the stove.

"Because nobody can make them how I want them," I mumble, subconsciously leaning into his touch.

"Mm," he hums, nodding slightly. He observes intently for a few minutes, watching me slice the potatoes and fry them to a golden crisp and pull them out and place them on a plate. "This wouldn't have anything to do with the... *theory*... I have, would it?" He brushes his fingers over my lower stomach.

"No," I reply, too quickly. "I simply wanted a snack," I nod once, affirmatively, "That is all." He knows he's never going to get me to say it, it just isn't true.

His eyes flash white, his palm sliding over my stomach. "Eowyn," he whispers, stepping closer.

I shake my head, flipping the potatoes with a pair of tongs. "I would know," I cut him off. I will not be having this conversation again.

"Baby, *you know*," he chuckles, "you just won't say it." His magic tugs at mine while he leans in to rest his chin on my shoulder. I glance at him from the corner of my eye briefly. "Eowyn," he drums his fingers against me, almost expectantly. "Come on, baby girl, stop," he brings his other hand up and pulls the tongs from my hand. He removes the pan from the stove and pulls the rest of the potato slices out of the beef fat. He lays them on the plate before bringing his attention back to me. "Humor me. Just let Amabel check, please," he places his hands on my hips and tugs me closer to him.

I sigh, finally conceding. "I'm taking this," I grab the plate of the chips.

He laughs again, this one pulling a short giggle from me in response. "You can bring it, *but*," he gently takes the plate and sets it back onto the counter.

I pout, *"but?"*

His eyes meet mine again before dropping to look at my lips. "Don't do that," he whispers, *almost* groaning. He brings a hand up to cup my jaw and runs his thumb along my bottom lip. "I can't stand it," he pulls my lip down before releasing it and watching it snap back up to cover my teeth.

"I'm hungry," I whine, bouncing on the balls of my feet slightly.

Windsor's fingers slide down my arm and he settles both hands on my waist. *"Oh baby,"* the growl rips through his chest while his hands tighten on my hips. "I know, you're hungry, but-" I whine even louder this time, cutting him off, my hands gripping the lapels of his jacket. He bites down on his bottom lip as he watches my childish antics. *"But,* I need you to let Amabel check first... *Please."* He pulls me flush against him.

I slide my hands to his shoulders and nod. "Alright," I agree.

"Mm, that's it?" He leans down and brushes his nose against mine. "I don't get anymore whining or..." he swallows, his eyes dipping to rake over me from my toes, back to my eyes. *"Protesting?"* He nudges my nose with his again. I hum, allowing my eyes to flutter closed. He chuckles lowly, his hand on my face tensing as he tilts my head up slightly. "Look at you," his lips dance against mine. I open my eyes, only to meet his. "So beautiful when you're wanting something from me," he lifts his hands to my hair. He pulls the two pins out of the top knot, watching the silver curls fall over my shoulders.

I take the chance to playfully hit his nose with mine in retaliation. "I always want something from you," I admit softly.

He tucks the pins into the breast pocket on the inside of his jacket and looks back up at me. "It makes sense why you're always so goddamn gorgeous all the time then, doesn't it?" His other hand pats my waist before he reaches for the plate. "Come on, I know better than to keep you waiting for your snacks, *as of recently."* He mutters the last part under his breath when I take a step back.

I roll my eyes and watch him start toward the doors. I keep my feet cemented to my spot with another deep frown on my face. He glances over his shoulder and stops when he sees I'm not following him. He turns to face me, holding the plate in one hand, the other coming up to rub against the stubble on his chin. He stares at me for a moment before nodding and setting the plate on the counter by the door. I quirk an eyebrow as he starts back toward me.

"I know what you want," he chuckles huskily, grabbing me and sitting me on the counter next to the stove.

I bite down on my bottom lip. "Oh yeah?" I tilt my head to the side, tauntingly.

He grins,"oh yeah," he murmurs, one of his hands sliding around my back. "I know just what my pretty little vermillion wants right now," he leans forward, his chest now flush against mine.

"And what's that, dear husband?" I tease gently. He smiles wickedly, bringing his arm from behind me. I glance down, "don't you-" I cut myself off when he shoves a Norang fruit and Omra frosted pastry into my face. I blow out a huff, bringing my hand up to dab the frosting off of my chin. He bursts into a fit of laughter, leaning forward and licking the frosting off of my face. "Stop it," I grumble, pushing against his chest. He howls again before pressing both of his palms flat against my back as he continues lapping at my chin. "Windsor, stop," I breathe out a laugh. He moves up to my lips, capturing mine in a fiery kiss. I roll my eyes and relax into his arms as I kiss him back. He pulls away after a few heartbears, another shit eating grin plastered on his face. "I married a child," I scoff, crossing my arms over my chest.

He licks his lips, settling his hands on either side of me. "A child?" He gasps dramatically.

I roll my lips together, attempting to contain my smile. *"A child,"* I raise my eyebrows challengingly.

"I'll show you a child," he *yanks* me forward, tossing me over his shoulder with his arm hooked around my knees.

"Windsor!" I shriek out a laugh, hitting his back playfully. He rumbles out a satisfied sigh, snatching the plate of chips from the marble surface and stalking toward the door. "Put me down," I lift my head to attempt to look at him.

"No," he smirks.

I straighten my spine, lifting myself upright. "At least let me sit on your shoulder," I huff out.

His smirk widens into a full on grin and he loosens his grip slightly. "Go ahead," he urges. I shift slightly and he pulls me the rest of the way, sitting my backside on his right shoulder. He closes his arm around my legs again and starts up the steps. "You really don't think you're-"

"No," I cut him off quickly, "I do not."

Windsor leans down and bites the outside of my thigh lightly. I gently tug at the ends of his hair until he releases me. "I don't believe you," he declares as he reaches the top of the steps. "I think you *know*," he squeezes his arm around my thighs gently, lifting the plate to my lap.

I hum, grabbing a chip and popping it into my mouth. "Where are we going?" I ask as he turns down a hallway, opposite the royal wing.

I grab another chip and lower it to his lips. He smiles, leaning forward and wrapping his lips around my fingers. I release the chip and he lets go of my fingers with a pop. "Thanks, baby," he mumbles before chewing and swallowing the chip. "I'm taking you to see Amabel, like I said," he points to a door a few feet away. "That's her office."

My eyes follow his finger and I take in the sight of the plain white door we approach, with a single red line through the middle. "I didn't know she had an office in the Palace," I frown down at my husband.

Windsor stops in front of the door and grabs the plate from me. He slowly lowers himself to his knees, using his other hand to help me stand from his shoulder. "We have been so busy since your arrival that you've hardly had time to explore the Palace. My hope with allowing Ri-Zahn to stay is that you will have more time to do as you please, when you wish to do so," he lifts the plate of chips between us. "Especially if this is what I think it is."

I sneer and roll my eyes, reaching up to knock my fist against the door. "Come in!" Amabel calls sweetly. I don't waste another breath before pushing open the door and stepping in. I glance around to take in the small office, everything so white and shining. "Your Majesties, what can I do for you?" Amabel's voice pulls me back to reality and I zero in on the Healer.

"Her Majesty is-"

I cut Windsor off with a sharp glare. He sighs heavily and sets the chips down on the counter before falling onto a white sofa against the wall. I turn back to Amabel with a small smile. "Windsor has an... *idea*... in his head and needs someone other than me to tell him that he's *wrong*," I raise my eyebrows at her.

She nods, quickly grasping onto the information. "Please, lie down," she gestures to the couch where Windsor sits. I walk over and stand in front of him. He grins up at me, patting both of his hands against his thighs. I roll my eyes once more, lying down on my back, with my head in his lap. His left hand immediately falls into my hair, combing his fingers through the strands he'd pulled from my updo earlier. "This will be super quick, Your Majesty," Amabel says softly, kneeling next to the sofa. I suck in a sharp breath as soon as her fingers press into my lower stomach. She quickly retracts her hands and looks up at me.

"What?" I lift my head to meet her wide eyes.

"My Empress," she releases a breathy laugh, shaking her head. Windsor clenches his hand into a fist in my hair, pulling my head back down to his lap. I look up at him, my lips parting as soon as the words fall from the Healer's mouth. "You are, *indeed*, with child."

www.ingramcontent.com/pod-product-compliance
Lightning Source LLC
Chambersburg PA
CBHW022141010726

47493CB00002B/290